W9-BJA-328

Cupid is definitely working overtime in this collection of love stories from three of Arabesque's most popular authors. These stories are guaranteed to bring a warm feeling of love to all readers and anticipation of their own encounter with CUPID'S ARROW.

CUPID'S ARROW

Layle Giusto
Doris Johnson
Jacquelin Thomas

ARABESQUE
BET BOOKS

BET Publications, LLC
www.msbet.com
www.arabesquebooks.com

ARABESQUE BOOKS are published by

BET Publications, LLC
c/o BET BOOKS
One BET Plaza
1900 W Place NE
Washington, D.C. 20018-1211

First Printing: February, 2000
10 9 8 7 6 5 4 3 2 1

Printed in the United States of America

Contents

Maleka and the Sheik
Layle Giusto

This novel is dedicated to the incredibly patient, talented, and supportive people at both Black Entertainment Television, Incorporated, and Kensington Publishing Corporation. People such as Karen Thomas, Tomasita Ortiz, Jessica McLean, and all those whose names I have never learned who have been involved with this book.

Thank you all

One

What a hunk!

It was a cold and blustery late January day in Paris. Twenty-five-year-old Maleka Darling should have been too cold to notice the person who stood in front of her. But she liked to think that she never overlooked a great looking man. Her eyes had been drawn to this one immediately. In a word, he was spectacular.

She had been walking along with her head down, hands tucked in her pockets, feeling sorry for herself. After having gone to a lot of trouble to visit Morocco, she was stuck in Paris during the cold. She had bought a wardrobe of clothes suitable for an Arabian country, suffered through various nasty vaccinations, obtained a visitor's visa, and then had to cancel everything because she'd run out of money and couldn't afford the trip. The tour group had left without her. Her whole vacation would be a waste. At least, she thought, wanting to take her mind off those thoughts, there was still the Valentine's Day dance at the Fashion Students' Lounge. She could attend that, though, chances of finding an escort were highly unlikely.

Well, none of that mattered right now. And daydreaming about the Valentine's Day dance was a waste of time. It was very likely that another intern, who wasn't the least interested in her, would be her escort.

That was when she looked up and saw him.

He was about thirty-one and stood with a contingent of

men who appeared to be from either the Near East or North Africa. They were waiting on the sidewalk in front of the Paris Ritz-Ultra, located on the Avenue Des Champs Elysees. It was one of the most prestigious establishments in the world.

The men wore long, flowing, white robes. The robes were called gandourahs, she remembered. On their heads were white kerchiefs secured with heavy black cords wound around their foreheads. They all managed to wear sunglasses in the winter weather without appearing odd. They looked as if, between them, they owned most of the oil wells on the planet.

She was captivated by the way he handled his over-six-foot frame. It was the first thing that caught her attention. He had the predatory stride of a panther, with the most incredible grace, while still making you totally aware that he was all male. His skin was a richer, darker bronze when compared with the other men.

He made her think of stories from the Arabian Nights and racing across the Arabian Desert on horseback—which was a joke because she'd never been on a horse in her life.

A sheik; the word jumped into her mind. That's what he reminded her of—an oil-rich sheik.

She had been so absorbed that she almost plowed into someone. It was a man who kept her from falling and he smiled flirtatiously. He stared down at her clothes and said, "Magnificent!" She smiled and looked at him from the sides of her eyes and apologized for bumping into him.

When she turned back, it was to see the doormen and several bellhops rush to assist the gorgeous sheik. In their eagerness to assist him, they overlooked others who were waiting.

For some reason, she felt that he'd been staring at her, too, and she found it strange. Why she felt that way she didn't know. Men and women often stared at her. It wasn't because she was beautiful; she knew she was far too short to be considered beautiful. Somehow he didn't seem the type to flirt with her. He was too cool and aloof.

She wondered if he'd say *"bonjour"* and how his voice would sound. Actually, she only guessed that he looked at her. For, while the other men wore dark glasses, he wore reflective aviator lenses.

Much as she hated to admit it, her height had become an issue in her life. After the age of twelve, much to her disappointment, Maleka had never grown another inch. She was five-foot-one-quarter-inch in a family where both her parents and her only brother were six footers. As a child she had felt that she lived in a land of giants and had longed to wake up one morning to find herself tall and stately. No such luck. She had feared that she would be ignored and, from an early age, had decided that she would never allow this to happen. Even today, her family would often treat her as if she were a child. She didn't mind this so much from her father, Russell Darling, but found it hard to take from her mother, Mildred. And as for her brother, Bobby, he was seven years her junior. There was no way she would let him get away with that.

She was slimly built with curving breasts and hips. The one quality she had always appreciated was her smooth ebony-hued complexion. It was inherited from her paternal grandmother, an indomitable woman who had raised five sons all by herself.

No, Maleka knew it wasn't beauty that people stared at. It was the clothes she wore. And she was quite proud of those clothes. They were all designer originals and all created by herself.

Today, she wore a magenta miniskirt that showed added leg through slits up the side. Her blouse was bright yellow. The fabric was handmade Himalayan felt. Indeed, it was sort of outlandish, but it was also new and exciting.

Over this, her coat was long, also slashed up both sides and back. She believed in the total pulled together look. No element was left to chance, no matter how small. She went to extremes, mixing colors that frightened many.

Even underwear had to work. And for that look, hair was very important. Sometimes, she wondered why she hadn't become a hairstylist. Her latest do was one with geometrical braids that swirled and curled and stuck out at all angles.

What most people did not realize was that such an outfit as she wore that day was not one that she tried to sell. It was simply an attention getter—a conversation piece. She was only too aware that most women wanted clothes that were more subdued.

Although she knew her designs were good, no one was beating down the door to buy her stuff, yet. It was frustrating. However, she had won one competition. Only a year before, the most phenomenal thing had happened to her—the dream of a lifetime. She had won the coveted Artiste in French Fashion Award. Each year, the prize was given for excellence to a relative newcomer in the fashion business. The prize was a full year internship at the couture house of your choice. It was a real coup, coming after years of serious study.

The fashion world was a highly competitive one. She had been in France for a year and had learned much during that time. In the daytime, she worked on other people's designs, but on her own time, she was a walking billboard for her own. Many of her fellow interns did the same.

It had been a year of long hours, working to get things ready for private and public showings. A year in which she hadn't had much of a social life. That was why she didn't have a date for the upcoming dance. But she wasn't complaining. Despite the hard work, it was a great opportunity.

As she surreptitiously watched the sheik, she had the weirdest feeling. She could have sworn that she'd seen him before. *Probably in the newspapers,* she thought.

Instead of entering through the door, he stepped back, bowed, and gestured for her to go first. A sigh escaped her. Wouldn't it be something if she could show up on the arm of a guy like that? She gave him a big, bright smile and, throwing her shoulders back, sauntered through the door.

And it was at that moment—with her first sight of the lobby—that she remembered why she had come to the Paris Ritz-Ultra that day. It was to meet her mother, who, only the evening before, had called to say that she was in Paris, staying at the Ritz.

An image of her mother, Mildred Darling, with a disapproving facial expression, jumped into her mind's eye. Her instinctive smile congealed on her face and she glanced around guiltily. It wouldn't do for her mother to catch her grinning at the man like a Cheshire Cat. That would bring on lecture number one million ninety-nine about how she was a chronic flirt. *Not true.*

Okay, maybe, it was a *little* true. Sometimes she did allow her gaze to wander and yes, she did smile a lot, but that was all it ever amounted to. And what was wrong with smiling? Anyway, the only reason she had looked at the man was because she had been thinking of the big dance.

It wasn't that she was a flirt, exactly, but she considered having an appreciation of good-looking men to be part of her fashion sense. Sometimes men were like accessories. That thought had her looking over her shoulder, again. Heaven forbid that her mother should ever hear her say that. It reminded her of her childhood when she often wondered if her mother could read her mind.

She realized that after a full year of living in Paris and being totally on her own, she was falling right back into the habits of her childhood. Why was she worrying about her mother? She hadn't thought like that in months. She loved her statuesque mother, but what a nuisance the woman could be at times. Her mother was incapable of understanding that life was different for a short person. Besides, flirting got her noticed and, as she intended to be famous some day, being noticed was very important.

Inside the lobby, she sensed the men walking behind her and had a powerful urge to strut her stuff. She didn't— just in case her mother *was* near. The last thing she needed was to have her mother observe that. Besides, there was always the possibility that she would fall on her face.

Already knowing her mother's room number, she walked toward the elevators. The sheik glanced briefly her way as he sauntered past. His ever-present attendants followed closely, surrounding him. Attentive hotel staff escorted them to a space where a new clerk magically appeared, specifically to assist them.

Humph, she thought. Although the French had had their troubles with their old colonies, they still had moments of being very tolerant and cosmopolitan. Yet, they were not to be toyed with. It wouldn't take much for the onlookers to start muttering about his group getting preferential treatment. The French occasionally loved dramatic street scenes. The only thing that saved the men was that everyone watched the sheik—especially women. He was as gorgeous as a movie star. One woman appeared so absorbed that she actually leaned over the desk to get a better look, totally ignoring her customer.

Maleka shook her head and continued on her way to the elevators. As she went, she caught sight of a display through a pricey glass storefront and ambled over for a better look. It was a display of Valentine's Day knickknacks. In France, the holiday had originally been named after a saint and, although people exchanged cards and gifts, it was pretty tame compared to the commercialism in America.

She leaned closer to get a better look. But on sight of an overpriced piece of fluff, a nagging thought took shape. It was something she had been puzzling over since hearing from her mother. She straightened and looked around. When she first entered the lobby, she had been distracted by the handsome sheik, but now she became fully aware of her surroundings.

It was absolutely impressive. Although it was not the original Ritz, it was still in the same class. It was likely one of the city's most expensive hotels. It was certainly the most elegant. Those thoughts made her shrug in puzzlement.

Either her parents had hit the lottery or something very queer was up. How had her mother ever convinced her father, who wasn't a tightfisted man, only a prudent one, to splurge his life's savings upon these digs? Her next question was how he had been convinced to take the trip at all. Her father was a quiet, laid-back man who enjoyed his creature comforts. Her parents had met twenty-six years ago in Paris. Her father had been in the Armed Forces, stationed here while her mother had been with a traveling song and dance troupe. He didn't travel much anymore. The whole thing struck her as very odd, but she fully intended to get to the bottom of it.

Two

Maleka glanced at her watch, noting that it was a few moments before noon. There was no danger that she was late. Her appointment—if you could call it that—was for six hours later. They were to have an early dinner according to her mother. No one expected her at this time. Actually, it was better for her because since being in France, she had taken to eating her biggest meal for lunch rather than for dinner. It was cheaper that way.

However, that was not the true reason for her being early. The true reason was that it was an attempt to uncover whatever was going on. Her parents had arrived in Paris almost a week earlier and last evening was the first that she'd heard of this. They had spent that time in total secrecy from her. She was determined to find out what was going on.

She loved her parents and the news of their arrival had given her a moment of spontaneous pleasure. It had been almost a year since last she had seen them. However, that initial response soon vanished, to be followed by annoyance. They were checking up on her. Considering that she wasn't a child anymore, it was aggravating. Plus, her mother would never admit to it. Of course, she knew that her dad still considered her his little girl, but that was all right. Besides, he never denied it. She knew that she could always tease him into good humor and because of that she made concessions for him. Her mother was a different matter altogether. The older woman watched like a hawk and never missed anything.

Not receiving an explanation for her parents' sudden trip aroused her curiosity even further and, although her mother had sworn she had come alone, Maleka couldn't help believing that her father was there, too. When she'd hung up, the niggling doubt had mushroomed into resentment. They'd probably even brought Bobby to baby-sit her. It was just too aggravating. While it was true that she missed them and would enjoy seeing them, she was still going to give them a piece of her mind. She was a grown woman and had already been in France for months. They had no right treating her like she was incompetent.

That's what came of being short, she thought. People didn't respect you. Heck, they didn't even notice you half the time unless you did something outlandish.

She left the Valentine display and walked to the elevators, only to see that the sheik and his entourage were already there. Some rather fanciful thoughts ran through her head as she approached them. The guards glanced toward her and she wondered if they were made uneasy by her presence. Maybe they thought she was part of a kidnapping gang. From there, her imagination jumped to thoughts of their swinging broad swords overhead and attacking her.

She felt foolish for those thoughts when she came abreast and the men bowed and smiled charmingly. One of them, a bearded man, said, "Cold day, isn't it?"

"Yes, it certainly is," she answered, glad to escape from her imagination and crazy images of being chopped to pieces by fanatical bodyguards. She felt sheepish for letting her thoughts run wild like that.

"In my country, the sun always shines." The others smiled and nodded in agreement at this—all of them except the snooty sheik. All she got from him was the reflection of her image in his glasses. He yawned, looking bored and disinterested.

"It shines especially on beautiful women," another of the men spoke in a softened voice.

"Oh, does it?" she twittered, deciding to take that as a compliment. Her mouth went on automatic pilot and turned up in what must have been a huge, silly grin. "How lucky for the women of your country." Now the sheik's mouth turned down in a sneer.

Oh, well, she sighed, forget that fantasy of him taking her to the dance. She went back to chatting about the weather with the other men. They gestured for her to move to the front where she could precede them onto the elevator. Even the gorgeous one bowed. He looked incredibly innocent and sweet-tempered.

She smiled and stepped forward. From the corner of her vision, she saw the sheik move. She was just turning to see what he was doing when she went flying—right into two strong male arms.

She could have sworn that someone had tripped her but that thought soon flew out of her mind along with every other reasonable thought she had. She looked up, recognizing that those strong male arms belonged to the gorgeous sheik. Her mouth went dry and her tongue stuck to the roof of her mouth. He must have taken off his glasses for she noticed that he had the most gorgeous brown eyes she had ever seen. His eyelashes were so long and thick that she kept expecting to feel the wind they created whenever he blinked.

She decided the quickest way to get a little attention was to go limp and act more hurt than she was. She sighed and raised one limp wrist, trying to appear frail. She even let her eyelids drift slowly closed. Then she peeked at him through her lashes. She was doing pretty well there for a moment.

The bearded man spoke to the sheik in soft accented French. "You've bagged yourself a young Cassiopia."

This flattered her more than she wanted to admit. But before she could take a deep breath, the sheik responded by unceremoniously hoisting her onto her feet, sneering,

"More like a little something that washed up with the Euro-trash."

"I beg your pardon," she said, giving him the special, 'talk to my palm' gesture. "Don't you know it's rude to call people Euro-trash?" She would have said more except she was a little wobbly on her feet. Besides, at that moment, an elevator opened. A bellhop motioned for the men to enter. It was a private car and they quickly disappeared behind the whispering door.

It was some minutes later before she was able to enter another elevator and go to her parents' room. Her mother opened the door. After a moment of surprise at her presence, the older woman appeared none too pleased at seeing her. Her glance took in the long leg that could be seen through the slit in the floor-length coat.

"Maleka, that skirt's too short," were the first words out of her mother's mouth. She never paid any attention to her mother's opinion on clothes. Her mom was inclined to be ultra-conservative in her dress. That was all right, but it wasn't Maleka's style. "It's a miracle you don't freeze to death. And I thought our meeting was for later today, for dinner."

"I just couldn't wait to see all of you," Maleka said sweetly, as she walked in, her eyes searching for her father. The room was small, but even so, Maleka was certain that it cost a fortune. It was beautiful. It was nothing like her little rooms that she rented out of someone else's apartment.

"You're lucky you caught me. In another moment, I'd have been gone," Mildred went on, turning back into the room. Then she shot a frown toward Maleka. "Couldn't wait to see all of who?"

"You, Daddy, and Bobby, of course."

Her mother sighed. "I told you that I came alone."

"Oh, yes. You did say that, didn't you?"

While it was true that her mother had insisted that Dad and Bobby hadn't come, not for one moment did Maleka believe that. Knowing her family, they always traveled together. This time, she'd catch them spying on her. To keep her mother off guard, she went on the defensive.

"Mom, you said that you were happy when I got the opportunity to study in Paris."

"I *am* glad, Maleka. I know what a wonderful opportunity this is for you."

"Then why are you checking up on me?"

"I've already told you that this trip has nothing to do with you."

Yeah, I'll bet, Maleka thought. She tiptoed to the closet, snatched it open, and peered in. There were only a few clothes hanging there. She didn't see anything that belonged to her father but she wasn't convinced yet.

"That so?" Maleka said, eyeing a door off to the side. She suspected it led to the bathroom. Slowly, in an attempt to act casual, she inched toward it.

"Maleka," her mother said, sounding impatient, just after she burst into the bathroom. "Would you care to tell me what you're doing?"

Feeling foolish now, Maleka said, "I was looking for Daddy. Where is he? He went out, right?"

Mildred stood with arms akimbo, tapping her foot. One eyebrow raised as she spoke annoyingly slowly. "Your father's not here. He didn't come and I'm not spying on you. So would you kindly stop challenging shadows?"

"Just checking," Maleka said, eyeing the bed. She had a brief urge to look under the ruffles but restrained herself. There was no way her dignified father would crawl under a bed. She hated to admit it, but she felt a little let down when she realized that her father really hadn't come. "Personally, I think it's a good idea for you to try your own wings. It's high time you stopped twisting your father and your brother around your little finger. And every other male you can make a fool of, too." Her mother mumbled that last bit.

"I don't make fools of men."

It was quite aggravating the way her mother was inclined to believe the worst of her.

"It doesn't matter right now," her mother said. "I have important business to accomplish. I thought we made arrangements for you to come tonight for dinner. What are you doing here now?"

"I told you. I thought Daddy was here and I wanted to catch him in the act."

"Oh, Maleka, grow up. I told you, I've come to meet with an old friend who lives here in Paris."

"How was I to know you still had friends in Paris? The only person I ever heard you mention who lived here was . . . ," excitement ran through her, ". . . Lisandra Orian, the world famous opera diva!" Maleka shrieked. "Is that who you're here to see?"

Ever since Maleka could remember, her mother had spoken of Lisandra, telling stories of how they had both performed in the Burke Troupe. It was a black American song and dance troupe that traveled across Europe during the early seventies. Although Lisandra had studied opera, in the troupe she sang jazz and popular music. It wasn't until later that she had finally gotten her break into the classics.

"If you must know," her mother sighed, "it *is* Lisandra."

"But you always said you hated her."

"I never said any such thing." She had the grace to look a little discomfited when Maleka looked askew at this and added, "What I meant was that sometimes we didn't see eye to eye."

"But you two made up. Great. When are you going?" Her mother looked absolutely trapped. Maleka's entire antenna was at attention. Something was going on here. "You're going to see her right now?" When her mother failed to answer, she said, "I'm going, too."

"Not this time. Lisandra and I have something terribly important to discuss and . . ."

"I promise I won't get in your way. I'll be still as a mouse until you're ready to introduce us."

"No way. You've never been still in your life."

"Mom, you can't hold me back on this. Think of my career. Meeting Lisandra Orian could be just the boost that I need. Suppose she loves my things and insists that only I should dress her? Think of the publicity."

"Somehow, I can't see her with a bare leg sticking out of a coat in the dead of winter."

"This," she pointed to herself, "is from my line for the young and trendy. It has to be outlandish or no one would notice me. Besides, my leg's not bare."

"Humph, there's little chance that will ever happen to you."

"For someone like Lisandra, famous, stately, mature, I have another line."

"Okay, far be it from me to put a damper on your career. Besides, I know there's little hope you'll change your mind once you've made it up, but I need to speak with her privately, first. You can wait here until I call you to come."

This was not going the way she wanted. But before she could protest, her mother picked up a large box that was lying on the bed. It was very peculiar to watch. It seemed as if Mildred didn't want Maleka to notice the box and, in her anxiety, was clumsy in her attempt to hold it. The box opened and the contents spilled out on the floor. Maleka had traipsed around to pick it up but stopped dead.

There exposed in tissue wrapping was the most scrumptious mink coat that Maleka had ever seen. She knew her mouth fell open but she was too stunned to care.

"Is that a mink?" Her voice was reverent.

"Well . . ." Her mother's pale beige complexion turned pink in embarrassment.

"But you always disapproved of animal furs."

"I can't stand it when Lisandra tries to lord it all over me."

"And how did you convince Daddy to buy you a mink?"

"I'll discuss that later," Mildred said, turning away quickly.

"Daddy doesn't know," Maleka said, as the realization dawned on her.

"It's only rented."

That was the biggest shock of all. Maleka knew her mother as a woman, blunt in her honesty. Certainly, she never allowed herself to associate with people that she didn't approve of. Here she was planning to pass off a rented mink as her own and to a woman who she'd never gotten along with. Something was definitely going on here and Maleka was more determined than ever to uncover it, no matter what the consequences were.

She flopped down on her mother's bed and crossed one shapely leg over the other. "Gee, I wonder what Daddy would think about this." Not even for a moment did Maleka doubt that it was pure blackmail.

Her mother sighed and rolled her eyes upward in what was obviously a quick prayer. "Someday, you'll have a daughter just like you and then . . ." Maleka knew she had won.

On the elevator going up to Lisandra's room, Maleka was aware of her mother's anxiety, which she attributed to nervousness at seeing Lisandra after such a long time. On Lisandra's floor, the door opened and they stepped into the corridor. There stood the same group of burly body-guards that Maleka had seen in the lobby. The men were at the elevator door—obviously to check out whoever stepped out. They were also outside the corridor quietly talking. She craned her neck, looking for the hunk, but he wasn't there. They smiled and bowed to her.

"Don't forget, you're going to be quiet while I speak with Lisandra," her mother said, distracting her. Her mother tapped lightly on the door. It was quite a revelation to see her mother pat her hair and shift from one foot to the other in the short wait for the door to open.

The door swung inward and there stood Lisandra Orian, the world-famous diva. The woman was both tall and sub-stantial. She had smooth brown skin that had a peach-like luster. Her long, wavy black hair hung down her back. A fabulously expensive white silk caftan, richly embroidered in gold, covered her from her neck to toes. Even here, the woman had a presence.

"Mildred!" the world-renowned voice boomed. Even in an ordinary conversation, you could recognize that voice. Maleka had a momentary vision of crystal cracking. "How wonderful of you to come. It's been years." The two older women almost touched cheeks. "You're looking . . . quite marvelous," Lisandra said, her eyes narrowed, as she appeared to calculate the value of the rented mink.

"Thank you, darling," Maleka's mother answered. The two women stepped back from each other and Mildred preened herself and smoothed the place where Lisandra's fingers had touched the coat. "You're looking"—Here Mildred gazed at the white silk caftan—"well, yourself."

It was quite amusing to Maleka, who watched the antics of the two older women. Then Lisandra turned to her.

"And this must be Maleka! I haven't seen you since you were in diapers. You're beautiful."

Mildred turned to look at her and Maleka had the feeling that her mother had forgotten all about her. Reluctantly, Mildred answered, "Yes, she wanted to meet you."

Something in the way her mother said it made it sound as if she wanted to add that she didn't know why anyone would be anxious to meet Lisandra Orian. Lisandra seemed to get the message.

"Really, how sweet, let me look at you, child—absolutely gorgeous. She takes after your husband, Mildred." Maleka figured it was payback for her mother's remark. The diva warming to it now, went on, "And I can see from that smile and those big eyes that she's a flirt. Just like you were too, Mildred. Honey, let me tell you, your mother was the biggest flirt on three continents. What a heartbreaker, she was. And could she dance the hooch." Maleka glanced incredulously at her mother, who had begun to fan herself. "And will you look at that skirt. Why, it's as short as your mother used to wear. Remember, Mildred?"

"Humph," Mildred snorted.

Maleka looked at her mother with fresh eyes. Mildred looked terribly uncomfortable with Lisandra's words. *She is probably peeved because Lisandra gave away her old secrets,* Maleka thought.

"This is wonderful," Lisandra gushed. "Ahmad just arrived only a few moments ago. The children haven't seen each other since they were in the crib." Maleka wondered who Ahmad was. But then she remembered reading about a son born to Lisandra and her very rich Arab lover.

"You mean since Maleka was in the crib. Ahmad's much older than she is."

Her mother made it sound as if it were Lisandra who was "old."

"Umm," Lisandra said, her nose tightening a little. "Not that much older. Only a few years." Then she turned to Maleka. "Come darling, I'm just dying for you to meet my only son again. You two used to be such good friends. Ahmad." She called to someone out of sight. Turning back to Maleka, she said, "You probably won't remember him after all these years."

A tall, absolutely gorgeous man stepped into the sitting room. He had thick, dark, curly hair and smooth golden-brown skin. Thick dark eyebrows were like raven wings over incredible brown eyes. His body was perfection, with broad shoulders and a tapering waist. He was wearing a cream-colored silk shirt opened at the throat with slim-legged tan pants and fine brown leather knee-high boots. He looked as if he had just ridden in from the desert and jumped off a sleek black steed. It was those thoughts that made her recognize him.

It was the sheik!

Although he was dressed differently and didn't have the reflector glasses, it had to be the same man that she had seen downstairs in the lobby with the bodyguards. It disoriented her. What was an Arab sheik doing in Lisandra's apartment? He had taken off his white robe and headdress, but she would have known him anywhere. It was the man who, she suspected had tripped her and said she'd washed up with the Euro-trash.

"Ahmad!" Maleka's mother shrieked. "You've grown so tall."

Despite her shock, she registered the remark about his height. *Just like my mother,* she thought, *all she can think of is how tall everyone is.*

"Ah, the incomparable Mildred," he responded.

"You remember me?" Mildred asked.

"How could I forget such a lovely, charming woman?" he replied, and kissed her hand.

Seeing her mother blush like a schoolgirl was quite a shock for Maleka. *It is certainly a day for learning about my mother,* Maleka thought.

"And this is my daughter, Maleka. Do you remember her? Of course, she was only an infant when last you saw her."

He turned a bored face to Maleka. "Oh, yes," he said, "I do remember her, vaguely. She hasn't changed at all." Then his mouth turned up in disapproval and he added, "Hasn't grown much, either."

It made Maleka see red, but she didn't say anything. Soon, they were all seated with a glass of sherry. They spent the obligatory moments talking about the Paris weather before Lisandra turned to Mildred.

"I was quite surprised when you called. Although I cannot help but feel you're too upset by this. Surely it's not part of the national treasury." Suddenly, Lisandra stopped and her eyes were riveted at a point over Maleka's shoulder. Maleka turned around to find her mother gesturing wildly. At being caught, Mildred tried to pretend that she was patting her hair into place.

Her mother was doing it again—treating her like a child. And right in front of that snooty sheik. It made her blood boil. But she'd show all of them not to discount her just because she was short.

Lisandra chuckled uneasily as she watched the undercurrents between Maleka and Mildred. "Well, anyway, I asked Ahmad to join us. He should be able to advise us on this big secret mission." Once again, Maleka sensed Mildred's frantic signaling to Lisandra. In total bewilderment, Lisandra said, "Let's eat. Surely, we can all agree to that."

Maleka was humiliated. It was bad enough to have her family treat her with the most incredible condescension, but to have them take it to outsiders was worse. And somehow, having her mother do it in front of Ahmad was intolerable.

However, her antenna4 went on full alert. *What,* she wondered, *is going on?*

Mildred tried to gloss over the moment by saying, "What a lovely suite this is. It's so large and comfortable."

"Why, this old place." Lisandra fell for the bait and preened a bit. "Lunch will be coming any moment, now."

Maleka could have spit. Obviously, whatever her mother's big secret was, it would have to wait until later. This, of course, made her all the more determined to find out exactly what her mother was up to.

When she looked over at the gorgeous Ahmad, it was to catch him watching her. He yawned broadly and glanced away. That didn't help her temper one bit. It almost seemed as if he were trying to say that he found her boring. After the remark about her size, this was just one more insult. She just wished she could think of a way to fix his bacon.

Three

The two older women warmed up to each other as the time passed. Soon they were laughing and telling old stories. Once Mildred leaned over and suddenly looked nostalgic. "Do you remember Emma, the concierge where we lived?"

At this, Maleka's ears perked up. She had heard her mother mention Emma, the concierge where she had lived many years earlier. When the letter arrived announcing that she'd won the fashion internship, Mildred had made an incredible effort to find exactly such an establishment, a building with a concierge in which Maleka could live. Her mother had been disappointed. Paris had changed in the years since her mother had lived there. The traditional concierge had just about disappeared.

However, Mildred was not to be thwarted. Failing to obtain what she wanted, she had found a fairly good substitute. It was a room that was part of a large apartment. The rules weren't too strict because this was a whole new century. But Maleka couldn't have men stay overnight. Not that this mattered, because as hard as Maleka worked she didn't have time for relationships. That was part of the reason that she allowed herself her little flirtations.

"How could I ever forget wicked old Emma?" Lisandra responded. "What an old witch."

"Oh, I don't know. She wasn't that bad," Mildred said, sounding a bit wistful.

"You hated that old bat. You were always finding ways to avoid her."

Maleka was shocked to hear this revelation. According to what Mildred had claimed, old Emma had been a beloved jewel. "I thought you loved her," Maleka said.

"I was young and I didn't understand," her mother said, looking slightly shame-faced.

Lisandra let out a big hoot. "You understood enough to know she was always spoiling our fun. Remember, she used to sneak around trying to catch men in our rooms?"

"I never had men in my room," Mildred protested.

"What about when Russell was stationed here?"

"Well, I married him."

"Oh, but you weren't married then."

"Well," Mildred answered, a little sheepish, "Emma was concerned for our welfare. After all, we were vulnerable young women in a foreign country. And our grasp on the language left a lot to be desired."

"That's not what you used to say," Lisandra countered. "Back then you swore she was just a frustrated old battle-axe."

"Never mind what I used to say," Mildred rushed in to add. Then with a hasty glance in Maleka's direction, she added, "Now that I have children of my own, I can understand. Emma was a truly caring person who took good care of us."

With this, Lisandra glanced at Maleka, too. Suddenly, she seemed to catch on and said, "Yes, of course, you're right. I don't know what we'd have done without the woman. She was an absolute saint."

But if her mother thought she had quieted Lisandra's tendency to speak her mind, she was wrong, Maleka realized when the diva spoke.

"But you didn't answer my question. Why is everything so secretive?" Lisandra asked, with her booming stage voice that carried to the rafters at the Met.

"Two weeks ago I received a letter," Mildred said with a strange intensity as she stared at Lisandra, "from Zeleke."

"Zeleke! How is that old charmer?" Whatever her mother had been trying to say to Lisandra, the diva obviously hadn't caught on. "I can't remember the last time I saw him. More than twenty years ago, surely. Oh, those were the days."

When her mother glanced at her, Maleka tried to look as innocent as she could. But Mildred didn't fall for it.

"I'll tell you later," Mildred said to Lisandra.

With that and the arrival of their lunch, her mother didn't say anything more about the big secret mission. A waiter entered with a small rolling table, which he set in the middle of the room. They waited quietly as he prepared the table.

Maleka glanced at Ahmad and when he looked back with his overly bored expression, she deliberately crossed one shapely leg over the other. That caught his attention for a split second. He stared at her bare knees briefly. When he glanced up at her face again, she gave him her 'come hither' smile. He yawned again. She could have stamped her foot.

When they sat at the table, Ahmad walked around her chair. Suddenly, a napkin floated down to cover the expanse of thigh that showed beneath the hem of her skirt. When she looked up, he had a perfectly innocent facial expression and went to sit at his place. Conversation at lunch was unremarkable, though Maleka kept wishing that she'd hear something more about the secret mission.

Maleka noticed something curious about the psychic crosscurrents at lunch. She had a feeling that Ahmad and his mother had been arguing earlier, just as she and Mildred had. Also, as the old hostilities between the two older women had not totally faded; the talk was either between her mother and Ahmad or Lisandra and Maleka.

Maleka suspected that later she would find the whole thing very funny. However, at that moment, she was rather distracted with trying to keep a sneaky eye on the sheik, while still finding out what all the talk about a big secret was. She decided to pour on the charm with Lisandra, hoping that the diva would tell all in time. Instead Lisandra did what all her parents' friends did when she was a kid. She chatted on and on about her career.

After lunch, despite all Maleka's efforts, her mother dragged Lisandra away, leaving her in the room with Ahmad. At first she sat as close to the other room as she could manage, hoping to overhear their conversation. When that didn't work, she decided to get close to Ahmad. Perhaps, despite his acting as if she bored him to tears, she could pump him for information—like who this Zeleke was. She stood and started to walk past him to take a seat on the other side.

Just as she came close to him, he smiled charmingly, appearing all innocent grace as he lifted one booted leg. She went flying, coming to land across his lap. His strong thighs cut into her abdomen and her face was parallel to the floor. This time she had no doubt. He had tripped her!

She struggled to get up from the awkward position but didn't seem to be getting anywhere. He wasn't helping much, either. She found herself staring into his fantastic eyes. They were a deep, soulful brown. She was mesmerized. Her breath caught in her chest.

He looked down his nose at her and said, "I do wish you'd stop throwing yourself at my feet. You're really not my type, and I already have a harem that's quite full, thank you."

"Harem! You have a harem? How many wives do you have?" she asked, aghast. She was interested despite herself and, in her shock, went still from her struggles. She was still lying across his lap. Curiously, she thought that her spirits did a little nose dive at his statement.

"I'm not married yet, but I do have a few concubines. Forty-nine of them—concubines that is—to be exact. I'm going to stop when I reach fifty. So there's room for one more."

"Oh, that's disgusting." He released her at this and she slipped off his lap. Now she was on her knees at his feet. "Just what I'd expect someone like you to say. And I didn't throw myself at you, you tripped me."

"Of course, I didn't trip you. You walked right into me. Besides, why are you so upset? At your height, you're already very close to the ground. You certainly don't have that far to fall." That made her want to spit, but now she was determined to ignore him. She couldn't stand arrogant men and this one took the cake. That's when he asked. "What about you? Are you married?"

"No, I'm not," she answered, trying to show her disdain. "I'm concentrating on my career. But when I do marry, it will be to my soulmate. There won't be any 'concubines' to cloud *our* relationship. We will be devoted only to each other."

"Really? And how do you intend to catch this great prize?"

"Excuse me," she said, one hand akimbo. "But I won't be catching my mate. It will be a mutual meeting of minds, hearts, and spirits. We'll fall in love."

"I hope you're right, but . . ."

"But what?" she said, biting the bait despite her intentions to ignore him.

"It's just that a man usually wants a woman to be like"—Here he stopped to shrug and hold his hands out—"like his own little secret."

"What do you mean?"

He glanced down at the long expanse of leg that showed under her very brief skirt. "You show so much of yourself. Aren't you worried that your soul mate will think that you've exposed yourself to the world?"

"Maybe men in your country think like that, but in mine, women dress to please themselves."

"Well, if you say so." He stood up swiftly and, taking her under her arms, lifted her to her feet. His movement was so sudden that it made her head spin. While he was pure beauty and grace, she landed with a clumsy thump on weakened knees. To steady herself, she held onto him. When she realized what she was doing, she jerked her hands away and went to sit nearby.

It would have done her so much good to tell him off but if she did, she might never find out what her mother was hiding. Obviously, since he was invited to this lunch, he was going to find out and she didn't want to sabotage her own efforts. So, she sank into the chair and smiled at him again. It was always smarter to use a little honey instead of vinegar.

"What did that man say about me?" she asked.

"What man?"

"The bearded one that was with you downstairs. He spoke French. Sometimes my French is a bit sketchy." While that was true enough, she had understood perfectly what was said. "He said something about Cassiopia."

"Oh, you mean Yustafa. He said you looked like a modern Cassiopia."

"Oh," she said, and straightened her shoulders.

"Cassiopia," he said, "was a beautiful African queen in Greek mythology. The goddesses were so jealous of her that they chained her to a chair. At night if you look up you can see a constellation of stars named after her."

"I know that, thank you." She made a mental note to find out more about the ancient story in the library.

"Well"—he looked her up and down—"that Yustafa never did have much sense and he's nearly blind as a bat—too vain to wear his glasses, you see."

Oh, he was the most infuriating man she had ever known. She was tempted to forget all about her decision to pump him for information and tell him off instead. But before she could do either, the door to the room with Lisandra and Mildred opened. Lisandra stepped into view. Mildred could be seen over the opera singer's shoulder. Whatever her mother had said, Lisandra looked alarmed and worried.

"Ahmad," she beckoned to her son, "would you step in here for a moment?" Ahmad flowed out of the low chair. It was a wonder. Whenever he wasn't near her, he was as graceful as a jungle cat. Then, looking at Maleka, Lisandra said, "I'm sorry about this, dear, but would you excuse us for a few moments more?"

Her mother wasn't as kind as Lisandra, but gave her a stern look before adding, "Just remember, Maleka, you promised not to make a sound."

Maleka felt absolutely mutinous. While it was true that she'd promised not to get in the way, she hadn't expected them to have some big secret that they kept from her.

When the three of them went into the other room and closed the door, she found herself staring at the closed door, feeling rejected. She sat there for a long moment, trying to be quiet, but suddenly that closed door began to signify all her childhood feelings of inadequacy.

It brought back all the frustration of being short in a family of tall people, of spending her life watching them talk to each other over her head. That was why she always seemed to need so much attention, why she flirted with men, and did the outlandish things that annoyed her mother. Of course, she had to be fair. It was also responsible for her being assertive and that was a good thing. But she wouldn't let that small factor appease her rising temper today.

She stood up and walked quietly to listen at the door. She couldn't hear much, but what she did hear was fascinating as well as puzzling.

". . . We must help him . . . it's insane. You need professionals to do this . . . a national treasure . . . can't let it fall into the wrong hands . . . antiquity hunters . . . war lords . . ."

Try as she could, Maleka wasn't able to make much

sense out of any of it. However, she did understand that both the women were asking Ahmad to do something very important and obviously, he was reluctant. Humph, what did they expect from that stuck-up fop? How could anyone expect him to do anything heroic? It probably meant that he'd be away from his women for a few nights. He should be glad for the rest. Trying to keep up with all those females must be exhausting. Although, she had to admit, he didn't look the least bit tired.

Four

Finally, it was beginning to make sense. From what Maleka could hear, her mother truly hadn't come to check up on her. The trip was to deliver some important object to an old friend. Lisandra had been called upon to help, as had the snooty sheik. She still didn't know why they were so secretive.

She found it impossible to believe that there was any big treasure involved. This was her mother here, a totally conservative, law-abiding woman. Also, there were times when her mother exaggerated things.

The whole thing annoyed her. Why hadn't they asked her? Here she had been living in the country for months and her mother hadn't even considered asking for her help. It was as if she was still a kid. After being in the city for a week, her mother hadn't called until last night. She was so fed up with everyone assuming that because she was small, she was also helpless. She was quite capable.

That's when she made up her mind that she would be included this time. When they became quiet, she rushed to sit down, just barely making it before the door opened and the three of them came out.

Ahmad went to sprawl into an upholstered chair, one leg hooked over the arm rest. As she had come to expect, he was all male grace. He seemed totally absorbed in the study of his perfect fingernails, but something told her he was not as cool as he appeared. She stood with her back to him determined to show that she could ignore him too. She heard him yawn behind her. Oh, how she ached to deliver one good swift kick to his shins. With her clodhopper soles, he'd regret it.

"I'm truly sorry, darling," Lisandra said, apologizing again.

"Don't worry, Maleka understands," Mildred said.

I don't understand at all, Maleka thought. She wanted to stomp like a child in the middle of the floor, but didn't. Instead, she took a deep breath and without further ado, launched her offensive. "So, where do we start?"

"What?" Both women spoke together as they turned to stare at her.

Hoping she had enough of the key words to make them believe she knew everything, she said, "We don't want it to fall into the wrong hands. It could be a national treasure, after all."

They stared at her as if she had just grown a second head. When she stepped back to include Ahmad, he was no longer yawning. His peeved scowl let her know that this time he heard her every word.

"You listened at the door," her mother shrieked. "I should have known you wouldn't keep your promise."

After mentally crossing her fingers, Maleka plowed on, "Okay, I'm sorry about that, but why not use me, too? I think it would be poetic for the children of Zeleke's two best friends to come to his aid . . ." Both women gasped. By mentioning Zeleke's name, she had taken a gamble, and from everyone's expression, she had hit pay dirt. Behind her, she sensed the very obnoxious Ahmad go dangerously still. She went on, "You need as much help as you can get."

Her words seemed to set them in a tizzy. In their agitation, they spoke to each other over her head. She seemed to be on a level with their navels. This only made her more determined.

Nothing could have infuriated her more. It was something that she noticed years ago about tall people. They spoke only to those on their level or taller.

Ahmad was the first to recover. He stood with both hands on his hips. He looked so menacing that she had to fight back the urge to cringe. His voice vibrated with quiet intensity. "This is not a game. What we said was confidential."

Having to look up that high to him soured her temper even further. *What a bully he is, and who asked his opinion? He's got some nerve. If he knew me better, he'd know that trying to intimidate me is the worst thing anyone could do. But at least he isn't yawning anymore.*

"I'm only offering to help," she said, smiling sweetly in the face of his fury.

"Well," her mother said, "you can't go."

Go, she thought. Go where? She hadn't heard anything about them going any place. There was more to this than she thought. She sensed that this was a good time to make a strategic retreat. Before going on, she needed to know more.

"I understand perfectly, Mother," Maleka said, taking a softer approach. "I simply want all of you to understand that I'm here for you. That I can be as much help as the sheik, here." The word had come out before she thought.

"Sheik?" Lisandra said, with her mouth open in shock. She rounded on Ahmad to say, "What's she talking about?"

He shrugged, looking puzzled by her statement, too. Of course, no one knew that she kept imagining him as a desert sheik. And she had no intention of letting them know, either. That was her secret. Before he could answer, Lisandra turned to her, waiting for an explanation. Maleka felt like a complete fool and wondered how she could talk her way out of this. She said by way of explaining, "Oh, it's nothing—Ahmad was just telling me about his concubines and . . ."

"Concubines!" Lisandra flopped backward into an upholstered chair and fanned herself with her hand. When she recovered a bit, she glared at Ahmad and demanded, "What concubines?"

He looked discomfited and Maleka's mother frowned at *her* in annoyance. It took some time before things calmed down. She had no idea what Ahmad told his mother but Maleka had to admit that she was pleased to see him on the spot instead of her. Both mothers were definitely in great form that day.

Later, after a quick glance at his watch, Ahmad stood to take his leave. He went to his mother and kissed her on both cheeks with a gentle, "Maman."

Lisandra answered, saying, "Yes. Do remember to come over tomorrow," she paused and then continued sarcastically, "sheik."

Then he walked to Mildred, who held her hand out to him, saying, "Ahmad, it's been a pleasure after all these years."

He took Mildred's hand and raised it for another continental kiss. "Enchanted, Madame."

Humph, Maleka thought, who does he think he is, a movie star? However, she couldn't help but be impressed by his flawless French.

When he walked toward her, he looked over her head. Then he lowered his glance to say, "Oh, there you are—short, aren't you?" He yawned, barely covering his mouth in time.

His behaving as if she were too small and boring didn't daunt her. She stuck out her hand to be kissed. He gave her a limp handshake. She wanted to stomp on his toes. With his good-byes said, he threw his desert sheik robes over his shoulder and sauntered toward the door. Sure enough, when he opened the door, his entourage of attendants jumped to attention.

"How could you have embarrassed me like that?" Her mother harangued her all the way down in the elevator and into her room. "You outdid yourself when you eavesdropped on a private conversation. And after swearing that you'd behave."

"I only offered to help and you were all falling over that . . . ,"—oops, she'd almost said sheik again—"that Ahmad."

"Maleka, you're too old to behave like a spoiled brat. Sibling rivalry at twenty-five?"

"Why are you talking about sibling rivalry? He's no brother of mine. But why didn't you ask *me* for help? I know Paris like the back of my hand. And I can do anything that he can."

"This isn't something that I wanted my daughter involved with, for one thing. Also, please don't think that I didn't notice your throwing yourself at the poor man in your usual disgraceful manner."

"I wasn't throwing myself at him. How can you take his side? You should know that he's always tripping me."

That stopped her mother's tirade. "What are you talking about?"

"He tripped me in the lobby and then upstairs in Lisandra's suite."

"Oh, Maleka, sometimes I think you'll do anything for attention. When are you going to grow up?"

Ordinarily, that statement would have caused her to start a slow burn. But today, she could see that anger would get her nowhere. She decided to approach more carefully. "Well, perhaps I am taking it too seriously." Then, aiming for the most innocent face she could manage, she said, "And I'm sorry that I upset you, Mother. But I do want to help."

Mildred did a double take at her acquiescence but seemed mollified. "Well, it's a very delicate situation. It needs careful handling."

"I can see that," she said. "But tell me about Ahmad. Lisandra said we'd met before?"

"Yes, but you couldn't have been more than two years old, with him only eight. He's grown up so handsome, hasn't he?" Mildred said, evidently glad to change the subject. "He was born before I joined the Burke Troupe. I don't know much about that time. I heard that Lisandra had returned to America for a short time and then came back to Paris. I knew Ahmad's father, but it was many years before I knew about Ahmad. By the time I saw him, I was back in the States. One day Lisandra, who was in the States temporarily, came to visit and brought him."

Maleka was silent for a few minutes and when she spoke again, it was to refer back to the meeting at Lisandra's. "Where's Ahmad going?" She tried to sound casual.

"Oh, no, you don't," her mother said. "I thought you knew everything. I'm not going to tell you that, so just forget it."

"Alright. Maybe I did get carried away there. But you know how much I hate it when you treat me like a child. It would be much better if only you'd be open with me."

"This is important and it involves someone else."

"I know, you already said that. I wonder what Daddy would think about it?"

"Okay, okay," her mother said, conceding. "I'll tell you part of the story if it will make you stop interfering. You must promise not to sabotage this."

"Mother, I wouldn't dream of sabotaging anything. I only want to help."

"You can help by not mixing into it."

"At least tell me some of it. That way, I won't be so curious." She almost crossed her fingers at this because it wasn't quite true. It wasn't just curiosity. She really wanted to help. She wanted to prove that she could.

"Okay, here goes. Twenty-seven years ago, when I was here in Paris, I met blacks from all over the world. It was a fascinating time. This will sound a little strange to you now, but back then, many African-Americans didn't know much about people in other parts of the world. Maybe some of the men who'd been in the Armed Forces knew but not the rest of us. And as for blacks in other countries, we knew next to nothing. Being in Europe was an education.

"We were young and terribly interested in politics. America itself was going through a lot of political upheaval. It was a time when blacks all over the world were on the move—Africans, the French, the British, Italians, and many more. Africa was a continent in turmoil. In Africa there were countries newly freed from colonial rule, while others were fighting for their independence. Many governments were unstable and seemed to change daily.

"Ethiopia, believe it or not, was one of the more stable ones at that time. They had reverted to their monarchy after World War II. But things were fermenting there, too, as history soon proved.

"Lisandra and I were with the Burke Troupe. We were fiercely interested in politics. There was a young man, an Ethiopian, who used to follow our performances.

"It was during this time of the early seventies that I met Zeleke."

"Your old boyfriend?"

Mildred sighed. "Not my boyfriend—my friend. We all knew him. He used to come every night to see us. He was a young Ethiopian diplomat, working at their embassy here in Paris.

"Anyway, your father was stationed here at that same time, as you already know. After I married your father and returned to the States, I lost touch with Zeleke. Then one day about fifteen years ago, he came to visit me."

"In America?"

"Yes. It was just out of the blue. He showed up on our doorstep, carrying a large shopping bag. Of course, I was pleased to see him. It had been a long time. I was surprised, too.

"We talked for hours about old times and he stayed for dinner and to see your dad. But he seemed troubled, worried. Then he asked me if I'd keep his package for a few days. He told me it was artifacts that had been in his family for many years and that he wanted to return them to Ethiopia. Had it been anyone but Zeleke, I would have refused. But I'd always been fond of him. Besides, I believed him, and didn't believe that it was anything that he'd gotten illegally. I knew that his family had been important people in his country. I decided that I'd do it. He stayed for dinner and your dad, who had always liked Zeleke, was pleased to see him too.

"After he left that day, I never saw him again. I put the package away and, although I made some inquiries for him, I kept it, expecting him to claim it."

"Did you look at the stuff? Is it some sort of treasure?"

"Yes, I did look at it, but if it's treasure, *I* couldn't see it. It was just an old wooden box. Inside there were a few pieces of old dried-out strips of leather. There was some writing on the leather—symbols in their language. Much of it was too old and faded to decipher. I've seen better pieces in moderately priced art stores."

Maleka was a little disappointed. She wanted it to be treasure. "Well, you never know. Only an expert could really tell."

"Maybe you're right. Anyway, after all this time, about three weeks ago, Zeleke called and asked about the package. He was in Paris and explained that he hadn't been able to collect the package because of problems. He asked me to bring it. He felt that he would be watched and the heirloom would fall into the wrong hands. He wants it to be placed in national archives and feared it might fall into the hands of antiquity hunters or the warlords."

"Warlords?" She shivered. That sounded so strange to her American ears.

"Well, he didn't say it. That was my thought," her mother admitted. "He did request that I travel by way of a specific cruise ship. He had a friend on board who would be able to bring the box into France."

"Mom! That sounds like smuggling!"

"Shh. I know what it sounds like." Mildred wrung her hands at this. "I guess I got caught up remembering the old days. There was a frenetic quality of political activity back then. So much was going on."

"You mean you were smuggling back then?"

"No! But we were always talking about aiding foreign freedom fighters. So many African nations were just becoming independent. We were all doing things that—well, that were unwise. And besides, I didn't want to desert an old friend."

This was news to Maleka. She had known her mother was politically active but she would never have thought of her as going that far out on a limb. "What kind of things did you do?"

The question seemed to make her mother calm down. "That was a long time ago. I was young and foolish. It's now that I'm worried about."

"Where is the heirloom?"

"I left it with Zeleke's friend, the steward, on the ship."

"I thought Zeleke said it was valuable. Can you trust the steward?"

"I certainly hope so. Zeleke recommended him. Anyway, what could I do if he did steal it? I'll be happy to turn the darn thing over to Zeleke and wash my hands of it."

"But you never did catch up with Zeleke?"

"If only I had, I'd be on my way home by now. I've been here for over a week and haven't been able to find him. He no longer lives at the address he gave me. That's why I had to bring Lisandra into this. I figured she's been in Paris for so long, she would know how to find him."

"Does she?"

"No, that's why she brought Ahmad into it. She says he'll be able to find Zeleke, and that although he doesn't deal much in antiquities, he does have contacts. He owns an import-export business. I'm praying that he can help."

"That fop? I doubt it." Then another thought occurred. "I'm still having trouble believing that you'd get involved in this."

Her mother sank down onto the bed. For a split second, she seemed on the verge of crying. It was such a shock for Maleka—she had never seen her mother so upset. "Believe me, I regret it. I'm not the young woman who loved playing political games that I used to be. Now do you understand why I don't want you getting involved?"

All of her life Maleka had seen her mother as a storm trooper. But today Mildred seemed so vulnerable. This was a side of her that she'd never seen before. She knew that she couldn't just walk away, especially now that she could see how difficult it was for her mother.

"Can you trust Ahmad? Why do you think he can do anything? Chances are he doesn't have any energy after his wives get finished with him."

"Wives? Concubines?" Her mother threw up her hands. "Maleka, what are you talking about? How do you know these things?"

"Oh, don't worry about that. You have enough on your mind."

She couldn't get away from the realization that she had never seen her mother so upset. And if her dad ever found out about this, he'd hit the roof. While she had been trying to get information about their problem, not for a minute had she thought it was anything as serious as this. It seemed so incongruous to think of her mother involved in anything like this.

While she might not see eye-to-eye with her mother, she certainly didn't want her to get into any trouble for trying to help a friend. It certainly was something to think of. Her mother smuggling? Good Lord, it sounded incredible.

Several hours later, Maleka left her mother's room. Riding the Paris subway to a little bistro on the left bank, she couldn't get the whole story out of her mind.

There she met up with several friends and joined them to while away the evening. Had the weather been warmer, they would have sat at the outdoor tables and indulged in a little people watching.

The restaurant was run by a relocated Algerian family that still held onto the trappings and attitudes of North Africa. It always made her think how strange the human dilemma was. While in Algeria, many black people were adamantly French, yet when they were forced to migrate to France, they became just as adamantly North African.

There was a forced gaiety about the group, which wasn't unusual. They were like herself, fashion students and neophytes, struggling to start a career. There was talk about the next showings, each of them trying to sound more knowledgeable than they were. Maleka found herself distracted, remembering Ahmad. She couldn't join in with her friends' usual talk. Her concern over her mother's problem continued to disturb her. She left earlier than was her usual wont and traveled on the Metro back to the East Bank and her small living quarters, or her little garret, as she thought of it.

As a girl, she had read biographies of famous artists and musicians of the eighteenth and nineteenth centuries. Many of them had struggled in the early days of their careers, living in poorly heated garrets. Her little room reminded her of those old stories. She had always loved it.

As she dressed for bed, her thoughts wandered over today's luncheon. Besides her concern for her mother's predicament, she couldn't stop thinking of Ahmad. Her fascination with him and his forty-nine concubines upset her, especially when she had to remind herself that it had nothing to do with her. It was then that she realized that she didn't even know his last name.

Now that she had some distance, she remembered that she had heard about him. They called him the American prince. The stories had been sparse, obviously in an attempt to protect his privacy, but she did remember that his father was an Arab sheik. If she remembered correctly, Lisandra had never married her Arab lover and Ahmad had spent much of his childhood in the States. This, of course, was why he spoke totally unaccented English.

The other thought that bothered her was the realization that she found him so incredibly attractive. Usually, she stayed away from the male chauvinist types.

That night as she prepared for bed, she observed her geometrical braids in the mirror. She turned her head to see them at another angle. She liked them, but she was getting tired of them, and she wondered what the sheik thought of them. Then she said aloud, "Forget him. Who cares what he thinks?" She tied a scarf around her head to protect the braids while she slept. She was still mulling over the incident when she slipped into sleep that night.

The next day was Saturday and it was the telephone that dragged her into the real world. She had been wallowing in delicious dreams of riding horseback across the Arabian desert with an absolutely gorgeous sheik. It didn't take much genius to figure out who that was.

Bleary-eyed, she fumbled and picked up the phone. Mildred's voice totally erased the remnants of the dream.

"Maleka? I've just received some information about Zeleke. So I'm going to see if I can catch up with him this afternoon."

"You're not expecting any trouble, are you?" she asked.

"No, there shouldn't be any problem."

"Mom, why don't you wait for me to go with you?"

"Nonsense. What for? This is just a meeting. Once I've met him, I can be finished with the whole thing." That was good to hear. "But first," Mildred went on, "I'm going to have breakfast with Lisandra this morning and I have to do another errand after that. But how about we go to one of the museums tomorrow? I'd hate for us to have no time together while I'm here."

She knew that her mother was trying to make amends for yesterday. "Sounds good."

Hanging up, she rubbed her eyes. Then she noticed something. There on the bedside table was a little packet. It contained her passport, visa, and the documentation to prove that she had received certain inoculations—all the papers she had needed for her canceled trip. Then she thought of meeting Ahmad yesterday. Wasn't it funny that although her trip was tabled, she had still had the opportunity to meet a desert sheik? Okay, maybe he wasn't really a sheik, but he was close.

She sank back on the pillow and tried to recall the

dream that she'd been having. Suddenly, the phone woke her again. Maleka bolted into a sitting position and grabbed it.

Immediately she recognized Lisandra's booming voice. "Darling, your mother was just here for breakfast. Why don't you come for a nice late lunch? We could have a little chat before we eat. I agree wholeheartedly with you and believe you shouldn't be left out of this—situation. I think your mother can be an alarmist sometimes. Also, I'd just love to see your designs. Why don't you bring some of your sketches. Shall we say, one-ish?"

She peered at the alarm clock at her bedside. "One o'clock sounds good."

When she hung up, she rushed out of bed. It was almost eleven and she'd better get hopping if she was going to get dressed and make a grand entrance.

Not till she was in the shower did she remember the second dream of that morning. She had fallen back to sleep after speaking with her mother. Only this time she didn't dream about desert sheiks but about various people who chased her across the desert, trying to pry a valuable treasure out of her hands. Ahmad was in this one, too. Instead of coming to rescue her, he had lounged on priceless carpets and dallied with dozens of beautiful women. These thoughts were so foolish that she quickly pushed them away and thought of the implications of taking her designs to Lisandra.

The implications did not escape her. Her career would truly be launched if she could sell her designs to the famous woman. Maleka dressed with the utmost of care. This time Maleka wore things that were more conservative—a tweed jacket with a flattering short skirt. She didn't want to look too trendy. Not all her designs were outlandish. Those were just to get the public's notice and maybe to aggravate her mother. But, who knew? Someday it might get her coverage in the newspapers, too.

It occurred to her that the opera singer was doing a great deal of entertaining—lunch yesterday, breakfast and lunch today, but that was probably the way great opera singers did things. It was providential for her to call though, and Maleka couldn't help wondering why.

Standing in the hallway, waiting for the diva to open the door, Maleka mused upon the relationship between Lisandra and her mother. It was obvious that the two women were in competition on some level. Quite possibly, Lisandra's inviting her to lunch was a little swipe at her mother, and yet, she was hoping that she'd learn something.

The diva wore another fabulous caftan, this one sea green, over her ample body. She had a long gold-colored silk scarf that wrapped around her neck and hung down her back. Her long, silky, wavy hair was twisted up and wound around her elegant head. When Maleka looked at the still handsome woman, she could see where Ahmad got some of his good looks, but she realized that he must also look very much like his father. Her mind immediately began to work on clothes that would show the older woman's elegant carriage.

"Come in, darling. I'm so glad you could come. Lunch will be a little later. It will just be you and me today, at least for awhile. Why don't we have a little chat and get acquainted? And let me see your sketches," she said, indicating the portfolio that Maleka had brought.

They sat on one of the antique couches. "I brought some that I call the City Woman," Maleka said, and pulled out a sketch.

"Oh, let me see," Lisandra said. "Isn't this smart? As you must know, fashion is terribly important to me."

The talk went on for a while before Lisandra said, "I suppose you've probably heard those old stories about when your mother and I worked with the Burke Troupe."

"I have heard a few. I always loved them. Those must have been exciting times."

"They certainly were. It was during the seventies and so much was going on in the world. We were young then and so caught up in everything. And your mother—what a beauty she was. You don't actually look like her but you do remind me of a younger Mildred. What fire she had. How the men adored her. She was statuesque and had such a presence—like another Josephine Baker. I do believe that Zeleke was half in love with her, too. But of course, all of that changed when your father came on the scene. He was stationed here for a while and that's how they met."

"Yes, they told me that."

"Zeleke was a dashing young flirt attached to the Ethiopian embassy." She stopped, staring off into space for a long moment. "But I've heard stories. People say he's not that same man anymore. They say he's changed."

"Changed?" Maleka prompted.

Lisandra didn't answer the question but only said, "Yes. Those were pivotal times in all of our lives." From there, the diva went on to regale her with more of her memories of that earlier time. Although the stories were fascinating, Maleka found herself looking around at the fabulous suite and thinking that it was the second day in a row that she had dined there. And that thought made her wonder why.

Not why about the first time—she knew how she'd blackmailed herself into yesterday's lunch—but why had Lisandra invited her today? Her earlier thought about the competition between the women seemed too silly to have gotten her invited today.

It was at that moment that Lisandra seemed to awaken from her thoughtful state. She laid the sketches aside and gazed into Maleka's eyes. "I suppose you're wondering why I've brought you here to hear these old boring stories." Lisandra said.

"Oh, I'm not bored."

"Well," the older woman waved off Maleka's protests and said, "I did want to talk with you about something else."

"Yes?"

"Something you said yesterday made me think that you had met Ahmad before."

"Oh, no, I'd just seen him in the lobby." When the

older woman looked puzzled, Maleka went on, "I tripped over his feet."

"That's all? How strange. You seemed to have known each other or to have had a shared past."

"Well, down in the lobby, he was annoyed and said I'd washed up with the Euro-trash."

"Ahmad said that? Very interesting, but you know, that doesn't sound like him at all. Well, never mind, I think he likes you." The statement made no sense and it was Maleka's turn to stare in puzzlement. "You know, likes you as in a man with a woman," Lisandra said, trying to explain.

Maleka was shocked. "Lisandra, I hate to contradict you, but I seriously doubt that. He goes out of his way to tell me that he *doesn't* find me attractive."

"That only makes me more convinced. It's my experience that when a man goes out of his way to speak with an attractive woman, it's because he's interested in her."

While Maleka could see there might have been a small general grain of truth in what Lisandra said, she knew there was no such chink in Ahmad's armor.

"He was with a group of men and they were all very nice. But he wasn't the least bit interested in me, believe me."

"We'll see. And speaking of those men you mention, it's because of them that I have invited you here again today."

"I don't understand."

Lisandra stared off at the puddles of sunlight that came through the lace curtains into the room before she answered. Then she sighed and looked at Maleka before getting up and walking to a little wine cabinet. "Well, it's a long story. Let's have a little sherry." She returned with a bottle and two small crystal glasses.

After pouring the sherry, she sat and looked pensive for a few moments before speaking. "I rarely indulge in sherry. It's bad for my voice, but today I need a little prop." Then she took a cigarette from the fine ceramic dish on the coffee table. "Do you mind? I'll only take a few puffs," she asked.

Maleka, who usually avoided cigarette smoke, nodded, feeling that the older woman needed to unburden herself today.

Lisandra sat back, blowing smoke upward. "It was several years before your mother joined the Burke Troupe that it happened. It was before I finally got into opera. I was a young unpolished girl from Louisiana when I met Hakime Mousoud. He was as handsome as a young prince in a fairy tale and swept me off my feet."

A soft dreamy look came over the great diva's face. "We fell in love and had a mad passionate affair on three continents. It was glorious. I loved him with every fiber of my being. When I was with him, I felt like a goddess.

"But there was a snake in our paradise. At first, it seemed so inconsequential. We laughed at it. But the truth was that we had serious cultural differences. He wanted to marry me, but for some reason, I kept delaying. You see, his culture allowed him four wives and as many concubines as he could afford.

"While he didn't seem interested in this, I wasn't comfortable with it. You know, they even had a woman that traveled with them. She was bought for him. To share the man that I loved with other women was more than I could have tolerated. As the time passed, I found myself less and less willing to take a chance. Also, I didn't want to risk that my freedom to follow my own star would be curtailed. Then something happened that made me realize that it was no longer just my feelings at stake—something that our love couldn't surmount.

"I became pregnant with Ahmad. This was how my decision was made for me. I wanted my son to be American. I couldn't have understood it any other way. It probably sounds narrow minded now. But back then I thought he'd be better off as an American. It was an interesting time. I was seeing a great deal of the world and it was an incredible experience. But a part of me never left the bayou.

"I didn't tell Hakime that I was pregnant, but left and returned to my parents. Ahmad was born there. I stayed in America for two years before returning to Paris. That's when I met your mother.

"I didn't tell anyone that I was pregnant when I left the troupe to go home. My parents raised Ahmad while I pursued my career, traveling a great deal, especially here in Europe.

"Hakime and I became lovers again, but this time it wasn't the same. Too much had happened. I didn't want him to find out about our child, and he never quite trusted me for leaving him as I did. Our relationship was never the same. In this new climate, I became more focused upon my career and soon was singing the type of music that I wanted. Hakime and I drifted apart. Now, I suspect that was inevitable, but then it was painful.

"My career grew and no one knew that I had a child. That didn't come out for many years. During that interval, Ahmad had had no connection with his father. But when I became better known, it was discovered by a gossip columnist. The story was reported by a newspaper.

"When Hakime learned of Ahmad, he was ten years old. By then the dye was cast; he was an American. Hakime insisted that he should be acknowledged as Ahmad's father and I felt guilty enough to allow it. There was an immediate rapport between the two of them. Ahmad went to live with his father and stayed there, except for visits with me, until he was college age.

"Perhaps I made a mistake. Other western women have made the adjustment. But still, I wanted my son's roots to be in the same country as my own were. Perhaps I was selfish, but it's too late to change any of that now. It's well known that men in Hakime's culture don't have the same attitude toward women. I felt that if Ahmad was that type of man, that I'd lose him, and I didn't want to lose my only child. In America, black women have a great deal of control over their families. This is not always true in other cultures.

"Then there was my career. To make it in this business, you need a healthy appreciation of yourself, and I've never had a lack of ego. I wasn't too sure that Hakime wouldn't interfere in it at some point. Even during the days when I worked in other areas and full of passion for Hakime, I was still an opera singer at heart."

At this she paused and gave a small shrug. "But then, I guess this couldn't mean much to you. You're a modern woman and probably already know that the world is always in turmoil. But to me it was new.

"I've grown more knowledgeable now that I've lived on three continents. And, as you can see, I eventually settled in France for my career."

"Yes," Maleka said, nodding.

"In the fifteen years since that, Ahmad has lived in America and owns an extremely prosperous import-export business. He also travels a great deal, going from America to here and to North Africa several times during the year. My son's an American but he became the product of both cultures in the end."

"Are you sorry about that?" Maleka asked.

"No, I'm not that foolish. Actually, I can see that it's by far the better compromise. Besides, he's an independent personality, allowing neither his father nor myself much say in his life. But as his life's a good one, what can either of us say? Of course, his father would love to see Ahmad be the total Arab male, but I suspect that will never happen. However, I guess I still don't want to lose my only child."

Maleka thought of the forty-nine concubines and, as had been true since yesterday, she felt a pang of disappointment. However, she didn't mention that. It was Lisandra who brought up the topic.

"I was wondering about those concubines that you mentioned yesterday."

It was such a change of pace that it caught Maleka unprepared. The sherry went down the wrong way and she started coughing. Lisandra began thumping her on the back. It only made matters worse, because it was doubly hard to concentrate on coughing while still trying to dodge the older woman's heavy hand. When she could finally catch her breath, she said, "Oh, I don't know anything about *them.*"

"Actually, I am inclined to believe that he was . . . what's the old saying, 'pulling your leg'?"

It was such an easy way out that she jumped on the woman's statement. "You know, I believe you're right." She said it to reassure Lisandra. But she personally believed that such a handsome man would indeed have no problems keeping concubines.

"*You* could find out for sure," the diva said.

"Me! What do you mean, find out?"

"You know, sort of feel him out."

"Feel him out?" Those words brought a very graphic image of her touching Ahmad. She nearly started choking again. To erase the mental image, she said, "But why would he tell me anything?" However, remembering his conversation yesterday, she had the distinct impression that he enjoyed telling her about it.

"He told you yesterday. Just get him to start talking again."

"Lisandra, I'd love to help you, but I'd be stepping over my limits to do something like that."

"Yes, yes, my dear. You're . . ."

The telephone rang in the other room, cutting off whatever the woman was going to say. "I'll be right back," she said, going into the next room. There Maleka heard her talking on the phone, "Yes, please come in about an hour," and hung up.

Just as Lisandra returned, a knock sounded at the door. She glanced at her watch and said, "I think that's our lunch. You must be starved."

"Actually," Maleka said, quite sincerely, "I was enjoying listening to your memories of the past." And she was, although she had been thrown about the woman's talk of Ahmad's concubines.

Once again, they waited in silence as the waiter finished

setting up for lunch. When he was done, Lisandra said, "We'll serve ourselves as we did yesterday. Do you mind?"

"That's fine," she answered, trying to sound at ease. It wasn't often that she got the opportunity to dine in such elegance.

The food was great. Her only disappointment was that Lisandra didn't return to the story about her love affair with the Arab sheik. Instead the conversation rambled on about various topics as they ate. They were finished and had set the cart outside in the corridor when Maleka's thoughts went back on the older woman asking her to feel Ahmad out.

Suddenly, there was a knock at the door.

"That must be Ahmad," Lisandra said, glancing at her watch.

"Ahmad?"

"Oh, yes. I asked him to join us after lunch. You don't mind, do you?"

Suddenly, she felt flushed. Her breathing sped up and her palms felt sweaty. It was as if she was getting ready to fight—or maybe to make love? "Oh, no," she replied. "It's no problem for me."

He strode in confidently, wearing western clothes—a long dark trench coat over khaki pants and a cream-colored silk shirt. His feet were clad in dark brown leather boots. The man looked so fantastic that she figured he could wear an old burlap sack and still look incredible.

After kissing Lisandra on both cheeks in the French manner, he turned to her and bowed. "Mademoiselle."

As ordinary as the word was, it was the nicest thing that he'd ever said to her. However, it was the weirdest thing but even in that small greeting, he seemed to mock her. "Bonjour," she said, reluctantly.

"Would you like something, Ahmad?" Lisandra said, indicating the bottle of sherry. He waved no, and went to sprawl in one of the chairs. "I'm so glad you were able to come because . . ." The telephone rang in the other room. Lisandra gave an impatient huff and left to answer it.

Ahmad looked over at Maleka, his eyes traveling over her exposed, stocking-clad knees. As usual, he looked bored. "I realize that at your age, you're probably getting quite anxious to catch a husband."

"As I told you before, I'm not the least bit interested in *catching* a husband. And what's wrong with my age?"

"You're getting kind of up there."

"At twenty-five? I beg your pardon."

"Okay, if you say so. But I do hope you're not trying to ingratiate yourself with my mother. You're wasting your time trying to get her to speak to me for you. I've already explained that you're not my type. I prefer my women to be a little more . . ." He seemed to run out of words and used his hands, indicating both a taller and more full figured woman.

"Jeeze, you're conceited. I am *not* trying to woo your mother. And I'm certainly not the least bit interested in *you.*"

"Then what are you doing here?"

"Your mother invited me to lunch. She happens to like me."

"Hah, don't forget she's a world famous diva."

"What's that got to do with it?"

"Divas are notorious for their huge egos."

"So?"

"Can't you see? A little thing like you would never cause a woman of my mother's ego to feel the least bit threatened. That's why she likes you."

"I think that's a perfectly ghastly thing to say about your mother."

"Don't listen if you don't want to." He yawned broadly and stood up.

"Would you stop that!"

"Stop what?" He looked too innocent and picked up a throw pillow from the couch.

"Yawning like that, as if I'm boring you to tears."

"I was yawning because I didn't get much sleep last night. I called my concubines to cheer them up because I've been away so long."

She couldn't help wrinkling her nose in disgust. "I think it's ridiculous that one man thinks he can keep up with all those women." As soon as the words were out of her mouth, she remembered Lisandra asking her to find out what was going on with him.

"It works out all right. I can rise to the occasion when I'm inspired. My father had me schooled in ways to please a woman . . ."

"Schooled? Who did you practice on?"

"Oh, I had plenty of excellent teachers."

"How old were you?"

"About ten or so. I started late."

She jerked her hand up in her tell-it-to-the-hand pose, saying, "Please, don't tell me any more. I find that appalling. It's disgusting to turn little boys into callous users of women."

He shook his head. "How someone as sweet and submissive as your mother could have given birth to such a misbegotten woman . . ."

"Sweet and submissive. Hah! Are you a bad judge of character, which doesn't surprise me at all—you're batting a thousand. You should know in my mother's last incarnation, she was a war lord in the army of Shaka Zulu."

"Maybe if you didn't wear those clothes that show all your wares, you'd get a mate quicker." He walked around her chair.

"Would you stop saying that?" She was distracted by a small soft object landing in her lap. It startled her. Glancing down, she saw the small colorful couch pillow there. He had dropped it into her lap, effectively covering her knees and thighs. She looked up quickly to see him staring out the window and behaving as if nothing had happened.

Lisandra entered the room at that moment and they both turned toward her. It was only then that she realized how silly the whole thing was. He was just baiting her, of course, and for some reason, she couldn't seem to stop herself from responding.

She suspected that the older woman had caught the whole scene, for she stared at the pillow and her eyebrows rose. Maleka feared that this would cause Lisandra to feel even more justified in her belief that Ahmad was personally interested in her. Hah, what a joke that was. She knew better. Mr. Snooty sheik was just trying to tell her that she was showing too much leg. She placed the pillow on the couch, trying not to make too big a thing over it.

"That was your mother, Maleka," Lisandra said. "She didn't get to see Zeleke. So I've just spoken with my friend, Lord Hunnicut, about this problem. He's an old dear friend and quite respected at the U.K. embassy. I've asked him to help."

"Maman, that wasn't smart," Ahmad said. "Suppose this is an heirloom?"

"I trust James Hunnicut implicitly."

"Nevertheless," he went on, "the less people that know about this, the better. Our worst nightmare would be to have antiquities hunters get wind of this. And it could cost us our necks if we ran foul of any warlords."

"I don't believe they're antiquities. Would Zeleke allow real family heirlooms to molder in Mildred's basement? Mildred misunderstood him. You don't know her like I do. She was always overly dramatic," Lisandra said.

"What about his government? They won't take kindly to his having taken it out of the country."

"But he's trying to return it now. Besides, they're family possessions."

"He told Mildred that they were valuable."

"How do you know Mildred didn't misunderstand him?"

"Suppose you're wrong. We shouldn't be taking any chances. It's best to assume the worst."

Lisandra lifted her hands to him. "Hear me out. James suggests that I come to the embassy this evening. There's going to be a small soiree. There will be people there from

Zeleke's embassy. He feels I could connect with someone who might know his whereabouts. I'm unable to attend at this last minute, so I made arrangements for you," here she spoke to Ahmad, "to attend in my stead." Then she turned to look at Maleka and said, "Maleka will accompany you."

"That's out of the question!" He shot out of the chair to stand with fists on his hips. "I told you that I was going to use some rather . . . seamy sources to find him."

Maleka had been listening to all of this with her head swinging from side to side as if she were at a tennis match. And she was as shocked as Ahmad at Lisandra's announcement. However, even in her shock, she still resented Ahmad's reaction.

Lisandra went on unperturbed. "I know you said that, but there's nothing seamy about the U.K. embassy."

"Suppose it goes further than you're expecting?" he insisted.

"Nonsense. This is just a little social gathering at the embassy. Nothing can happen. If you feel so strongly about it, then I'll just have to cancel my appointment and go, myself—with Maleka."

He raked a furious glance in Maleka's direction. "I guess you're the one who put her up to this." He sneered at her.

"I didn't know any more about it than you did."

"Maleka had nothing to do with this. It's a done deal. I've already made the arrangements with Lord Hunnicut and he's offered to help, and he's expecting her. Do you think you'll be able to attend, Maleka?"

"I certainly will," she hurried to assure the older woman, and tried not to look too smug at Ahmad's chagrin. "I have just the outfit to wear." She could have sworn that Mr. Snooty muttered something at this.

He looked as if he wanted to refuse outright. Instead, he exhaled and said, "We don't really know what's going on and it could be dangerous."

"O posh! Why should it be dangerous? Zeleke was always

a mild, sweet person—a little flirtatious but a pussy cat. He wouldn't be involved in anything illegal."

Maleka remembered Lisandra saying that Zeleke was a changed man and wondered. Maybe he had been a pussy cat but what was he now?

"I protest this," Ahmad said, sounding more impatient than ever.

"I tell you it will be all right. And Maleka will be a big help. She's bright and personable. With her along it will allay everyone's suspicion. And that's final," she added, when Ahmad seemed ready to balk further.

Maleka couldn't help smiling. She wanted to hug Lisandra but tried to appear as cool as she could. Besides, she wanted to go. She had to look out for her mother's interest. "I think it's a good idea," she said.

That obnoxious Ahmad actually snorted. Part of her wanted to tell him off but she managed to hold on.

At Lisandra's insistence, Ahmad drove her home in his little shiny red Fiat. Then he left to go to his own place and get dressed.

She raced up the stairs, her mind desperately trying to think of what she could wear. She spent some time pawing through her small closet for the perfect dress. There wasn't a lot to choose from. It was rare that she went to events such as this one. Then in a flash she decided. She pulled out a dress that was wrapped in tissue and hung in the back of her closet. It was one of her own originals, and she had planned it for a part of a showing—if such a time should ever occur.

Laying the dress across the bed, she took a long look in the mirror. She was tired of the braids. On an impulse, she took them out. Her hair was a thick mass of crinkly waves that touched her shoulders. She hadn't worn it like that lately and decided to leave it. A quick glance at her watch and she knew she had time for a relaxing bath instead of a shower. The steam would also help fix the crinkly waves.

Sooner than she expected, Ahmad was back, fully

dressed in a tuxedo. He wore a white kerchief on his head with a black cord. He looked absolutely sumptuous. Once again, she felt a pang of wishing that she could get him to escort her to the Valentine's Dance.

She had just come out of the tub when she heard the doorbell. "Come in; I won't be long." She led him to her room. "This has to remain open," she said, indicating the door. "It's house rules."

There was a hint of a smile on his lips as one eyebrow rose, but he only said, "No problem."

He walked around her little room, making everything appear smaller. Looking around, he examined her little knick knacks and especially checked her books. Then he settled into a chair and scanned through one of her books. She was dying to see the title but didn't want to let him see her curiosity. There was something terribly intimate about his going through her small library and reading her books. She felt as if he could look into her heart.

Having him watching made her feel all thumbs. Finally, she took the things that she had planned to wear and went back into the bathroom to get dressed. It wasn't one of her more outlandish outfits, because she suspected that it wasn't a time for her to be too conspicuous. It was a pretty simple red sequined sheath with spaghetti straps and a short skirt. It had a jacket to keep her from freezing.

She took meticulous care to put on her makeup and fix her hair. Stepping back, she was pleased. It felt great to be going to such a posh do because she could advertise her own stuff.

Ahmad looked up. Although his scrutiny made her a little anxious, she still felt like a million dollars. It was the dress that did it. She knew it was one of her more successful designs. She walked into the room. He sat there still looking at her, not saying a word. The thought that her design had made him speechless filtered into her mind. She inhaled a heady breath of air. But his next words changed that.

"Are you going to wear that dress?" he asked, disapproval dripping from the words.

"Yes, what do you think?" she asked.

"I think you need to change into something more . . . just put on *more* clothes."

"Why do I need more clothes? We're going to the British embassy. It won't be a problem there. Besides, this dress is quite acceptable. It isn't that revealing. Maybe you're uncomfortable with it because it makes me look too sexy?" This last remark she said with sarcastic sweetness.

"Me, uncomfortable? It doesn't mean a thing to me. But there may be people at the party who will find it offensive."

"Oh, give me a break. This is Paris, not a country where women are put in harems."

"Either you change or you're not going."

"I will not change, and your mother said that I *have* to go—that you need a disguise."

"Disguise? When people wear disguises they're usually trying to be inconspicuous. That outfit stands out like a neon light. You will draw eyes from blocks away."

"You think so?" She glanced at herself in the mirror and turned from side to side. "It does make me look sexy."

He rolled his eyes upward. "I wouldn't take it that far. And I don't give a hoot what my mother says. She can be as foolish as you. Suppose the top falls down?"

"Don't worry, it won't." She threw her shoulders back.

Ahmad stopped short to stare at her chest. Then he turned away as if distracted and said, "How you ever expect to get married after you've destroyed your reputation and credibility as a respectable maiden . . ."

"Ahmad, please. Let's not get on that again. Also, I have no intention of marrying at this time. And I'd never choose a husband who couldn't accept a dress like this."

"Can't you pull it up?" he asked.

"Oh, all right," she said ungraciously and tugged it upward. Of course, when she pulled it up, it got shorter at the bottom.

He stared down at her legs and said, "Never mind."

"I do have a jacket for it." She handed it to him and turned around for him to help her. She had done it deliberately, hoping to get a rise out of him.

He held it as she slipped her arms through the sleeves. He stood behind her and she could have sworn that she felt his body heat through the sequins. His finger lightly grazed her throat. Gently, he pulled the collar close. His warm breath lifted the tendrils of hair from her face. When this was done, both his hands rested on her shoulders. They stood like that for a long moment. She could not have moved even if her life had depended upon it. Finally, his hands dropped from her shoulders and she felt as if she had lost some wondrous gift.

He stepped back, saying, "We'd better be going."

Whatever her reason was for handing him the jacket didn't matter, for it was *her* breath that caught in her throat. He looked as cool as he wanted to be.

Five

The ride to the party wasn't particularly long but it seemed like forever. If she had been flirting with him in her room, he got his revenge in his car. First, he came around to help her into the car and strap her into the seat belt. He took an agonizingly long time to do it, too. When he leaned over her, she could smell his tantalizing after-shave. Once again, she was captivated by his eyelashes. They were long and abundant. Heat suffused her body where his hands brushed over her flesh. When he was finished, he turned and looked her full in the eyes. It was a mesmerizing, intoxicating moment.

By the time they arrived at the party she was a wreck. She had to stand and take several deep breaths to regain her composure.

Everything was already in progress. People from all over the world were in attendance. It was an absolutely fascinating sight. Famous faces loomed everywhere—diplomats whose words were valued by multitudes, powerful government dignitaries, oil rulers. She was rubbing shoulders with people whose opinions were respected by kings and presidents and prime ministers. It was intoxicating to be in the presence of so much power. She was as awed as any school kid.

But not only the powerful were represented that night. There were also spiritual leaders. She noticed several East African Orthodox priests, garbed in their long black robes and hats that resembled graduation caps. They stood to one side, as if careful not to usurp any attention from the diplomats.

She took another deep breath and removed her jacket. She wanted people to see her dress. This was the best advertising she'd ever had.

James Hunnicut, Lisandra's friend, was the first person to greet them. When Ahmad introduced them, he took Maleka's hand and said, "You are everything that Lisandra said. She insisted that I take good care of you."

She was so thrilled to be talking to one of Britain's peers of the realm that she almost fell over her feet. "Thank you," she twittered, and was disgusted to see Ahmad roll his eyes at her.

They hadn't been there too long before a diminutive Asian man came up to her. He was all smiles and Oriental bows. "My dear, are you with the Ghanian group?"

"No, I'm not," she responded.

"Too bad." He went away, sadly shaking his head.

There was a wide variety of hors d'oeuvres and other edibles. Although there was one main area for the food, someone had cleverly placed buffet tables at various spots throughout the rooms. It cut back on people bunching in one spot.

She followed Ahmad to one of the main buffet tables and glanced around, wondering what to sample. Everything looked delicious.

"Try this," he said, offering a dab of caviar on a wedge of toast.

Her reaction was spontaneous. "Those are fish eggs!" She held up her hands and wrinkled her nose. "It's against my principles to eat the unborn babies of any species. No wonder our environment is in trouble," she said.

"Bet you had a nice American breakfast of bacon and eggs this morning," he said, biting a piece of the toast.

"With all that cholesterol? No way. How can people kiss each other after eating that?"

He leaned toward her, his face coming alarmingly close. "Were you thinking of kissing me?" he asked.

She was stalled like the proverbial deer caught in someone's headlights, staring at his mouth. Then she forced her attention away and took a small step back. "I was speaking generally."

"Oh, good, because I'd have had to get into the mood first."

"Believe me, if I ever kissed you, you would be in the mood immediately," she said.

"Really? Want to prove that?"

The challenge warmed her right down to her very toes. Their little war that had begun in her room was escalating. What, she wondered, would he do if she were to press her mouth to his? The powerful temptation rattled her. But turning away, she forced herself to focus on putting food onto her plate. She tried to sound totally at ease when she said, "No way, beluga breath." But if she did sound unaffected, it still took all her control to steady her hand enough to fill her plate.

His challenge rang in her thoughts after that. The only reason she hadn't taken him up on it was because she suspected that he hadn't meant it. Still, she couldn't keep her imagination from spinning out a scene that was hot enough to melt her brain.

They were at the soiree to meet people, yet she didn't want to part from him. Part of her wanted to escape. Part of her brain whispered that there was danger if she stayed close to him. But another part couldn't keep away.

She remembered Lisandra's asking her to find out about his concubines. And although she knew this was none of anyone's business, she was curious enough to want to know.

"Tell me about your concubines," she said.

He looked down at her with one eyebrow raised. "What would you like to know?"

"You said they were from all over the world."

"Yes." He started ticking them off on his fingers.

"There's Yin-yin. She speaks Mandarin. And Utter, who's Dutch. And . . ."

Already, she regretted asking. She cut in, "I guess they learn Arabic?"

"Oh, no. It's rare for them not to know English or French. And usually they teach me their native language. That's how I've become proficient in so many languages. Communication is important with lovers," he said smugly.

Lord, how nauseating the man could be. No matter what Lisandra asked, there was no way she could listen to this. They separated and each went to mingle with different people. Each time she looked up, Ahmad would be in a different group, and each time, she heard him speak in a different language. It was obvious that he was having a high old time.

The nerve of him trying to keep her from attending. Where was the danger that he'd mentioned? Ha. The only danger she could see was that all the women who congregated around him might blow him away with all their heavy breathing. It would be a cold day in hell the next time she believed him.

Later that evening, they were standing together, holding the usual champagne glasses. "Where is this man that we're supposed to meet?" she asked.

"He hasn't arrived," Ahmad said. He looked around casually. "And to be honest, I don't think he's coming."

A handsome older man, holding a drink, came up to her, speaking in an unfamiliar language. She guessed his accent to be Eastern European.

"I'm sorry but I don't understand you," she said, when he launched into a spate of strange sounding words.

"Oh, you're American. I thought you were Somalian. Let me introduce myself. I am Johannes Von Wendt. Do you know that you resemble that beautiful model, Iman?" He took her hand and kissed it.

She was so tickled at the attention that she turned her

biggest smile on him after first checking to see if Ahmad had heard. The talk was just banter, but he was charming.

She was aware that he kept gazing down her dress front. But by this time, she had replaced her jacket so there wasn't a lot for him to see. She took a deep breath at one point and he stopped speaking to stare raptly at her breasts, grinning in expectation. It didn't take a rocket scientist to figure that he was hoping her dress top would fall down. It was a small thing, but she was reminded that even famous important men sometimes behaved foolishly. Ahmad had noticed too, and he grumbled something from behind her.

Then a peculiar thing happened. Ahmad was no longer at her back but had come to stand beside the man. She glanced at him and he smiled back, so sweetly and innocently. A funny feeling went up her spine and she found herself wanting to step back. Suddenly the older man seemed to bump into Ahmad. His drink spilled and somehow he managed to step into it, which sent him sliding across the floor.

Fortunately, Ahmad caught him and set him back onto his feet. It had all occurred so quickly that she still hadn't figured out what had happened. However, there was no damage done. But strangely enough, the man turned a look of total puzzlement upon Ahmad and quickly took himself away.

"What happened there, for pete's sake?"

"How should I know? He just bumped into me. He was probably too busy looking down the front of your dress."

"I can't believe how clumsy you are. You could have caused a diplomatic incident," she said.

"Oh, I don't think so," he said, gazing into his drink. "Maybe what I should have done was drop a few ice cubes." He glanced pointedly down at her dress and smiled innocently.

She wasn't sure but that sounded like a threat. Her hands flew to cover the top of her dress. "I'm going to the powder room," she said, and sauntered away.

When she returned, Ahmad was across the room talking with several women. Every few minutes, a burst of feminine laughter erupted from them. They seemed to hang onto his every word. And to think her mother believed that he would save that treasure. What a joke. It was a good thing she had insisted upon coming.

The same diminutive Oriental man who had approached her earlier came up again. He smiled broadly. "I am Nado Tanaka, and what is your name? You said you're not from Ghana, but you didn't tell me where you are from."

"My name is Maleka Darling and I'm an American."

"Ah, your name is Darling? Isn't that an English endearment? No wonder you have such a lovely smile. Your name suits you. I wish I could have brought my camera." He held both hands up in front of his face as if he were looking through the viewfinder of a camera. "You are a perfect subject."

"Oh, thank you," she gushed, totally flattered. She glanced around, wishing that Ahmad had heard.

"Come," he said, taking her hand. "Let us sit over there. I want you to tell me all about yourself." He led her to a row of chairs placed at the side of one wall. Near Mr. Tanaka's elbow was a table, which was part of the buffet. A bowl of salad greens sat there.

He pulled his chair close to hers, sitting so close that their legs were almost touching. As he talked, he kept leaning over and tapping her knee for emphasis. "Now, tell me. Where in America is your home and how do you like Paris?"

They had been chatting merrily for some minutes when she looked up and spied Ahmad approaching. He came up and introduced himself. Mr. Tanaka stood and the two men went into a curious little ceremony of smiling and bowing to each other. They conversed and Mr. Tanaka turned to her, saying, "He speaks excellent Japanese."

Eventually, Mr. Tanaka sat and, once there, continued his habit of tapping her knee at frequent opportunities. Suddenly, Ahmad smiled benevolently down on them. That smile made her uneasy.

She saw what came next from the corner of her eye. At first, there seemed almost to be a gentle shifting of air. Looking up, she caught another of Ahmad's spectacularly innocent facial expressions. But when he gracefully stepped to the side, her antenna went on alert. She had seen him move that way several times in the last two days and each time something had happened. Twice she had tripped, and once it had been someone else, she thought, remembering the earlier scene with the gentleman who said she looked like Iman.

Instinct made her bolt from her chair. Once out of the firing range, she glanced around, wondering what was going to happen. This time, she wasn't going to take any chances. She intended to save herself. Whatever it was would probably make her look like a fool.

Sure enough, lettuce leaves tumbled down on the spot where she had been sitting. She was definitely getting better. Not a drop had landed on her.

Poor Mr. Tanaka wasn't so lucky. He was still pretending to look through the viewfinder of his imaginary camera. When Maleka moved, he actually leaned closer, putting himself right in the path of the missile that was aimed at her—the huge bowl of salad greens. It was as if it moved in slow motion.

She watched in horror as the whole bowl upturned onto his lap. The older man's facial expression would have been funny if she hadn't been so furious at Ahmad.

It was pure good luck that there had been no salad dressing on the lettuce. In the end, once Mr. Tanaka was sponged off, he and Ahmad returned to their smiling-bowing ritual. However, the little man hastily took his leave after a short incomprehensible conversation with Ahmad.

"What did you two talk about?" she asked, suspicious.

"I'm not sure, my Japanese was never very good, but I think it was something about the evil eye."

"Do the Japanese have a belief in the evil eye?"

"Doesn't every culture have one?"

"You didn't tell him it was my fault—did you?"

"Why would I do that?" His expression was too innocent for her satisfaction.

"Why is it that every time you come near me, I have an accident? Are you sure you're not doing it deliberately?"

"Me?"

"Maybe you really like me and don't want to admit that you're jealous." To this he laughed uproariously and she hastened to say, "All right, forget I said that."

"However, I am a little concerned for you."

"Why?"

"You see, Mr. Tanaka already has a wife."

"So what?" she responded, and then in curiosity asked, "You don't mean that beautiful young creature that he's talking with?"

"Where?" he asked, looking around.

"Over there," she pointed.

"Oh, no, that's his concubine."

"That nice little old man? How disgusting. She's probably only after his money."

"I'm sure he doesn't mind that. After all, *I've* always found her quite charming."

"Oh, for pete's sake," she said, and started to walk away.

"You're not jealous, are you?" he said, catching her arm and keeping her from leaving.

"Jealous of who? You?"

"Maybe just a little?"

"You wish." She stomped away.

* * *

Later, he came up to her. "Still angry with me?"

"Angry with you? Who said I was angry? Nothing you do has the least effect on me."

"Good," he murmured. His voice made shivers race up and down her spine and her knees nearly buckled. "It's time for us to leave."

"Leave? But I thought you didn't see our contact."

"Our contact, you're calling him? Sounds like you've been reading espionage novels."

"Whatever," she waved her hand. "You know what I mean."

"No, I didn't see him, but I don't want to waste any more time here. I'll take you home."

"Oh," she said, feeling disappointed. Having been all psyched up, she felt let down now. Also, it meant the end of her evening out with Ahmad.

Ahmad went to collect their coats and she went looking to take her leave of their host.

"Lord Hunnicut, we are leaving now and I want to thank you for having us," she said, extending her hand to him.

"My dear," he responded, taking her hand in both of his. "I'm so sorry that I wasn't able to spend more time with you. But I guess it's as they say—all's well that ends well. I am glad that you met your man."

"Met our man?" she parroted. It took a moment for her to catch on.

"Yes, Ahmad tells me you have arranged a meeting for tonight. Jolly good, that's what I always say."

She didn't want him to see her surprise. "Yes, that's what I always say, too," she muttered vaguely.

But he sensed something, for he said, "Don't tell me that I didn't hear it right?"

"Oh, yes. You heard right. We're going to meet tonight."

After that Ahmad came up and also said good-bye to Lord Hunnicut. He glanced warily at her but didn't say anything. She smiled in sweet innocence up at him. Two could play that game.

Once they were in his car, the truce was off.

"Okay, let's hear it," he said.

"You liar! You were going to dump me at home and go on to meet our contact."

"Listen, it's just as I feared. This is turning into a dicey situation. I told you it could happen. Where I have to go tonight, you don't want to be."

"Oh, yes, I do. Don't forget, it's *my* mother's problem. I have no intention of letting you freeze me out."

"Don't be ridiculous. Bow out gracefully while you can."

"There's nothing ridiculous about it. And I'm not quitting. For all I know, you probably can't even handle it. You're always tripping people with your big feet and doing other things like that."

"I absolutely refuse to let you come with me."

She rolled her window down. "How are you going to stop me?" He looked at her in pure fury. She felt almost as if sparks shot from his eyes. "And don't think you can manhandle me. I'll yell bloody murder and get you arrested."

He glanced impatiently at his watch. "Maleka, I don't have time for this."

She glared at him and smoothed her skirt down casually. Then she said with sickening sweetness, "Then start the car and let's be on our way."

He turned the ignition in the motor and let out such a stream of curses that she thought of the phrase, "turned the air blue."

They stopped at his place briefly, where he exchanged his red Fiat for a less showy low black sports car in which the engine purred with just a whisper. Once on their way, he glanced up in the rearview mirror repeatedly. She looked back at the street behind them, wondering what he was watching.

"Are you trying to hint that we're being followed?"

"I didn't say that," he hissed through his teeth. But she watched him after that.

Next, they traveled north to the Montmartre district where the beautiful cathedral of Sacre Coeur, The Sacred Heart, stood high on a hill. In contrast, it was also a place of a rather seedy history. In recent years, some of this has changed as rising property values have made inroads into the area, much of it being renovated.

But the bar that Ahmad took her to was still a garish, seedy shake joint. It was dark, crowded, and smoke filled—the kind of dark that made you feel like you had just stepped into a velvet black fog. The scant pin-pricks of light that shone from above actually made things worse. They illuminated only patches of the customers' faces, making them look distorted. Maleka felt as if she were walking through a cave filled with monsters.

Whatever made Ahmad think they could spot their contact here was a mystery. He could have sat right next to them and still have been invisible.

Almost as soon as she entered, her eyes and her throat began to sting from the cigarette smoke. When Ahmad insisted that they check their coats, she wanted to renege. She had serious doubts about handing her coat over in a place like that but she went along with it. She knew he was already annoyed enough with her.

As it had been in the embassy, the clientele she could see was international. Customers sat at round tables. A mean, scruffy-looking waiter ushered them to a table located near the front. Following behind the man, she could barely see and was forced to move cautiously through a sea of tough-looking men. Many of them leered at her. Suddenly, she wished that she'd worn a dress that covered her from head to toe.

One man leaned so far in front of her that she couldn't pass him. He smiled evilly and whispered something incomprehensible.

Ahmad loomed up from behind her, saying, "Move along, my darling."

His darling. Humph. Who did he think he was fooling? She realized that it sounded as if he were calling her sweet names, but she knew better. Still, she was terribly glad that he was there. The man gave Ahmad one look and leaned back in his chair, and they continued to their table.

It wasn't the sort of place that she would have gone to had she been alone. Finally they were seated at a table close to the front where there was a cleared circular space that she figured would be used for entertainment.

Once seated, Ahmad ordered drinks. Although she had eaten hors d'oeuvres at the party, finger foods weren't very filling. She was starved and felt as if she could eat an elephant. Yet, she was glad that he didn't order anything else. In the dark, she couldn't even read the menu. Besides, the place didn't look too kosher and there was no way of telling what the kitchen looked like. Quite likely there were creepy crawly things.

Ahmad glanced around casually and spoke to the waiter as he collected the menus. "Is Snake-Eyes here tonight?"

After a brief hesitation, the man answered, "Who's asking?"

"Tell him that the Rock wants to speak with him."

She tried to appear like everything was fine with her, but at the mention of someone called Snake-Eyes and hearing his strange alias, she couldn't stop herself from being startled.

Once the waiter was gone, she hissed, "Why are you calling yourself the Rock? And who's Snake-Eyes?"

"Don't worry about that. Just act natural."

"I *am* acting natural."

"Like hell you are. Even in this dark I can see your eyes bug out."

She suspected that he was right and tried to ease up a bit. But that didn't stop her questions. "What makes you think our contact will be here?"

"This is where I was told that he usually comes."

She couldn't help shuddering as she peered through the darkness. "It's a peculiar place."

"Don't complain now. I warned you not to come. Besides, we won't be here that long."

"I wasn't complaining. I was only making an observation. And we can stay as long as we need. I'm not the least bit worried."

"Are you trying to say that you come to places like this all the time?"

"Maybe not all the time, but I come whenever I feel like it." She only hoped that the lie was convincing, because she wouldn't have been caught dead in a place like this if she hadn't been trying to prove that she could handle anything that Ahmad could.

"Sure, I'll bet you do."

She was terribly annoyed with him at this. Why his apparent disbelief set her teeth on edge, she wasn't sure. After all, it *was* a lie. Nevertheless, she didn't want to appear uncomfortable so she leaned back and looked around, trying to appear relaxed. She even smiled at the people at the next table. She thought they were women, but with so little light it could have been anyone.

She was determined not to react to his making fun of her. Glancing around at the many smoking customers she wished that she had one of those artificial cigarettes that people used to quit smoking. Then she would look right at home. Although she didn't smoke, there were times when it seemed the perfect accessory. Right at that moment it would have lent her an air of sophisticated decadence.

The drinks came and within a few minutes a rather disreputable man with a black patch over one eye appeared out of the dark. He was so menacing looking that she couldn't believe he was real. He looked like a character out of a scary movie. Surely people like this didn't really exist, and certainly not ones named Snake-Eyes. That was just too much to believe.

Whatever lingering doubts she'd had evaporated when

the man spoke. "What a rare pleasure," he said to Ahmad. His accented voice was soft and cultured. When he looked at her, he said, "Ah, you bring a friend, a beautiful friend."

It was then that she began to believe that Ahmad was putting her on—that he'd brought her to this dive to scare her off. Well, he could think again. She knew all about these tourists' joints where the waiters dressed in costumes. If this wasn't a costume, she'd eat her hat.

Ahmad said, "Maleka, I want you to meet Snake-Eyes."

The man inclined his head stiffly toward her. The more she thought about it, the more certain she was that Ahmad was trying to trick her. She decided to show him that he couldn't scare her off with this obvious ploy.

She smiled and pushed out her hand to the man. "So nice to meet you, Snake-Eyes," she said.

Ahmad looked surprised, as if he hadn't expected her to be friendly. Snake Eyes, too, had expected her to be put off by his appearance. For a split second, he drew back. But then he smiled. That smile changed him completely. He no longer looked like a pirate. Now, he was just a man with an eye patch. She was totally disarmed and smiled again.

He took her hand and bowing gallantly said, "For you, lovely one, I am Annan."

He sat with them. "Rock, you old dog, where did you find this rare and beautiful creature?"

"Oh," Ahmad said, "she's a young nun from the local convent."

Her mouth fell open. She was as surprised by this statement as Snake-Eyes, who yelped, "Nun?" He crossed himself. "What's she doing in a place like this?"

"We'll talk about that. It's part of the situation that I told you about."

Snake-Eyes shook his head and cast one long lingering glance at her. "Too bad," he said sadly. Then he moved away from her and spoke quietly with Ahmad. He never looked in her direction again.

She was annoyed enough to spit nails but didn't deny Ahmad's remark about her. Maybe this was important to their disguise. Anyway, she didn't want to take any chances.

Six

She forgot all about Ahmad's telling Snake-Eyes that she was a nun when the spotlight flooded across the center of the floor. In swept a voluptuous woman clad in a scanty, diaphanous fabric that revealed more than it hid. The woman, a beautiful creature, stood with arms raised. She had a jewel in her navel. The audience went wild. At first there was a roar of recognition. They clapped and called out. Yet, the crowd wasn't what Maleka would have expected. Yes, it was mostly men and yes, they were raucous. But there were no obscene cat-calls. They were respectful. True, she'd never been to anything of this sort but she had thought they'd be rowdy.

A hush built up slowly as the clapping lessened. The woman stood absolutely still. When everyone was quiet she began to dance. Her movements were slow and her hips moved sinuously. Her abdomen seemed to have a life of its own. It appeared to be divided into four separate sections, and she could move each section either individually, in unison, or even in opposite directions. The jewel winked in and out with her movements. Maleka suddenly realized that she was not watching a strip-tease act. She was watching performance art. She gained respect.

The first dancer was followed by a second and a third, each more incredible than the last. In the end, the third dancer spied Ahmad and slunk over to give him a special performance. He laughed and clapped at her every move.

She swirled around his chair, enfolding the two of them in her veils. The crowd went wild at this.

Maleka, who had been enjoying herself until this moment, felt annoyed at this maneuver. The last thing that conceited man needed was special attention from such a beautiful woman. He was probably measuring her for that number fifty spot in his harem. Maleka was tempted to lift the veil and see what they were doing. She would only be doing it for his mother. After all, hadn't Lisandra asked her to find out what was happening with him? Somehow, she knew that this was only an excuse to interfere and managed to restrain herself.

At the end of the third dancer's number, there was an invitation for audience participation. The dancer pulled Ahmad onto the floor to dance with her. Then the other dancers returned and invited everyone to join them. Maleka couldn't resist it. If Ahmad could get up there and do it, so could she. Jumping up to join the people, she totally forgot her early fears. It was mostly men who moved to dance in the clearing. There was no way she could do the dances those women did, but she knew a few things. Before long, there were almost as many men around her as around the belly dancers. However, that didn't last long, for Ahmad came and collected her.

"Do you know what a spectacle you're making of yourself?"

"Me? What about you? And everyone else was dancing, too."

"Men, you mean?"

"I saw a few women out there. And you have some nerve talking about me. 'People in disguise have to be discreet,' she mimicked him. "There was nothing discreet about the way you flirted with that belly dancer. It was positively disgusting."

"Oh, I was just interviewing her for a place in my harem."

"She's so fat."

"She's what I like to refer to as a whole lot of woman."

Suddenly, the air seemed to go out of her. She felt as if she were walking on very thin ice. What was she doing here? It wasn't that she'd led a completely selfish life, but in a way her mother was right. Why was she so determined to get in on this situation? Didn't she have enough challenge with the fashion internship? Heck yes. The Fashion and Design House of Vito Genovese got a full sixty-hour work week out of her. And hard hours they were, too.

Why was she knocking herself out to spend her short vacation doing something crazy like this? Who did she think she was—a secret agent? If everyone else thought Ahmad could handle the situation, why didn't she simply let him get to it?

So she wanted to help her mother. That was okay. It was even all right that she felt the need to prove herself. But surely she wasn't doing all this because of a handsome man?

She admitted that she adored good-looking men, but she'd never let herself be a complete fool over one before. Why was she acting different this time?

Tomorrow, she'd bow out of this. No one wanted her here anyway. Maybe Lisandra wanted her to keep an eye on Ahmad, but as far as she could see, he didn't need it. Not for a moment did she believe he was as clumsy as he pretended. No one who moved as gracefully as he did could be that much of a klutz. He didn't need anyone watching over him. Also, he was positively rude with the way he told her to buzz off. She didn't need this. Lisandra would have to find another way to keep tabs on him.

Somewhere during the dancing, Snake-Eyes had left them. When he returned, he leaned over and whispered something to Ahmad. After the man had left, Ahmad leaned toward her and said in a low voice, "We're going to have to leave here now."

"Huh?" she said, too distracted by her own thoughts to respond quickly.

"In a few minutes, we're going to leave through the back way. Be ready to move—and do exactly what—I say."

"Oh, please. I'm tired of all this play acting . . ."

"Now," he insisted.

Suddenly, he grabbed her arm and jumped up, dragging her along with him. They rushed out a different way than they had come. Fortunately for her he was in front, because in the dark, she would have been bumping into things.

They ran through the kitchen toward the back. Even in the urgency of the moment, she took a quick look around the kitchen. It was spotless—not a creepy crawler to be seen.

In record time, they were at the back door. "Wait," she said, holding back.

"We can't stop," he said.

She leaned down to remove her heels. They dashed through the door and into a dank, dark alley. Still he hauled her after him. She felt as if her feet never touched the ground. They exited the alley and raced for half a block. Suddenly, he stopped and she realized they were in front of his low, dark car. Someone had moved it while they were in the club. The sight of Snake-Eyes, standing at the driver's side explained that. The engine was already running.

He pushed her into the passenger seat and vaulted over the hood to sit in the driver's seat. "Buckle up!" he roared at her.

She was so rattled that it took several attempts before she could lock the seat belt. The tires screeched as they tore rubber, getting out of there. He searched the streets behind them through the rearview mirror. After about twenty minutes, he seemed to relax a bit.

By this time she was exhilarated. The dash out of the club had driven her sad thoughts out of her mind. When she laughed, he glanced toward her and laughed, too.

"What was that all about? What happened? Why did we have to leave like that?"

"I thought we picked up a tail at the embassy and I wanted to dump whoever it was."

"You're kidding, right?"

"Who knows, maybe I imagined it." They laughed together like conspirators. It was the nicest few moments she had spent with him.

At her apartment, he took her up the stairs and waited while she fished her keys out of her purse. He took them from her and opened the door. But when she would have gone inside, he turned her to face him. Her heart leaped in her chest until she feared that it would break through her rib cage.

He touched her cheek with one gentle finger. "You've been very brave tonight."

"I know you didn't want me to go."

"Maybe I was wrong."

"But someone did chase us."

"Did you see them?"

"No, but . . ."

"Don't worry, I was just dodging shadows." He kissed her softly. *It has to be nerves,* she tried to convince herself. *That's what it is. It couldn't have been that kiss. Surely, in real life, kisses don't do that.* But for some reason, her bones turned into water.

She put both arms around his neck and pressed herself into him. He deepened the kiss, holding her tenderly as if he held a flower. "You are a very beautiful woman."

"But I thought you said . . ."

"Don't worry about what I said."

He kissed her again, this time deeper. An answering gnawing need blossomed deep within her. They clung together briefly. Then he released her with seemingly great reluctance and glanced at the door. It was then that she remembered she couldn't have men in her room—at least not in the way she wanted right at that moment.

"You can't come in," she whispered. "We're not allowed to have men in our rooms after ten at night and never with the door closed." She'd never said more difficult words. She wanted him to take her to his place, any place.

Instead, he smiled and shrugged. "It's kismet, I suppose.

Something that's not meant to be—at least, not tonight. But that is all right. When we come together, it will be perfect." That was some consolation. He expected them to come together. She sighed.

"Good night, little Maleka." He gently placed his lips on hers again. His words made her feel safe and cherished.

They parted and she went in. She lay in bed for a long time, remembering every moment of the scene in front of the door. It was like something out of a dream. When she went to sleep, she dreamt of languorously lying on carpets in some Arabian fairy tale.

She awoke, feeling deliriously sensual. Stretching both arms overhead, she indulged herself in delicious memories of the night before. Everything seemed to come back to her—even the wonderful way that Ahmad smelled. It also brought back the same hunger. More than anything she wished that she'd given herself to him last night. Even this morning, she had not fully recovered from his kisses. She rolled over and hugged her pillow, wishing she could go back to sleep and dream about him. Just at that moment, the phone rang.

"Maleka, this is Lisandra," the woman said, unnecessarily. There was no way she could have missed that voice, even over the phone. "I thought you were going to stay with Ahmad on this thing."

"I am," she answered, still mired in soft fuzzy memories of last night.

"I just called his room. Last night he made arrangements to meet Zeleke in Morocco and he's gone already."

"What!" That got her attention. She peered at the bedside clock. It said ten o'clock. "He couldn't be."

"I got the whole story out of Yustafa this morning. Yustafa said that you were followed and had to run. Was that true?"

That dog. That snake. He'd probably set up this whole story so that he could tell everyone how dangerous it had been. But she knew the truth. After he'd even admitted that it was just dodging shadows. What was worse was that he'd played on her emotions, knowing he was going to do this today. Her throat clogged up and she could barely talk. What a fool she had been to fall for his smooth act when all he was thinking about was tricking her. Tears stung the back of her eyes. She had an almost overwhelming urge to pull the covers over her head and bawl like a baby.

She couldn't believe how betrayed she felt. Imagine a few kisses doing that to her. She'd never been more affected by a man in her whole life.

When she didn't speak, Lisandra went on, "Maybe it's for the best. I'm beginning to think it might truly be too dangerous for you. We don't need you running through Pigalle at night."

"What do you mean? I thought you said they were exaggerating the danger just to keep me from going."

"Mildred said that we should hire professionals to do this job, only I didn't trust them and neither did she, to tell the truth. Ahmad says it's too dangerous for you, too. Maybe he's right. I'm sorry, Maleka, but I can't help thinking that maybe we should let it go. Suppose Ahmad's right and it's too dangerous for you?"

"Too dangerous for me but not for him, right?"

"Too dangerous for both of you."

"I think he's fooled you. Remember, I was there last night. I never saw anyone chasing us."

"Maybe that's so, but I'm sorry I got him involved in this. I'll be worried until he returns."

A sudden mental image of the beautiful Ahmad lying bloody in some North African alley jumped into her thoughts. It sent cold dread through her. Suppose there was real danger. She sat up at the side of the bed.

"If only we knew where he was going," she said, idly.

"I do know—Morocco."

Maleka's eyes fell upon the little packet with her passport. She remembered Ahmad saying that last night was kismet. Well, maybe this was kismet too. "I'm going," she told Lisandra. The decision had been made instinctively.

"How can you?"

"I have everything I need for a trip to Morocco except a ticket and information where to meet up with him."

"But, but . . ." For once the diva was speechless. Then after a short pause, she said, "I can hire a plane to take you to the same place where Ahmad will leave for the North African coast. How long will it take you to pack?"

"I'm already packed," she said, remembering the clothes that she had bought for her own trip.

Another moment of silence. Then Lisandra spoke. "Are you sure you want to do this?" And at Maleka's answer, she said, "He has to stop to collect the box. That might hold him up long enough for you to catch up."

When the plane landed, she grabbed her bags and bolted through the door as soon as she could. There was another plane parked across the tarmac. Hopefully it was the one she wanted. She rushed to the attendant there.

"You have Lisandra Orian's chartered plane?"

"This is it. It's ready to go. We're just waiting for our passenger."

With shoulders back, she informed him, "I'm the passenger. One of them," she corrected.

He glanced down at the sheath of papers he held. "I don't have your name here."

"Yes, you do. I heard her make the arrangements. I am Maleka Darling, couturier extraordinaire."

He glanced down at the tacky jeans and oversized shirt that she was wearing. "But I thought you'd cancelled. I got a message this morning that there would only be one person."

"Well, obviously you got the wrong message. I'm going."

"I was quite specifically told that you—"

"Excuse me," she held her palm up to him, "no discussion. There's been a mistake. If *I* don't go, Ms. Orian will cancel the whole trip. Everything will stop without me."

"Okay, okay. Let me take your bag."

She walked up the steps and chose one of the four seats for herself. Not long thereafter, she heard Ahmad's voice down on the tarmac.

"Who?" he bellowed. Her stomach did a little turn. She could hear the attendant's voice but not what he said. "I told you she wasn't going," Ahmad roared in response.

The next thing she heard was male footfalls rushing up the stairs into the plane. Ahmad stormed in and stood over her—in absolute fury. "What the devil are you doing here?"

Seeing him there in living color brought back that kiss from last night, and anger flowed through her. She was no longer queasy about facing him. She was a woman scorned and he'd better watch his step.

She stood to confront him. "You tried to leave me. And you lied to Yustafa, knowing that he'd tell Lisandra that crazy story. You know nothing happened last night, that no one chased us."

His mouth tightened and he raised one eyebrow. Slanting his head to the side, he said, "Are you sure that's the only reason that you're angry? Maybe you're just a little frustrated that I didn't finish what I started in front of your door."

"Ha. You wish." She waved her hand at him. "If you think I'd let a few inconsequential kisses turn my head, think again."

He placed both fists on his hips. "I absolutely refuse to allow you to follow me around, interfering with what I have to do."

"It has nothing to do with you and I'm not following you. I'm looking out for *my* mother's interest."

"Your mother was quite satisfied to let me handle it."

"That's because my mother pays too much attention to height and not enough to substance."

"Will you give up on this? The Sahara is no place for a woman like you to be."

"What's wrong with a woman like me?"

"You've never had any hardship in your life. You're pampered and soft."

"I am not soft. And I'm going to Morocco. Also, as I explained to the pilot, without me there will be no trip. I'll see to that," she said, trying to sound syrupy sweet.

He folded his arms across his chest. He looked stubborn and unmovable. "That's it. We're not going."

She hissed through her teeth, "If you try to stop now, I'll make such a scene that everyone will know what you're doing."

He looked cornered and fit to burst. "Okay. But only if you accept that I'm running this show. I don't have time to fight with you. You'll have to follow my orders and do everything that I say, without hesitation."

"Oh, all right," she said, ungraciously.

Pointing his finger at her, he said, "You are a willful spoiled woman. Your father should have warmed your bottom and broken you of this trait."

Later, when they were already in the air, she asked, "Where is the box? Did you pick it up? What did you do with it?"

"None of your business."

They avoided each other during the trip and there were no further incidents. They flew south with the Atlantic Ocean on the right. It was a deep Prussian blue and sprayed white frothy waves. The Atlas Mountains were visible, looking like giant upturned ragged cones of grey and dull yellow with pale streaks of snow at their tops. Beyond the mountains lay the Sahara Desert—where nothing moved. It seemed to stretch out forever.

The aircraft came to rest outside the terminal and they stepped out into the shocking, oppressive heat. They lined up to go through the immigration procedures. She looked around at the other travelers. Morocco was also a city of many racial and ethnic groups. It was even more exotic than Paris, for there were people in colorful native garb as well as those in western clothes. Present were the usual group of priests, wearing black robes. There were large gatherings of Moors dressed in traditional outfits of thick cotton that was dyed indigo blue. She wondered if they were hot in the stiff heavy fabric. The colors combined with the cacophony of so many diverse languages made it an overwhelming experience. She was dizzy trying to see everything. She was excited to be in Morocco after not being able to get here before. Granted the circumstances were wildly different, but it was still a wonderful experience.

Ahmad walked behind her as they approached customs. She lugged her own baggage, refusing to ask for any help. He didn't offer any, either. However, he did see the camera that was hanging around her neck.

"Why did you bring that? This isn't a vacation," he said, sounding peevish.

"This was a gift from my dad. He wanted me to photograph my whole stay."

"I don't think he meant *this* trip."

"It's a good disguise and makes me look like a tourist. Besides, I wanted to take it on this trip."

"No one's going to have time to guard that camera."

"Don't be silly. I'll keep it with me. Why would we need to guard it?"

"Okay, I leave it on your head. Don't look at me if it gets you in trouble."

"What trouble? Everybody has a camera," she said, looking around.

"We'll see."

While going through customs was tedious, it did come to an end, eventually. They took a cab to a local hotel, which was quite lovely to look at. She was glad to get into her room, where the bathroom was done in blue and gold mosaics. She had just gotten out of the tub when Ahmad knocked on the door.

He came with a black garment thrown over his arm. "I've bought this for you."

"What is it?" She was still wary. Not since they'd met up had there been any mention of last night. It wasn't something that she wanted to talk about. She felt used and betrayed to realize that he'd used his sex appeal to lull her into relaxing her vigil.

He held it up. "I want you to wear this." It was a loose black dress that was meant to cover her from head to toe.

"Are you crazy? Anyway, I bought clothes—the type of clothes that I was told to wear here. They're sedate and modest."

"Who told you that?"

"A travel agent who booked tours here."

"You forget, this is not a tour. A black American woman traveling in North Africa is going to draw attention. Which reminds me, you've got to keep your mouth shut or you'll blow our cover."

"Oh, for pete's sake. Give it to me." She snatched the dress out of his hand.

She went into the bathroom and pulled the dress over her head. There was a head covering that went with it. She had to braid her bushy hair to fit under it. In the end, she resembled a dumpy little crow.

She exited and went to stand in front of him. "Well, how does it look? I hope you're happy; it's a hundred and ten degrees in here. Black holds the heat. Couldn't we make it white?"

He laughed and walked around her. She turned with him until he stopped her.

"Walk over there," he said, pointing a little distance away. She walked to where he'd pointed and turned around only to find him laughing.

"What's so funny? What can you complain about now? I'm covered from head to toe."

"Yes, but do you have to walk like this?" He demonstrated with swaying hips.

"You can see that?"

"Yes. And you're standing too straight." He put his palms around her shoulders. "Soften up."

"But that'll make me look short!"

He started laughing more. "No, it won't. Haven't you

ever noticed that tall women slump? It'll make you appear taller."

"You think so?" She turned to the mirror and rounded her shoulders to see if she looked taller. Then she swung around and caught him with a suspicious sparkle in his eyes. "You're putting me on." She pulled off the head piece and suddenly they were both laughing.

The little scene took some of the bitterness from her heart, but she was still wary. While she realized that she was going to have to relax while they were together, she still felt gun-shy. But it wouldn't be forever. In a short time, they'd have delivered the box to Zeleke and she could go back to her real life.

Seven

They stood at the edge of the market with both of their suitcases at her feet. The pick-up area where they were to board a communal taxi was located a few yards ahead.

Tired and disgusted, she whispered, "Why do *I* have to carry everything?"

"Because it's part of your disguise. You're supposed to be a nice *submissive* North African housewife. It's your duty to carry the luggage," Ahmad said. "And besides, it's your own fault. You're the one who insisted that you had to come."

The man needs a good kick to the shins, she thought, wishing she were wearing her clodhopper shoes.

"Why can't we hire a car? Why do we have to travel with so many people?"

"This is Africa and we're not supposed to be rich people. We need to be inconspicuous."

"That's what you always say, but I don't believe you."

"Whether you believe me or not is not important. What is important is that you keep your promise to obey my orders. Otherwise the deal is off. Are you reneging already?"

In a huff, she picked up the bags and struggled toward the taxi stand. However, before she'd gone a few feet, he came up behind her and relieved her of their weight.

"Never mind," he said, "I'll do it."

"What about our disguise?" she challenged sarcastically.

"Allah will have to help us."

She smiled behind her black veil. Lisandra said that she wanted her son to be an American man and she had succeeded. He obviously couldn't tolerate seeing her carry the luggage.

After an incredible amount of haggling, they took a communal taxi. It was a dust-covered old-model Peugeot. There were rust spots aplenty and one door was wired to the frame. The driver was an irascible elderly man. They piled into it with six other people.

It took them six hours to arrive at their destination, and by that time Maleka was thoroughly sick of the crush and smells of communal travel. She was miserable having to wear the black head-covering and dress. It was almost enough to make her wish she'd stayed in Paris.

Maybe it would have been better if she'd been able to talk, but she was under strict orders from Ahmad not to open her mouth. He told the other passengers that she was deaf and mute. This meant that they tried to communicate by gesturing. All she could do was smile and nod her head. The whole time she sat in an agony of frustration. In the end, she was sure that her fellow passengers thought that she was not quite bright.

One thing she had noticed since arriving in Morocco was that living with sand was a way of life. It drifted through the streets, blew into the houses, painted highways, and frosted the traffic lights. But here in the small town of Chinquetti, it wasn't sand that they had to live with—it was the Sahara Desert.

"This way," Ahmad said, breaking through her reverie. He took one look at her and shouldered both bags.

They walked through several narrow, long, winding streets. Some of the streets were paved with cobblestones. It appeared peaceful, except for one street where there were several makeshift houses built from old timbers and flattened-out corrugated tin.

Despite their being carefully scrutinized by the people, it seemed a tranquil place. The people were nomads who had been forced to abandon their lifestyle in the Sahara when the Great Drought came some years before. Some of them had never recovered financially. Moorish women with their strange, blue-tinted skin, that came from the dye in their clothes, watched them curiously.

They stopped at a single-roomed house of stone, standing at the end of one street. On one side a staircase ran to the roof. There was a small area at the back for washing. She thought they'd better find a laundromat or they were in serious trouble. The cooking facilities were beyond her. Fortunately, Ahmad brought their food in daily. The only furniture was a rolled up mattress pad and carpet.

From the window, you could see a sea of sand dunes. They ranged in color from ivory to cream to amber and ran down to a stream. Theland around the stream was the only green area and divided the town into halves. Palm trees grew around it.

By the time they'd been in the house for a week, she was ready to scream. She had to continue with the deaf-mute act, and it was a strain. She was dying for companionship. What was worse was that she was sleeping poorly. And when she did doze off, nightmares plagued her.

All of this made her cling to Ahmad as if he were the only other person on earth. Whenever he had to leave, she felt on the verge of tears. Originally, he had worn native dress in order to blend in. He had spent time in the desert, wearing his robe, topped by a burnoose—a hood that protected him from the sun.

And she, who had always loved native dress, found herself feeling strange around him. She chalked it up to the claustrophobia and isolation of her situation. Somehow he had noticed her reaction and had begun to wear a safari jacket and khaki pants. It helped a little, but not much.

Although she hated to admit it, she knew the trip had been a mistake. He traveled locally in an attempt to contact Zeleke. Although he made many contacts, he'd not found

Zeleke. She couldn't even go with him because women didn't travel freely with men. It was enough to send her into the doldrums.

The only thing that kept her from going insane was that she had taken to venturing outside in the early mornings before it became too hot. At first she had thought that she would enjoy walking to the town well, but Ahmad had arranged for a boy to bring them water every day, so she didn't need to go. She had hoped that seeing other people would relieve some of her frustration, even if she couldn't talk with them.

On the first morning that she went out, she had had a particularly bad night, sleeping only in short fits. Ahmad had been gone for more than twenty-four hours and she felt as if she were in solitary confinement.

She walked to the well, which was a sort of town meeting place for the women, but it was deserted. She drew up some water, sat at the side, and took a drink. It was surprisingly clear and sweet. Now that she was no longer trying to sleep, suddenly she felt extremely tired and drowsy. Her eyelids seemed too heavy too keep open. But she shook herself awake. She had no intentions of falling asleep in the public square of a strange African village.

As she sat there, an elderly man hobbled up. He was dressed in a long black robe, with a black burnoose over his head. He looked tired and dehydrated and too weak to draw up any water for himself.

He gestured to her, signaling that he wanted water, so she drew some up for him. When he had finished, he said, *"Merci."*

Hearing the French threw her for a moment. Then she reminded herself that for many, French was like a second national language in North Africa. It was only in some of the smaller towns that you didn't hear the language. Hearing the word brought a welcome respite. It fed her hunger to talk with someone. She answered in French, saying, "You're welcome."

"Where do you come from, daughter?" he asked.

"From the north," she said, trying to keep it vague.

"Come sit with me here," he said, patting the space beside him. It was a curious request coming from an African man. As a rule, they were quite careful in their dealings with women who were not family. "I am a stranger in this land, too," he said, gazing far off at the mountains in the distance.

That surprised her, because she had thought him vaguely familiar and assumed that she'd seen him in the village.

The old man's command of the language was much better than hers, though he sometimes mixed tenses and used funny combinations. Then he turned back to her, saying, "I guess that's why I like to look at the Atlas Mountains. They don't truly look like the mountains of my country but they remind me a little. There's a very special place in the foothills here. It's called Abba Applaudir. Have you ever heard of it?"

"No, I haven't."

"You must go there someday. You will feel relieved of your burdens."

"Yes," she answered, still vague.

They talked for a while before he took his leave and was off. She regretted seeing him go. It had been such a pleasure to talk with someone, even if she did have to watch her every word.

The next thing she knew she awoke from sleep, still sitting in the same place where the old man had left her. She jumped up and looked around, totally disoriented. She wasn't even sure that the incident had been real. It was possible that she had fallen asleep and dreamt the whole thing. She tried to remember what the old man had said, but found that the combination of French and patois, a local language, had confused her.

After that experience, she didn't walk to the well anymore. She feared that she might fall asleep again. Mostly, she walked to the small market place located in the middle of town. It consisted of a central plaza that was paved with cobblestones. The plaza was surrounded by two-story stone buildings. There were two arches, one facing east and one west. The west led to the house where they stayed. It resembled a European feudal town and, according to local history, it had been used for the slave trade.

She never bought much because she didn't feel comfortable counting in their coins. And, in fact, she didn't even dare show too much money. But one day an old woman sitting on a blanket caught her eye. Spread out on the blanket were various items, among which was one familiar jar. It was a famous American brand of a hair relaxer. She almost couldn't believe her eyes. Just seeing it perked her spirits up. She gestured, asking the price, and counted out the coins. She hoped that it was the right amount.

Carrying her find back to the house, she cradled it carefully as if it were a precious jewel. Her excitement was monumental. She was going to perm her hair. That would make it more comfortable in the heat under her headdress.

Back at the house, she removed her black crow gown and donned her shorts. She decided to wait until it was dark to start. Then the temperature would be cooler. However, she collected water in several pots in the meantime.

It was several hours later. Just as Maleka was in the middle of working the cream through her hair, Ahmad burst through the door. She was so frightened that had she not been sitting on the floor, she'd have fallen on her face. He blew out the flame in the lamp. It was still relatively light, for bright moonlight shone into the room. He went to look through the window. She watched him, wondering at his actions.

"We've got to get out of here, tonight," he said, in a low voice.

"What is it?" she asked, pitching her voice low to match his.

Whatever he saw at the window seemed to reassure him

for he relaxed a bit and walked toward her. "There was someone following me. I seem to have lost them for the moment but it's time for us to go." That's when he noticed that she had not moved. "What are you doing? What is that stuff you're putting on your head?"

"I'm perming my hair."

"You're what? Never mind; it doesn't matter. I've made arrangements for us to leave tonight."

"I can't stop right this minute."

"Yes, this minute."

"I can't leave until I've rinsed it all out."

"For pete's sake, what is that gook?"

"That gook makes my hair easy to manage. I'll be cooler in this heat."

"Why would a beautiful woman ruin the lovely hair that Allah has given her just to make herself look different?"

"You think that I'm beautiful, Ahmad?"

"Umm . . . that was a rhetorical question."

"Huh," she said peeved. "You'll have to wait, because I'm not moving until this is finished."

"Couldn't you have done this at another time?"

"How was I to know you'd come in tonight with another of your imaginary chases?"

"Imaginary? I don't think so. We could be in danger of losing life and limb and you're worried about putting that gook on and ruining your hair."

"Well, you're the one saying that I'll never get a husband. Now I'm trying to make the best of everything, and you're still complaining."

"I thought you didn't want a husband."

"I don't. I was only using that as an example."

Some sound made him jerk to face the window. "I'll be right back. Finish with that. When I return, we have to go." He slipped through the door.

It was time to rinse the cream out and she ducked her head in one of the pots. While she was at it, she thought she heard a noise on the steps going up to the roof. Then she heard what sounded like a single thump. Her eyes almost bugged out of her head. What could it be? Visions of antiquity hunters and warlords went through her mind.

Ahmad ducked his head in the door, saying, "Are you ready yet?"

"Almost. Just a minute more. What was that sound?" But he was gone before she'd finished.

Seeing him looking so calm made her relax a bit. *There aren't any antiquities thieves or warlords. That's just something he used to scare me,* she thought. Her next thought was that it was more likely to be someone trying to steal his wallet. But that thought was as scary as the first one.

She started rinsing furiously, praying that Ahmad was safe and that he wouldn't leave her.

She heard another thump just as she wrapped a drying cloth around her head. Ahmad leaned through the door. "Are you ready now?"

"Yes," she said, running to join him at the door.

He took her hand and they raced through the narrow, winding, moonlit street. It wasn't until she felt the cool air on her thighs that she realized that she'd forgotten her black crow's outfit.

They came to the central plaza and stood in a doorway set into a two-story stone building. "Stay here," he said.

"Ahmad, don't leave me," she whispered, but he was already gone.

It was at that moment that a cloud covered the moonlight and the plaza was doused in blackness. She tried to do what he said and remain perfectly still, but it seemed as if there were little sounds from all over the square. The longer she waited, the more frightened she became. Finally when a little light shone out from a break in the clouds, she had to move. She started walking along the way she had seen him disappear.

"Ahmad. Ahmad," she called, in a loud whisper. Now she was disoriented and totally bewildered as to where she should go. The only thing she knew was the walk back to the house but she was afraid to go back there.

That's when she saw the two men.

She had almost missed them because they were both dressed in black, their heads wrapped in black hoods. They sat atop incredibly muscular, sleek black horses—steeds, she thought inanely, because they were so beautiful. The men leaned together and appeared to be talking, though she couldn't hear anything. Then they parted and one went under the east arch. The other stood facing her.

She was standing there in plain view when the moon came out of the clouds. Her heart jumped into her throat and her hands were suddenly clammy. Her knees trembled and she felt rooted to the spot.

Suddenly, the horse reared up and the rider stood tall in the saddle. Even though she felt herself in great danger, she was aware of the breathtaking beauty of horse and rider. He was like a centaur, like a graceful shadow. Slowly, she started back-pedaling. She was terrified that any sudden movement would have him after her.

All at once, horse and rider took off, speeding around the little square like a dark streak of lightning. Once again, the horse stood up on his hind legs. This time the rider gave a loud blood-curdling yell. Without further ado, she turned and took off in a pell mell race toward the west arch. Hoofbeats gained on her. He moved in front of her, cutting off her escape through the arch, and she turned and sprinted for the other side. She never missed a beat and didn't even feel it when she lost her sandal.

Once again, he cut off her exit but he stopped chasing her. It gave her a chance to catch her breath. Perspiration rolled off her in sheets of water. Not chancing turning away, she moved slowly backward toward the plaza. Horse and rider stood facing her. When she had a little distance, she whirled and once again headed toward the west arch.

Like a shot he was after her. He came at a breakneck speed, leaning low on the horse's neck, whooping his banshee yell. Knowing her attempt at escape was fruitless, she still kept going. Any moment she expected to be crushed under the horse's hooves.

Suddenly she found herself suspended in the air. He

held her by the waistband of her shorts. Her feet dangled as she frantically tried to right herself. Then she was shoved across his saddle. The air whooshed out of her and she landed like a sack of potatoes.

Although she had been frightened out of her wits, she had not made a sound in all this time. But now, as soon as she could draw a breath, she opened her mouth and bellowed at the top of her lungs, "Ahmad! Help!"

"Would you shut up," Ahmad's familiar voice said, coming from behind the face covering of the rider.

"Ahmad, is that you?" she asked, peering at him. He yanked the black covering from his face. She was never so glad to see anyone in her life, but for some reason that's not what came out of her mouth. "You scared the mess out of me like that."

"Oh, *you* were scared?"

"Well, I didn't really mean scared. And where did you get those clothes?"

"I appropriated them."

"The horse, too?! Oh, this is terrible! Aren't we in enough trouble without you doing something stupid like that?"

"Like what?"

"Stealing someone's gorgeous horse? Even I can see that horse is worth a fortune. I happen to like both my hands and I have no intention of losing them because of you."

He threw his hood over her head, "Oh, shut up. Forget your hands. With your infernal chatter, it's a wonder we haven't both lost our heads."

"We're a lot more likely to lose something with your taking this horse than with my talking. And why did you keep riding around like that, making that appalling noise?"

"I was getting the horse warmed up."

"Hah! You were showing off."

"I was not."

"Yes, you were—showing off for me."

Then without any reason, Ahmad nudged the horse and

they began to move much faster. Despite his arm around her waist, she was shaken all around as the horse's body took off.

He kept making that incredible blood-curdling whoop. It made her hair, damp as it was, stand on end. Then they turned on a dime as they rounded a corner and stopped. Somehow, Ahmad managed to quiet the horse, by whispers and caresses. As they remained motionless, the other black clad rider detached from the shadows and took off in the direction that they had been going.

As he rode off, he started making the same sound Ahmad had made. Maleka felt suddenly disoriented, as if she had fallen into a weird wonderland situation.

Good grief, I feel like Alice in Wonderland must have felt, only I'm not blonde.

"Who is that?" she asked, but didn't really have much interest. Somehow her mind wouldn't function.

"Hush," he hissed. "A friend. Don't worry about him."

When she would have said more, he grabbed her jaw with strong fingers and turned her face to his. Then he pressed his hard demanding mouth on hers. All rational thought became impossible. She went up in flames.

When he finally drew away, she sighed and her head slumped against his chest. She realized that her arms had gone around his waist sometime during the kiss. She would have loved to have said something smart aleck to put him in his place, but nothing came to her mind.

It was then that the second rider came alongside them. She had almost forgotten about him. He signaled to Ahmad and then rode off, making the same blood-curdling yell as he moved into the distance. Ahmad waved in the same signal and headed into the desert.

It was like her dream. They rode like the wind. Somewhere along the way, she lost the cloth she had wrapped around her drying hair, but she didn't know when. Once she learned to relax, she no longer felt jostled about by the horse. The desert air was cool and he wrapped her in his robe.

She felt as if she had found a secret place—a place that she had never even imagined existed. It seemed like the place that she had been searching for all her life. A place where she belonged—in Ahmad Mousoud's arms. She never wanted to leave that place.

They rode some miles before coming to an oasis. There they came to a courtyard built in the Moorish manner. Inside, stood a jewel of a house, all pale cream stone with ascending arches and lacy carvings. It was like something out of the *Arabian Nights*. It was quiet and there were guards posted around the structure—guards who seemed to recognize Ahmad and waved him through.

Eight

"Where are we?" she asked, as they walked through marble hallways. Awed by her surroundings, she suddenly realized how strange she must look in her shorts with her hair flying all over.

"We are at my cousin Abdul's home."

"Won't he mind if we just show up in the middle of the night?"

"In my cousin's house, I am always welcome." He strode through the corridors like a lithe panther. Quiet, self-effacing servants took them to a sumptuous sleeping area. The huge room was dominated by an extra-large round bed. It was covered in fine silk sheets and pillows. A netting hung from the ceiling. Sumptuous Oriental carpets covered every inch of the floor.

It was obvious that they would share the bed. She felt exultant. Her heart beat like a tom-tom drum that had gone mad. When the servants left, Ahmad came to her and thrust his fingers through her hair. Without asking any permission, he kissed her with a wild urgency. His demanding maleness made her feel as if she would melt. She threw her arms around his neck. The heat that rose between them threatened to set them aflame. Never in her life had she wanted a man like this. She opened herself to his kisses and his tongue entered her mouth. His hand moved to open the buttons of her shirt. It seemed to melt away, leaving her with only a bra on top. Then he sank his face between her breasts. She didn't want him to be clothed, either. She pulled his shirt up over his head. He slipped out of it as easily as if it were made of clouds and brought his mouth to kiss her neck. It sent delicious tremors through her body. Next he unbuttoned her shorts and they slid down her legs to puddle at her feet. Even as she stepped out of them, she was fumbling with the tie around his waist that held his pants. She was shocked at her eager response. No man had ever made her feel this way. He opened it for her and had stepped out of his pants before she even realized. He was nude before her. She was so absorbed in watching him and looking at every smooth corded muscle that she stood absolutely still. He stood momentarily to allow her to look but then soon returned to removing her bra and panties. When she was nude, he sank to his knees. It was his turn to look at her.

"You are beautiful," he murmured. He then rose up and, in one motion, swept her into his arms and carried her to the bed. He sank down with her still in his arms. She marveled at his strength and clung to him as if her very life depended upon remaining close.

There among the cushions, he rose on one arm to look at her again. She was proud to be nude before him and wanted to satisfy his every wish. He moved one hand to touch her breast and she moaned and arched up to him. He kissed her again as he kneaded one areola and then another. Her body seemed to have a life of its own. When his hand moved down to caress the flesh between her legs, she thought she would go insane. She marveled that he could make her feel this way—that he was so knowledgeable about her body—but these thoughts didn't last long. She was too desperate for release to think. He rolled between her legs and their two bodies became one. That moment was so exquisite that both of them moaned. The fiery heat within her built to a roaring fire and she cried out in ecstasy. Her cry was followed by his groan of release. Then she held onto him as she seemed to slowly float back to earth.

Just as she was drifting off to sleep, she felt that she had come home. It reminded her of their first kiss.

The next morning, she awoke and stared up at the netting that hung from the ceiling. When she stirred, she became aware of various minor aches and that the sheets were in disarray. Immediately, she remembered where she was and turned to find Ahmad.

He wasn't there.

She remembered how he'd left Paris the morning after their first kiss. She bolted up to a sitting position, only to have a small beautiful young woman hurry to the bedside. "Who are you?" she asked, bewildered.

The woman smiled down at her. "I am your servant while you're here." She stared about her. The young woman giggled. "Your man has left to do some business."

"Did he tell you that?"

"No, but that's what men always do, isn't it?"

Maleka jumped out of the bed and the girl hurried to assist. With great difficulty Maleka dismissed her after finding out where the bathroom was.

Suddenly, she felt ill at ease. Waking alone had brought back all the doubts of the last two weeks. Even the lovemaking was worrisome. He was too good at it! She thought about all those concubines and remembered him saying that he'd been schooled in the arts of pleasing women. *I can't believe I did that. Flirting was all right but falling into bed with a man who had multiple partners was downright stupid.*

Besides, it occurred to her that he had not been open with her, either. Not since she'd boarded that plane had he told her anything. He'd totally cut her out of the whole thing. There were too many unanswered questions. He had a lot to explain.

When Ahmad returned that night, she remained quiet until they were alone in the bedroom. It didn't matter that he looked tired; she wanted answers.

"What's going on?"

He threw up his hands. "Nothing, in case you haven't noticed. What's wrong with you?" he said.

"Wrong with me? What makes you think there's something wrong? Could it be because you've had me locked up in solitary confinement for weeks? Or that you used some pretty nasty terrorist tactics with that fancy horse of yours. Not to mention that you double-teamed me with that other rider. Or maybe it's because after you reduced me to a poor brainwashed creature, you then proceeded to seduce me?"

"Seduce you?" he said, ignoring all the other accusations. "You were all over me."

She gave him the hand. "I don't care to discuss that right now. I want to know what's going on, and why haven't we found Zeleke yet? There's been more than enough time."

At this, he seemed deflated. "Maybe you're right, but he hasn't contacted me."

"Where was he supposed to meet you?"

"At that same house that you call solitary confinement. When he didn't show, I tried to find him, but to no avail."

"So, who was the other rider?"

"Annan. The man you know as Snake-Eyes."

"What's he doing here?"

"He brought the box."

"You trusted him with it? I thought you said he was a pirate."

"He is, but that didn't stop you from flirting with him."

"I won't even answer that." Yet, she thought of it afterward. Was Ahmad jealous? That thought crept into her mind but it was so impossible that she hurriedly squashed it. "Is the box here?"

He hesitated a moment. "Yes."

"Weren't you going to tell me any of this?"

"A woman like you has no business being mixed up in something like this."

"I can't believe it. Here, I've just given my body to the world's worst lecher and he can't be bothered to tell me anything!"

"Surely I can't be the world's worst."

She ignored that and said, "It's time for you to be open. Where have you been looking for Zeleke?"

He sprawled upon the circular bed and said, "I've been up and down this place, looking for something called, 'father approves.' "

" 'Father approves'—what is that?"

"If I knew we wouldn't be having this conversation. I've already taken longer on this than I intended. I do have a business to run."

She had a job to go to, too, she mused. But her mind kept going back to the phrase he'd given her, "father approves." She repeated it several times. For some reason, it teased her memory and made her unable to let it go. There was something about the phrase that she felt she should have recognized. But try as she would, she couldn't put her finger on it.

They called a truce after that and spoke no more about it. But as time to retire came, he undressed for bed.

"Excuse me," she intervened. "What are you doing?"

"Exactly what it looks like—getting ready for bed."

"We are not going to repeat last night," she said, arms crossed across her chest. "This is *my* bedroom. You'll need to go to your own."

"We both have to sleep here because I had to tell my cousin that you were my woman."

"How dare you?"

"If I hadn't said that, you would have been up for grabs."

"Why?"

"Because you're traveling alone with me. Unattached women in this country don't travel with strange men. They will label you as loose. A loose woman is considered fair game. And Abdul is always looking for new flesh to add to his harem."

That night she barely closed her eyes, she was so conscious of him lying in the same bed. It wasn't until the first signs of dawn that she dozed off. And when she woke some hours later, she suddenly remembered why the phrase about "father approves" rang a bell.

She rolled over and shook Ahmad awake. "I know what it means. It's 'Abba Applaudir.' "

He opened one bleary eye and said, "You are a most aggravating woman. I'd like to sleep."

"It's not 'father approves.' It's patois for 'father applauds.' You know, like in father claps, and it's on the eastern approach to the Atlas Mountains." He sat up, his face screwed up in intense concentration. "An old man dressed all in black spoke to me at the well in Chinquetti. He was a stranger to the area and he told me that I must visit Abba Applaudir. That it would relieve me of my burden."

"Why didn't you mention this?"

"I didn't know what he was talking about. You had gone out on one of your trips. And later, I thought that I'd been dreaming. Could that have been Zeleke?"

"Let's go," he said, and rolled out of the bed to get dressed.

She jumped up to join him. He spent a long time on the phone. Then he consulted with Abdul about directions before preparing for the journey. He played overseer as servants collected water, food, blankets, rope, and mountain climbing equipment. She hoped he didn't think *she* was going to climb any mountain. But she didn't mention this. He also had a gun, which at first frightened her.

"Why do we need that?" she asked, shrinking back.

"It's a flare gun. We're traveling in strange territory and I want to be prepared if we're lost at night."

There was also a pair of binoculars on a cord. This she confiscated. The gear was stacked in the jeep.

He handed her some tiny white pills and said, "Take them." They were salt tablets and she knew she needed them, but she was tempted to balk anyway because of the way in which he'd spoken. She was tired of his autocratic manner. Nothing would have pleased her more than to have the whole thing be over. But even as that thought occurred, she knew it wasn't true. Now that they were so close to their goal, she didn't want to leave him.

She would never be able to forget their one night. It would haunt her for the rest of her life. Indeed, she would never forget him, the American prince. Like something out of a fairy tale, it had been. It grieved her that it would soon end—that she would return to the fitting rooms of Vito Genovese's Fashion and Design House.

How she wished that Lisandra had been right—that he had been interested in her. Oh, she was all right for a moment of passion. But the truth was, she wanted more. And no way would she share the man she loved with fifty concubines.

When the jeep was packed, he opened the passenger door for her. Then he handed her the box. It was swaddled in several layers of soft flannel cloth.

She sat there in awe, unable to believe that she was actually holding it. Her mother had been right. It didn't look like treasure, but she sensed its antiquity—its great value. With a sense of reverence, she lifted the lid and gazed inside. There were several strips of old worn leather with strange markings on them. They were faded and, even had she understood the markings, she wouldn't have been able to read them. It was a little disappointing. But she wasn't sure what she had expected.

They rode west for several hours in the late afternoon. The mountains were silhouetted by the setting sun, a huge ball of fire. Soon they would be in the foothills. Behind them lay the desert, an incredible expanse of sand and rock. Unlike what she had expected, the desert wasn't all one color. There were areas of dark reddish-brown and beige and even grey in the immense stretch of undulating dunes. Water holes crisscrossed throughout, looking like coiled brown snakes. Nothing and no one moved. It seemed to stretch on forever.

The drive had been long and hot. The car had no air

conditioning and she had consumed quite a bit of the water. However, now with the approach of sunset it was getting cooler. She reached in the back and pulled the blanket to her.

They hadn't spoken much since she'd told him about the man at the well. In her boredom she had been using the binoculars to view off in the distance. She turned to observe the scenery behind and noticed a pale brown cloud that hovered on the road some distance behind them. She realized that Ahmad was observing it, too. He had been keeping a steady check on the road behind them the whole trip. Now he became tense and more vigilant.

"What is that?" she asked.

"Dust," he answered tersely. "There are cars behind us." Their speed increased and they left the cloud behind. But when she glanced behind them the next time, it had moved closer again. Whoever was behind them was keeping pace.

Their car sped up more. She glanced at the speedometer. They were traveling a lot faster than it felt. She didn't know a jeep could go that fast and realized that it must have had a souped-up motor. Her head swung from watching the speedometer to watching the dust cloud behind them.

Ahmad drove with the same cool efficiency that he used to control a horse. He kept them moving at a dizzying speed. She remembered that he'd been a race-car driver but still the speed frightened her. Although the terrain was a relatively unhampered surface, there were ruts and depressions where they could have fallen. Also, it was getting dark and becoming more dangerous by the moment.

All along she had half believed that the talk about people wanting to steal the box was just that—talk. And indeed, Ahmad had admitted to dodging shadows. Now, she didn't know any longer. She feared this time there was real danger. She didn't want it to be true. Not when they were so close to their goal.

"Are they after *us?*" she asked, her voice sounding shaky

in her own ears. She crossed her fingers, hoping he'd deny it.

"Could be." His brief answer was no comfort.

Although she didn't expect to see much, she watched the cloud behind them through the binoculars. Once or twice the car swerved at a turn. When this happened, the cars behind them would escape the dust briefly. In this way, she got brief glimpses of what looked like men in safari hats with what might have been weapons.

Cold dread rushed up her spine. She snatched the binoculars from her eyes and shook her head. Then she rubbed her eyes. Obviously, she was more rattled than she'd realized. For a split second the faces had looked familiar. But how could that be? Was the sun of this fantastic continent rattling her brain? Did everyone look familiar on this crazy quest?

"What did you see?" Ahmad asked, almost as if he'd read her mind.

"Nothing," she said, quickly, not wanting to sound as frightened as she was. He glanced at her but appeared too focused on his driving to question further.

Ahead, the mountains loomed right upon them. She couldn't see how they would escape from their pursuers once they were at the foothills. "What are we going to do?"

"We'll figure that out when we get there." Suddenly, he swerved and drove along the edge. Out of nowhere there was a narrow pass. He drove the car behind a rock that was surrounded by dense shrubbery and parked it there. Getting out of the car, he shoved the flare gun inside the waistband of his pants. Cradling the box in one arm as if it were a football, he grabbed her hand, saying, "Come on!" She dragged the blanket with her.

Once again, as had happened in Paris, he was running along dragging her behind him, only this time she knew they were fleeing more than just shadows.

"We may be able to hide if we can put some distance between us and the car." They ran along the foothills with her stumbling over rocks. Several times her ankle twisted and she nearly went down, but each time he held on to her. It seemed as if they would run forever, but soon they came near a shallow cave and he said, "In here." She scrambled inside on hands and knees with Ahmad coming right behind. They moved as far away from the opening as they could. It wasn't until that moment that she realized that she'd skinned her knees.

"Are you all right?" he whispered later, when he'd checked to see if they'd been followed.

"Yes," she said. She pressed against the wall, huddled in the blanket. He came and joined her, putting both arms around her. She felt better with his body heat surrounding her. "Too bad you didn't bring the rope. Not that I'm anything of a mountain climber, but it would have been something."

"It's too dark. Besides, mountain climbing with a novice would make too much noise. They'd be on us in a heart-beat."

"Do you think they'll find us?"

"Yes, but not right away."

"Oh, no, then they'll get the box and it will all be for nothing."

"Shhh." He touched her cheek. "It will be all right." He checked the flare gun at his waist.

What could they do with a flare gun? she wondered. For only a moment she wished it were real. That thought brought back what she had seen in the car. The men pursuing them quite likely had real guns.

"What did you see through the binoculars?"

She knew immediately what he meant. "I know it sounds funny, but I thought I saw those men from the British embassy—Mr. Tanaka and Mr. Von Wendt."

"You did."

"What?" She gulped.

"Shhh," he hissed. "It was them. They've been on our tail right from the beginning."

"Oh, my goodness. Is that why we ran from that nightclub?" When he admitted it, she added, "You told me we were dodging shadows."

"There wasn't any sense in your worrying about that. We did get away," he said, unperturbed by her agitation.

She shook her head. "I can't believe it. Mr. Tanaka? That nice old grandfather-type man?"

"I'm afraid so."

Her next thought came with cold fear. "Are they going to kill us?"

He took too long to answer and her heart rate went crazy. "They want the box."

"What are we going to do?" She wanted to cry but didn't want him to see what a coward she was.

Evidently, he'd taken her question at face value, for he answered, "We'll avoid them for as long as we can."

"Then what?"

"We'll decide that when we have to."

Lord, what she wanted was reassurances, and obviously he wasn't going to give too many of those, except his 'it will be all right.'

Several times, he left her there to go outside. She couldn't figure what he could see in the dark. Despite her fear, she had dozed off, for the next thing she knew, he was shaking her awake. "We may have to get out of here," he whispered near her ear. She heard faint sounds of men's voices. Then he hissed, "I'll be back."

"Ahmad," she whispered, stopping him. He turned back and she regretted that she could not see his face. She saw only his silhouette in the faint moonlight coming into the cave. She put her arms around his neck and kissed him. When she drew back, she said, "Be careful."

He touched her cheek and left. The men's voices seemed to be getting closer and she pressed against the wall of the shallow cave. She knew that anyone shining a flashlight into the cave would see her immediately. And that is what she thought had happened when she saw the whole outside light up. For a few moments it looked like broad daylight. Next a din of gunfire, shouting, hoofbeats, and whinnying horses split the air.

She cringed down on the ground, expecting any minute to feel bullets tear through her. It took her a while to realize that it wasn't the cave that was illuminated but the whole of the outside. And that the noise was coming from there, too.

The flare gun!

She scrambled to the opening and tried to look out without being seen. What she saw there sent her mind reeling. A full-fledged battle was in progress. The antiquity hunters were there but there was an even larger group. Heavily armed men, all in black and on horseback, were fighting the thieves. One of the antiquity hunters was near the front of the cave but before he could enter, Ahmad tackled him. Then Ahmad stood guarding the cave.

She snuck up to where he stood. "Who are those other men?"

"Warlords," he answered.

Oh, no, she thought, we're out of the frying pan into the fire. She clung to the box. But it wasn't only for the box's safety that she feared. It was for Ahmad and herself, too. It wasn't long before the men on horseback had rounded up all the others. Then the riders all reeled to face the cave. They were clad completely in black, including hoods that only showed slits for their eyes. Slowly they rode toward where Ahmad and Maleka stood, their rifles pointed upward. Ahmad pushed her behind him and stood to face them.

They stood silently in that manner for a long moment. Then one of the men, the leader, detached himself from the horde and rode up to confront Ahmad.

It was at that moment that she became unhinged. Suddenly, she feared that they would kill him. She was so upset by the events of the last couple of hours that she spoke before she thought. "Please, spare him! We're just humble travelers. Those men attacked us."

"And who are you, pretty one?" the leader asked, in a peculiarly familiar voice.

She remembered Ahmad saying she was his woman to keep her from being up for grabs. "I'm his woman," she said, pointing to Ahmad.

Everything went silent. The line of men on horseback looked at her through the slits in their hoods. Ahmad turned to stare down at her, one eyebrow raised.

The leader reached up and pulled off his hood. "I say, Rock, old man. Isn't this our little nun?"

It was Annan.

Later, she discovered that Ahmad had called Annan before they left Abdul's house, arranging for them to meet. Both Nado Tanaka and Johannes Von Wendt, whose names were aliases, were notorious antiquity thieves, known for robbing North African treasures.

Most important of all, they found Zeleke. He was in a small settlement close to where they'd had the confrontation with the antiquity hunters. It was the same elderly man that she had met at the well. However, this time she realized why he had looked familiar. He had been a part of the group of priests that she'd seen at the British Embassy party and also at customs when they'd first entered Morocco. Their every move had been monitored.

It was later, after Annan and his horde had removed the antiquity hunters, that they delivered the box to Zeleke. He took it with reverence and gently opened the lid.

"What are they?" she asked, referring to the leather strips.

"Ah, they tell about an old legend in my country," he explained.

"They must be very valuable," she said.

"Yes, more valuable than you could imagine. They tell of a great secret. A Biblical secret."

"Oh," she sighed. "They really are valuable. And the hunters knew that?"

"No, they don't know about that. They came for this." He touched something and a panel moved. A hitherto unknown compartment sprang open, revealing a small leather package. Zeleke picked this up and an antique gold filigree cross slipped out. He turned the cross toward her and there at its center was a red jewel the size of a robin's egg.

It looked bigger than any jewel she had ever seen in a museum, and she had once viewed the Hope Diamond. It glowed with a bright fiery light.

"Is that real?" She could barely get the words out.

"Yes."

Later, when they left Zeleke, she asked Ahmad, "Did you know about the cross?"

"I surmised it. I'd heard the story in my travels for my business."

But he hadn't told her, she thought. He hadn't shared much of any information. She realized that once again in her life, she'd felt left out. There was nothing for her here, she realized.

The next morning, after a sleepless night, she went outside in the cool mountain air. She had not seen Ahmad since the night before. The camp was quiet, except for one man who was packing things into a jeep. It was Annan.

She went to speak with him. "I'm sorry that we lied to you," she said.

"It wasn't *you* that lied. It was Rock."

"He was trying to protect my disguise," she said.

"Is that what he was trying to do?" he asked, looking dubious. "I thought it was something quite different." When she started to explain, he laughed, saying, "Do not worry. I understand totally."

She wanted to say more, for she suspected that he thought there was something between her and Ahmad, but she was too dispirited to argue. That's when she really looked at the jeep. "Are you going somewhere?" she asked impulsively.

"Yes, I am sailing to France today."

Suddenly, she blurted out, "Will you take me?"

"Take you? But I thought—"

"Please. I don't have any money, but you can trust me. I'll pay back the whole cost."

He glanced back at the house. "What about Ahmad?"

"He won't mind." Annan looked doubtful at this. "Please," she pushed on. "I must leave here."

"Alright." He laughed and shrugged. "This ought to get quite a rise out of him."

Two weeks later, Maleka was hard at work in the back room of Vito Genovese's Fashion and Design House. The place was chaotic. Everyone ran around, trying to do several things at once as they prepared for a special showing. She was hard at work, pinning sheaths of fabric to fit the lithe, slim model. As she did so, it suddenly occurred to her that something was missing. But what? Just as quickly the answer came: Envy. At one time she would have felt a twinge of envy for the reed slim, nearly six-foot beauty. But today that was gone. She had learned to respect herself and her height. Now, she knew she didn't have to be tall. Riding across the desert had shown that she could hold her own. It should have been a good feeling—and it was, except that she still ached for Ahmad.

Suddenly, there was a flurry of voices behind her. She shifted around to see what the disturbance was. Ahmad stood just inside the door. He started walking into the sewing room. Models ran, or seemed to consider running, but instead remained to smile enticingly at him. He smiled back but it was obvious that he wasn't truly interested. He strode through the women like a panther, his eyes searching every corner. Finally, he saw her. She was suddenly immobile. She could barely breathe. He walked toward her.

"What are you doing here?" she asked.

He took her hand and kissed it. "Surely, *you* don't need to ask that. I was on the verge of murdering Annan when I realized that he'd spirited you away. I couldn't stay away from you. You have become a part of me."

"Me? Why? If you think I'll be your fiftieth concubine, you can forget it."

"There are no concubines. There never were."

"No concubines?"

"No. You were right when you said I'm too American for the practice. I came because I love you."

A sigh went up in the room that she only half heard.

"You love me? When did you decide that?"

"From the moment I saw you standing in front of the Ritz-Ultra."

"Ha! If that's true, why were you so mean to me all that time?"

"Was I mean? I thought I was protecting myself from a cold-hearted flirt. I could see that you were a terrible tease and used to breaking men's hearts."

Suddenly, she realized that while she didn't believe she had ever broken anyone's heart, she had been very unconcerned with men's feelings. She remembered thinking that sometimes men were like accessories—something to be worn.

"You broke my heart in that first instant when you smiled at every man indiscriminately. Remember, I'm the son of an Arab. I grew jealous when you turned your wonderful charms upon all and sundry. Such a beauty is used to male admiration, I thought. She isn't going to pay me any attention. Maybe if I'm lucky, I'll get a few empty smiles. So, I decided to capture you by playing the cold-hearted dandy. For some weird reason, you women always love those types."

"Please," she protested. "What's with the 'you women?' And don't blame this on me."

"No, I don't. But I did figure the only way to get your attention was to play hard to get." He paused a moment. "I know you are very focused on your career, but I want to be in your life—I want to be that soulmate that you spoke of."

"Oh, Ahmad," she sighed, and went into his arms.

"By the way, I see posters advertising a Valentine's Day Dance. I hope you don't already have a date."

She wanted to jump up and down. Clasping her hands under her chin, she said, "No."

"Then allow me." He put out his arm for her to take. She took his arm and knew that she was grinning from ear to ear.

A Passionate Moment

Doris Johnson

Dedicated to Bonnie and Roderick, and to a marriage destined for a lifetime of love and happiness.

One

"Oh, look, Dan, there they are!" The woman rushed excitedly to the bin filled with colorful pillows, with the tall man close on her heels.

Verna Sinclair stood to one side holding a decorative silk pillow emblazoned with a dramatic orange and gold abstract design. She looked at the woman who was pawing through the pillows, tossing each aside in increasing dismay, then dejectedly turning to her companion with a distressful look. Realizing she was staring, Verna moved away, feeling sympathy for the woman but happy that her own search had been fruitful. Luckily, she'd discovered the mistaken sale of her pillow to Hager's Department Store in time and rushed in immediately after work, hoping that it was not too late. The companion piece was at home on her living room sofa. After finishing it, she'd forgotten to carry the pillow home from the boutique shop, and her aunt Neda had unwittingly sold it to Hager's store buyer. Relieved that retrieval of the pillow would complete her decorating ensemble, she carried it to the cashier. To her surprise, she was stopped by the woman's voice.

"Excuse me, miss, but where did you find that? Was it in with these?" Verna turned, wondering at the disappointment she heard. There were so many other beautiful choices to be made.

"I'm sorry," the woman continued, "but that is the exact color combination that I was looking for, and there doesn't seem to be any other like it."

Verna smiled. "No, I'm afraid this is the last of its kind. I'm sorry." She turned to leave and included the man in her smile, but he was looking at the young woman, who appeared near tears. Apparently disturbed at his companion's distress, his arm went around her shoulders as they turned to leave. Verna watched them go, then walked slowly toward the cashier, smoothing the textured silk. Standing in line, she saw them stop and look at other decorative objects in the fifth-floor boutique. Hager's was known for its international treasures and unique finds. Accessories for the home and wearable art did not last long, as eager customers scooped up the one-of-a-kind oddities. Verna was proud that her handcrafted pillows and other crafts from her aunt's store, The Cracked Teapot, were in elegant company. She knew the disappointment of the stranger very well because her aunt had received many calls from repeat customers, who, after asking for a duplicate of some item or other, then expressed their dismay when told of the exclusivity of most items in the store.

Unable to forget the unhappy face of the woman, Verna looked up and caught the pleasant smile and nod as the woman walked by, giving one last glance at the pillow.

"Oh, why not?" Verna murmured, leaving the line and going after the couple. *They're probably decorating their first apartment together,* she thought. *Guess my sofa will have to wait a bit longer to look complete.* She caught up to them at the elevator, just as the woman hurried into the nearby linen section.

"Excuse me," Verna said a little breathlessly, suddenly feeling a little awkward. The man turned to her in surprise. "I—I decided that I can wait until another shipment comes in." She extended the pillow. "Here, it's yours if you want it." She smiled at the astonished words of thanks she received.

Verna looked up at the man beside her elbow. She hadn't gotten a clear look at him before, but now, up close, the first thought she had was that his face was kind. Her eyes clouded with the memory of a time long past. She'd known and loved a face just like that. "You're welcome."

Dan Hunter was taken aback by the sudden look of sadness that appeared in the unselfish stranger's eyes and was amazed that the softly spoken words tickled his ears so sensuously. She was staring almost searchingly into his dark startled eyes, and he was drawn into hers almost as if by the spell of a magician's wand. He could see himself swimming in her wide-open stare, and the feeling of warmth and comfort was drugging. The alien feeling of peace was indescribable.

Verna blinked, and the feeling of weightlessness left her. She was actually still in Hager's—not orbiting the earth. The tall stranger had not moved but was looking at her as if she'd stunned him with her words. She too was speechless and, without another word, she turned and hurried toward the escalator. When she looked back, the woman had joined him, and they both stared at her until she disappeared from view.

Two

Four months later

Verna dodged the huge raindrops as she rushed from her black Altima through the back entrance of The Cracked Teapot. The door slammed shut as she shook herself off, water flying from her sopping-wet short black curls and her soaked cotton jacket.

"Whoosh. I hate getting wet." Verna peeled off the jacket and shed her shoes.

"You'd never know it the way you dash around in the rain without an umbrella every chance you get," Neda Hicks said to her niece. The thin, fiftyish woman with the mocha-colored skin and long, thin cornrows wound around her head smiled at the disgruntled young woman. She was in the midst of pouring herself a cup of tea and now prepared a cup of the strong English brew for Verna. "Here, drink this after you dry yourself off. Don't rush; Gregory's minding the front. It's been a little slow so far."

Verna groaned with pleasure as she slipped her dried feet into the old pair of sneakers that she wore while working in the shop and donned a long-sleeved cotton cobbler's coat. She knew she was foolish not to protect herself from the rain, which was too cold for mid-September.

"Mmm, thanks." The hot tea gliding down her throat hit the spot. Comforted, she raised a brow. "Michelle's not in yet?" Her cousin, Neda's daughter, was usually in the shop first thing on Saturdays. With her exuberant personality, she was the one that enticed the customers into buying the store's quality merchandise.

"She called, saying that she will be in around noon," replied Neda.

Verna raised a brow, then smiled. "Must have been more than a night out with the girls," she mused. "Glad I opted out," she added, sipping more of the warming beverage.

Neda glanced at her niece. "When are you going to stop doing that?" she asked softly. Her gaze slid to the sparkling diamond ring Verna still wore. "No one is going to blame you for laughing and smiling again. It won't be sacrilegious."

Verna lowered her long lashes, shielding the hurt in her dark eyes. "I know, you and Michelle are right." Her voice was low, and she stared into the cup as if seeking answers there. She didn't look up when she heard her aunt softly close the door behind her as she went into the front room of the store. Verna rinsed her cup then walked to her workspace in the large, brightly lit back room, where she and her aunt crafted many of the gift items. "Who puts a time limit on grief?" The question was merely a murmur and one to which Verna never had an answer.

The gold silk pillow that she picked up was nearing completion. The fabric was reminiscent of the bolt she'd used months ago to fashion pillows for her own home. Although not an exact match, the pillow would only complement the one that already occupied a place on her burnt-orange sofa. Once she sewed in the zipper and prepared the inside covering, it would be finished, and this time she would take it home with her.

Flustered suddenly at remembering the day she gave away her pillow to the stranger, she busied herself to forget, but the whir of the sewing machine only invited her to get lost in her thoughts. Until recently, she'd been successful in burying the image of the handsome man who had so totally mesmerized her. She'd been drawn into the depths of his deep brown eyes; then, after staring at his face, she had rushed away with her heavily charged emotions. She stopped the machine to adjust the fabric then began again. Not since her fiancé, Frank Parsons, had died had she thought romantically about another man. But that day in Hager's, she didn't know what had come over her, swooning over a married man. It had been hard not to notice the set of rings on the woman's finger. Pleased that she'd made the couple happy, Verna had put the incident from her mind until days ago when painful memories began to surface. The advent of September reminded her of her own engagement two years ago. In November, a scant two months later, Frank was dead of a massive heart attack.

The machine stopped, as did Verna's daydream, when the back door burst open and the whirlwind that was her cousin, Michelle Fieldings, flew inside.

"Ugh. What a deluge." Michelle imitated Verna's earlier movements in shaking the droplets off, but hers were shaken from an umbrella, which she put in the stand by the door.

Verna smiled at her cousin's dislike of getting wet. They had so many ways that were similar, and they both attributed it to growing up together since the death of Verna's parents when she was six.

"At least you have sense enough to cover yourself," Verna said.

Michelle removed her rubber boots and hung her raincoat next to Verna's wet jacket. "And you didn't, as usual," she observed, slipping on black velvet step-ins, then heading for the stove and the teakettle.

"No lectures, please," replied Verna. "Heard it already."

Michelle laughed. "Ma, huh? Serves you right. I'm glad you're not *my* nurse!"

"Never mind," grumbled Verna. "I get no complaints from my patients. Besides, what are you doing here before eleven? I heard your day was starting at noon."

"And yours would be too if you'd joined us. The girls and I went to Barry's Place after dinner."

"Dancing?" Verna sniffed. "I'm glad I didn't join you."

"You missed a good time, Verna," Michelle said, after sipping the hot tea. She pushed her shoulder-length brunette hair away from her face with an annoyed look at her cousin. "Dancing would do you a world of good. The way you and Frank used to tear it up, you'd think you'd gone lame after he died." Ignoring Verna's stricken look, Michelle continued. "Guess this is your day for lectures, sweetie, so don't close your ears. Last night while I was cutting my own rug, best I could in that jam-packed club, I couldn't help but think of you sitting home, mourning Frank's memory. I didn't know him as my sweetie-pie, but I knew him well enough to know that he would blow his stack at you revering him like a subject that's lost her king." She paused, and her light-brown wide-set eyes narrowed in her deep beige face. "After all, it was I who got you two together." Her eyes softened and the one-sided dimple in her cheek deepened when she smiled. She left the stool that she was perched on, went to her cousin, and kissed Verna on the forehead. At twenty-nine, she was only older by one year, but Michelle had assumed the role of mother hen when Verna came to live with them. She sat next to Verna and patted her shoulder. "It'll be two years soon, Verna," she said softly, and picked up Verna's hand. "Don't you realize that this rock tells available men that you're taken? You have to take off Frank's ring and put it away with your other cherished memories. You won't be dishonoring him. I promise you."

"I know, Michelle." Verna twisted the ring off her finger and held her hand away from her body. "I've tried this before. See how empty? That's the way I feel inside. It's like I've tossed aside what we once had." She replaced the ring. "It makes me feel connected."

"To what? A spirit? Frank's gone. You said it yourself—'What we once had.' It's time to think about making new memories with someone else." Michelle searched her cousin's face for signs of acceptance, but when Verna started looking for the right size foam filling for her pillow, she leaned back in her chair, feeling a little deflated.

Verna found what she wanted then returned to her worktable. She worked in silence then finally said, "I'm not angry with you, Michelle. I hear what you're saying. Maybe I need a little more time than some others."

Michelle smoothed her hair and checked herself in the full-length mirror before she joined her mother. She always dressed as smartly as she did for her nine-to-five job as a sales representative for one of Maryland's leading department stores. She wore a candy-apple-red short dress with short sleeves and a marbled orange and red scarf tied fashionably around her throat. "Maybe you do, Verna, but I'm not going to let you have the last word on this."

"When do you ever, Mother?" Verna teased.

Michelle laughed. "Never. You may be bigger than me, but I'm older."

"This is true," Verna said, looking approvingly at her petite cousin. Michelle was three-inches shorter than Verna's five-foot six-inch tall slim figure.

Michelle turned at the door. "I'll tell you what, Cousin," she said, thoughtfully.

Verna raised a cautious brow, listening for one of Michelle's great schemes.

"Suppose we take it slow, say a dinner with just you and me. Get you used to going out again. After almost two years of nothing but work, you'll feel like new money. Next we'll go with the girls." Michelle warmed to her own idea and her words came faster. "After a few dinners, we'll try the club scene." She held up a hand at the protests she saw coming. "I promise to stay away from places we all used to haunt." Before Verna could answer, she said, "Okay, next Friday, we have a date. Ma and Gregory can close the shop as usual at seven and we'll get an early start at six." Breathlessly, she said, "Good," and hurried to the front, closing the door firmly.

Verna had to take a deep breath, then laughed. No wonder that little dynamo was top-notch at her job. She wondered if Michelle's customers said yes to her sales pitches just to shut her up and get her out of their offices . . . until next time.

The following Friday at five o'clock, Verna was in the ladies' room at the Prince George's Family Health Clinic where she worked as a registered nurse. Located in Silver Springs, Maryland, she was a twenty-minute drive from Laurel, where she lived, only blocks away from her aunt's home where she grew up. Michelle had decided that the first venture out should be close to home after a full day's work and before a long Saturday at the shop. She'd found a new restaurant in Upper Marlboro that had begun to attract repeat customers. Word of mouth was creating booming business and they'd started a reservations policy. So rather than going home to change and risking being late, Verna brought her change of clothes to work. Always a casual dresser, probably subconsciously getting away from her usual uniform of white jacket and pants, she preferred blowsy, loose-fitting garments in natural blended fabrics, which were very colorful. She rarely wore white or pale blue. Her honey-gold complexion was complemented by bold colors and her wardrobe was filled with the hues that were reflected in her pillow designs. But tonight she chose to wear a fuji-silk pantsuit with wide legs and a fingertip length jacket that she left unbuttoned. The fuchsia sleeveless blouse was an exact match to her suit. A black, low-heeled, fabric shoe completed her ensemble.

Verna freshened her makeup, satisfied at the selection of cognac-red lipstick that she'd applied to her full lips. She made a face at the tiny pimple that threatened to break out under her dimpled chin, but shrugged it off. That was the least of her worries, as the rest of the skin on her oval face was flawless. The memory of Frank running his knuckles over her cheeks caused a pang. She used to get annoyed at the affectionate gesture, especially when they were out. Now, if only he . . . Verna shuttered at the thought and, gathering her things, hurried from the room and out the clinic door.

As Verna drove, she suddenly looked forward to this new and different activity on a Friday night. Normally, if she didn't go to the Georgetown, D.C. store to either help out in the front or work on her crafts, she'd shuck her work clothes, shower, then spend the night working on new designs; a routine she'd followed for almost two years. As long as she kept busy, she was fine. There was little time left to think about other things. Tonight was a chance to bring a new and sensible order to her life. She glanced at her hands on the steering wheel then quickly eyed the road steadily, resolving that there would be no regrets. The stone that usually sparkled on her left hand was missing. And for the first time, she did not feel empty inside.

Three

Dan Hunter was not looking forward to the date that he'd made last week. For the last few months he'd been going at a breakneck speed, putting some kind of order to his life, and tonight he felt that his fevered pace of living was telling on his thirty-five-year-old body. He'd made a commitment, but all he wanted to do this Friday night was sleep into Saturday afternoon. But since he was the one who'd initiated the call, as he'd done with all his recent dates, he had to keep his word. Breaking the date at this point was not an option; besides, he'd hate to think that he'd sunk that low. Determined, he'd do his best to show the lady a good time. He hoped that she didn't pick up on his disinterested attitude, or worse, think that she was the problem.

Dan knotted his tie. The navy and burgundy with gray and white square splatters complemented his blue shirt and navy, two-button suit. Satisfied that he cared enough to at least look good for the lady, he smoothed his thin mustache then headed for the door, nearly tripping over the living room furniture that he'd pushed into the hallway. The carpet was being delivered and laid the next day, which was another reason why he wanted to just chill out tonight. He locked the front door and tried to put a little jazz in his step as he walked across the grass to the garage. The passageway from inside was impassable and he wished that this sudden fever to decorate, making a house into a home, would hurry and burn itself out—before he did. Although the restaurant in Upper Marlboro was less than a fifteen-minute drive from his Largo home, he had to travel in the opposite direction for fifteen minutes to pick up his date. Thinking about that old "sleeping in the bed that you made" saying, he grunted and drove with a heavy foot—as if that would speed up the night. He lightened up when he found himself losing his concentration.

Dan could remember the exact moment his frenzied urges had started: the need to establish some permanency in his life. It was over four months ago, in Hager's, when he'd been stabbed in the heart by a pair of beautiful, dark, doe-shaped eyes that belonged to a brown angel. When she had disappeared down that escalator, she had disappeared from his life. There had been no need to try to find her because she was already taken. The shining diamond on her finger had told him that. His sister, Paula McMurray, had had to nudge him out of his euphoric state. When he'd come to, he had felt dazed. He remembered Paula's look of amazement. Obviously, she knew the same instant as he did what had happened to him.

"Oh, brother," Paula exclaimed. "Smack dab in the middle of a crowded department store on a Thursday night, my big brother was stabbed with Cupid's arrow! Now don't that beat all?" She grabbed her brother's arm and pulled him out of the flow of people traffic, to keep them both from getting trampled to death by the shoppers who brushed them aside with annoyed looks.

"What are you mumbling about?" grumbled Dan. But he knew exactly what she was saying. He had to jam his hands in his pockets to keep from rubbing his chest. Did he feel a burning sensation? The illusionary pain was just that, he thought. Unreal! He felt her propel him to the elevator and soon found himself in the store café. The hot coffee was jolting, and stimulated him back to reality.

"Whew! This hit the spot." Dan drank some more.

"Not like *she* did," Paula said, with a twinkle in her eyes. Then, serious, she patted his hand, which he moved restlessly up and down the shaft of the spoon. "I'm sorry, Brother. I don't mean to be mean or cutesy. But I never saw anything like that happen before. I mean, *see* it. Of course, when it happened to me, I *felt* it when Marvin and I locked eyes. But looking on when it happens to somebody else, is nothing but *weird.*"

Dan had to smile at his pretty younger sister. At thirty-one, she had been happily married to her husband going on four years now. Though still childless, they remained hopeful.

"Now that's one thing I can agree on with you," he remarked. Again suppressing the need to massage his chest, he tried to let the coffee soothe his insides. "Okay, you tell me what you saw and see if we're together on this thing."

"You saw something that you wanted and can't have. I saw the ring, too, Dan."

"Right," he agreed. He blew out a breath. "And for a split second, I wished that I had put it there. Couldn't have," he said, his voice dropping. "So, where does that leave me for the rest of my young life?" he tried to joke.

"Looking for another woman who can make you feel the same way," Paula said, as if there could be no other answer.

Dan snapped his fingers. "Just like that!" Deep down he knew that anyone else would always be second best.

"Dan, you're going to be an old man before you find a woman you love and settle down. At your age you should be taking your lady around, looking at condos or a house big enough for five—two grown-ups and three babies."

"I have a house," Dan grumbled.

"A rented house with option to buy! And not a stick of furniture anywhere, except in your bedroom and your basement workshop."

"That's not true. I have furniture."

"Humph, Ma's old sofa that was new when I was six-teen?" Paula rolled her eyes. "That's why you never invite women home. There's no decent place for you to sit and get your groove on properly."

Dan's eyebrows shot up. "All right, Paula," he growled. Was this his baby sister schooling him on romance?

Paula shucked off her brother's scowl. "The dining room is bare, the kitchen even worse, and all the bedrooms are nothing but store rooms for years of accumulated stuff! Your house is not a home but a warehouse. I think after three years of living there you can at least put a little of yourself in it." Then she smiled to soften her words. "I can help you get past those intimidating salespeople if you like. Some of them would sell you anything and you'd wind up with a place resembling a frat house."

Dan shrugged. "And after the transformation, what then, miss know-it-all?"

"Simple. We find you a wife."

And that was the beginning, Dan thought, as he picked up his date and drove to the restaurant. Mary Jennings was a lovely young woman, and he didn't remember what number date she was, but he knew without a doubt that she wasn't the one. He wouldn't be calling her again. Guilty relief flooded through him when she greeted him with the sniffles and apologized for requesting a short evening.

Dan drove in silence, wondering if the woman of his dreams was truly happy. He couldn't help but remember the haunted look in her eyes.

The crowd in Sampson's was dressed festively and affected the cheerful mood in the upscale restaurant as people ate. Murmurs of ebullient adjectives about the food floated past Verna's and Michelle's ears as they waited for their own dinners to be served. Scrumptious smells from the passing waitpersons' trays did nothing to lessen their anticipation or appetite.

Verna took a sip of the pink champagne that Michelle had specifically ordered for the occasion. "Good choice."

It was a California brand that she'd had in the past, but she didn't dwell on where or with whom—tonight was a new beginning.

"I'm glad you like it. My treat." Michelle eyed her cousin closely, as she'd done since they'd met outside the restaurant. There was no pretense in either attitude or voice and only sincerity in her conversation and interest in her surroundings. Feeling pleased with herself at maneuvering this first step in Verna's "coming out," Michelle savored her drink and tried to keep from salivating when the plates of food arrived. She was starved, and she felt certain that her normally hearty appetite for good cooking was going to be satiated.

The same words of praise that had reached their ears about the southern-style cuisine now became duplicate murmurs of appreciation from Verna and Michelle.

"Umm, tastes just like mine," Michelle sighed, as she bit into a succulent piece of pork chop.

"In your dreams, sweetie." Verna would have laughed if she hadn't had a mouthful of delicious lamb. Michelle was the world's worst cook and was often teased that her culinary skills, or lack thereof, was the primary cause of her husband Floyd divorcing her.

Miffed, Michelle washed down the meat with a sip of water. "I'll have you know, I've gotten better."

"How? A la LaBelle, taking your pots on the road with you? Bet the cities' bravest are put on alert by your hotels soon as your reservations are confirmed." Michelle was a frequent flyer traveling to many cities doing business for her company as a buyer. There were times during the last two years that Verna had envied her trips to fascinating cities.

"Very funny. I've been watching Ma as much as I can lately." Michelle sniffed. "Like I should've done years ago, just like you did." She ate some more of the tender pork.

Verna remembered very well the times she was underfoot in Aunt Neda's kitchen. "I'm just glad your mother had the patience to come home from work and cook, never minding me following her every move." She smiled. "One thing is certain . . . when my time comes it won't be due to keeling over from starvation."

"Be a sin and a shame if it were. Make me wanna wake you up and whip some sense into you."

The image made both women laugh at their silliness and they continued to enjoy their meal, talking quietly about a sundry of subjects but never touching on why they were out in the first place. Michelle observed that Verna hadn't thought twice about their morbid little joke.

Verna had excused herself, and Michelle, dessert finished, was enjoying a cup of coffee when she frowned and looked up. Without guessing, she knew that her eyes would meet those of the man who'd been staring at her and Verna all night. Seated two tables behind Verna's back, Michelle had watched the man watch them all evening, even though he was with someone. At first, she thought he was mistaking her for someone he knew, and she'd nodded slightly and smiled. He'd acknowledged her with a slight nod of his own but when, during the evening, she continually caught his stare, she became annoyed. *Men! And with a pretty date, too!*

Michelle watched the woman stand and murmur something and soon she passed by Michelle's table. Almost immediately the man rose and strode toward her.

"Have we met?" Michelle's voice was hard-edged.

"Excuse me, Miss, but I must speak with you. My name is Dan Hunter and, believe me, I have nothing in mind but to ask you one question privately. Would you please come to the bar, alone?" Dan searched the eyes of the woman, who eyed him with suspicion. "I swear. One question." When he noticed a blur of fuchsia at the doorway, he walked stiffly back to the table.

Michelle turned to see why Dan Hunter had left in such a hurry and saw Verna approaching. There was no indication on her face that she'd seen the visitor at the table making his strange request. Michelle stared at the man, but when he stood as his date returned, he did not glance

Michelle's way. Rather, he said a few words, then navigated himself in the opposite direction from their table and walked to the partitioned bar area.

Never one to let a mystery solve itself, Michelle, curious as a puppy discovering brand new slippers, made her excuses to Verna and made her own circuitous route to the clandestine meeting.

Dan held his breath, thinking that he'd go crazy if the petite young woman ignored his plea. He hoped that he hadn't sounded like a raving idiot but decided he had when she'd given him that incredible look. But this was a once in a lifetime opportunity and he'd be a fool to let it pass him by.

Over an hour ago, he and his date had barely been seated when he saw that angel of his dreams walk in with another woman. He thought he was seeing things and had done all he could to restrain himself from approaching their table. From his view of her and the gestures she made, he failed to see the sparkling ring on her finger. Was he only imagining? Was her finger really bare? While trying to carry on a decent conversation with Mary Jennings, he agonized over the possibility that his angel could be free. He had to know. And there was no way that he could leave this place without being sure.

With Mary becoming increasingly ill with harsh cold symptoms, Dan knew that they would be leaving soon. His chances were slim to none of meeting the beautiful stranger and putting to rest the gnawing in his gut. His chance came when Mary excused herself. It had to be now.

Dan was facing the bar, head down, not wanting to see whether he'd made a dent in the cool exterior of the shorter woman. He could only wait and pray.

He jumped at her voice. "My name is Michelle Fieldings."

Dan turned to face her. "Thank you," he breathed.

Michelle looked him over with a critical eye. She was excellent at her job and usually was a good judge of people—all except the man that she'd married of course, but that was another story. She'd long ago assessed that this man was highly intrigued by her cousin. Had they met somewhere before? she wondered.

"What's your question?"

Dan spoke quietly. "She's not wearing her ring. Is she still engaged or married?"

Michelle raised a brow at the underlying urgency. Was she looking at a man hopelessly in love—*or a stalker?* How had he known about Verna's ring unless he'd seen her wearing it? *What was she doing?* She stepped back, suddenly wary.

Dan saw the sudden look of fear on Michelle's face. He'd frightened her. *No wonder, you jerk,* he chastised himself. He could be the nightmare from Hell for all she knew. "Ms. Fieldings, please, I know I must be coming off as your worst horror show." He reached inside his breast pocket and pulled out his card. "Here. Take this, please. I swear I have no evil intentions. You can check me out up and down, inside out, if you want." He hesitated before turning to leave and solemnly said, "Thank you."

Michelle took a deep breath. *Please Lord, let this be right!* "Wait." He watched her carefully. "Her fiancé died." Dan threw her a grateful look and walked away. Michelle watched him go, suddenly feeling the sense of anxiety leave her. Was this a new twist on how to get a date? She must have been out of circulation a long time, she mused. Dan Hunter. Why was that name so familiar? She met hundreds of people in a year in her travels for the department store. Could he have been a customer? She glanced at the name and local address on the card. *Dan Hunter, Artist/Sculptures in Wood.* Michelle's jaw dropped. *That* Dan Hunter?

Michelle reached her table just as Dan and his date stood up to leave. *Made it,* she breathed.

Verna searched Michelle's flushed face. "What's wrong with you? You look like you ran into your ex. What a perfect ending to a perfect evening," she teased.

"I think it will be," Michelle mumbled. She took a drink

of water just as Dan and his date approached the table on their way out.

Verna moved to get up and as her foot shot out, she winced as a woman stumbled over it. "Oh, I'm sorry," she gasped. "Please excuse me."

Dan caught Mary before she fell and, when he looked down, he was caught by Verna's stare. He was mesmerized.

"Oh, hello, Mr. Hunter. It is Dan Hunter, isn't it?" Michelle said, smiling and extending her hand. To the woman who seemed a bit woozy, she said, "We're sorry, are you all right? Would you like to sit down for a moment?"

Verna, amazed, looked from the woman who appeared to be ill, to Dan Hunter, to her cousin, who seemed pleased to see this man—the man who, months ago, had looked into her eyes and had sent her senses reeling. And he and Michelle were acquainted!

Dan followed Michelle's lead. "No, but thank you. We really must be going, Ms. . . . Ms. . . ."

"Fieldings. Michelle Fieldings. And this is Verna Sinclair. Verna meet Dan Hunter, artist. And Mrs.?"

"Forgive me," Dan said. "Ms. Sinclair, Ms. Fieldings, meet Ms. Jennings."

Verna Sinclair. Magical, thought Dan. But when he turned to Verna, he was hit with the saddest look he'd ever seen. She appeared almost in tears. Then suddenly a look of anger blanketed her face. "Mr. Hunter. Ms. Jennings," she said tersely.

Before anyone could say anything else, Mary turned to Dan. "Please?" she implored in a raspy voice.

Dan could see the tiny beads of sweat beginning to dampen her forehead. Suddenly compassionate, he took her arm. "Sorry," he murmured, solicitously. Glancing at Michelle, he said, "Nice meeting you again, but we really must be going."

"Good-bye, Mr. Hunter. Maybe someday you'll drop by our crafts shop, The Cracked Teapot, in Georgetown. We could discuss displaying your work."

With a grateful look at Michelle and a nod to Verna Sinclair, Dan led Mary from the restaurant.

With blazing eyes, Verna watched them go.

"Now what in the world is wrong with you?" Michelle asked, wondering at the steam rising from her cousin's head.

"Men!" Verna scowled. "He's married."

"He is?" Michelle fell back in her chair.

"Yes. But not to her."

Four

Two weeks after Dan's living room carpet was laid and the old furniture thrown out, he sat on the floor in the big square room looking around in disgust. So much for his scheme, he thought. The deep beige carpet was the only result of his hasty resolution made months ago. He felt as deflated as last year's birthday balloons. After his four-month whirlwind activity, which had included dating every old girlfriend and wining and dining new women in a mad-dash, hare-brained effort to meet that special someone, he had come to a dead halt. By one chance in ten million he had learned the name of the woman that he'd fallen for but that he'd thought was promised to another. But more miraculous was that she was unspoken for. Exactly the news that had made his heart nearly leap from his chest. He had a chance! But what had he done with that piece of news? Not a damn thing!

Dan had his back against the cream-colored wall, legs stretched out and arms folded across his chest. Contemplating his action, or rather inaction, he knew why he hadn't made a move to find Verna Sinclair. It wasn't as if he had any searching to do, thanks to Ms. Fieldings. Surveying the empty room again, he knew that this was the reason. What did he have to offer to any woman? What kind of stability was there in his life? If he were to read anything into Ms. Fieldings's remarks, she and Verna had their own business. To his surprise, his name and his work were familiar to her, so they probably dealt in some sort of art. But with her own business, would Verna even want to deal with someone who until only five years ago didn't know where he fit in this world? With that thought, he had given up his foolish quest to find the right Mrs. Hunter.

But the gnawing feeling in his gut was a signal to Dan that he was wrong and just being pig-headed. His body syncopation couldn't be that far out into left field. *Man, why don't you get off your rump and do something? If you get kicked to the curb, face it and get on with the rest of your life!* Dan grunted. So much for his smarter-than-he-was alter ego. The man's got a point. Behaving like an immovable object begets absolutely nothing.

Dan hauled himself up off the floor and walked upstairs into the largest of the three bedrooms, which he'd made his. Since his sister's attack on his living conditions, he'd galvanized himself into properly furnishing the room. The room smelled of the newly purchased oak bedroom set that had come out of the factory where he worked. It had been no problem ordering the set and getting it delivered in a matter of weeks. As a matter of fact, the triple dresser and the highboy wardrobe looked like pieces he'd worked on himself. The queen-size sleigh bed was sturdy enough to hold his solid but lanky six-foot frame. The polished wood floor was left bare by choice, but Dan had allowed his sister to select the two rugs that flanked either side of the bed. At his "keep it simple" instruction, she had chosen an oriental-style design with a navy background and beige and cranberry-red highlights. The bedding was solid navy and the window panels, hanging from oak rods, were ivory. Scattered around the room were several African masks, which made perfect cover for the cream-colored walls. Now, when Dan came up from his basement workshop, he actually used his room for more than sleeping. He lived in it, and often lay in bed sketching new designs for his wood sculptures.

As he undressed, on the way to shower, he mused over

the fact that what had been a hobby for practically all his life had turned into an art form. One that had begun to pay him big bucks—and only three years after being "discovered." The water pelted his head and he had to stop chuckling before he drowned himself. But he couldn't help his constant amazement at how a thirteen-year-old boy's interest in whittling had turned into woodcarving and later, wood-sculpting. A "future giant," the powers-that-be were calling him.

Summers, he had been allowed to hang around Al Cunningham's furniture-making factory, cleaning up the wood chips and keeping the small place debris-free. When he was old enough to work, Al, the only black major factory owner in the District of Columbia, hired him and began to teach him the art of making quality wood furniture. By the time he was eighteen and a full-time employee, Dan was an accomplished woodcarver, making miniature animals for fun and earning a living making furniture. After a brief Army stint and various jobs, including one as a cruise-ship waiter, years later, at the age of thirty, Dan found himself back at Al's and back to his love of working with his hands. While in the service, he'd begun to branch out, making sculptures in wood depicting the human form. It was one such sculpture of a demure maiden that had put him on the map, so to speak. He'd sold it for a nominal price to a coworker, who'd given it to his wife who was an art teacher. From that, he began receiving requests and, after a gallery paid a phenomenal price for a mother and child sculpture, Dan realized then that his talent was to be called a hobby no more. He'd become an artist. Dan Hunter: sculptor. It was then that he'd desired a large workspace for his fledgling part-time business. Three years ago he'd rented the house where the garage was also at his disposal.

Dan got out of the shower and dressed casually in slacks, short-sleeve knit shirt, and blazer. He walked downstairs to the kitchen looking around with pride. Rented no more, he thought. Only four weeks ago, he'd had the closing that made the property his. It was part of his "organizing" to bring stability to his life. He reached for the telephone directory. Surely a place with a disarming name such as The Cracked Teapot would be bustling on a Saturday afternoon. As he dialed the number, he wondered if Verna Sinclair would answer. Then what?

Dan, without identifying himself to the male voice, asked for the hours and directions and hung up. He'd decided that he wanted an up-front and personal encounter. Anything else would be unacceptable. His future depended on him making a favorable impression. He hadn't liked the look Verna Sinclair had given him two weeks ago, and he had to know what lay behind the anger in her eyes—because it had without a doubt been directed at him.

Verna was in the shop alone and would be for the rest of the day. Gregory, the young part-timer, had had to leave unexpectedly but would try to make it back before closing. But by two in the afternoon, she had given up expecting him. She'd told her aunt that it wouldn't be a problem for her and Gregory to manage by themselves for one day. The shop was closed on Sundays. So her aunt had decided to accompany Michelle out of town on a buying trip from which they wouldn't return until Monday morning.

A sigh of relief escaped her lips when the last customer walked away happily with one of her aunt's Victorian-style creations. It was an old-fashioned silk sachet filled with delicate fragrances that was placed in closets and drawers for pleasant smells. There were a few leftovers from Valentine's Day, when the big-selling item had kept everyone busy crafting the small bags. Verna loved making the romantic bit of fluff. It reminded her of that lovers' holiday when Frank would surprise her with exquisite oddities that she still held dear. Only recently, she'd packed away those special gifts, in preparation for starting anew. It was time to begin making new memories. But the problem was that the couple she'd often thought about in the last few months—that woman who'd been so happy to get the pillow and the man who'd looked at his wife with affection—now brought a sour taste to her mouth. That same man, who'd acted so happy for his wife, was nothing but a philanderer. He had the boldness to squire his other woman about town to the newest popular restaurants for all to see. Suppose he'd run into his wife's friends? It was that chance meeting in Sampson's that had put a damper on Verna's thinking about starting a new relationship if the opportunity presented itself. After that look at a supposedly happily married couple, her expectations of meeting another trustworthy man went down to less than zero.

Verna huffed. What would his actions matter to a man like that anyway? Glancing toward the door and hoping that she would be free for a minute or two, she hurried to fix a cup of tea. The water was boiling, as she'd put the kettle on while her last customer was trying to make up her mind about her purchases. Now Verna rushed behind the door. She'd just sweetened the strong brew and taken a sip, when she heard the tinkle of the bell on the front door. Hastily taking another sip, she said "Here we go again." Maybe the customer would see, buy, then leave, after which, Verna would lock the door for a half-hour. She was starved and had to put food in her stomach before she passed out. She drew in a breath when she instantly recognized the tall figure scrutinizing the label on one of her pillows. She closed the door softly and entered the room.

"Mr. Hunter." She waved a hand. "Is there something I can help you with today?"

Dan looked up. "Ms. Sinclair." Dan inclined his head and looked quickly around.

Verna noticed and said, "My cousin is not here." After all, it was Michelle who had invited him to visit.

Dan would not be put off by the same look of anger that appeared on her face, or by her disinterested voice. In a quiet, firm voice he said, "It's you I came to visit, Ms. Sinclair." His stare was unwavering, even as she glared back at him with those beautiful dark-brown eyes.

Annoyed, Verna broke the stare. She was being pulled involuntarily to a place she did not want to go. She'd been there once before with him for a brief, uncontrollable moment. But now, she fortified herself.

"Whatever for?" Verna eyed the pillow that he held. "Is there something wrong with the pillow you and your wife purchased at Hager's? I'm sure you won't have a problem returning it. They do stand by their merchandise."

Wife? So that's it! Dan could hardly restrain himself from reaching out and pulling her into his arms. He quirked a brow and kept his voice steady. "I don't have a wife, Ms. Sinclair. The woman you saw me with in Hager's was my sister, Paula McMurray."

Verna's eyes widened. "Not married? Then . . ." Her voice trailed away as she walked behind the counter if only to put distance between them. She was certain that he could feel the tremble that went through her. *Could he be single? The other woman* . . . He finished her unspoken thought.

"In Sampson's? I asked a young woman to dinner and she accepted." Dan's eyes burned into Verna's. "Nothing more," he said, with emphasis.

"You're not . . ." She was interrupted again.

"No, I'm not." Dan kept his jacket closed in the very sure possibility that she could see his heart thumping. He sensed her discomfort and, more relaxed than he'd been in months, he backed away. The last thing that he wanted was to scare her off by making strong moves on her. She'd recently lost the man she loved and another man taking his place so soon was probably ludicrous to her.

"Ms. Sinclair," he started, just as the door opened. Two women and a man entered, all voicing opinions about something they'd seen in the window. Dan moved away while Verna excused herself. He didn't miss the questioning look she gave him. "I want to look around a bit, if you don't mind," he said in a low voice. Feeling encouraged at the small smile she gave him, he busied himself with perusing the items in the store.

Twenty minutes later, Verna closed the door behind the customers and locked it.

"Mr. Hunter," she said, "would you mind if I . . ." She faltered and brushed a hand across her forehead. "If you'll excuse me . . ."

Dan walked to her, concern covering his face. "What's wrong?"

Verna smiled at the worry in his voice. "Nothing that food won't cure. Usually my first meal of the day is taken before three in the afternoon."

He frowned. "You've eaten nothing all day?"

"Coffee this morning and two sips of tea just before you came in." She hesitated. "We close at six o'clock on Saturdays and I must eat something before then. It's just that I hate closing because this is one of the shop's busiest days, but I'm going to run next door and get a sandwich. I won't be long."

Dan frowned again. "And I interrupted your tea break." He thought for a second then said, "Suppose you let me get your sandwich and when I return, you can eat it in private while I entertain any customers that walk in." At her uncertainty, he added, "I promise you that I won't lose any business for you. I can enthrall them with my tales of searching the four corners of the world for their shopping pleasure." He swung his arm in a wide arc. "Like that ebony mask from Ghana," he said, squinting with one eye and nodding in wise fashion. "The haggling that I did to get it at a price for that one special customer wouldn't be believed." He turned to the colorful cushions and bolsters arranged in neat displays around the shop. "And the fabric." He unfurled a bolt of silk that was part of a display. "I searched for days in Milan for such a piece! And . . ."

"All right, all right!" Verna laughed, and her eyes twinkled when she held up a hand. "I'll accept your offer. Go, now," she said. She went to help him roll up the silk cloth. When she reached him, he stopped her.

"There's a condition," he said quietly.

"Why did I not know?" Verna asked, a trifle breathless. "What is it?"

"Have dinner with me after you lock up tonight."

"Tonight?" Verna was surprised, pleased, and confused all at once. She didn't know this man.

"I know what you're thinking, Verna." *How easily her name came to his lips.* "How else can two people get to know each other? Dinner is the conventional way. Afterward?" He shrugged. "If there's nothing there, then nothing's lost. It's goodnight and good-bye." He waited.

"I accept," Verna said softly. She took the bolt from his hands and positioned it in the display. When she turned to the expectant look he was giving her, she added, "Ham and Swiss cheese, with the works."

Dan's long stride carried him to the door and when he was out of view, a resounding "Yes!" flew from his mouth.

"No, I don't think so, Verna. After finding you again, I'm not about to let you out of my sight so fast." Dan was helping her into his car under her protests that she could follow him to the restaurant and then drive herself home afterward.

Verna realized that he was determined to put himself out for her so she suggested a restaurant in Georgetown that was trendy, served good food, and was quiet. She wanted to be able to talk without shouting to be heard over the usual noisy Saturday night fun-seekers, because she wanted to know more about Dan Hunter. In the space of the hour he'd spent with her earlier, she'd become intrigued and looked forward to their impromptu dinner date. He had been waiting outside when she locked the shop at six.

Verna was quiet for the next few minutes, thinking about what she was feeling. His gentle touch to her elbow a few seconds ago was unsettling. But only because she'd liked it. Where these feelings would take her, she didn't know. She couldn't know. Like Dan said, one can always say goodnight and good-bye. But deep down, she hoped that he'd spoken those words to someone else two weeks ago.

"What's the smile for?" Verna asked, smiling herself because his was so infectious. The devilish grin was made more so by the crooked smile that brought a dimple to life in the middle of his chin. The neatly trimmed mustache and shaded goatee enhanced the devil-may-care smile. They'd finished their meal and, both declining cocktails, sat leisurely over second cups of coffee.

Dan shook his head as his smile broadened, then quickly sobering, said, "I was just thinking about a saying you hear all the time. It goes something like, 'don't ever wish too hard for something because your wish might come true.' Well, I don't regret getting mine one bit."

Verna caught her breath. "And what wish were you granted?"

"Seeing you again." Dan held her stare.

"That's what you meant about finding me again?"

"Yes," Dan said quietly, never losing eye contact. "But, I never hoped for it to happen because you were engaged. I'd seen the ring."

"Michelle told me," Verna murmured. "Yet you still wished?"

"Not at first. I tried to forget you, but it wasn't working," Dan said. "That night in Sampson's, even before I picked up my date, I'd decided that it was no use. That that was to be my last date—at least for a long while, until I'd rid myself of the thought of you." He closed his eyes briefly. "But when you walked in, I was hit with the same feeling I'd had the first time. The bare ring finger did it for me." He shrugged. "And here we are."

Verna was nearly overcome. "I . . . I don't know what to say."

Dan offered a wry smile. "Can I give a little hint?"

Verna nodded.

"Say you'll see me again." He caught her hand and she

didn't pull away. Dan was encouraged to continue. "I know you lost your fiancé," he said in a low voice, "and I'm not asking you to forget that he ever existed. I just want to be there when you feel ready to begin a new life." He released her and busied his hand with his coffee cup. The softness of her skin and the delicate scent of flowers were sending the wrong excruciating messages to his brain. Weren't his senses smart enough to realize that he couldn't react? Almost instantly they went into high gear again when she caught his hand and held it.

"Dan. You must know by now that I felt the same way in Hager's. It was a moment that just . . . happened. I didn't know what to say or do. You were with your wife and I was confused about my feelings. It was the first time since . . . since I lost my fiancé that I felt that way." Dan squeezed her hand and she saw the compassion in his eyes. She was right about her first thoughts months ago. He was a kind man.

Verna was the one to hold on tightly. "Frank will have died two years ago in November," she said in a soft voice.

Dan looked at her in surprise. "Two years?"

Verna nodded. "I couldn't let go of the past. I was afraid to. Michelle had been trying to get me to start living again. She finally succeeded. I started by agreeing to have dinner with her."

Dan frowned. "But you weren't wearing your ring that night." He dared not speculate. "Was it because . . ."

"I'd decided to let Frank rest in peace. I still have my memories," Verna said, looking directly into Dan's eyes. She knew that her meaning was clear when he gave her an answering look. "And yes, I will see you again, if that's what you want."

"What I want?" Dan's voice was barely a croak. He coughed. "Look at me. You made me lose my voice."

Verna laughed. "Then it's not goodnight and goodbye?"

Dan cocked his head to one side. "Cynical words. Did I ever say that?" Then serious, he caught her other hand

and cupped her hands in his. "It's only been a few hours, but I feel that I know you; that we've met and talked like this in the past. But we never said 'good-bye.' Strange, isn't it?"

Verna's glistening eyes held a faraway look. "The world is strange. And I'm glad for that."

Dan was the first to disturb the sobering mood. "Let's get out of here," he said gruffly. He did not misread her look. As much as he wanted to kiss her delectable-looking mouth, he knew that she wanted the same. He breathed a silent prayer to whomever or whatever was responsible for that thing called Fate.

Verna stood in the driveway behind her parked car and waited while Dan parked and joined her. For the end of September, the weather was still warm, and tonight was gorgeous with the breeze enticing enough to want to linger out doors. The connecting townhouse that she'd purchased the year before she met Frank was separated from its neighbor by flowering bushes and a patch of grass. Verna was comfortable in the three-level house and was always happy to return to it. When Dan joined her, they silently walked to the door.

As comfortable as they had been at dinner, now both appeared to be lost in thoughts of their own. Verna hesitated to ask him in, but she wanted to prolong the evening. But what would that mean to him?

Dan saw her wrestling with her thoughts. He caught her hand, though his next words nearly stuck in his throat. "Verna, I know you're probably tired and want to call it a day, so I'll say goodnight." He was elated from her hand tightening in his. "Do you have to work tomorrow?" He'd been surprised when she revealed that she was a registered nurse and that working in the shop was a help to her aunt as well as a chance to pursue her hobby. His mirth had been silent. There's something to say about hobbies.

"No," Verna answered. "After church, I usually spend the day working on new designs."

"Then after church, would you mind taking a departure

from the usual? Spend the rest of the day with me." Dan's voice held a quiet urgency as his eyes probed hers.

Verna held his stare. Had she detected the heat in his eyes or was she imagining the desire that was there and then wasn't?

"I get back home around noon," she said softly. "Is that okay?"

Dan took an easy breath. "Perfect," he said. "I'll be here at twelve-thirty."

"Where are we going?"

"Suppose we plan that together. Dress casually, just in case, and don't eat."

Dan caught Verna by her shoulders and looked searchingly into her eyes. He kissed a spot somewhere between her temple and her cheek, then abruptly let her go. "Go inside, Verna. I'll see you tomorrow."

When the door closed behind her, Dan walked with a quick step to his car and drove away. His lips still smarted from that fleeting touch, and now he could stop guessing how he would feel after tasting her lips. One thing he knew for sure was that when it happened it had better be in a very discreet place.

Five

"So besides Bain's Artwork, where else have you sold your sculptures?" Verna asked. The prestigious D.C. dealer was known for carrying impressive works by local artists, which were prominently displayed with art by the best from around the world. Impressed with how he'd begun selling his wood sculptures, she listened with fascination. She enjoyed hearing the deep resonance of his voice. His face, she soon learned, was a mirror for his thoughts and moods. The animation and his glittering eyes bespoke of his love for his craft.

"Just call me Mr. International," Dan said, with a wink. The big grin on his face showed his excitement. "My buddy's wife sent two pieces to her nephew in Paris. He's a partner in an art gallery and he e-mailed her in caps. They sold in two weeks and, through word of mouth, the requests for commissioned pieces are coming in."

"Dan, that's wonderful. You must be very proud," Verna exclaimed, happy for him. They'd just finished eating dinner at Don Pablo, a popular restaurant in Laurel Lakes, a community park where they'd spent the day.

"Thank you," Dan said, catching her elbow and steering her out of the path of a toddler on a tricycle. The evening retained the warmth of the day and families and couples were enjoying the last days of summer. Earlier, at twelve-thirty, Dan had arrived with a packed lunch and a blanket. He promised her that he didn't do the cooking. After enjoying the spread of salads and sandwiches, they rented a paddleboat in which they lazed around the lake. The slow rhythmic gliding over the still water had put them both at ease, and they had talked quietly.

"But probably no more so than how you must have felt," Dan answered, with a purposeful look at her.

"Me?" Verna sounded surprised.

"Yes. The first time your work was bought by places like Hager's, you must have experienced the same rush." They reached Dan's car but stood leaning against it, neither wanting to leave. Dan smiled at her agreeing nod. Reluctantly, he helped her in the car and then joined her.

"I thought so," he said. Then, inclining his head, he asked, "Why is it that the pillow my sister bought didn't have the 'By V.S.' logo? I couldn't help but notice that the ones in your shop carried the label."

"Because the one your sister bought was not meant for sale," Verna replied. "I'd made it for myself." She explained the mistake.

Dan buckled his seat belt then turned to her with a thoughtful stare. "That's what you meant by catching the next shipment," he said.

Verna nodded. "Yes, but it wasn't a problem. I saw how much your sister wanted it, and I know that feeling of searching for and then finally spying that one perfect accessory. It's like the final, finishing touch that makes you feel complete."

"I can understand that."

Curious, Verna asked, "Is she pleased with her choice? Does it match her décor?"

Dan shook his head. "It was bought for our mother, who lives in Greenbelt. Paula decided that what my mother's house needed was a touch of color. It started with a rust-colored recliner. When it clashed with the navy, green, and white plaid sofa, new everything-else was necessary." Dan grinned. "Your pillow was the final 'must have' for the living room."

Verna laughed. "How does it look?"

Dan nodded in approval. "My mother isn't fussing anymore over her discarded plaid couch, so I think she's pleased with the new look."

"I'm glad it worked out," Verna responded.

Once arriving at Verna's and pulling up behind her car in the driveway, Dan turned off the ignition but made no move to get out. Instead, he turned to Verna, who was looking at him quizzically.

"Something wrong?" Verna noticed the shift in mood from carefree to somber. Although she couldn't quite put a name to her own feelings, she wasn't as exuberant as she'd been for most of the day. She could only guess that it came from the first pangs of impending separation. Did she have any right to feel this way?

"Nothing that seeing you again won't cure," Dan said quietly.

Verna swallowed. He was feeling the same, and she wasn't sure how that should make her feel. Were things happening too fast?

He gestured helplessly. "I don't know what to say to you." He turned away from her and looked out the window.

Verna saw his tension, evident in the tightening of his jaw muscles. "Tell me," she said, in an encouraging murmur.

Dan turned to face her. "I know and you know that you're a levelheaded person and not given to impulsive moves. You went out with me last night and again today, so you probably do feel comfortable with me. You put your trust in me that I'm not some kind of nut putting the fast moves on you with ulterior motives in mind—a guy who's liable to leave as fast as he came into your life."

Verna didn't know what to say, but her silence encouraged him to continue. She had a sudden feeling of apprehension without understanding why.

"I've told you that for four months, I've thought of you and the fact that you belonged to another man." Dan exhaled. "Since I couldn't have you, I tried to find you in other women. I finally gave up, thinking that I was acting the fool over a woman who'd become like a ghost figure— invisible and untouchable."

"Dan, but I'm not. I'm here."

He raked his chin hair then smoothed it. "I know. That's what scares the hell out of me." His gaze was searching. "But for how long? I used to psyche myself into thinking that if the opportunity presented itself and we'd finally meet, we'd find that the chemistry was all wrong between us . . . and that would be the end of my silly dreaming." He took her hand, covering it with his. "But that's not the case, Verna. You're all I'd hoped for and more. To see you, to be so near, to smell that mind-burning scent that you wear, your voice . . . all the real things that blow my dreams to smithereens."

Verna drew a deep breath. "What are you saying, Dan?" she asked, a little breathless.

Dan dropped her hand and put a little distance between them. He wanted to watch her face. "I don't want to be content with just seeing you," he answered. His voice had grown husky. "I want a relationship, a serious relationship. I want to love you, Verna."

Verna's eyes widened. Love? How could she think of loving another man, so soon after just mentally burying the love of her life? *Sacrilegious!* The word screamed at her.

Dan saw the result of his frankly spoken words. He knew the risk he took by baring his soul, but he had to let her know. He couldn't see her and pretend that they were getting to know each other before settling into a comfortable relationship. He already knew where his heart lay. As sure as he knew his own name, he knew that there couldn't possibly be another woman for him. Not ever.

Verna moved to get out of the car. "Please come inside, Dan. We can't end things sitting out here."

End? What is she talking about? Dan was silent when he followed her to the door and then inside. He heard her say something about fixing coffee after inviting him to sit in the living room. His thoughts moved in slow motion as he vaguely sensed that the room was her. It moved with vibrant color, as she did. Hues of gold, shades of reds and oranges dominated the space without being overbearing. Soon Verna returned and they watched each other for long moments while sipping the hot brew that singed their lips. Finally Dan spoke.

"Verna, I know that you are just beginning to venture out to seek new meaning to your life. You couldn't possibly know that there was some guy out there ready and waiting to take you on some whirlwind romantic adventure . . . even before you could catch your breath. Or even waiting to see if you wanted another relationship." Pausing, Dan said, "I guess that I don't want to think about the time when you do decide . . . that I won't be that guy."

"Dan, how can I even say that? Being with another man, now, I can't think that way. Beyond trying to live normally, to put a halt to my reclusive life, I've not progressed that far."

Dan listened, sympathetic to her dilemma, but he couldn't let her go on thinking that she wasn't ready for him or any other man. He'd already seen that she was and he didn't want to take a chance on losing her while she groped for whatever she thought would make her come alive again.

"Verna, can you deny that you didn't feel something when we first met?" he asked, making his tone non-threatening.

"I can't deny that, Dan." She held on to her mug like a lifeline.

"Yesterday, I wanted to kiss you and you wanted to kiss me. Can you deny that?" Dan would not let her avert her gaze. His eyes bore into hers.

"No," Verna whispered. He spoke the truth. Last night in the restaurant she'd wanted to feel his lips on hers. She'd wanted to feel more than the soft peck on her cheek. Yes, she did want to know what he tasted like. And she knew by that admission that she was a mass of contradictions.

Verna felt him take the mug from her hands and set it on the table in front of them. He stood and, grasping her hands, pulled her up close to him.

Dan held Verna's hands at her side, looking at her with serious eyes. He nearly let her go at the soft, pleading look in her eyes that was in total conflict with the involuntary twitch of her full lips and the tiny movement of her hips against his. Her body was telling her to obey her natural biological instincts while her intelligence was screaming no. When her lips parted, Dan closed his eyes against the surge of heat that sped through him. He bent his head and kissed her.

Verna, raised on her toes, leaned into him and welcomed the touch she'd desired. Her arms went around his neck and she wasn't sure whether it was his or her moan that escaped. He wrapped his arms around her waist gently, almost as if she would break, and his lips on hers were soft and tender, unbearably sweet. Verna caressed his strong neck and shoulders and as he deepened the kiss, she held him fast.

Verna. You were only a dream, but now, I have you. Dan's hold on her tightened and his kiss became aggressive, sure, and exploring. Nothing could have prepared him for the sensations that attacked him. The one thought that plagued him was that this was the end as she'd implied. Not on his life, he vowed. Instantly realizing that his actions were crucial if he was to win her, he knew that he had to put a hold on his emotions. She was still tender inside. After a moment he released her, giving her a kiss on her forehead.

For a fleeting moment, Verna felt that she was in that place she'd traveled to months ago. Only now this was real, and suddenly she was scared. She stepped back, giving herself distance from this stranger who'd awakened her emotions. She sat down and looked at Dan, who took a seat across from her. Vaguely she wondered if he too felt that need for distance.

Dan watched the uncertainty that overtook her, causing

her to sit on the edge of the seat with hands clasping her knees. The pose was meant to be one of calm and nonchalance but he knew better.

"I'd wanted to do that since the first time I saw you," he said quietly. "Does that bother you?"

Verna's stare was direct and so was her reply, although her heart was still beating rapidly. "No, it doesn't bother me. And it didn't." It wasn't exactly a lie, she thought. But she couldn't confess to him how deeply she'd been affected.

"Then you're not backing away from me? Are you still okay about seeing me again?"

Verna closed her eyes briefly while trying to formulate her thoughts into a sensible answer. "Yes, I do want to see you again, Dan, but . . ."

"Not as intensely as this," he finished for her.

Surprised, Verna said, "Yes." She unclenched her knees and sat back, her lips parting in a soft smile.

Body language is so telling, thought Dan. Remembering his purpose, he too relaxed, but so as not to mislead her, he said in a sure voice, "At least for now."

"For now," Verna agreed.

"I guess I can live with that for a while." Moving to sit beside her, Dan cupped her chin and after giving her a soul-searching look, pressed his lips against hers, savoring again the sweet softness of her mouth and her delightfully warm tongue that wiggled into his mouth. Reluctantly, he pulled away. "Remember, only for a while." He stood up. "I should go," he said, catching her hand.

At the door, Verna touched his arm. "Thanks for understanding."

Dan only nodded. "I'll call, Verna."

The door closed behind him and Verna remained there wondering what that last look had meant. For the first time in the short hours that she'd known him, she'd been unable to see the light in his eyes.

* * *

Almost two weeks later, Verna finally told herself that she was the world's biggest fool. Laughing instead of crying about her silly hours spent with a handsome stranger was the only way she didn't constantly berate herself. Her aunt Neda used to say that swallowing salty tears did nothing but turn a good heart sour.

Verna turned out the kitchen light. After a light meal of a tuna salad sandwich and a cup of herb tea, she went upstairs to her workroom. She'd made one of the two bedrooms into her workspace, because she felt lonely working downstairs in the finished basement. Now, when she was through, she only had to walk steps to the master bedroom.

It was still early and another long night yawned ahead. Since when had she become so aware of her nights being endless? She had always come home from work, prepared a good meal, then hurried to work on her designs. Or, she would go to the shop. But in the past weeks, if she'd spent four nights there, it was a lot. Her behavior was enough for Michelle and her aunt to question whether she was feeling all right. Verna always answered firmly that she was just fine, because Michelle was the last one she wanted to tell about her folly with Dan Hunter. Once, Michelle had wondered out loud why Dan Hunter had never visited the shop. Verna had guiltily changed the subject, relieved that she hadn't shared her misadventures with her cousin.

The quiet hum of the dishwasher and the low whirring of the sewing machine were joined by the ringing of the telephone. Verna frowned but stayed where she was, continuing to sew the ivory-colored damask fabric. Long ago, she'd moved the telephone from her workroom because she'd ruined many a piece while talking on the phone. Now it was in her bedroom on the nightstand. Thinking it was Michelle for the second time tonight, Verna continued to sew, deciding to let the machine answer. Tomorrow was soon enough to talk about nothing with her cousin again.

"Verna, this is Dan."

Pause.

"Verna, you're thinking I'm playing with you, but nothing could be further from the truth. I want to see you. I'll call again tomorrow night."

The sewing machine started again. *Tomorrow night? Why in the world would he want to do that?*

Verna finished sewing the last side of the pillow cover. She ran her hand over the textured silk, satisfied with the perfectly shaped heart. Holding mauve silk piping against it, she smiled a tiny smile. Ivory and mauve: Perfect colors for Valentine's Day. Before she and her aunt Neda were through, there would be hundreds of such items in these and other romantic colors. Early October was not too soon to start preparing for the most romantic day of the year. Another wan smile appeared. For a few brief foolish hours she'd almost believed that someday, that lovers' day would once more come to mean something to her. Her emotions had been stirred . . . for a moment. Now Dan Hunter was gone as fleetingly as he'd come. Just as he'd said.

Why call her now? Refusing to speculate on the reasoning of a handsome stranger, whom she'd probably never see again, Verna went and cleared the message. And hoped that just as easily she would be able to erase the image of his kind face and the sensuous touch of his mouth and hands.

Six

The following night, Verna was in the shop, tidying up the back room while her aunt was busy locking up. It had been busy for a Thursday, but as always, her aunt didn't complain about that and counted her blessings. The tinkle of the front doorbell brought a frown to Verna's face. She'd thought the door was locked. It was with surprise that she saw her aunt in the doorway looking puzzled.

"Do you know a Mr. Dan Hunter?"

Verna nodded. "Was that him who came in just now?"

Neda Hicks eyed her niece. "He says he wants to see you."

Hesitating for a second, Verna said, "I'm finished back here. How about you?"

"Finished," Neda said, indicating the bag of receipts tucked under her arm.

"Okay, then we're out of here." Verna put on her heavy nubby wool sweater and picked up her shoulder bag.

"What about Mr. Hunter?"

"We can say goodnight to him on the way out."

Neda, always alert to Michelle's and Verna's moods since they were little girls, never was bamboozled by them. Years ago they'd caught on and simply stopped. She'd come to be their confidante in most things, and listened without imposing her own views on them, especially in affairs of the heart. The only time she'd interfered with Verna was when she told her to put the pain of losing Frank behind her. With the appearance of the young man tonight, maybe Verna had done just that. But the indifference her niece was displaying was not encouraging.

"Ready, Aunt?" Verna asked.

Neda had on her coat. "I'm ready." They went to the front of the shop.

"Hello, Dan," Verna said. "This is my aunt, Neda Hicks, owner of the shop."

"Hello, Verna." Dan nodded to the older woman. "Yes, we've met."

Neda watched the looks pass between the two young people that said much more than their lips. "Well, I'm going to say goodnight, Verna. Mr. Hunter, maybe you'll come again sometime? See what our little place has to offer."

Dan looked at Neda. Was he reading something into her words? But the woman stepped outside with Verna and he followed. The metal gates were secured and locked. He watched Verna walk her aunt to the car, say goodnight, and watch her drive away. Then Verna turned to Dan. She was standing next to her own car, looking at him expectantly. He strode toward her.

"I owe you an apology. Will you hear me out before you refuse?"

Verna leaned against her car and, tilting her head to look into his eyes, wondered at the absence of contrition in his voice. Though he was asking to apologize to her, he wasn't acting ready to wolf down a whole humble pie. Intrigued by what he could possibly tell her, she nodded.

"Certainly. I'd love to hear what you have to say." Verna settled herself in a more relaxed position, crossing her feet at the ankles.

Dan noticed and he knew what she was doing. He'd hurt her badly. "Not here, Verna," he said. "Have you eaten?"

"I don't want to have dinner with you, Dan." Verna straightened up and folded her arms across her chest.

"I can understand that. But I want to talk to you, not at you with a sidewalk full of passersby listening in." He gestured to a small café across the street. "Would you refuse a hot drink?"

"No." Verna glanced at her watch. "I guess I have a little time for that."

Her meaning very clear, Dan didn't attempt to touch her as they walked across the street in silence.

The waitress brought two large mugs of the house coffee, a rich, dark Brazilian brew, then left.

Dan watched Verna sip then look at him expectantly. "How've you been?"

Verna set her mug down. "No light talk, Dan, please." Cupping her mug, she added, "This won't last long."

Dan's jaw tightened. "I'm sorry I've hurt you, Verna."

"That's debatable," she replied.

"Don't do that," he said. His voice was sharp.

"What do you expect from me?"

"To listen as you promised."

Verna lifted a shoulder. "Okay. You have my attention."

Dan eyed her carefully. Although her tone was indifferent, he could see in her face that she was curious about what he had to say.

His voice was low-keyed and even. "The Monday that I was to call you—well, that night, I was still at the plant. Didn't leave there until midnight trying to sort things out. That morning when I had arrived, the place hadn't been opened and the workers were standing around grumbling about production falling behind, and how the other managers and I were going to be on their butts all day." He smiled at the memory. "My boss, Al Cunningham, for as long as I've known him, opened up the plant every morning at six o'clock. Never late, no matter what the weather was like. Well, I opened up and my partner saw to getting everything running while I called Al's wife. There was no answer at their home, and no explanation on the answering machine." He spread his hand. "We didn't know what to think or where to start looking for answers. All we could do was wait. I was going nuts speculating and was about to start calling the area hospitals when his wife, Yvette, called." Dan rubbed his forehead, wearily. "Al had locked his front door and then dropped on his front steps. He'd suffered a stroke. When Yvette happened to glance out the window and saw his car still in the driveway, she rushed outside and saw him lying there."

Verna was awash with compassion for the stranger. And his wife! What a shock she must have experienced. "Did he . . . survive?" Briefly her thoughts went to a similar time in her own life.

"He's alive." Dan's voice turned bitter. "Just barely," he added. "He's paralyzed completely on his left side from his neck down."

"I'm sorry," Verna murmured. "You were close?"

"I've known him since I was thirteen. He's more like one of my older brothers than a father figure," Dan answered. "More than that," he continued, "he's my mentor."

After a short silence, Verna asked, "What's the prognosis?" In her profession she'd seen the devastating after-effects and the toll they took on the patients and their families. She knew that it was a waiting game, as Dan's next words confirmed.

He shrugged. "Yvette is just waiting. The coma that he'd fallen into lasted four days and she was happy to see him open his eyes. But later, in private, she cried in my arms. She saw the frustration in his eyes. If Al can't sometimes work on the floor, shaping that wood with the guys, he'll feel that his life is over."

Verna knew that Dan was the same. He'd told her that he was a hands-on manager, working alongside the skilled craftsmen. The thrill of crafting lumps of stiff wood into warm, polished things of beauty was something he'd never want to stop doing.

"Will his wife close the plant?"

Dan stared at her with a pained look. "Never. That's her husband's life. He started it from nothing and it's grown into a successful, respected business that employs a good many people—some of the best-skilled men you won't find just anywhere."

"So what has she decided to do?"

"Yvette asked me to take over, at least for now, until she can think clearly about what to do." He paused. "I've been running it with the help of another manager. The administrative assistant, Patrice Nichols, is also a world of help. She's been with Al for ten years now and knows what makes the place tick."

For the first time, Dan let his weariness show and Verna realized how fatigued he must have felt. "Have you seen Al?"

"Almost every night," Dan answered. "He needs reassuring that the plant is still running and orders are being filled on time. And it helps Yvette to know that someone's there when she's not."

"They have no children?"

Dan frowned. "A son, my age. We went into the Army together and came home together. But his experience was one he could have done without. He came home a drug addict. The streets eventually ate him up. He died several years ago."

Verna said seriously, "Then, you're like their son."

Dan splayed his hands. "They think so," he said quietly.

After two mugs of coffee, they had finally ordered sandwiches and now they ate in silence. When Dan finished, he pushed his plate away and stared at Verna, who couldn't help but see the anguish in his eyes. He was still bothered, so she felt compelled to put his mind at ease.

"With all that trauma, I understand what a hectic two weeks you've had," Verna said, in a low voice. "I accept your apology, Dan."

"Thanks for understanding," Dan answered. His eyes darkened, despairing to tell her the rest of what was on his mind. But after his passionate display two weeks ago, he owed her the truth of what he was feeling.

Verna watched him fighting with his emotions. "What else?"

Grateful for her perception, he drew in a deep breath. "I swear, I feel like I'm beginning my life all over again."

"In what way?" Her tone empathized with his apparent frustration.

Dan didn't answer, but instead signaled for the check. "Can we get out of here?"

It wasn't long before they were outside. The weather was nippy, but not enough to chase strollers on Wisconsin Avenue indoors.

"Let's walk a bit," Verna suggested. She pulled her sweater closed and Dan zipped up his windbreaker.

"First, let me say that during all the bedlam that was taking place, I didn't forget about you. I could have found some minutes in my days and nights to call." Dan looked down at her profile but could find nothing in her manner to indicate what she was thinking. "I chose not to."

Verna continued to walk beside him, mulling over his confession. Instead of addressing it, she said, "Your life is beginning all over again. What did you mean?"

Dan kept his hands in his pockets to keep from grabbing her into his arms. But since he had no right, he kept pace with her.

"I've already told you that after years of flailing about I finally found my niche with my art." When Verna nodded, he continued. "The calls for my stuff have been a godsend." He grimaced. "Al told me that it was time to consider an agent. He feels I'm giving the stuff away."

"Maybe he's right," Verna said, giving the idea some thought.

"Well, I think we can just scratch that idea."

"Why?" She stopped to stare up at him with curious eyes.

"Because I've decided to pull back on my art for now. I'm refusing all new commissions." Dan exhaled. "I'm committed to complete quite a number of pieces and after they're finished, I'm going to quit for a while."

Verna sucked in her breath. "You're going to do what?"

Her voice was incredulous. "For what good reason?" she asked.

Dan was surprised at her violent reaction. Without presuming that it was because she cared, he said, "I owe it to a friend. Al would do it for me." They continued walking. "Running a large plant, keeping it the success that it is, is no easy undertaking." He paused. "Besides, I'm not stopping altogether, just putting it on ice."

Verna was stunned. Though she had yet to see his work, she knew that his inner animation would wither if he couldn't create his sculptures. She swallowed her accusatory outburst, then asked, "What does your decision have to do with me?"

Dan saw a curbside bench and led her to it. Sitting beside her, he said in a quiet voice, "The last time I saw you, I made some promises—statements that would have you believe, as I believed then, that I wanted no other woman in my life but you. And that I didn't want you to be drawn to other men. I wanted you for myself."

"How has that changed?" Verna asked, wondering if she really wanted to know.

Dan caught her gaze. "I was going to court the hell out of you, Verna. Like I told you, I was going to be there whenever you decided that you even wanted to look at another guy—forget about getting serious about one." He lifted a shoulder. "But now?" He said in disgust, "I can't ask you to sit home waiting for a call that may not come because I got tied up at the plant or I'm in the basement or the garage carving my butt off to keep a customer happy." He snorted. "If that's not a sure turn-off for a new relationship between a man and a woman, I guess I don't know what is."

Verna was not usually at a loss for words, but his admission left her speechless. She had not given any thought beyond just getting to know him well enough to explore her deeper feelings. But he'd obviously planned from the beginning to make her a permanent part of his life. What was his ulterior plan? Live-in roommate? Marriage? His voice interrupted her racing thoughts.

"That's what I meant by beginning all over again. It's as if I can't get to that place where I want to be, especially for that certain lady."

Dan spread his hands, palms face up. "That's it," he said. "I thought that a phone call wouldn't do it for me."

Verna turned to look at him. "Are you saying that you don't want to call me again?"

"No!" Dan exploded, a black look settling over his face.

"Then, I'm confused, Dan," she said. "What is it that you want from me?"

The words seem to stick in his throat, but Dan said, "It's not fair to ask you to see me exclusively when you do decide to go out again." He took a deep breath. "It . . . just might be that there could be someone else out there that you would . . ." He couldn't voice the words.

"Fall in love with again?" Verna said in a soft voice.

God, help him, he thought, trying to shutter the image of her with someone else. "Yes," he replied, trying to sound as normal as his gut-wrenching feelings would permit. What in the world was he doing? The woman who was staring at him with those soulful eyes was the woman he'd fallen in love with! And he was asking her to see other guys!

Dan stood. "I think we should call it a night." He held out his hand and she took it. They began the walk back to their cars. "Now I've totally confused you," Dan said.

Verna had to smile. "I admit that I've never run into anyone before with such a unique technique for building, then ending, a relationship. Especially while it's still under construction. It's rather refreshing."

Dan stopped and caught her arm. "Verna, don't play." His eyes probed hers. "Does this mean that you still want to give this thing a go? You're ready to try us out?"

Verna laughed. "Sounds like we're new clothes. But, yes, I'm ready."

Dan caught her arm again. "Under one condition," he said.

"Condition?"

His throat nearly constricted. "I meant what I said before. I won't hold you to exclusivity."

Verna thought for a moment. "Okay. I guess I can live with that." They had reached her car. She took her keys from her bag and beeped open the lock. Before opening the door, she looked at him, curious. "I suppose this works two ways?"

Dan frowned. "What does?"

"Everything." Verna shrugged. "The exclusivity condition. Calling."

His frown deepened. "Well, I suppose, well, yes," he finally said.

Verna nodded. "Good." She got behind the wheel. "Talk to you soon, Dan."

Dan waved as she pulled off.

"She wants me to see other women?" he grumbled. He snorted at the ludicrous thought. For him, she was the one. And one day she was going to know it without any doubt. And her seeing other men? He'd have to rethink that plan. Real fast!

Seven

A week later, a sudden shift brought cold, wet weather to the region. The missing sun turned moods and tempers as gray and dark as the dreary days. Verna's mood was no exception, and she was glad to see Friday come and end with no emergencies that would keep her overtime. She was anxious to get home and climb into a tub of hot, scented water and soak the weariness from her bones.

She'd closed her office door, being one of the last to leave she opened it again at the ringing of the phone.

"Prince George's Family Health," Verna said, hoping that the frown that was on her face was absent from her voice.

"Girl, it's a good thing that I don't need your services," Michelle said, her shaped eyebrows rising. "You sound just as gloomy as the rest of D.C."

"Michelle, I should be in my car as we speak," Verna answered, impatience tingeing her voice.

"Verna, it's Friday. Loosen up." Michelle was exasperated. All week she'd gotten nothing but the answering machine whenever she'd tried her cousin at home. "If you'd picked up instead of listening to my sweet voice we wouldn't be having this conversation now."

"We're not having this conversation now, either," replied Verna. "I'll call you when I get home. I'm tired and I want to get out of here."

"Oh, no, you don't," Michelle said quickly. "I won't be home. I've been calling so you can join us tonight. There's a private art party and I'm told that Dan Hunter's work is being exhibited. Thought you might want to attend, since you've already met the artist, albeit so fleetingly."

Fleetingly? Guilt held Verna's tongue. Dan Hunter was still her secret. Even after her last meeting with him, she'd still chosen not to tell Michelle, and she knew the reason why. Because this past week she'd questioned her own motives for agreeing to see him again. She'd realized that she wanted a meaningful and lasting relationship with Dan. Once she had confessed that to herself, she'd decided that this weekend she would share her feelings. Now, she thought, the opportunity had presented itself. But tomorrow morning at the shop would be soon enough.

Michelle repeated her question. "Are you listening? What do you say? Want to meet us there?"

Verna thought, then said, "No, I'm too tired. You all go on. Another time."

"There won't be another time," Michelle answered. "Private, I said." Then she added, "You're too tired lately. Better get yourself checked out, girl."

"My health's fine," snapped Verna. "It's that big order you sent Aunt Neda's way that's keeping me up all hours of the night."

Michelle laughed. "Isn't that fantastic?" Her voice was gleeful. "Last summer while I was in New York, I showed your work to two sisters who have a bad boutique in Brooklyn. They're twins and as different as two people could be. The sour one said no immediately, but the bright one, Vicki, said she'd let me know."

"Humph. She let you know, all right. Are you certain she wants the order this Christmas, not next?"

"Tsk, tsk. Sarcasm doesn't become you, cousin dear. Besides, Ma can use the money, and your work and The Cracked Teapot will have a new market."

"True," replied Verna. "I'm appreciative, but you

An important message from the ARABESQUE Editor

Dear Arabesque Reader,

Because you've chosen to read one of our Arabesque romance novels, we'd like to say "thank you"! And, as a special way to thank you, we've selected four more of the books you love so well to send you for only $1.99.

Please enjoy them with our compliments, and thank you for continuing to enjoy Arabesque...the soul of romance.

Karen Thomas
Senior Editor,
Arabesque Romance Novels

SPECIAL OFFER!
4 BOOKS FOR ONLY $1.99

ARABESQUE

A PRODUCT OF

BET BOOKS

3 QUICK STEPS
TO RECEIVE YOUR "THANK YOU" GIFT
FROM THE EDITOR

Send back this card and you'll receive 4 Arabesque novels! These books have a combined cover price of $20.00 or more, but they are yours to keep for a mere $1.99.

There's no catch. You're under no obligation to buy anything. We charge only $1.99 for the books (plus $1.50 for shipping and handling). And you don't have to make any minimum number of purchases—not even one!

We hope that after receiving your books you'll want to remain an Arabesque subscriber. But the choice is yours to continue or cancel, anytime at all! So why not take us up on our invitation to receive 4 Arabesque Romance Novels, with no risk of any kind. You'll be glad you did!

Call us
TOLL-FREE
at 1-888-345-BOOK

The deep voice startled her. "Beg your pardon?"

"My lady would have done the same thing," Thomas Woods said, throwing her a slow smile. "I would have insisted."

Verna studied the serious face and weighed his and Michelle's words against her suspicions. Her shoulders settled and she smiled for the first time. "Thanks," she said.

"Thanks, Thomas," Michelle said, as they kissed cheeks. To Verna she said, "You're going to love this exhibit. I'm glad you changed your mind."

Verna smiled at Thomas when he nodded to them and went to join a group of friends, who appeared to be in spirited conversation over a five-foot tall abstract carving.

Michelle's eyes sparkled. She grabbed Verna's hand and pulled her into the spacious room where passing waiters offered drinks and hors d'oeuvres. She took a glass of champagne and Verna did the same. "Several of the artists are here and very willing to talk about their work."

"Really?" Verna sipped her champagne, appreciating the strong nutty flavor. "I wonder if . . ."

"Yes," Michelle interrupted excitedly. "Dan Hunter is here."

"Here?" Verna's eyes widened. "But . . ." She looked around the crowded room.

"I saw him across the room and he recognized me and waved," Michelle said, craning her neck. "But he's disappeared." She frowned, but only for a second, when she took Verna's elbow and moved her toward the chattering crowd. "Let me introduce you to our host."

Verna stopped. If Dan was here, then she'd have to tell Michelle now that she knew the man. Otherwise, she'd never hear the end of it.

Michelle looked strangely at her cousin, who steered them to a quiet space by the town house's floor to ceiling window, but remained silent. When they were alone, she said, "What?"

Swallowing and giving Michelle a direct stare, she said, "I've already met Dan Hunter."

Michelle let out a breath. "Is that all? Girl, you had me worried. Of course you met him the night that . . ."

"No, Michelle," Verna interrupted. "Really met him. We . . . we've had dinner and he's . . . been to my place."

Michelle's mouth gaped open, but all she could do was stare and listen for once, her penchant for fast talk temporarily stymied by Verna's amazing tale.

"Well, I'll be!"

A slow smile spread across Verna's features. "Don't tell me, for once I've shut your mouth?" Then, worriedly, "You're not mad?"

Finally finding her tongue, Michelle said in a soft voice, a trace of mist at the corner of her eyes, "No."

"You're not?" Verna was disbelieving.

Michelle smiled. She hadn't been wrong in following her gut feelings that night in Sampson's. "No," she repeated. "These last two years I could only imagine what you were going through. I lost my man but that was because he was a jerk and I tossed him out. You had no control over losing yours." She cleared the lump in her throat. "I just wish happy days ahead for you."

Verna had trouble keeping her own eyes dry and busied herself with finishing the last of the champagne. Both she and Michelle set their empty glasses on the tray of a passing waiter.

"Hello, again. I thought I recognized you." The pleasant-voiced woman smiled at Verna and Michelle who looked at her in surprise. She added, looking at Verna, "Hager's? The pillow?"

Dan Hunter's sister! Verna smiled and extended her hand. "Yes, I remember. How are you? I'm Verna Sinclair and this is my cousin, Michelle Fieldings."

"Paula McMurray. Pleased to meet you, and you too Ms. Fieldings." Turning to Verna, she said, "Finally. I was wondering when we were going to meet. I asked Dan where you were the minute he walked in the door. I've been asking him to bring you over for dinner, but I swear that man knows nothing but work and more work. But anyway, I want to thank you again for the pillow . . ." She stopped and gave a short merry laugh that matched the merriment in her twinkling light brown eyes.

Michelle and Verna looked at the pretty woman in amazement—Verna, because she'd finally met another woman who could keep up with her cousin in the chatter department, and Michelle because she'd never met anyone who matched her own mile-a-minute mouth.

Michelle smiled and stuck out her hand. "Pleased to meet you. And call me Michelle." She winked. "I think we're going to get to know each other rather well, don't you?"

Paula's smile broadened as she shook the hand of each of the women.

Verna could only look surprised and suddenly felt a warm fluttering in her chest. Had she come to mean that much to him that he'd shared their meeting with his sister? It appeared obvious that they were very close. She followed Paula's and Michelle's look behind her.

"Ladies." Dan's greeting acknowledged all three women, but his eyes speared Verna's.

"Dan," Paula said. "Where did you disappear to?" She stopped when her brother only nodded her way but continued to stare at the surprised Verna. Catching Michelle's eye, she said, "How about making ourselves scarce?"

Michelle looked from Verna to Dan and with a quick smile said, "Best idea I'll hear tonight." Without another word, she hooked her arm in Paula's and they sauntered away, both suddenly falling into excited conversation.

"Dan, I'm surprised that you're here," Verna said. She wondered at his quiet air and the lack of spontaneity in his greeting. Was he really overdoing it both at home and at work?

"It was a last minute decision for me." Dan spoke quietly. His eyes still searched hers. "I received a call that required me to be here tonight." He broke the stare briefly as his look encompassed the room. "I didn't think it fair to call you at the last minute, so I came alone. Now, I'm regretting my decision." He eyed her again. "I would have liked to have been the one escorting you tonight."

"Escorting me?" Verna frowned. "Dan, what are you talking about? I came with . . ." She stopped. "You saw me come in?"

"Yes."

So that's it! He's jealous, Verna thought. "You think I have a date?" She was suddenly feeling amused at the situation.

Dan raised a brow. "Yes." He wondered what she was finding so funny. He didn't see a damn thing amusing when he saw her on the arm of the good-looking brother.

Verna was enjoying herself. "You really came alone?"

Dan scowled. "Of course I did!"

"But, you could have brought someone else, Dan. I thought that it would be okay for us to see other people." Verna looked up at him and smiled. "Right?"

Dan's look darkened. "Right!" he growled.

"Oh, that's what I *thought* we'd agreed upon." Verna saw the pained look flash across his face and her heart melted. She'd never been a game-player and wouldn't know how to start to save her soul. Giving up her little tease, she said, "This was a last minute decision for me too, Dan. Michelle arranged everything. I don't have a date."

Dan's chest deflated with the expulsion of air that rushed from his mouth. She was alone. "You're not with anyone?"

"No," replied Verna. "Did you want me to be?"

"I don't find that funny, Verna," Dan responded in a low voice. "And on second thought, remind me to have my head examined." He gave her a meaningful look when she stared up at him with innocent eyes. "I think you know exactly what I'm referring to."

This time, Verna did smile. "Our agreement?"

"It's a dead issue. Gone. Forgotten. Never even existed. I never thought it up." He looked at her expectantly. "All right with you?"

"Now *that* I can agree on," Verna answered, a soft smile parting her lips.

Dan suppressed a groan. "I want to kiss you, woman." His voice was a husky whisper. Instead, he caught her hand and pulled her close to his side, sliding his arm around her waist. He bent to whisper in her ear. "Later?"

Verna's body reacted to his nearness more than she anticipated. She wasn't prepared for the heat that sped through her, causing her cheeks to flush at her response when she leaned into him. She'd felt a stirring in those secret places that had been cold for so long. Was she really ready for what Dan was offering?

Dan felt Verna's hesitation and, immediately sensing her discomfort, released her.

"Are you all right?" he asked.

Unsure of the steadiness of her voice, Verna simply nodded.

Dan frowned but didn't pursue her sudden shift in mood. He felt he understood.

"Have you looked around yet?" he asked easily, his tone a vast change from the sexy one of a moment ago. His strategy was the right one because he saw the tension leave her shoulders.

"Not yet," Verna replied, looking at the wall art. "I'm still anxious to see a fabulous 'Dan Hunter' piece."

"Then you have no further to look than right behind you . . ." He looked up at the man who clapped him on the back.

"Dan, here you are. Monopolizing you, is he, Ms. . . . ?"

"Sinclair. Verna Sinclair," Dan said to the dark, robust man with white hair and a startling equally-white walrus mustache. "Verna, this is our host, Justin Pinchback."

"My pleasure, Ms. Sinclair," said the art connoisseur, in a booming voice that came from the bottom of his belly. He looked with an appraising eye at Verna. "If I didn't know any better, I'd swear you were the model for one of Hunter's sculptures." He pulled on his mustache. "Humph. No, the flesh and blood model is more beautiful." He kissed Verna's hand. "More beautiful, my dear." He bowed. "Would you mind if I borrow this young man for a minute?"

Verna smiled at the old-world manner of the man. "No, sir," she answered, not surprised at her address. His demeanor almost commanded the title of respect. She watched the older man—she guessed him to be over seventy—spirit Dan across the room to a group of older men. She instantly liked the old man and wondered at his foreign accent.

Turning her attention to what Dan had been about to show her, she saw a sculpture that appeared to be about fifteen or sixteen inches tall.

Verna could only stare in awe at the breathtaking figure. *And he wants to cut back on creating?* She was incredulous. The abstract figure of a woman in a reddish-brown wood stared back at her—no, it wasn't staring, because there was no face—only the illusion of one. No eyes, mouth, or nose, but one could see in the oblong face a sense of movement created by the flowing lines of the whole piece. The robed figure had its arms crossed over the breasts, the hands grasping each shoulder. The face was in profile, the chin turned slightly upward. Peering at the card beside it, Verna saw the name of the sculpture: Yearning.

Moved by what she'd seen and felt, Verna threaded her way slowly through the crowd, wondering about the other pieces that were on exhibit. She was glad that Dan was preoccupied because she'd wanted to see his work without him near. Why, she couldn't answer. Maybe because she knew the artist and felt a kinship. But, whatever the reason, she was unprepared for her reaction. It was the same as when she finished a particularly difficult bolster or pillow that was part of a decorative ensemble. Knowing she'd done exceptional work, a feeling of complete satisfaction stole over her, and she would smile inwardly and wait for Aunt Neda and Michelle to laud her creations. Secretly, she wished that she could listen in to the private comments made by the eventual consumer of her work. Now, looking at Dan's work, it was with a special connection that she felt drawn toward him.

Admiring the paintings and sculptures of the other exhibiting artists, Verna found another of Dan's sculptures. The work was of two figures standing in a dance position.

"So, what do you think?" Dan had followed Verna's slow walk around the room and now stood behind her watching her reaction.

Without turning, Verna murmured, "Beautiful." When he moved closer to her side, she looked up at him. "Who are they?"

"My mother and my sister."

"Paula?"

"Yes. She's the youngest and the only girl," Dan answered. "I have two older brothers." He looked at the sculpture with a smile. "My mother was teaching Paula how to dance when she was about nine or ten."

The fondness in his voice made Verna realize that she'd been right. He was close to his family. "You've really captured them in a carefree tender moment. The memory must have been pretty strong for you to have remembered so vividly."

Dan shrugged. "This is one of the first pieces I started when I really knew what I wanted to do with my life. It took a long time to finish because I was never satisfied with the way it was shaping up, until one day, I saw them as clearly as I had way back when."

"The wood you selected is just perfect," Verna said. "The light color brings out the exhilaration of the subject. What kind is it?"

"Beechwood," Dan answered. "Although the grain isn't as interesting as some others, I felt this wood was the best to express my meaning."

Verna looked at him with serious eyes. "I haven't seen your other pieces yet, Dan, but I don't have to, to know that you've a great talent." Her voice was just as serious when she said softly, "Are you still thinking of putting a hold on your career?"

Dan's eyes clouded, but he answered in a firm voice, "My plans haven't changed, Verna." He saw her disapproval at his response. "I have no choice," he added, in defense.

Verna bristled. "We all have choices, Dan. Sometimes we make them in haste and are hesitant to rethink the decisions we've made."

His jaw tightening, Dan answered, "Are you saying that my helping a friend is wrong?"

Verna saw his mounting annoyance with her frankness, but she felt strongly about her feelings. "No, not wrong, but little thought went into making your decision. It was more emotional than sensible."

"Now, you are wrong," Dan said, surprised that she didn't understand his position. "Don't tell me that you've never been faced with a do-or-die situation where your ultimate decision meant self-sacrifice?"

"Sacrifice?" Verna's eyes darkened at his implication that she was selfish. After the decision she'd made when Frank had proposed?

Dan saw the sudden anger in her eyes and had a need to know what caused it. In the hours he'd spent in her company, he hadn't noticed a tendency toward self-centeredness. But something he'd said bothered her.

"Why are you angry?" he asked.

"Because you don't know me well enough to put labels on me."

Dan held her stare. "Then, we'll have to change that, won't we?"

Michelle and Paula were just in time to hear the heated exchange and they passed surprised looks. Michelle spoke first.

"Verna, Paula is meeting her husband, Marvin, at Barry's and she's asked us to join them." She gave the couple a skeptical look. "I wouldn't mind dancing a bit. But if you'd rather not, I'll drop you home and then join them."

Verna shook her head. "I think not, Michelle, but dropping me first would be too much trouble, wouldn't it? Barry's is not exactly around the corner from me."

Paula looked at her brother's masked face. "Dan? How about it? Care to join us? The night's still young," she said, wondering what went on between the two somber people.

"No, Paula. Thanks, but I'm calling it a night."

Paula brightened. "Verna, would you mind very much if my brother took you home?" She gave her a rueful smile. "I'm sorry you can't join us. I'd love for you to meet my husband, and I'm sure he'd love to meet the person behind such exquisite creations." She looked expectantly from Verna to her brother. "Dan, would you mind?"

Verna protested, with a look at Dan. "That's not necessary. I can manage," she said.

Dan eyed her. "Of that, I have no doubt, but I would like to take you home, if you don't mind."

Michelle jumped in before Verna could respond. "Dan, thanks." She asked her cousin, "Okay?"

Verna finally nodded in agreement, unwilling to spoil the night for Michelle.

"Perfect!" Michelle gave Verna a peck on the cheek. "See you tomorrow?"

After saying goodnight to the two women, Dan turned to Verna, who was silently watching him.

"Would you like to leave now?" he asked.

"Yes."

"Then I'll find Justin and say good night for both of us," Dan said. "Wait here."

The first five minutes of their ride was spent in silence as Dan drove toward Verna's home. He glanced at her but could read nothing of what she was thinking.

Dan broke the silence. "What were we about to get into back there?"

Verna looked over at him. "We were arguing."

"We don't know each other well enough for that."

"Then we'll have to change that, won't we?" Verna said

quietly. Her minute anger at him earlier had subsided, although her feelings were unchanged.

Dan was just as serious when he asked, "You mean that?"

"Yes."

After a thoughtful moment, Dan pulled into a vacant spot on a near-empty street and, idled the engine.

Verna looked at the unfamiliar surroundings then at Dan, curious.

"Verna, maybe you'll tell me what angered you, but that's your decision," Dan said. "But, I want you to know more about me so that you'll understand where I'm coming from. Right now, I want that more than anything." He hesitated. "Would you mind if we stopped by my place first? There's something I want you to see."

Verna felt that each time she saw him she learned more about him—and, startlingly, herself. She was perfectly comfortable with her positive response.

"No, Dan," she answered. "I won't mind."

Relieved, Dan pulled away from the curb. "I promise not to keep you long," he said.

But, an hour later, Verna had forgotten about that promise. They were still in Dan's basement workshop, her questions nonstop. She was propped on a backless stool, watching as Dan secured his latest piece to a holding vice.

"So what is that device called?" she asked.

Dan looked up for a second and flashed a smile before continuing to work. "You sound like you really want to know," he teased.

Verna's hands clasped her crossed knees. Her foot stopped swinging as she looked at him. "I do want to know, Dan." Her brow rose. "Isn't that why I'm here?"

Dan felt his temperature rise again at the huskiness in her voice. It was all he could do to concentrate on why he'd brought her here in the first place. But her nearness was driving him nuts. Was she asking him something that had nothing to do with his work? He looked at her briefly, but her face was devoid of any hidden meaning.

"This is called a G-cramp," he answered. "Just another

method of holding the wood while I carve. It's like the other vices you've already seen, but I like this best for smaller pieces."

Verna nodded. "So the bench screw on the table in the garage wouldn't be suitable?"

"Uh-uh," Dan answered, pleased that she'd remembered. She was really interested. "It would hold the wood firmly to the workbench, but it would prevent me from moving the wood around so I can see it from different angles while I work."

"But wasn't it in the garage where you did the roughing out with the bandsaw?" Verna asked. "Or did you use one of the gouges?" She'd been amazed at the number of tools he used, the gouges and chisels lined up neatly being the most in number.

"The bandsaw," Dan said. "The size timber that I ordered for the piece was too large for my idea, and that power tool came in handy for eliminating a lot of the waste." He straightened up after securing the piece of basswood in the position he wanted. "A lot of carvers frown on the use of power tools, but I'm all for using the newest in technology whenever I can. Makes a lot of sense to me." He stared pointedly at Verna. "Saves valuable time for some other pleasurable pursuits."

Verna colored at the inference to their relationship. She slipped off the stool and walked over to where he stood. Looking down at the rough outline, she said, "Can I touch?"

"Sure." Dan wondered if she was aware of what their close proximity did to his senses. But, as before, she appeared to be oblivious. "Won't hurt a thing," he exhaled.

Verna rubbed her finger lightly over the black crayon outline, tracing the spirals of what was to be gouged into a flame. Already she could see the blithe movement of the dancing fire. She looked up at him. "It's uncanny." A tremor went through her.

"What is?" Dan said, husky-voiced.

"It's only a chunk of wood now but soon it will come

to life," Verna said. Turning away from the heat she saw rising in his eyes, she added, "I can see and almost feel the fire."

Dan closed his eyes briefly. When he opened them, he stared at her steadily. "You do understand," he said.

Verna stared back. Slowly, she shook her head. "No."

Taken aback, Dan said, "What?"

"It's not you I don't understand, Dan," Verna said, looking around the wood and tool-filled workshop.

"What do you mean?"

Verna sighed. "You brought me here to understand what you're all about." She glanced down at the work in progress. "I *see* you in all of this. But, I am baffled by the emotional decision that you've made. How can you just give all of this up?"

Dan watched her walk around the room again looking at other figures in various stages of development. Then she walked to the stairs. Apparently she was ready to leave, he thought. He followed her and they walked upstairs in silence.

After turning out the light and closing the door to the basement, he turned to her.

"Can I get you something before we leave? Wine? Coffee?"

"Coffee would be fine, thanks." Verna sat down at the kitchen table. She sensed his annoyance with her last remarks.

Dan sat down across from her. "All that you've seen is the reason that I'm not giving it up, Verna." He spoke in a strong, firm voice. "That's what I was hoping you'd see and understand. That it's a part of me. I'm not just walking away from it, as you want to believe."

Verna heard the determination in his voice and remembered a time when she'd been just as determined. Putting a career on hold, as one would believe, was not always the best or the easiest way. She met his stare. "Have you given yourself a deadline? I mean, how long do you propose to lock up your workshop after you've finished these projects?"

Dan shook his head. "You really believe that I'm kidding myself, don't you? That I'm not going to ever begin again once I stop."

Verna did not look away from his piercing gaze. "Yes," she answered.

Dan studied her face. "Is that what you did, Verna?" he asked softly. "Is that the reason you're so certain that I'm giving up my dream?"

Verna was surprised and was on the verge of denying what he'd already guessed.

"It seems so long ago," she said softly. She accepted the mug of coffee from Dan and sipped gingerly. "Mm, hot," she said.

Dan drank and watched her, waiting until she was ready to continue. Whatever had happened had affected her strongly.

Verna cupped the mug, warming her hands. "I love being a nurse," she said. "I'm a good one, too, but I decided too late to follow my mind and change my direction."

Dan's voice was encouraging. "What happened?"

Verna smiled. "My hobby happened. I'd discovered my talent for home design in my first year of nursing school but decided that a hobby was not a valid enough reason to throw away money already spent on schooling myself." She lifted a shoulder. "Besides, how would I sustain myself? My aunt and uncle have done their share in raising me. So I stayed with my first career choice."

"And you've regretted the decision you made?"

"At times," Verna answered, truthfully. "I always told myself that next year—it was always next year—I would enroll in design school. I was determined. Then, when I did decide to start, I became engaged. Since Frank was finishing up his master's program, I dropped out. The money I saved could be used to begin our future."

Dan kept the surprise from his eyes. She'd unselfishly put her own dreams on hold!

Verna looked at Dan. "Things do have a way of working out, though." She shrugged again. "Who knows? Maybe I would have hated interior design school and been a wash out."

Dan said, "I can't see that." His eyes and voice were serious.

Verna nodded her thanks at the compliment. She stared into the mug of mocha-colored liquid. "Now, without any planning at all or years of schooling, I'm doing what I love to do. It just fell into place for me." A smile brightened her face. " 'Designs By V.S.' are sought by some of the most prestigious stores in the region."

Dan caught her smile. "Are you happy, now?" The sudden shadow that flickered across her face quickly made him aware of his thoughtless question. How could she be without the man she had intended to marry?

Verna saw his annoyance with himself. "I'm okay, Dan. But, yes, I'm happy now, with both careers."

"Even though one day you wouldn't mind giving up one for the other?"

"Yes," she replied. "If that were to happen, I'd love that, too." Her eyes suddenly darkened. "That's why I feel that . . ."

Dan finished her sentence. ". . . I'm making a big mistake in putting my carving on hold."

Verna bent her head and studied the swirls of cold liquid left in her mug. "It's such a waste of your talent, Dan. Time has a way of not waiting for us until *we're* ready."

Dan didn't speak for several seconds as he regarded the fascinating woman sitting across from him. He'd wanted her to understand him, and he was the one who'd learned so much more about her. Whether she was ready to admit it to herself or not, she cared about him.

"Verna?" He'd moved closer to her. When she lifted her eyes to his, he reached over and, with his knuckles, tenderly touched her cheek then brushed his lips against the hidden dimple. "Thanks for sharing that," he murmured. "I promise I'll think about what you said."

"Hmm." Suddenly Verna smiled and the dimples appeared. Her eyes twinkled.

"I don't know whether I want to believe your promises," she said.

He gave her a quizzical look.

"What was it that you said, oh, about two hours ago? 'This won't take long' . . ."

Dan laughed, then kissed both holes in her cheeks. His voice was a seductive hush when he spoke. "If you keep throwing those smiles my way, I know I won't renege on my next promise." He captured her lips in a tender kiss, but she pulled away.

Verna gazed at him. "What promise?" she asked, in a smoky voice.

While Dan gave her a look that was filled with secret promises, he stood and pulled her up, catching her close to his body. He whispered in her ear, "Not yet, sweetheart." He felt her shudder and held her tightly. "Not yet," he murmured against her curls, as her arms wound around his neck. He captured her warm moist lips again and wondered when—no, how long—he'd have to wait before he really could utter that ultimate promise.

Eight

"Well, aren't you going to share? Or is last night going to be a secret, too?" Michelle teased her cousin. She was sitting on the bed in Verna's huge bedroom watching her put the finishing touches to her makeup. "And tonight?" she added.

Verna scrutinized her face then turned off the vanity table lamp. She swung around and said, "No more secrets, Michelle. I promise." A smile crossed her lips. *Promises!*

"Oh? Then what's that mysterious little smile for?" accused Michelle.

"That's not a secret. That's private." Verna's smile broadened.

"Like that, huh?" Michelle studied Verna's face, noticing for the first time that the haunted look she'd carried for two years had disappeared. The tightness around her mouth was gone, taking with it the frown wrinkles. She looked radiant. "You really like him, don't you?" Michelle asked, all teasing gone from her voice.

Verna thought for just a second. There was no need to hide her true feelings from the woman who'd stuck by her side, being her friend through the bad times.

"Yes," Verna answered. "Very much." She joined Michelle on the bed. "In fact, I'm . . . I'm . . ."

"Falling for him?" Michelle asked softly.

"Fast and hard," replied Verna. She stared into Michelle's light-brown eyes. "At first, I denied what I was feeling. From the beginning—in Hager's, and then the evening he came to the shop. I . . . I thought that I was dishonoring Frank's memory."

"Until you realized that you weren't."

"Right," sighed Verna. "Like you said, Frank's dead. I accept that. But I didn't know how I'd feel loving someone else. When the thought crossed my mind and when Dan took me into his arms, I started to back off, but fast." She hesitated. "He noticed and then he backed off, I suppose so as not to turn me off."

Michelle looked at Verna with understanding. "And now you don't want him to treat you like fragile porcelain."

"Correct. We shared a lot of thoughts last night and I know we've become closer," Verna admitted. "I'm . . . I want this relationship to work."

Michelle put her arm around Verna's shoulders and gave her a quick hug. "It will, girl. Just continue to be natural and honest with each other and things will fall into place." She looked at her watch. "He's coming at eight, right? Then I best be going because it's almost that now." She eyed Verna. "You look quite smashing, my dear," she said, in a haughty voice. Then normally, "If my brother's trying to take it slow with you, you certainly aren't making it easy on him to keep his cool act goin' on."

Verna was dressed in a long-sleeve, fire-engine-red silk dress that showed some thigh. The scoop neck showed off her bosom alluringly. Her throat was bare and she wore dangling onyx spheres in her ears.

"Where are you going, anyway?" asked Michelle.

"Dinner and dancing."

"Dancing?" Michelle laughed. "Humph. Talk to me tomorrow, girl!" Still laughing, she hurried down the stairs. "I'll let myself out."

Verna smiled at her mischievous cousin and walked slowly down the stairs to wait for Dan. Michelle's thoughts mirrored her own. After last night's steamy kisses in his kitchen and then again at her door, she'd been ready for more of Dan's touch. But he'd embraced her sweetly and said good night. At the sound of the bell, Verna walked to the door, wondering what tonight would bring. Her body was already responding to her thoughts of being held in his arms as they danced. When she opened the door, her pulse quickened at the sight of him. It had only been overnight, but she realized in the split second that their eyes met that she'd missed him. Yes, she thought, this is right.

Dan's eyes smoldered as he stepped inside and closed the door. She took his breath away. He could only stare at her bare throat and hungered to taste the thin, honey-gold-colored skin. Her full lips were moist and inviting and he remembered their taste. Was it only hours ago?

"You're beautiful." His voice was intense, strong, yet, as oddly gentle as the look he gave her.

Verna watched the sensuous movement of his lips and when he took a step toward her, she slipped easily into his arms. "Dan," she whispered.

Enfolding her, Dan's arms were crushing around her waist as he bent to claim her lips. He devoured their soft fullness, his thrusting tongue searching for that inner softness that fueled his passion for her. When her arms tightened around him and her hands slid down to his buttocks, holding his fullness firmly to her, the scream in his throat escaped as a groan.

"Verna," he croaked through his scorched throat. "Verna, sweetheart." He was raining kisses on her neck, her throat and caught her lips again as he fondled her breasts. The clothing, hampering his goal, caught him up short and, breathing hard, Dan pulled back, putting distance between their heated bodies, but he didn't release her. His hands caressed the small of her back.

Verna's breath came in spurts as she looked dazedly up at Dan. She didn't have to ask what was wrong. She knew from the remorseful look on his face what he was thinking—that he was moving too fast. Verna slipped out of his arms and straightened her dress.

"My hair is probably a mess," she said lightly, taking his hand and walking into the living room. "I won't be long."

When she returned a short time later, makeup freshened and hair fluffed out, she handed him a glass of ice water.

"You sounded a little hoarse." Her eyes twinkled.

Dan drank half a glass before speaking. Her amusement did not escape his sharp eye. He stood up and reached for her hand. Glowering at her, he said, "Let's go eat, Verna Sinclair."

The month of November came in acting like it was May but soon righted itself, bringing with it a spate of colds and flu symptoms. It was nonstop throat cultures, shots, and pill-pushing at the center. On Wednesday of the third week, Verna was exhausted. Earlier, she'd called Dan and broken their date for the evening. Besides the job, she'd been feeling out of sorts herself. She knew she wasn't coming down with anything, but the reason for her sudden melancholia wouldn't allow her to be with Dan tonight. Today was the second anniversary of Frank's death.

Verna had tried to tell herself that she was over mourning, but, try as she would, every thought she had when she woke up this morning was of Frank. Images of happy times flashed before her and in between patients she found herself tearing up. It had gotten so bad that the doctor had wanted to examine her. Somehow she'd made it through the day—barely. By the time she arrived home, Verna had developed a headache that brought tears to her eyes. Downing aspirin for the pain, and foregoing dinner, she went upstairs and flung herself across the bed in the darkened room.

The ringing of the phone startled Verna from a deep sleep. She turned on the table lamp and looked at the clock. It was nearly seven o'clock. She'd slept for an hour and a half. But her head no longer felt like a little old shoemaker was hammering away inside.

"Hello," she muttered.

"Verna, it's Michelle." She paused. "Are you all right? You sounded a little out of it at work this morning." Although they hadn't spoken of it, they both knew what day it was.

Verna heard the meaning behind her question. "I'm fine, Michelle. I was asleep." She propped herself up. "Was Aunt Neda looking for me tonight? I swear I couldn't make my body take another step."

"No," Michelle answered. "You know Ma loves when you come but she makes out fine. I went by to help her close up. She thinks you're working too hard anyway." She laughed a little guiltily. "I suppose I'm partly responsible for that, huh?"

Verna laughed with her. "Guilty," she agreed. "What's going on, Michelle?" She knew her cousin well enough to know that she'd called for a reason.

"Dan called the shop looking for you. He was concerned about you not feeling well," Michelle said. "Verna?"

"I heard you," answered Verna.

"You didn't want to be with him tonight?"

"Something like that."

There was a brief silence.

Michelle spoke softly. "I can understand that." She paused. "Did you explain to Dan?"

"No. Did you?"

"That's not for me to do, Verna."

Verna apologized for her abruptness. "Forget I said that."

"Done," Michelle replied, without animosity. She suspected that the day had taken its toll on Verna and she was trying hard to cope. But what she shouldn't do was shut out the man who was obviously very much in love with her. The two occasions that Michelle, Paula, and her husband had had dinner with Dan and Verna, a baby would have been able to see that the man was crazy in love.

"Hold on a minute, Michelle, someone's beeping me," Verna said.

"No," Michelle said hurriedly, "take the call. I just

wanted to shout at ya. I'll call tomorrow. 'Night." She hung up, hoping that it was Dan that she'd cleared the line for.

"Hello?"

"It's Dan, Verna." He spoke in a low unhurried tone. "How are you feeling?"

The sound of his voice brought back all of the pain and doubt she'd experienced earlier. Her temples throbbed.

"Verna?"

"Better," Verna lied. "I rested for awhile and it was the best thing for me to do." She put a smile in her voice. "I'm sorry about tonight," she lied again. But how could she tell this new man in her life that today she felt the acute pain of losing the old? She couldn't hurt him. "Now I'm wide awake and maybe I can get a little something done tonight."

Dan frowned. "You mean work?"

"Yes."

There was a long pause before Dan finally said, "Okay, Verna, I'll call you tomorrow. Don't work too long." He hung up. Always alert to the sound of her voice and the many expressions of her beautiful face, Dan had sensed her wish to end the conversation.

Since she'd called him at the plant to cancel their evening, he'd known then that something was wrong, though she'd denied being ill. It hadn't taken him long to figure out what it was. The fact that she hadn't gone to the shop confirmed his suspicions.

Dan left the living room and went to the kitchen. Minutes later he was back on the couch, beer mug and bottle in hand. He poured, watched the foam settle, and took a long swallow. Since he'd already intended to take the night off, he didn't have the urge to go downstairs to work. He'd been sitting on the couch, sketching an idea for a figure that he knew he'd never get to start, at least for a long while. He'd tossed it aside because he couldn't get Verna off his mind.

Even before the arrival of November he had thought briefly of the effect the month would have on her. He'd made it his business to call her every day and see her as much as possible. She'd been nothing but her pleasant, playful self. Until Sunday, when he'd kissed her goodnight. She'd gotten that sad look in her eyes—one he hadn't seen since that day in Hager's. The days following, she held short, but light, conversations. So he hadn't really been surprised at her call. She didn't want to see him this evening.

"Today must be the day," Dan said. He emptied the bottle and drank deeply. "How can I compete with you, Frank?" he asked the empty room. "You stole her heart first."

Thanksgiving Day was a cold blustery affair with gloomy skies that threatened rain. Dan had spent the evening with his family. His brothers and their families, Paula and Marvin all piled up in their mother's house in Greenbelt. As usual, it was a raucous, happy time with his young niece and nephews commanding the attention of the adults.

Dan turned from the living room window and stood surveying the scene. His oldest brother, Samuel Hunter, and his wife, Jessica, had two children, eight-and nine-year-old sons, Otto and Micah. He grinned at the way eight-year-old Otto, who was slight of frame, tried to best his brother in any and everything, usually getting the upper hand. Darlene, the five-year-old daughter of his brother, Jeremy, and his wife, Ruby, was the cutie-pie of the family. Although she could have been, she was unspoiled by the massive attention that she got from the whole family—especially from Paula and Marvin, who were still trying for one of their own.

Paula was watching her youngest brother. All during dinner he'd fended off questions from his teasing brothers about the absence of a serious love interest. They'd heard he had been seeing someone and thought Thanksgiving was the perfect time to show her off to the family. Paula had told them to back off, and the teasing had stopped. She joined Dan at the window.

"Did you invite her?" she asked in a low voice.

Dan looked at his sister and nodded. "She's with her family."

"Will you see her later?"

Dan shrugged. "Hadn't planned to."

Paula's eyes flashed at her brother's uncharacteristic defeatist attitude. "What's wrong with you?" she asked in a whisper. All she needed was for her older brothers to get wind of what they were talking about. "You want to lose her?"

Dan's lips curled at that. "Lose? I never had her." His eyes darkened. "Frank's still around, apparently."

"You can't believe that!" Paula hissed. Exasperated, she said, "He's gone, and you're here. Now you tell me that you don't have the edge! If you let her walk into the arms of someone else, you've nobody to blame but yourself." Paula's voice had risen and, ignoring Samuel's curious stare, she said in lower tones, "She's young, pretty, and ripe for loving. You've got to show her that you're the one to bring her back to life." She paused. "When I see her with you, I know that I'm looking at a woman in love. Only, she doesn't know it or is refusing to acknowledge it."

Dan gave a wry smile. "Then you see more than I do. At one point I thought the same thing. But now, I'm having second thoughts."

Paula sighed. "Then if you don't lose those thoughts, Dan, you'll lose her."

Friday, the day after Thanksgiving Day, supposedly the biggest shopping day of the Christmas season, was hectic at the Cunningham Furniture factory. Dan and the rest of Al's staff had done a fantastic job of filling orders and shipping them out on time. The minimal complaints from customers about mixed-up orders or damaged pieces always came as a blessing in the business. In two weeks, the plant would close until after New Year's Day. The need to complete the remaining orders promised in time for the holiday was paramount, and no vacations or leaves were approved during this time. Longtime staff was already used to the routine and newer members didn't mind since they would be home with their families during the long holiday.

Dan, who'd been using Al's office since he assumed running of the operation, was sitting on the edge of the desk, arms folded, as he watched his boss slowly roll himself about the room in his wheelchair. Al's wife, Yvette, sat in Al's chair, watching, a proud smile on her lips. Both Dan and Yvette were not surprised at the astounding progress Al had made in the weeks he'd been at home. The paralysis had diminished to the point where he could move his left side, but haltingly. Today was the first day that Al had been to the office, and Dan looked at him proudly. He'd come to personally hand each staff member a bonus check.

Al Cunningham had never been a very large man and looked even smaller in stature in the wheelchair. But his illness had done nothing to dampen his zest for living nor had it lessened his awareness of what went on around him. What he'd seen today nearly brought tears to his eyes. And he knew he had Dan to thank. The actual conditions of his factory lent credence to the weekly reports he'd received. He lifted his dark eyes to Dan, who was watching him carefully.

Al said gruffly, "You don't have to watch me like a hawk, boy. I'm not going to fall out of my chair." He sniffed. "I got pretty good control over this thing."

Yvette and Dan exchanged looks.

Dan lifted a brow. "What do you think?" he said to Yvette. "Should we believe him?"

Yvette, a petite older woman who allowed her hair to stay gray, also raised a skeptical brow. "I think so," she said slowly. "Provided we leave here in the next hour. You know. Overconfidence?"

"Humph. Stop talking about me like I'm a block of wood." Al's eyes softened as he looked at Dan. He sniffed again. "Now just give me those checks and let's get this over with." With the box of envelopes balanced on Al's knees, Dan wheeled the older man out of the office and onto the floor, where the whole staff was assembled. He stood to one side with the other managers and listened while Al thanked everyone and wished them a happy holiday. He then called each one by name and shook his or her hand. The long process had tired the weakened man and Dan wheeled him back inside the office.

Yvette said, "I think that's enough for the day. Time to go home."

Al looked at his wife and shook his head in agreement. "No argument, here, honey," he said, a little tiredly. "I want to say something to Dan first. Would you give me a minute?"

When his wife closed the door softly behind her, Al waved a hand to Dan. "Sit down, son. My neck is getting tired looking up at you."

Dan sat behind the desk, wondering what was on his boss's mind. He waited.

"You're fired!"

Dan sat up straight. "What?" His brows were knitted into a frown.

Al laughed. "Thought that'd wake you up."

"What are you talking about, Al?"

"Me and Yvette pulled a fast one on you, son." He raised his good hand. "Don't go getting hot and mad. We've been interviewing for my position and yours. We think we've found the right person, and he'll be starting when we open back up in the New Year."

Dan was speechless. "You're selling the factory?"

"No," Al exploded. "Did you hear me say 'sell'? A manager! Someone to take my place permanently. Something that I'm not going to allow you to continue to do."

Dan spread his hands helplessly. "But, I thought you were satisfied. The place is in tip-top shape!"

Al slapped the arm of his chair in frustration. "It's the best it's been in as far as I can see! And at whose expense?

Yours!" His voice softened. "When's the last time you carved something, son?"

"What?" Dan looked surprised. "I have two more pieces to finish to fulfill prior commitments," he said. "Why?"

"Me and Yvette read about you. Pretty big spread. People are talking and wondering where this Dan Hunter's been all these years." Pride was shining in Al's eyes as he continued. "We know how you've cut off your art for this." His look was meant to encompass the factory. "We're not going to let you end your career just as it's beginning." He gave a short laugh. "Especially since you've finally found yourself. I swear you must have had more jobs in your young life than that guy on TV who just jumped into other people's shoes week after week." He chuckled. "Wonder where that fellow finally wound up."

Dan smiled, but his look turned serious. "So, you don't want me here anymore?" he asked quietly.

"No, except on a weekly basis, as a consultant." Al looked thoughtful. "Don't consultants demand more money? Anyway," he said, without waiting for an answer, "you'll be getting a raise. You gotta eat and keep that roof over your head. Even with all the work you'll be getting after that article, we don't want you to be a starving artist until the dough starts coming in."

Dan looked around. "Consultant? What am I supposed to consult, and with whom?"

Al rolled his eyes. "How am I supposed to know?" he wolfed. "Come in once a week, bother the new manager, look around to see that he's doing what you would do. I don't know. Just consult!" He started toward the door. "Come help me out of here, before Yvette pounces on both of us."

Dan got up as if in a daze. He opened the door to find Yvette about to open it.

"See? What'd I tell ya?" Al said, with a mock frown. To his wife he said, "All right, all right. I told him, so stop worrying. You're looking at the new consultant and the next greatest whittler you ever laid eyes on."

* * *

Dan watched Yvette drive off in the van, then went back to the office and closed the door. He was overwhelmed; his thoughts collided around in his head like oversized marbles. A page over the intercom soon brought him back to reality. He sighed and stood up. Consultant or not, he still had a business to run for the next two weeks. He left the office wondering if his love life would ever become so ordered. He winced at the thought as he remembered Paula's words: *"If you let her walk into the arms of someone else, you've nobody to blame but yourself."*

Knowing now that there could be no other man for Verna, Dan knew that he had to show her what she was refusing to admit to herself—that she had fallen in love with him. He had to convince her soon, before it was too late, and she reverted to her reclusive lifestyle.

It was with new impetus that he walked the floor, pushing the workers to capacity. He was preparing himself for the hours and days ahead. As with his staff, he wasn't going to give himself any slack as far as pursuing the love of his life. He thought about the pretty little things that she was crafting for the biggest lover's holiday of the year.

Dan's chest swelled. For the first time in his adult life he was going to make it his business to be with a special someone on that day. As fate would have it, he'd never been with anyone that he could call his Valentine—a lady to whom he could say, "Be mine." Now that he'd found her, Dan would be the world's biggest fool if he lost her.

A determined look crossed his face and then a small smile, as he tested the words on his lips. "Verna, I love you. Be my Valentine?"

Dan laughed out loud when the office manager raised her brows as she walked by him.

Nine

On Saturday, Verna awoke feeling headachy, and worse, grumpy. "Great," she mumbled. "Just what Aunt Neda needs for her holiday shoppers—staff with an attitude."

After a shower and some food in her stomach, she felt better but decided against going to the shop. Her day would be more productive if spent at home. If she called her aunt now, she would catch her before she left the house.

"Is everything all right?" a concerned Neda asked, when she heard her niece's voice.

"Sure, Aunt Neda," Verna reassured her. "I decided to stay in today to get more accomplished, but I just remembered Michelle is still in New York. Do you have enough people to lend a hand? Otherwise, I'll come in later."

Neda didn't like the tone she heard. It sounded as lifeless as it had on Thursday.

"No, don't do that, Verna," she said. "I have two people here with me. You're better off working at home today." She hesitated before saying, "I wouldn't mind seeing you later tonight after we close up. Stop by for some dessert. You might just want to get out for some fresh air. Unless you have a date or something, of course."

Verna heard the real question in her aunt's hopeful voice. "I'll be in all day, Aunt Neda. Besides, your desserts are doing harm already and it's weeks 'til New Year's," she said, with a laugh. After adding in a soft voice, "Don't worry. I'm fine," she said good-bye and hung up.

Standing in front of the bedroom mirror, she looked herself in the eyes. "How fine are you really?" she whispered to her reflection. The depths of her deep brown eyes told her the truth. For days now she knew that she was falling back into her old routine. Nurse by day, designer by night. As she'd done for almost two years, she left no room for thought other than her immediate task. She knew it had started even before the night she'd canceled her date with Dan: on the anniversary of her lover's death. The days leading up to that day she'd been distant with Dan. And when he'd invited her to meet his family on Thanksgiving, she'd declined, and they hadn't spoken since. She wasn't surprised that he hadn't called. How much ice water in the face does a person need to wake up? Of course he hadn't called!

Verna sat on the foot of the bed then lay down, staring at the ceiling, acting as if she'd find answers there. Or maybe the questions, because she already knew that the answers lay in her heart; she just couldn't face them. How could she tell one man that she was falling in love with him while the spirit of another still haunted her? On so many occasions she'd wanted to throw herself into Dan's arms, and have him love her wildly, and stop being so cautious about making the move to love her. She knew that he was waiting for that right moment: the moment when all thoughts of her former lover had disappeared.

Verna closed her eyes. Dan had been right all along. The last time he'd held her in his arms, kissing her passionately, Frank had come between them! Was it because of the upcoming anniversary that she'd felt his presence so strongly? Verna's eyes flew open at the memory. Anguish marred her features. Had she been fooling herself all along that she could fall in love again? She'd been tested and failed. Her eyes watered when she thought about the old "true love" saying—*only one time around!*

The ringing of the phone brought her upright and she answered it quickly.

"Hello."

Michelle frowned. "Ma said you're staying home to work. Are you all right?"

Verna sighed. "Yes," she said, patiently. "I'm all right."

The frown was transferred to Michelle's voice when she responded, "Well, you certainly don't sound like it, girl! I told you to come up here with me yesterday morning. You sure could have used this three-day break."

Exasperation took over. "And like I told you yesterday, I couldn't get the time off." Verna added, "Are *you* all right? Why are you calling?"

Overlooking the obvious brush-off, Michelle answered, "I'm at Vicki's Creations. They are going nuts over the twelve pillows I brought to them. Verna, they're going to go! The sisters are keeping four for themselves. Now what did I tell you?"

Verna caught the excitement in Michelle's voice, but her thoughts only moments before the phone rang were inhibiting. She could only muster a dull, "That's wonderful." A worried frown wrinkled her forehead. "But you did tell them about the remainder of the order?" She'd hate to lose a new market because she reneged on the order.

"Don't worry about it," Michelle answered. "I explained that you could only give them eight more because of your Valentine's Day crafts." She gave an excited laugh. "Vicki said she understands but wants you to include her. She'll buy at least twenty of whatever you're making, sight unseen. That lovers' day is big here, and Vicki says it's guaranteed she won't have one of those items left in her store." Michelle added, "Hmm, maybe I'm looking for a new husband in the wrong state! Wonder what my chances are if I relocate?"

That brought a chuckle from Verna. "And leave your parents behind? I don't know what I'd do with the three of you looking like little lost lambs without each other."

Michelle sobered. "Don't forget about yourself, cousin."

Quickly, she said, "Take a break, Verna. Get out of there today even if you jog around a few blocks. I'll call you tomorrow night when I get back." She hung up before she got teary-eyed. Verna was her sister. How could she think of herself as being anything else but?

Michelle was right, Verna thought, rubbing her eyes. A break would do her some good. She'd been working nonstop and now it was three in the afternoon. As usual, she'd skipped lunch and was starving. She left her workroom and went into the bedroom to change. Instead of scrounging around in the fridge, she would grab a bite at the mini-mall and stretch her limbs at the same time.

Verna was pleased at the amount of work she'd done, and she toyed with the idea of quitting for the day. Maybe she'd even stay out longer, take in a movie, and call it a day. The more she thought about it, the better she liked the idea.

A half-hour later, Verna was dressed in casual slacks, oversize sweater, and wool jacket. A bright red cap covered her short curls. She breathed in the cold air and nearly choked on it, thankful that it was not moist. The crispness was encouraging, and soon she wended her way through the Saturday traffic, unmindful of the hurried drivers. She had no particular time to get to where she was going, so she let them pass her by without a care.

She parked in the mall lot and found a luncheonette that made good sandwiches. After purchasing a sandwich and a container of tea, she decided to eat outdoors. She walked until she found an empty bench. Actually, all the benches were empty except for a few pot-bellied pigeons pecking around for food. Passersby looked at her strangely, a lone figure eating and drinking hungrily in the cold. Verna looked amused at the glances of sympathy she got from some and obvious disgust from others, all thinking that she was down and out and had just received a handout from a kind stranger. She was tempted to take her cap off and set it beside her. Who knew? Might make the price of her movie ticket.

Inwardly chastising herself for poking fun at those less fortunate than herself, her mood sobered. She tossed her trash and stretched. After taking a walk around the outdoor mall, maybe browsing inside TJ Maxx, she would be ready to drive to the movies, and hoped that there would be something worth sitting through. Minutes into her walk, her cell phone rang. She reached into her bag for it, hoping that her aunt was okay.

"Hello?"

"Verna, it's Dan."

"Dan?" Verna asked, surprised. "Is everything okay?"

"Yes," Dan reassured her. "I stopped by the shop but your aunt told me you were working at home today." He paused. "I called there."

"Oh," was all Verna could say. He sounded strange.

"I took a chance calling this number." He paused again. "Are you sure nothing's wrong?"

"Nothing's wrong, Dan," Verna responded.

"I miss you."

Verna wanted to respond in kind, but her tongue got stuck in her throat. Shouldn't she stop lying to herself now? Her good feelings were beginning to wane as she warred with herself.

"Verna?"

"Yes?"

"I want to see you."

"Dan, I don't know if that would be such a good idea right now."

"Don't say no, Verna. Just for a little while. I promise."

Verna couldn't help herself. She laughed. "Promise?"

Dan laughed at himself. "There I go again, right?" In a rush, he asked, "Where are you?"

"Hilltop Shopping Center."

"I'm ten minutes from you. Would you wait there?"

"From here? You're not working?" She thought not finding her at the shop, he would surely have gone back home, to finish up the last of his commitments. Aloud, she said, "You're taking a break, too?"

"Something like that," Dan said. "More than a break, you can say."

Verna frowned. "Why? What's happened?"

"I've been fired," Dan said, too casually.

"What?" Her mind raced. "From the company? Mr. Cunningham did that to you?" Anger flashed in her eyes. "How could he . . ."

"Verna," Dan interrupted, "I can explain. Would you wait for me there? That is, if you don't have any other plans."

"No," she answered, still annoyed with his news. "I was on my way to take in a movie. I . . . I can wait for you." She told him where she'd be and then ended the connection. All she could think of was the ungrateful "old friend" and "mentor" that would do this to a hardworking, caring man like Dan. She was glad it was cold outside, because she was fuming on the inside.

Dan must have been driving while talking to her, because five minutes later she saw him pull into the parking lot and drive toward her. She left the bench and went to meet him. When he got out of the black Volvo and locked it, looking around for her, her heart sank and self-doubt spiraled inside of her, twisting her insides into a searing flame that emulated Dan's carving. Was it so easy for her to deny her feelings when he wasn't in sight of her? Facing him, could she continue to lie to herself?

Dan saw Verna's wave and waved back, watching her walk to him. When she reached him, he caught his breath, praying on his decision. Exactly how he felt was the way he would act—no more pulling back. And the way he felt right now was to feel her in his arms. She was so close, smelling of cold air, and a fresh scent that reminded him of spicy fruit.

He caught her close and hugged her. "Hello. I've missed you," he muttered, against her wool cap. She was startled because she hesitated, smothered against his chest. When he felt her arms around his waist, he was heartened. Now all he had to do was act as naturally as he could. This was a new beginning for them whether she realized it or not.

Verna was surprised to hear herself murmur, "Me, too, Dan." She closed her eyes and then released him.

Dan and Verna exchanged long looks.

It was Dan who broke the silence, reluctant to let her go, but being sensible, and a man with a mission, he let her step back. "Are you late for the show?"

"No. I'm just going. I have no schedule and nothing in mind to see," Verna answered.

"Want some company?" he asked casually.

"I'd like that." She was not lying to herself.

"Which one were you going to? Should we take both cars or should I drive and then bring you back?"

Verna thought. "Um, no, this place will be deserted, and I wouldn't want to leave the car here all that time. Suppose we both drive to the Hoyt-Bowie Cineplex since it's not far from either of us. This way, we'll only be twenty minutes from home."

"Sounds like a plan," Dan answered. "Where're you parked?"

Verna pointed, and as he walked her to her car, she said, "When are you going to tell me?"

Dan took her hand and put it into the crook of his arm. "After the movie. Over dinner?" He grinned his satisfaction when, after a slight hesitation, she nodded her agreement.

The plan to see a movie fizzled when they arrived to find long waiting lines for the popular shows, and over an hour wait for one they did want to see. Neither of them were enthusiastic about the offerings, so they opted to scrap the idea. They decided to mall-walk until both were hungry enough to eat dinner.

At the Annapolis Mall, at five-thirty, Verna scurried to a

bench and plopped down. She wanted to kick off her walking sneakers and wiggle her toes.

Dan sat beside her. "Tired?" She'd long ago pocketed her cap and removed her jacket in the overheated complex. Her face was flushed, but her eyes sparkled, and he had a feeling that she'd enjoyed herself.

"And then some," Verna answered. "I don't believe we spent over two hours in here."

"I do," he said, indicating the shopping bags in front of his feet. They bulged with bedding. "Thanks for your assistance, mademoiselle." He squinted one eye at the bags. "I don't know that if I was alone I would have chosen those colors, though," he said, doubtfully.

Verna gave the once-over to the cellophane-wrapped puffy comforter. The two sets of matching linen filled another bag. The vibrant colors fairly burst with life. She rolled her eyes. "Dan, you're an artist and do wonderful things with color. Why are you balking about living with it?"

Dan cocked a brow. "But, red?"

Verna sniffed. "Carmine and wine," she said.

"Now who's the artist? Fancy names for a vivid red and burgundy," he teased.

"You'll see," persisted Verna. "The carmine paisley and the reversible wine will be a change. You did say that some of the colors are in the rugs beside your bed."

Dan was still skeptical. "This is true," he remarked. "But, I know someone who'll be accompanying me back here to return them if it doesn't work!"

Verna grinned. Her eyes glimmered with an I-don't-think-so look. "Trust me. It'll work. When I see the bed dressed, you're going to owe me one," she said. She tossed her head back and laughed.

Dan's eyes flickered. She doesn't know what she's just said! Smoothly ignoring her remark, he said, "I think everyone's got the colors of the season on the brain, anyway." Changing the subject, he asked, "Hungry yet?" They'd both stopped for cold drinks and Verna had had a strawberry milkshake that she'd complained filled her up.

Serious, Verna replied, "Yes. Then will you tell me?" He hadn't mentioned a word about his firing and she hadn't asked him. After all, he'd promised.

Once outside, Dan had forgotten they were in separate cars since they'd both driven from the theater to the shopping center. His agitation obviously showed.

"The cars?" Verna asked. She saw that he was annoyed.

"As luck would have it," Dan said, frustrated. "Haven't we done this before?"

Verna remembered. "We have," she answered, looking around at the crowded lot. "Where did you have in mind to eat dinner?" She frowned. "Trying to stay together getting out of here is next to impossible."

"You're right," Dan agreed, but he tried not to show his disappointment. All he needed was for her to back out now, giving up their idea as a bad decision in this madness. He couldn't end the day now. For the past few hours he was sure that even she didn't realize how relaxed she'd become.

"Verna, suppose we drive to my place. You park, then hop into my car, and we'll go eat at a small place I know in the neighborhood. It won't be crowded and the food is good."

"Okay," Verna agreed, after a second. "That'll work. Now don't leave me stranded if I take too long to get there with this monster mad traffic."

As if he would! Dan bent and kissed her mouth. "Bite your tongue," he whispered. "Or do you want me to do it for you?"

Verna blushed as she unlocked her door and slipped behind the wheel. "See you soon," she murmured.

Dan drove thoughtfully through the stop-and-go traffic. He knew that the opportunity was at hand to let Verna know how much he loved her. Was she in love with him? He knew that without a doubt, now. If, in her subconscious, she knew it, how much longer before she would finally face the truth? That's where he would help her all he could. It was hard to believe how his luck was shaping up—his taking the day off, her deciding to do the same, meeting tonight. How much luck can a guy ask for? When he rolled up to his house and saw the Altima, he pulled into the driveway and cut the engine. The only sound in the quiet community was the hammering of his heart against the walls of his chest.

Verna got out of the car as Dan waited for her to get into his. She felt a little embarrassed as she approached him.

"Dan, would you mind if I used your bathroom to freshen up a bit? I feel the mall all over me," she explained.

"Sure, that's not a problem." He popped the trunk of his car open and took out his shopping bags. "May as well take these inside now."

Inside, Dan led her to the master bath on the upper floor. "Just a second," he said, peeking inside. "Inspection." He picked up a towel that was draped over the tub, threw it in the hamper, and hung a gray terry cloth robe behind the door.

"Okay. All yours. There's towels there in the basket and fresh soap under the sink."

"Thanks, I won't be long."

"Take your time. I'll be downstairs." He left before she closed the door.

Dan used the half-bath on the main floor to do his own freshening up, then, taking his purchases, went upstairs to change sweaters. He dumped the linen on the bed and after pulling a black turtleneck over his head, he gave a critical stare from the bed to the floor, then pictured the whole ensemble.

"Hmm, not bad," he muttered. "That'll work. That will work!"

Verna, freshly scrubbed, applied makeup and combed her hair. Refreshed, she folded the towels over the tub and before leaving, admired again the simple décor. The floor and wall tiles were soft beige with a subtle, alabaster swirl pattern. The tub and other fixtures were a matching beige ceramic, and Dan used burgundy, white, and navy bath linen. Navy scatter rugs covered the floor.

"Very nice," she murmured, and turned out the light.

Dan was waiting for Verna in the living room. He stood and held out her jacket, as she walked to him. "Ready?" he asked, helping her into it. He caught the same whiff of fresh, spicy fruit, and he briefly closed his eyes against the warmth that sped through him at her nearness. *It was time to get out of this house!*

Verna took another sip of the full-bodied white wine that Dan had suggested. She was all Chardonnayed out and wanted something different.

"This is a great taste, though I haven't heard of this grape," Verna said

Dan smiled. "Glad you like it." He looked around the cozy restaurant that boasted good American fare. He said, "No fancy preparation, but mouth-watering food. The chef is also very knowledgeable about wines and keeps a varied list. One night he introduced me to a group of wine people who were in town for a convention. They'd been visiting our Maryland vineyards."

Verna asked, "Vineyards? Oh, that's right, we do have a couple of those down here."

"About three or four," Dan acknowledged. "It was the one sister in the group, a sommelier from New York City who really knew her stuff. Her name was Sydney Cox and the chef told me later that she's got quite a fine reputation in the business."

Verna looked pleased. "A female wine connoisseur? Rare birds," she responded, with a big smile. "I'm happy for her."

Dan nodded. "So am I." He gestured at the bottle. "She turned me on to the Pouilly-Fume." He laughed at Verna's slaughter of the word. "Say, 'pwee foo may,' " Dan instructed.

Verna laughed. "Whatever." She finished her glass and Dan replenished it from the bottle he'd ordered. "Half," she said. "I have to drive myself home."

His expression grew serious. "One day we're going to get this act together."

"We will." Said almost absently, she drank more of the wine and looked around the room with pleasure.

Another slip of the subconscious. Dan curbed the urge to grin like a silly fool but managed to hold it to a smile. *She's so unaware,* he thought.

After a short silence, Verna set her glass down. "So, tell me that getting fired is a blessing and you're going to spend your days and nights carving up a storm."

Dan held her gaze. In answer to her right-on-the-money statement, he said, "Correct."

Verna, who'd been joking, looked at him like he'd gone crazy. "What did you say?"

Dan's smile broadened. "I'll be doing exactly that. Except for the one day a week I'll be at the plant."

Before she exploded, Dan explained what had happened when Al and Yvette visited the company the day before.

Verna could only shake her head in amazement. A sheepish look clouded her face. "I owe your friend an apology."

"How's that?" Dan was in the dark.

"Because I called him a few choice words." Verna's look was accusing. "You misled me, Dan Hunter, had me thinking those horrible things about that man and his wife! I wanted to tell Mr. Cunningham where to go and how fast!"

Dan didn't respond to her outburst, but sat back against his chair, regarding her thoughtfully.

His silence couldn't be ignored. Verna searched his eyes, wondering at his sudden sober mood. Had she said something? It was he who should apologize to her for his tease. "What?" she said, suddenly flustered at his probing stare.

"You really care that much?" He spoke above a whisper.

"Of course I care . . ." Verna stopped. "Oh . . . ," she said, almost inaudibly.

At that moment, everything Dan had ever felt for her welled up inside of him until he thought he'd take to the air. He wanted to hold her and love her like she'd never been loved before. If only she would let him!

Verna felt miserable. What was she saying? Was it fair to him to start something she knew she couldn't finish? If he made love to her, would Frank's face swim before her again? She couldn't take that chance. She nearly flinched from the touch of Dan's hand on hers.

"Verna, look at me."

The low command was like a tender kiss floating from his lips to hers. She caught her breath then raised her eyes to his. Verna couldn't run from his naked stare. *He loved her.*

Dan held her gaze. "Don't deny us, sweetheart."

"Oh, Dan," she whispered, "I . . . I can't . . ."

"Shh," Dan murmured. "Don't say it. Once spoken, it becomes true." He released her hand and signaled for the check.

The ride to Dan's house was a somber one. Verna clutched his free hand for a good part of the ten-minute drive. When she released him, she'd wondered if she wanted to hold onto him lest her fears crippled her.

Dan was parked in the driveway watching her. She'd been struggling with her emotions since they left the restaurant and he didn't interfere. Now he asked, "Are you all right?"

Verna nodded. "I think I'll go now."

"Home?"

"Yes," Verna answered.

Dan studied her for a moment. "Okay," he finally said.

At her car, Verna turned to Dan, who stood beside her. He was holding her hand, and suddenly Verna pulled herself into his arms. "Dan," she whispered, her voice catching as he caught her.

Dan hugged her tightly, waiting until the trembling stopped. He cupped her chin, forcing her to meet his eyes. "You don't really want to go, do you, sweetheart?"

"No," Verna answered, shaken with the depths of emotion that she felt for this man. "I want to stay." Her voice shook.

"You know what will happen once we're inside, don't you Verna?"

"You'll love me."

Dan's look was smoldering. "I won't take what's not offered."

Verna's stare was unwavering. "Let's go inside, Dan."

Ten

Dan was pent-up with emotion as he helped her off with her jacket, then dropped it on a living room chair. His movements were slow and deliberate. There was all the time in the world to make her feel safe in his arms. She was looking up at him and he could see the doubt enter her eyes then quickly disappear. Understanding what she must be feeling, his heart constricted, yet he knew that she wanted him as much as he wanted her.

Dan brushed his knuckles over her face then kissed her. "Verna." His voice lowered in volume. "I want you and you must know that I would never do anything to cause you more pain." He looked steadily into her eyes. "I love you."

Verna closed her eyes and her breathing slackened. Weakened, she slumped against him, her head resting on his chest. The beating of his heart filled her eardrums and she wondered if he could feel hers. "I know, Dan," she mumbled, against his sweater. She lifted her head. "That's why I'm so afraid. I don't want to hurt you because of it." She whispered, "I've fallen in love with you."

Dan saw the moistness in the corners of her eyes and he kissed her damp lashes. "I know you have, sweetheart," he whispered, kissing her cheeks and then the tip of her nose. "Don't think about anything but us and the love we feel for each other."

Verna was filled up. "Dan," she murmured, then kissed

his sensuous mouth. Her kiss was soft and tender and, with his hands moving over her back, warming her thoroughly, she strengthened the kiss, while calling his name.

Dan felt her need and responded, accepting her aggressive tongue into his mouth, suckling it as he deepened their kiss. He slipped his hands beneath her sweater and unhooked her bra, allowing the fullness of her breasts to fill his hands.

"God, Verna," he rasped, "you feel so good." She stepped back and lifted the sweater over her head, causing the lace bra to fall to the floor. The sweater landed on top of it, and Dan bent his head and kissed her breasts. The berry-brown nodules peaked under his hot tongue and he groaned his pleasure.

Verna was on fire, and she strained, twisting to fit herself into his burgeoning erection. "Dan." Her throat burned and her voice cracked. She found it hard to speak.

But Dan was feeling her need, and he tore his lips from her breasts and without a word, guided her up the stairs. In the bedroom, he pushed the new linen off the bed and onto the floor and pulled back the comforter. Gently, he eased her onto the bed and continued to disrobe her. When she lay undressed before him, he drank his fill of her nakedness. He could already see the minute pulsing of her womanhood, ready to be relieved of its own fullness.

"You're a gorgeous woman, sweetheart," he murmured. He was sitting beside her, and he ran his fingers down her body, lingering over her breasts, flecking the taut nipples, then traced the outline of her curves, over her hips, her thighs, and slid the flat of his palm over her smooth calves.

"I knew you'd feel this way," he rasped. "Smooth all over, creamy skin, and as warm on the outside as you are on the inside. Beautiful, in and out." His hand skimmed the hairs between her thighs and the moistness drove him wild. She squirmed at his touch and her eyes pleaded with him.

"Dan," Verna murmured, "you're teasing me."

Dan stood up and undressed swiftly, until he, too, was

naked. He turned from her for a few seconds. "Not any-more, sweetness." He was prepared to love her.

Verna's bold look took in his total maleness, her gaze sweeping over the strong, lean, muscled body. As he bent over her, she touched the hairs on his chest and caressed his nipples. When he shuddered at the touch, it went through her fingertips, and she grasped his waist and pulled him down on top of her. She crushed his mouth to hers.

Dan nearly yelled when his naked body touched hers. She was on fire and he was singed. She was trying to guide his erection into her, and he lost all reason when he touched her fingers in aiding her. His thrust was forceful and he yelled, calling her name when her hips rose to meet his powerful plunge.

Verna's temples throbbed violently, and tears formed behind her eyelids as she gave her body freely to him. As if from afar, she listened to the love songs he whispered in her ear, while his hands played the same melodies all over her, resulting in sweet torture. All too soon she felt his climax, and her body shivered violently with their joint descent. Verna's hips sank and her legs slid limply from his. She didn't want to let him go and felt the cold air when he eased himself to her side.

Dan's chest heaved as he lay on his back, eyes closed. He'd been humbled by her display of love for him. She was natural and uninhibited, playing out her powerful emotions. No longer could she deny what existed between them. Finally, he opened his eyes. She was so still.

"Verna?" He propped himself up on one elbow. Her eyes were closed.

Verna refused to look, fearful of what she might see. Her body still tingled from Dan's exquisite lovemaking; it had never felt so alive! It was that thought that prevented her from opening her eyes. Would *his* image be there?

"Verna," Dan said, in a firm voice. "Open your eyes, sweetheart." He kissed her eyelids. "Please?"

Verna slowly opened her eyes and turned to Dan. All

she saw was his worried face, and his love for her. Nothing more! Almost afraid of what she didn't see, she blinked. Only Dan's face was there. Slowly, a smile appeared. And then, she raised up a little and kissed his mouth. "I love you," she said.

Dan breathed easy. He gathered her in his arms and kissed her back. "Don't ever stop," he muttered. "I wouldn't know what to do without you, love."

Verna snuggled closer with droopy eyelids, feeling herself drift into a lover's sleep. "Dan?" Then, wide-eyed, she looked at him. "It is you," she murmured. She closed her eyes.

Dan's lips brushed her forehead. "Always," he whispered.

It was past midnight when Dan awoke. He guessed from Verna's even breathing that she was still asleep. She didn't stir when he turned on the light nor when he sat up.

Now he knew how hard she must have been working at her job and her lucrative hobby, obviously giving a hundred and ten percent to both. She was knocked out. Not to mention the mental strain of trying to sort out her feelings toward him.

Dan eased out of the bed, refusing to wake her because he knew that she'd insist on driving herself home. He'd let her sleep and worry about her annoyed response later. As quietly as he could, he picked up the packaged linen and left the room with it, leaving the light on. Waking up in his bed would be startling enough.

Verna stretched then turned over to peer at the clock. Her eyes flew open at the unfamiliar surroundings. She sat up, flung her legs over the side of the bed, and stared at the bedside clock again. After six in the morning? "Oh my God," she said. "Oh, my God." She'd slept through the night! Suddenly aware of her nakedness, Verna blushed and pulled the covers over her. She couldn't imagine what Dan could be thinking. Where was he? Too embarrassed to stay in the bed and too embarrassed to go looking for him with nothing but her slacks on, she stayed where she was. Her bra and sweater were downstairs in the living room and the scene of how they got there was very vivid in her mind. She groaned. The sound of Dan's footsteps and his soft whistle made her scrunch down even farther beneath the blanket.

Dan appeared in the doorway. "Good morning," he said, cheerfully. "I thought I heard you stirring up here." Amused at her shyness, holding the covers up to her throat, he laid her clothes on the bed. He bent and kissed her. "Sleep well?"

Verna glowered at his sunny disposition. "Why didn't you wake me? I spent the night!"

Dan grinned. "Not a morning person, I see." He winked at her and went to his closet to take out a lightweight robe. "Hmm, we'll have to arrange our schedules a bit, but we should be able to manage with few problems." He gave her the robe. "I'll wait until you shower before I finish breakfast, but the coffee's made if you want a cup now."

Verna stared at him. "Dan, have you gone mad?"

"Uh, huh," he answered. "Happened overnight." He walked to the door. "Oh, I forgot to ask. Do you eat heavy or light in the morning? Lumberjack pancakes or continental?"

"Lu . . . lumberjack," Verna finally sputtered.

"Good. Me too." He winked at her again. "You'll find everything you need in the bathroom. Take your time."

She listened until the happy whistling faded into the rooms downstairs. As if a whirlwind had just hit, Verna shook her head until it cleared. But the feeling was short-lived. "Manage?" she said. "Manage what?"

Close to seven o'clock, Verna went downstairs looking for Dan and found him in the kitchen sitting at the table reading the Sunday papers. He was drinking coffee, and he smiled and stood up when he heard her at the door.

"Good morning, again," he said, after reaching her and planting a kiss on her forehead. "Come, sit down." His arm snaked around her waist as he drew her toward the table.

"Good morning, Dan." He was dressed in jeans and a T-shirt and Verna caught his bare arm, thinking that he smelled more delectable than the delicious smells coming from the stove. His firm touch made her skin tingle from remembrances of last night. Her slight squeeze caused the thumb of his splayed hand to brush against her breast.

Dan felt her shudder but chose to ignore it. He wanted to play down, not heighten, her discomfort. She sat down and he poured coffee.

"Dan," Verna said, after taking a sip of the hot beverage. "You should have awakened me." Wrinkles creased her forehead. "What will your neighbors think?"

"My neighbors?" Dan's grin erupted into a belly laugh. "They're probably saying right now, 'it's about time that boy found himself somebody. Maybe now he'll stop all that fool bangin' and sawin' all hours of the night.' "

Verna smiled. "You really do that?"

"Fried, scrambled, or over?" Dan was at the stove, cracking open eggs.

"Scrambled."

"To answer your question, I do. When I get to working, I lose track of time. Don't you, sometimes?" He flipped the eggs onto a plate, removed a platter of pancakes and sausages from the oven, and set them on the table.

"A lot," Verna admitted. "Mm, smells good." If she didn't have an appetite before, she did now. The golden-brown pancakes looked too fluffy and perfect to eat. "Mm, tastes even better," Verna added, after eating the first bite.

"Thank you, mademoiselle. Do make a mean flapjack, have to admit." Dan's fork stopped midway. "How're yours by the way? I could eat these things every morning, you should know."

Verna sputtered on a sip of coffee. "Wha . . . what do

you mean?" Was this inference the same as his "manage" statement, earlier? What was he thinking?

Dan got up. "More coffee?" he asked. He refilled both cups and sat down again, looking at her carefully. While she was sleeping, he'd weighed everything he was about to say, more than a dozen times.

"I think you know what I mean, sweetheart." Dan did not try to thrill her with a sexy tone or distract her with a charming smile.

His quiet voice and riveting look caused an ominous feeling to overcome Verna—like someone walking over her grave, as Michelle would say. Was she ready to hear what he had to say? And how was she going to respond?

Verna held his direct stare. Her voice matched his steady one. "I believe I do, Dan."

"Then you know I love you and I want you."

"Yes. I know that," she murmured.

"Since I admitted that to you weeks ago," Dan said, "my feelings have only grown deeper. Getting to know you, and last night, finally loving you, has brought a sense of," he sought the right word, "of fullness, no, completeness to my life."

"Dan, you shouldn't . . ."

His low voice interrupted. "Let me, Verna." He continued when she sank back in her chair, eyeing him speculatively.

"I've told you all there is to know about me, and what I've left out probably isn't important." Dan saw the shadow of her long lashes sweep her cheeks. Was he frightening her? Determination spurred him on. "The things that I don't know about you will be exciting to discover." He smoothed his goatee and his eyes glittered. "Or maybe dangerous," he said, lightly. "Like knowing you're a morning grump." He smiled. "Which makes me look forward to our nights."

Verna had to smile at that.

Amusement covered his features. "If my mother only knew what buying a new couch would do for her youngest son, she'd have redecorated years ago," he said. "If Paula hadn't been such a stubborn little perfectionist in hunting down the 'finishing touch' as she called it, I would never have been in Hager's that day. But you were there, I was there, and I fell for you, instantly. In a short five months, my life has changed. I have my work, my career. And I have the love of a beautiful woman." His voice dropped. "Finally, I'm in a place where I want to be."

Dan's look never wavered. "And right now, you're where I want you to be—here, with me, and I never want you to leave. Will you marry me, Verna?"

Verna knew the words were coming even before they formed on his lips. But before she could speak, Dan held up his hand.

"Wait. Don't answer that." There was no humor in his request. "I'm not trying to be funny, Verna, just hear me out." He had her complete attention. "I want to hear your answer and I pray that it is the one that I'm hoping for, but I don't want to know now, today, or tomorrow."

"Dan, I don't understand." Verna's mental state was in a tizzy.

"Let me try to explain. I know it sounds crazy, but it's the only way to let you know how much I love you." Then he smiled. "I guess you're wondering what other kind of crazy suggestion is going to pop out of my mouth." Once more, he was serious. He stood and held out his hand and she took it. Dan led her to the living room where they sat in separate seats.

He saw that she was trying hard not to interrupt, and he only hoped that she would really listen to him and try to understand.

"When you fell asleep in my arms last night, you'd have thought I was a kid lost in an ice cream factory. When I knew that you would wake up in my bed in the morning, I realized that I had to let you know that that was where I wanted you to be every morning—for the rest of my life."

Verna remembered his body, moist and warm from their lovemaking.

Dan's eyes clouded. "But," he gave a wry smile, "I had a problem."

"Problem?" She looked puzzled.

"Yes," Dan said, somberly. "My timing."

Verna knew.

Dan hesitated. "Proposing to you so soon after the anniversary of your fiancé's death. It would become a date associated with a painful memory. I want us to be special and apart from the past." He gestured in frustration. "I also didn't want you to think that I was insensitive to your feelings. But if I had let you walk out of here this morning without letting you know that I want you as my wife, I would have been a fool."

Verna was shaken at the depth of his emotional confession. "Excuse me," she murmured. Once in the small bathroom near the kitchen, she stood with her back plastered against the door and took deep breaths. After a minute, she doused her face with cold water and, patting it dry, stared at her reflection, knowing the truth of her feelings would be there. Verna was not disappointed. *She wanted to be Mrs. Dan Hunter!*

"I do," she whispered to her pained image. "More than I thought would have been possible!" Verna folded her arms and hugged herself. What should she do? she asked herself. Was this really another chance at happiness? Would something else happen to snatch it out of her grasp? No—impossible—he's so young: Only thirty-five. But her other lover had been even younger. Gone from her at thirty-one!

Verna dropped down on the edge of the toilet seat and held her head in her hands, kneading her throbbing temples. Several minutes passed before she stood up and rinsed her face again. She knew what she'd decided, but at his request, she'd wait.

Sadly, Verna remembered something someone once said to her after Frank's death. At the time she thought the woman was cold and callous, and Verna recalled her instant distaste for the thoughtless remark. But, as time passed, Verna had to admit the woman had spoken the truth.

"We are *all here but only a minute,"* Verna whispered.

Dan had cleared the table and the dishwasher was humming when he heard Verna open the bathroom door. He tossed the dishtowel on the counter and waited. She'd taken a long time to gather her composure, and he'd started second-guessing his decision to bare his soul. She was still a tender individual, and he could only imagine what was going on in her head. Dan scowled. If he'd been Frank, he didn't know that he'd ever want her to forget him with some other guy. "But, I *am* that guy," he muttered.

"Dan?" Verna said softly. She had watched him warring with himself.

"Okay?" Dan stayed where he was, not knowing what to expect.

Verna nodded. "I'm okay," she answered. After a careful look, she tilted her head. "Are you?"

Breathing deep, he replied in a gruff voice, "That depends."

"On my answer?"

"No," Dan answered slowly. "I don't want to know that now. But, I wondered if I came on too strong, after all." He shrugged. "You know, acting like the relentless bulldog with tunnel-vision."

Verna smiled at the comparison and the vision was hilarious. Dan? Fat and squat and head closer to the ground than to the sky? The man she'd fallen in love with was more like the sleek greyhound—long and lean with a thick muscled chest.

Dan was surprised at her smile and wondered what she found so amusing. He was nearly bowled over when he found himself wrapping his arms around her as she came to him and snuggled against his chest.

Should he even ask? Dan just held her, needing her as much as she wanted his comfort.

Verna accepted the haven he offered. After a while, she

lifted her head. "Definitely not a bulldog," she said, in a throaty voice.

Dan kissed the tip of her nose. "No? What then?" he queried.

"More of a racer, I think."

Mulling that over, Dan said, "Oh, yeah?" Then, gravely, "Right now, I'm not so sure."

Verna kissed his dimpled chin. "Be sure," she said.

Dan studied her. He was aware of her relaxed body, and her face was free of frowns. "Feel like talking?"

Verna nodded. "Yes." Arms entwined, they returned to the living room.

This time they sat side by side on the sofa, hands comfortably clasped.

"Everything smells new," Verna said, giving an admiring look around. She ran a hand over the smooth-textured tan leather sofa. The whole room done in contemporary style in inviting earth tones was warm and pleasing to the eye.

Dan grinned. "The result of my 'getting it together' period a few months ago. Like it?"

"Mm, cozy," Verna answered, approvingly.

"I'm glad," Dan said, warmly. He gently cupped her chin and bent to kiss her lips. He didn't linger and reluctantly sat back. "Tell me what you were thinking, Verna," he said. His thumb was making little circles on the back of her hand. He wanted the connection and he felt that she did, too.

"All that you said before rang so true, Dan, that I wonder why you had to say them at all. We could have done a mental telepathy thing." Verna answered the squeeze to her hand with one of her own. "You said that you were in the place that you want to be, that you have the love of a beautiful woman. Well, it took me a long time to admit it to myself . . . and to you . . . but knowing that I had the love of a beautiful man—a beautiful person—I wanted to be in that place with you. When you invited me to become your wife, be a permanent fixture in your space, I was overwhelmed, to say the least." She paused. "I had to see the truth of what I was feeling at that moment."

"And what did you see, Verna?" Dan's tone was gentle.

"My love for you," she murmured. "There's no denying that. But . . ."

"You don't want to give me your answer yet," Dan finished for her. "I meant what I said," he said firmly. "I don't want to know."

"I think you suspect my answer," Verna replied, gently. "Like I said, your words hit home." Her eyes clouded. "But, your proposal now, in this month, would always be a bittersweet memory." She gave him a sad look. "I also want us to have our own special memories."

Dan could breathe again. She didn't say no! He kissed her, then brushed her eyelids with his thumb, as if chasing away the sadness that lingered. "We will, sweetheart, we will," he whispered.

Verna heard the huskiness in his voice, and she realized the anguish he must be feeling. She laid her head on his shoulder.

After a silent moment, a thought came to Dan. Once she accepted his proposal, and he had no doubts about that, they would be engaged. That meant a ring. A ring! How would she react when he put it on her finger? As hard as it was going to be for them, he knew memories ran deep. She couldn't help but remember another time when a man slipped a ring on her finger. Suddenly, he wondered if he would find comparisons in everything he said or did for her. Is that a healthy sign? Normal?

Verna sensed Dan's agitation. She sat up. "What is it?"

He had no reason to keep his thoughts from her, since they both welcomed the honesty between them.

"I was thinking that if you give me the answer I'm hoping for, well, do you have a particular style of ring that . . ." He never finished because she gave a violent shudder and moved away from him.

"Verna, what's wrong?" Dan asked quietly.

"Ring?" Already memories were surfacing. How could

she accept another ring? What was she going to do with the one that was in her keepsake box? She was shaking her head.

"Yes, a ring," Dan said calmly. "An engagement ring."

Verna continued to shake her head. "No ring," she said, choking over her words. "No more rings."

Stunned, Dan could only watch her with amazement. He'd expected some emotion but not this violent reaction. It struck him, then. Is she still in love with her dead fiancé? No, Dan argued with himself. He didn't believe that. Not after her confession to him, and her sweet, sweet, lovemaking. She loved *him!*

The emotional outburst was gone as quickly as it had come when Verna realized how she must have hurt him. "Dan, I'm sorry," she apologized. "I didn't see that coming. I thought I had put all that behind me." She felt miserable at the look in his eyes. He doubted her. "I made a mess, didn't I?"

Dan put a halt to his wandering thoughts and regarded her thoughtfully. "Nothing that we can't straighten out," he answered, slowly. "You had a strong, honest reaction to something that means a lot to you."

"Meant," Verna said, with emphasis. "That's part of my past, now. But," she smiled ruefully, "some things are not so easily forgotten."

"Some things aren't meant to be," said Dan. He looked away. "You need more time to deal with your feelings." His tone was resigned. "Maybe you should put that on the shelf. I told you, bad timing."

Verna's heart sank. "Your proposal?"

"Yes." He saw the brief shadow. "Would it bother you so much?"

It was seconds before she answered, "Very much."

Dan didn't answer but wondered how far he should pursue this. He'd taken a chance, going as far as he had, ignorant of the consequences. Maybe it was time to let it go for now.

Verna tugged on the hem of her sweater as she stood up. "I should go before *my* neighbors raise a brow."

Dan stood. "Going to try and make church?"

"No. I'm a little late for that. I intended to work today, anyway." She shook her head. "I don't believe that Christmas is just three and a half weeks away."

"And New Years. And then, Valentine's Day. Not too long after that, here comes Halloween again, signaling Thanksgiving."

Verna smiled. "It's like rushing to beat the clock before time catches you."

Dan gave her a wry smile. "Right," he said. He touched her cheek. "Are you all right, Verna?" Then, "You'll think about . . . the future?"

Covering his hand with hers, Verna held it to her face and closed her eyes. *I pray to God I will be,* she breathed, silently. "I'm fine, Dan, and I won't forget about our future."

Our future! He shielded his joy with a question. "Will you be working all day?" He wanted to see her again.

"I have to," Verna replied. "There's an order that must be completed before the end of the week." She smiled. "After all, those things should be in the stores now, not being delivered on Christmas Eve."

"I hear you," Dan replied, helping her into her jacket. At the door, he pulled her close and hugged her. "I miss you already," he whispered in her ear.

Verna shivered from his warm breath tickling her ear. "Me, too." Inexplicably, a sense of fear washed over her. She hugged him a little longer, a little tighter, then released him to his sudden look of surprise. "I'll call you, love." She left.

After Verna left, Dan felt restless. Although he knew that he should follow her lead and get to work on his carvings, he fell into a melancholy mood. All he wanted to do was to sit and think about her and the last hours they'd spent together. He looked around the living room and could envision her being there for always. In the kitchen, he could see her sitting at the table, laughing, her eyes sparkling at something he'd said. Upstairs, he stood at the door of his bedroom, staring at the bed. He recalled the hours she'd spent in his arms, and he couldn't ever see her spending her nights somewhere else. She belonged here, with him. He went back downstairs into the kitchen and opened double louvered doors that one would assume was a closet. But it was the space for his laundry room. When he'd moved his workroom into the basement he found that wood dust filled the air and eventually settled on his clothesbasket and freshly laundered clothes. He'd had the work area built and had his appliances moved upstairs.

Dan opened the door of the dryer and removed the freshly laundered linen. While Verna was sleeping, he'd washed and dried the new linen before putting them on his bed, a practice he'd learned from his mother. The sheets smelled like fresh air and sunshine, and he was reminded of Verna's fluffy cap of curls when he'd met her in the parking lot the day before. Upstairs, after making up the bed with the colorful set, he stepped back. The hues were bright but not outlandish, he thought. They blended in, giving the room a look of warmth that was in keeping with the spirit of the season.

As Dan looked around, he knew that he would never look at the bedding without thinking of how it had gotten there. He'd remember Verna. The thought came to him that this was one of the things that would become a memory. *Memories.* He realized that they'd begun to build their own—something that she'd done with her former lover. Thoughtful, he left the room.

Drinking reheated coffee, pondering over his discovery, an idea began formulating in Dan's mind. He had to give her something new and different—memories of her own that she would cherish, and that would become more important than any from her past. The urge to work was very strong as Dan left the kitchen and went downstairs to the basement.

I'll call you, love. The words kept rolling over in Dan's mind as he worked to finish his carving. Verna's endearment had taken him by surprise. It was the first time she'd called him anything other than his name. *Love!* He liked the way it had slid smoothly over her tongue. Natural. Uninhibited. Only some of her attributes that he loved.

Dan chipped away at the figure with his gouge and mallet. The voluptuous female form was finally beginning to take shape, and the vision he'd sketched out was becoming a hard reality. He ran his fingers over the wood. A chestnut, it wasn't as hard as some woods that he used and though it had a tendency to split, he liked the distinct grain, and it always gave a good finish. The Maryland couple who had commissioned the piece were successful art gallery owners. They'd sent Dan a photograph hoping that he would capture the attitude of an African peasant woman. Refusing to copy work, and only after lengthy discussions, he drew pictures of their vision and his. Once a final sketch was agreed upon, he went to work.

The urgency of his thoughts prodded Dan to work fast but carefully. Sculpting was definitely a case for the adage, "haste makes waste." Yet, he was anxious to complete the piece and move on to his final commitment, which was already in the grueling sanding and finishing stage. Then he would be free to begin the next work of art that was taking shape in his mind's eye. Quickly, estimating the time required to complete it, he grimaced. Forget about giving it to her for her birthday, which was in December, or even trying to make it a Christmas present!

Dan stopped chipping and closed his eyes, mentally trying to see his inventory of wood in the garage. Shaking his head, he swore softly, knowing that he didn't have what he wanted. If he couldn't find what he needed at the local lumberyard, he'd have to mail order from his supplier, and that could cut into the time needed to finish it. Or maybe he'd find what he needed at the plant. At the worst scenario, he would be rushing to complete it in February. With that thought, something clicked, and Dan laid down his tools. Excitedly, he got up and jammed his hands in his jeans-pockets, while he paced the floor, kicking aside wood chips.

"February!" He slapped his forehead. "What an idiot you are, man." He plopped down on the stool again. How long had it been since he was lamenting that he'd never had that significant other to call his Valentine? "Well, that's in the past," he said, picking up his tools again.

A smile touched his lips. He didn't need a special time to call Verna his sweetheart, but, on the lovers' day that would be here only a nod after Christmas Day, she would know it without a doubt. If she accepted his wearable work of art, he'd be giving her his heart, and she would be giving him the world.

Eleven

After arriving home and soaking in a hot tub, Verna dressed in wide-legged cotton drawstring pants and an oversize long-sleeved T-shirt. Her mood after leaving Dan's was one of melancholia. It was definitely not the reaction one expected from a woman who'd just received a proposal for marriage. It was strange, she thought. Why wasn't she happier?

Instead of immediately going to her workroom, Verna had a sudden urge to cook. It seemed as if she'd become a stranger in her own kitchen these past few weeks. While she peeled potatoes, washed vegetables, and seared a roast, her thoughts were as nimble as her fingers. Through the flash pictures in her mind, she was journeying from her life then to her life now, weighing her successes and her failures. She was a success in that she was a single woman, property-owner, managing to sustain herself in a comfortable lifestyle. She was a failure in that she didn't, or wouldn't, pursue her professional career goals in obtaining her degree in interior design, a conquest that would have garnered her both professional and monetary rewards. She was successful in that, surprisingly, her hobby had become a lucrative enterprise and was self-fulfilling; a failure in that she couldn't come to grips with the emotional upheaval that tore her apart two years ago and that now was threatening to interfere with her love for a man who wanted her.

Almost three hours after she started, Verna had prepared a feast with no one but herself to enjoy it. She removed two cake pans from the oven and, while they cooled, proceeded to whip up the chocolate icing and mocha filling. She looked at the food with dismay. What had she been thinking? Freezing leftovers wasn't a favorite pastime and rather than come home and zap stuff in the microwave, she was quick to stop and bring something in with her. No cleanup and she'd get to her workroom that much sooner.

The potato salad was in the fridge and the candied yams, collards with mustards, were still on the stove, while the baked beans cooked slowly. A veal roast was in a warming pan. The only thing she hadn't made was corn bread, because she loved it swimming in butter and always overindulged herself.

Verna grinned, thinking about the food she'd cooked. "Just listen to yourself, silly girl. Talking about overindulging." A big laugh flew out of her mouth. Deciding to work while the cake cooled, she turned out the light and left the kitchen. She felt lightweight, as if the cooking activity had eased her troubled thoughts.

The burnished-gold silk embroidered fabric that she'd already cut to make four pillows was ready for the silken twisted cord and the tassels. When she picked up a square, the metallic fibers glimmered like precious metals. Verna planned to make each identical to the other and hoped that they would be sold in pairs.

She worked quickly and had finished sewing two pillows before she remembered the cake. Twenty minutes after removing the beans and icing the cake, she was back upstairs. At this rate, she thought, all four would be complete by tonight and then she'd cut the last four squares, completing the order.

While Verna worked, a sudden smile appeared as she stopped and scrutinized her accomplishments. "If I'd have thought doing flashbacks of my life would propel me like this, I would've developed that technique ages ago," she said to the still room. The small smile remained while she continued her task.

Funny how the smell of good food affected one's moods, Verna thought, feeling more serene. Gone was the earlier, gloomy self-assessment, replaced by a more philosophical vein of thinking. Deep within, she was happy with herself and not disgruntled with the choices she'd made. She knew that walking through life was not always striding on pristine paths or beaches. In the words of the great Langston Hughes, "life ain't no crystal stair," she thought. It was what a body made for oneself carving out a special place.

Verna sewed on the last gold tassel for the last pillow. She pulled the cool silken threads through her fingers, liking the smooth, tactile sensation. *Special place!* Was that part of her conversation with Dan? She knew it was and smiled because they were both honest enough to admit that they loved and wanted each other.

As far as making that final commitment to their love and future relationship, it was she who was allowing her fears to cast doubt in his mind about her love for him. Her superstition about accepting a ring as an engagement token would probably seem so ridiculous to some. But for her, it was real. Two months after receiving a diamond ring, her lover was dead. She wanted this new man in her life as her husband, but she didn't want his traditional gift of love. Who said she had to have such a token anyway? Maybe in time, as she grew older, she would laugh at herself, hopefully with her oldest daughter, who would become the recipient of any diamonds Verna had received over the years. But with those there would be no association with sad remembrances.

Verna put the last pillow down next to the others. The muslin interlinings were already encasing the prefabricated square foam shapes. She gave a critical eye to all four, picking them up and squeezing them. Depending on the fabric, shape, and eventual use, she sometimes used goose-down fill or synthetic polyester fiberfill for her pillows. But since the foam retained shape better, she favored it more. Carefully, she slipped the shapes into the colorful silk covers. After slip-stitching the openings closed, she was finished.

Standing and stretching to the ceiling, Verna was happily tired. She turned out the light, padded to the bedroom, and plopped down across the bed, belly first.

"Umm, you feel good, bed," she groaned. Her eyelids drooped, but a look at the clock made her get up. It was nearly five-thirty and she'd yet to eat anything since breakfast. Besides, if she didn't refrigerate her food, she'd have to toss it out before the night was over.

In the bathroom, Verna splashed cold water over her face and fluffed her hair. Eyeing her casual clothes, she suddenly wanted to dress and eat her fabulous dinner at the table instead of at her usual place in front of the TV. She did a quick wash-up and spritzed herself with a lush Oriental scent with bergamot and jasmine tones. Padding to the bedroom, she pulled out a flowing caftan with a V-neck. The brilliant emerald green and gold cloth swirled around her ankles.

"Hmm, ready for a date, looks like," her reflection said. "My man is home working, just like I am," she answered herself back.

"This would be a sin," she said, looking at the food. Without another thought, she picked up the phone in the kitchen.

"Hey, Michelle," Verna said, when her cousin picked up.

"Hey, Verna, what's up?" Michelle rubbed her eyes.

"Not too much. You sleeping? When did you get in?"

"About two hours ago. The flight was delayed and when I hit the door, the bed grabbed me. It's where I am now." Michelle paused. "You worked all day?"

"For a good part of it, anyway," Verna replied, a little hesitant.

Michelle's ears perked up. "Really? And what did you do the other part?"

"Well, I spent a few hours cooking, and that's why I'm calling you," she said in a rush, remembering the early hours. Already, Michelle's antennae were up.

"After you made breakfast you stayed in the kitchen cooking?"

"Well, actually I didn't make breakfast. But, yes, I worked some and cooked some. And that's where you come in. Girl, you have to come over here and have dinner with me. Otherwise it's dog food."

"What? Not *your* food." Her stomach was reacting already. "What'd you make?" When Verna finished telling her, she groaned. "Oh, no, stop. You're torturing me."

"So will you come and have dinner with me?" Verna asked.

"Oh, Verna, I can't. I have to pack again. Tomorrow morning I have a corporate meeting, and then I have to catch a four o'clock flight to Seattle. I'll be there for three days."

Verna felt deflated. She wanted the company and conversation of her lively cousin. "Oh."

"I'm sorry, I would love to sit up chatting. But, don't you dare throw that food away!" Michelle said. "I know you don't like freezing it, but I want some of everything, especially those greens and baked beans. Too bad the potato salad will have to go."

Verna sighed. "Okay, will do. So enjoy your trip and call me when you get back."

"Thanks, it's three days of meetings, so I don't know how much fun I'll have." She paused. "You're not seeing Dan tonight? That man will *not* have a problem getting rid of your food for you."

Verna laughed. "I already know that, but he's working the rest of the day just like me."

Michelle thought, then said, "The *rest* of the day?" She grinned when her brain clicked. "So, you two met for breakfast?"

"Okay Sleuth Fieldings," Verna said. "Yes, we had breakfast this morning." She felt the next question coming, so she added, "At his place."

After a moment of silence, Michelle said, all laughter gone from her voice, "I'm happy for you, Verna. You and Dan are so right for each other. Go for it, girl." She hung up.

Verna ate her meal quietly and in elegance at the dining room table. For company, she had her reflective thoughts—of Dan and the night she'd spent in his arms and her ever deepening feelings for him. She looked around the room thoughtfully, mentally imagining him in this space. Would they live here as man and wife? Where would he work? His sculptures required so much room. *Her* work required a separate room. She imagined herself living and working in his space. So many changes, she thought, as she began to clear the table. But then, life is all about change.

As if suddenly realizing what she was doing, a soft laugh escaped. "Girl, you haven't said 'I do' yet and you're already divvying up living quarters!" Her eyes softened. "But Dan already knows my answer," she whispered.

Timing. It's all about timing, Verna thought, as she filled the dishwasher then washed the sink-full of pots. When she finished, she turned out the light and went upstairs. She knew exactly when she would formally accept Dan's proposal. They would be building special memories. And Verna discovered something else as she entered her workroom. The next time she made love to Dan, there would be no other image floating before her. It was something that she just knew—no—*felt,* in her heart. She'd finally let go of the spirit of her former lover.

Later, when Verna was in bed, she recalled Michelle's words.

Verna knew that she and Dan *were* right for each other and believed that they would be a couple for as long as she breathed.

* * *

Dan stamped his feet and clapped his hands against the cold, waiting for Verna to open the door. "Whew," he said, when he blew inside. "Hi, gorgeous. Ready?" He bent and kissed her lips.

Verna kissed him back, long and steady. "You're freezing," she finally managed to say. "It's that cold out?"

"Mm, you keep warming me up like this and we can forget about going back out there, sweetheart." Dan nibbled her ear. He protested when she pulled away.

Verna blew in his ear, knowing he'd pull her back. She loved to see him shudder and his eyes heat up with passion for her. He didn't disappoint her and she swayed back, wrapping her arms around his neck. His kiss was sweet, then urgent, as she felt his passion. "Mm, you taste good," she murmured, against his mouth.

Dan lifted his head, giving her a quizzical look. "Does that mean you don't want the special birthday dinner I have planned for you?"

Verna laughed and pulled away. "You don't taste *that* good," she said.

"Is that so?" Dan looked hurt.

Verna opened the closet and got her coat. Her eyes twinkled. "That hurt little-boy look won't work this time," she said. "I'm too hungry."

Dan's eyes glittered. "You are?"

Verna blushed.

Dan laughed and kissed her nose. "Come on, birthday girl. I promise we can pick this up where we left off—later."

"Promise?" Verna locked the door then caught his hand.

"Always," Dan answered. When they were in the car, he bent and kissed her lips.

It was the Saturday before Christmas and Verna's twenty-ninth birthday. For weeks, Dan kept checking with her to make sure she didn't make other plans. She kept reassuring him that the day was all his. She chuckled to herself—as if all her free days hadn't been his in the weeks following Thanksgiving.

Dan noticed her secret smile. He took his hand off the wheel and chucked her under her chin. "What's that mysterious smile about?" he said softly.

Verna caught his finger and kissed it. "You," she answered, with a soft finality.

Dan knew he wasn't going to get any more so he smiled and drove. He had a few surprises of his own.

The Sequoia restaurant on K street in Georgetown was literally lit up like a Christmas tree. Hundreds of twinkling lights in the surrounding trees were ablaze.

Verna's eyes sparkled, lighting up her face, as Dan waited his turn to pull into the parking lot. He knew that it would be crowded and was glad he'd made early plans for this night.

"Better close your eyes, sweetheart," Dan whispered.

"Why?"

"Because your eyes are putting those lights to shame," he answered. "Surprised?"

"You know I am. So this is why you kept putting off coming here," she accused. "And you told me the food wasn't all that great!"

Dan pulled into the parking lot and soon they were in the elevator. "Had to tell you something," he said. "For a while there, I thought you'd come without me."

Once inside, Dan spoke quietly to the hostess and they were led upstairs.

They were seated in a secluded area in the room known as 'The Bubble.' It overlooked the Potomac River and was all glass and crystal chandeliers.

Verna had never dined in the restaurant but had heard so much about it. It was simply something that she'd never gotten around to doing, and now she was glad she'd procrastinated.

"This is so romantic," she murmured to Dan. She blushed because he was staring at her with such an intense look that she was certain other diners couldn't help but notice. But it was obvious he didn't care, because he took her hands and held them across the table.

"You're beautiful." Dan released her hands only because the wine server arrived with the champagne, and Dan began the ritual of tasting and smelling. When he approved, the flutes were filled and the server left.

Dan touched his glass to Verna's. "Happy birthday again, sweetheart. Here's to a long and happy life." His eyes flickered for a second.

Verna was deeply touched. She sipped and then held on to her glass when she set it down. Her gaze was locked with his, and his instant sadness did not go unnoticed, especially since she knew the reason behind it. He'd never once repeated his proposal, waiting until she was ready to give her answer. But each day that they'd become closer, even after their lovemaking, she could sense that he wanted her answer.

She'd decided weeks ago that her birthday would be the day that she accepted—and what better place than this? Unknowingly, Dan had provided the perfect setting.

Dan drank his champagne, wondering what had happened to suddenly sober his love. And was that a tear in the corner of her eye? He'd thought that she would be pleasantly surprised.

"Something wrong, sweetheart?" he asked. He set his glass down.

Verna shook her head, and this time it was she who reached across the table to take his hands in hers. "Everything is right with me. And I do hope to have a long and happy life—with you, Dan. As your wife. Yes, I will marry you."

"What?" Dan was flabbergasted. He fell back against his chair. And then he closed his eyes and rubbed his forehead. Clearly shaken, he looked at her. He could only muster, "I thought you'd decided against it."

"Because we are so happy together?" Verna asked, in a low voice.

Dan nodded. "I thought that you'd become . . ."

"Complacent?" suggested Verna.

"Something like that." Dan was still stunned. He was

the one to be giving surprises tonight and she'd dropped the bomb.

He got up and walked to her and pulled her into his arms. He bent and kissed her lips. After a second he let her go, winking at her embarrassment. Dan turned to the other patrons, who were looking and smiling.

"She's agreed to marry me, folks," he said, with a big grin, then laughed at the applause.

Verna smiled and waved to the well-wishers.

Dan waited until she was composed. "I love you," he said.

"I love you," Verna replied.

Later, refusing dessert, coffee was all Verna and Dan could manage.

"The meal was marvelous," Verna said. "This was a treat."

"No, you are," Dan said, husky-voiced. He reached into his pocket, took out a small black box, and pushed it toward her. "Happy birthday, Verna."

Verna opened the box. "Oh."

Dan watched her pick up the watch and turn it over in her hand. He only wished that it could be the diamonds he wanted to put on her finger. Maybe, one day.

"Dan, it's beautiful." The sterling-silver face with a circlet of turquoise and lapis lazuli was shining brightly against the bed of black velvet. The two gemstones were separated with slivers of sterling. The work of art glittered brightly.

Verna slid it over her hand and adjusted it on the long black sleeve of her jersey-knit dress. She held out her arm. "My birthstone. It's absolutely stunning. Thank you."

Dan saw that she was really pleased and he felt better. "You're welcome," he responded. *One day soon, you'll have diamonds,* he thought.

Verna was in the ladies' room, fluffing her hair, when a young woman walked up to her, excitement shining in her hazel eyes.

"Oh, congratulations," she said. "I heard your fiancé.

He's so handsome," she gushed. Then she held up her hand. "My boyfriend proposed to me, too. Isn't it gorgeous?" She turned her hand until the light caught the diamond facets. "Can I see yours?"

For an instant, Verna's face clouded. Serenely, she said, "Your ring is very beautiful, dear. I hope you'll be very happy." She held up her bare left hand. "I'm a nontraditionalist." She smiled at the astonished young woman and left the room.

Dan stood up as she approached. "You okay?" He thought he detected a shadow.

Verna kissed his dimpled chin then his lips. "Never better, love," Verna murmured. "Can we go home now?"

Dan read the message. He smiled. "We're almost there."

Twelve

"Engaged!" Michelle yelled over the phone. "When?"

That's a good question. "I accepted on my birthday," Verna finally said. Did she really have to explain to anyone else? In her mind she'd been engaged from the time Dan had proposed in November.

"I'm coming over tonight to see your ring. Did you select it or . . . ?"

Verna stopped her. "Michelle," she said quietly, "I didn't want a ring." The finality in her voice spoke volumes.

Immediately Michelle understood. "Gotcha." Her voice was subdued. "Have you discussed a date?"

"We talked about it, but nothing's been decided," Verna replied. "We like the idea of getting married on an island in the Caribbean. It's not like I have hundreds of people to invite."

Michelle thought of the big wedding Verna and Frank had been planning. His family was large. "Is that what you want?"

"It's my dream," Verna responded softly.

"Then make it come true," answered Michelle. "I'll help you in any way that I can. Will it be soon?"

"Probably right after the holiday hustle and bustle. We don't want to wait, so maybe February or early March." She paused. "We want to be together, Michelle. All the logistics of where to live and all that stuff will work itself out as we go along. But wherever it is, we'll have a place to call home."

Michelle smiled at the happiness she heard in her cousin's voice. "And that's wherever you'll be."

Christmas Day was cold, yet warm. Verna had been welcomed into Dan's family without the stiffness of first meetings, and today, so had Verna's small family. She looked around the large living room of Dan's mother's house. Michelle was at her best, talking with Paula and Marvin while the Hunter brothers and their wives joined in. Her aunt and uncle had taken to Mrs. Hunter and they were having an animated discussion while the youngsters were noisily comparing their presents.

Dan was standing with Verna, his arm loosely around her shoulders. "Happy?"

"Very," Verna smiled up at him. "You have a wonderful family." She looked suspiciously at him. "Did you know that they were going to turn this into an engagement party for us?"

Dan grinned. "Paula could never keep a secret." He watched his sister, who waved when she caught his stare. "She and Michelle are thick as thieves, aren't they?"

"Two of a kind and inseparable," Verna said, with affection.

Dan spoke in a voice only for her ears. "Would it look bad if we left a little early?"

Verna whispered back, "We're engaged. They'll understand."

An awesome shudder went through Dan's body as he fell to her side. The blood pounded in his brain as he sought to catch his breath. Verna's hand caressed his stomach and a guttural moan escaped. "Verna, sweet, I'm not ready for that." He kissed her curls then, eyes closed, sank against the pillows. "You're incredible, sweetheart."

Verna's breathing was quieting. The fire and passion that raged through her body was slowly dissipating. But her body still craved him and she wanted him to know it. She continued to massage him, her hands finding the contours and the crevices. She bent her head and suckled his rock-hard nipples. "I want you again," she murmured. She lifted her head and smiled wickedly. "Do you think you can get ready by the time I return?" She slid out of the bed and shamelessly stood naked before him.

Dan felt the heat in his loins. "Verna," he rasped.

Verna winked and slinked from the room.

Dan's eyes smoldered when seconds later he watched her return. "Come here, you tease," he muttered. When he held her atop him, he said, "Are *you* ready?"

There was no way that Verna could deny that she was. His erection pressing into her took her breath away, but she managed to whisper, "For you? Always, my love."

Soon after New Year's, as expected, the days got longer and lighter. The warmth of the holiday season disappeared, only to uncover bad tempers and rudeness associated with after-Christmas bill paying. But Verna and Dan were oblivious. The first two weeks of January they hardly saw each other but spoke daily over the phone, making plans.

Verna was sorting her Valentine's Day crafts, getting an order ready for shipment. The huge display she and Michelle had set up in the shop won oohs and ahs from the customers, and they were already selling faster than she'd expected.

"Aunt Neda," Verna said, "do you think we made enough?" It was the second Saturday in January, and her aunt had to keep rearranging the shelves and the display cases as the items disappeared.

Neda laughed. "You worry too much. The idea is not to have *any* left, Verna. After the fourteenth of February, I don't want to see another tussie mussie or frilly lace sachet." Her eyes twinkled. "That idea you had for the church pews was a winner. Did I tell you a woman called back? She wants to order a dozen tussies for her wedding in July."

"Really?" Verna was excited. "Did you tell her yes?"

"Of course not. I had to ask you first." Neda appeared indignant.

Verna was crestfallen. "Oh, Aunt Neda. You should have."

"I'm just kidding you, baby," Neda said. "Of course I placed the order."

"You did?" Verna brightened. "Don't do that," she scolded. "That will become a longtime customer, I hope."

Neda smiled. "You're really happy with your decision, aren't you?"

"Yes, I am," Verna said, with an answering smile. "Dan and I have discussed it and I plan to work part-time at the clinic and do my pillows and crafts at home. That way, when our baby arrives, nothing will change." She grinned. "Saves zillions in child-care."

Neda caught her excitement. "You and Dan plan to have children right away?"

"Immediately!" Verna blushed and her aunt chuckled. "Uh, yes, starting with our honeymoon, actually."

"Nassau, Bahamas," Neda mused. "You kids sure do things differently nowadays."

Verna gave her aunt a quick hug. "I'm glad you'll be there."

"Wouldn't miss your wedding day, baby."

Verna returned to a buying customer. The heart-shaped ivory and mauve moiré silk pillow was one of Verna's favorites. Her chest puffed with pride.

Dan was relieved. He walked around his workbench viewing his work from all angles, his critical eye looking for the merest imperfection. He ran his fingers over the smooth yew wood, checking for any hidden wet spots from the varnish. Satisfied, he grinned, and the tenseness left his shoulders. His engagement gift for Verna was almost ready. Carefully wrapping it in a soft cloth, he skipped up the basement stairs to use the phone. Fifteen minutes later he left the house. The jeweler would be waiting.

The day before Valentine's Day, Neda and Michelle objected violently to Verna stepping foot into the shop.

"Are you crazy, girl?" Michelle said. "It's being handled. Besides, we're closing early because everything is practically gone! I don't believe you wanting to come in here on Valentine's Day! And you flying off the day after to get married! Go on and have your day of beauty, and the next time I see you will be in Nassau."

On Valentine's Day, Dan was as skittish as a newborn lion cub. The wine server had just left and Dan could hardly find his tongue. Here it was, that day for lovers and he was finally living his dream. A chance meeting had led him to his sweetheart.

Verna looked pleased. They were in "The Bubble" in the Sequoia restaurant—the place where she'd accepted Dan's proposal. Tomorrow she was to become his wife, and what better place and time than to celebrate on this romantic lovers' day? She'd never been happier.

"Dan, I wouldn't want to be any other place. This is special to me," she said softly.

Dan smiled at her. *At last. Memories for us.* He was finally settled and he held his glass up for a toast. "And to me, sweetheart," he said. "To all our special memories."

When she set her glass down, Verna looked curious when Dan slid his chair next to hers. He slipped his hand in his pocket and pulled out a red velvet pouch.

"Sweetheart, this was made with all the love I have for you." Dan opened the drawstring, took out the jewel, and handed it to her. "My heart is in there," he murmured. "Happy Valentine's Day, Verna."

Verna gasped. The gold chain glittered, and the small, highly polished, amber-colored wood hearts dangled and sparkled with two large, round white diamonds. The hearts were entwined as though they were one. The brilliant stones were embedded in each center. Tears sprung to Verna's eyes and her voice trembled. "Dan, it's so beautiful. Where . . . when did you find the time?"

Dan was nearly choked up himself seeing the naked love for him in her eyes.

"All those days and nights that I couldn't be with you, love." He took it from her trembling hands. "Let me do that."

Verna fingered the pendant as it lay inside her V-shape neckline.

Dan kissed her, then returned his chair to its place across from her. He wanted to see if it did her justice.

"Perfect!" he murmured. The wood against her honey-gold skin looked just as he'd envisioned. And he'd finally given her diamonds. "You're perfect, love."

Verna wiped her glistening lashes. "Our engagement?" she murmured. Her fingers still caressed the diamonds.

Dan held her gaze. "Yes." He held out his hand and she squeezed it tightly.

"And memories?"

Dan kissed the palm of her hand. "Our special memories."

Dear Reader,

I hope Verna and Dan's story filled you with the spirit and love of Valentine's Day. Verna found it almost impossible to pack away cherished memories of her dead lover. She was of the mind that love doesn't strike twice in the same place. But Dan was of the mind that she was wrong and set out to convince her. With patience, love and the honesty to say what was in his heart, he won the love of his life. I'm sure if they could speak, you would hear them say—be kind to yourself—and think again about deferring your dreams.

Please look for PRECIOUS HEART very soon. I hope that Diamond Drew and Steven Rumford will touch your heart. I always welcome your comments, so please write and include a stamped envelope for a reply.

Thanks for sharing,

Doris Johnson
P.O. Box 130370
Springfield Gardens, NY 11413
e-mail: *Bessdj@aol.com*

Heart to Heart

Jacquelin Thomas

As always, I have to acknowledge the man who has been my best friend, lover, and father to our children. You have given me so much, but nothing compares to the giving of your heart. Saying thank you is hardly enough, so I give you my love in return.

One

The hair on the back of Jillian Ransom's neck stood up. A flicker of apprehension coursed through her as she searched the crowd of people bustling around her in the passenger terminal of the Houston airport. She hunted for the source behind the disturbing quakes in her serenity. She felt the sudden prickle of recognition. That woman! Her eyes landed on a woman standing a few feet away from her. Jillian went rigid with shock. It couldn't be—could it?

Her stomach clenched, Jillian picked up her carry-on and rushed toward the woman. She tried to call out but couldn't, her voice so filled with emotion. Her mind a crazy mixture of hope and fear, Jillian refused to take her eyes off the woman. Although her hair was longer, it had to be *her*. It had to be Kaitlin, her sister. She seemed agitated—almost as if she didn't want to board the waiting plane. A man was trying to calm her. Disbelief shook Jillian. Who on earth was he, and why was he with Kaitlin? Jillian's heart raced as she watched him usher Kaitlin along the busy corridor.

Before she could break into a run, someone clapped a hand upon her shoulder, and Jillian was stopped in her tracks by the steel-like grip. Whirling around in anger, she snapped, "What the—" Jillian stopped short. It was John Sanders, a family friend. Talking fast, she managed to say, "John, you're not going to believe this, but

I just saw Kaitlin. If we hurry, we can catch up with her . . ." Impaled by his steady gaze, she didn't finish her sentence. Jillian knew what was coming next. She stared sullenly ahead, her chin assuming an independent tilt.

"You probably saw someone who reminded you of her. You know she's dead. It's been six months. Think about it. Why would she be in Houston? If she could, I know Kaitlin would be home with you and the rest of the family. She wouldn't leave you all wondering."

She couldn't keep the frustration out of her voice. "You're right, John. I sound like Matt now, don't I?"

"I thought Ray and Garrick were trying to get him to leave Phoenix and come home."

Jillian nodded. "Matt's convinced she's still alive. God knows I wish he were right." She glanced over her shoulder in the direction that the woman had gone. "She looked so much like Kaitlin. She even walked like her. It was strange, John. Even before I saw her, I felt her presence . . ." Jillian shook her head sadly. "I know I sound insane."

"No, you don't," John assured her. "You and your sister were close. I understand what you're feeling. You're still grieving for her." He reached over and took her carry-on. "Let me lug this for you. It looks kind of heavy."

"It is." Jillian flashed him a smile of thanks. She was glad to be relieved of the burden. "Well, enough of me and my hysterics. What are you doing here in Houston?" she asked, although Jillian was pretty sure she already knew.

"I was here visiting my parents. They celebrated their fiftieth wedding anniversary this past weekend and my mother's birthday. They were married on her birthday. Dad said he did it to save himself a lot of grief in the long run."

Jillian was mildly surprised. She'd assumed his visit involved a weekend liaison with one of his many women. "That's cute. I think Prescott had the same idea with Mary. Her birthday is next week, and they were also married in January."

"Hey, it's not a bad idea. Now how about you? What are you doing here?" He looked her over seductively.

Smiling, Jillian replied, "I was here for a physical therapist convention." She glanced down at the plane ticket in her hand. "This is my gate."

"Looks like we're on the same flight home. Would you mind if we sat together?"

Jillian shook her head. "No, of course not." She took a seat while John spoke with a TWA representative about their seat assignments.

From where she was sitting, Jillian studied him. She knew he was thirty-six, four years older than she. John stood there, dressed in an expensive suit and looking devilishly handsome. She took in his tempting, attractive male physique. The set of his chin suggested a stubborn streak. His dark hair was cut short and lightly flecked with gray throughout. The salt-and-pepper effect complimented the soft toffee color of his skin.

John glanced over and caught her watching him. Jillian thought she detected laughter in his eyes, but she couldn't be sure. When he winked broadly at her, she warmed over like a schoolgirl in the throes of puppy love. His magnetism captivated her; however, John was a temptation she could not afford.

Holding his head high with pride, John made his approach. She pretended not to notice when he dropped down beside her.

"You know, I noticed earlier that you had this funny little smile on your face. What was that all about?"

"What are you talking about?"

"When you asked about my being here in Houston." A sparkle of humor crossed Jillian's face. "Oh. Well, it's no secret how much you love being a single man. I figured you were here visiting one of your many women."

John broke into laughter. "You've been listening to your brother."

Inclining her head, Jillian asked, "Is that your way of saying that it's not true?"

"It's not true. I'm not a player."

"Right. And I've grown three heads. Practically every time I've seen you, you've been with a different woman."

"I don't think that's true."

"It is. Matter of fact, I've never even seen you with the same wife twice."

John roared with laughter. "Hey, wait a minute. I've only been married twice. Now you know my first wife and I had a lot of problems—she couldn't leave other men alone."

Jillian nodded. "And your second one was straight crazy."

"Debra was on crack real bad back then, but I saw her a week ago and she looked good."

"Is she off the drugs now?"

"That's what she said, but she's said that many times before. For her sake, I hope she's telling the truth." Leaning closer to her, John whispered, "You know, they say that the third time's the charm."

She gazed into his warm brown eyes. "So, you're looking for wife number three?"

"Who knows. I might be. Are you interested in applying?"

Shaking her head, Jillian replied, "I think I'll pass. You're too much for me."

His gaze was as soft as a caress. "I think you just might be what I need."

"John, are you ever serious?" Jillian asked. She was not about to be swept away by the warmth of his words. She'd had her share of philandering men and wanted to move forward with her life. After all, she had an eight-year-old daughter at home. Jillian wanted to lead by example. This did not include bringing home a string of men.

"What would you say if I told you I'm very serious?"

Smiling, Jillian rose to her feet. "I'd say it's time we boarded the plane." She headed toward the door leading to the passenger transport vehicle. She could hear John laughing behind her.

Los Angeles, California

"I'm so glad to be back home." Trying to stifle her yawn, Jillian covered her mouth with her hand. "Please excuse me, John. I'm so tired."

"Me, too. I've ordered a car to pick me up. Need a lift?"

"No, someone will be here to pick me up." She embraced him quickly. "It's so good to see you again. You made the flight go faster for me."

"For me, too. I'm hoping to see more of you. And I don't mean just at the family gatherings on Sundays." Scratching his chin thoughtfully, John asked, "I've been asking you out for what—ten years now? And you keep saying no."

"Well you were either getting out of a marriage or we were both dating other people. The timing's been off. I think maybe it's a sign that we should just leave things the way they are. We'd probably make better friends than lovers anyway."

"I don't agree. I think we should see where it takes us." His eyes clung to hers as if analyzing her reaction.

Jillian reached for her carry-on, saying, "John, I need to get home to my daughter. I'll see you around."

"You know, I never figured you for a chicken."

She regarded him, resisting the urge to bite her lips. Jillian was not about to let this man bait her.

Seemingly amused, John leaned over and kissed her

lightly on the cheek. "I'm sure we'll be seeing each other soon."

In a surprising move, he walked away from her without another word.

Jillian watched him leave. A part of her wanted to call John back, but pride kept her from doing so. Slinging the leather strap of her carry-on across her shoulder, she turned to walk in the other direction.

"Jillian, right here."

Looking in the direction from which the voice had come, Jillian broke into a smile when she spotted her brother. "Hello, Ray." She hugged him tightly. "Thanks for picking me up."

"No problem. How was your trip?" He reached for her bag.

"Wonderful, but I'm glad to be home. You wouldn't believe who was on the plane with me."

Ray inclined his head. "Who?"

"Your friend, the player."

His eyes registered surprise. "John was on the plane?"

Jillian nodded. "He was in Houston visiting his parents."

"That's right. They moved there about two years ago, I think. Right before his grandmother died." Ray scanned her face. "I'm sure you two had a lot to talk about."

"Why would you say that?"

"I know John is attracted to you. I'm sure he spent the entire flight trying to ask you out."

Jillian couldn't hide her smile.

"See? I know the man."

Deciding to change the subject, she asked, "How's my baby?"

"Leah's fine. She was Carrie's little helper." Ray led her through the airport exit doors. He didn't speak again until they were in the car.

"So, what did you tell John?"

"What are you talking about?"

"Did you agree to go out with him?"

Her long lashes flew up and Jillian met his eyes. "No, I didn't, but what is it to you anyway?" Why was she feeling so defensive? she wondered.

"I was just asking, that's all."

For the remainder of the ride to Ray's house, Jillian stared out of the window. There was no way she'd ever consider dating John. They could never be more than friends, she thought sadly.

Carrie greeted them as soon as they entered the two-story house in Westwood. She stood on tiptoe to kiss her husband before reaching to embrace Jillian. "How was your trip?"

"Good. That is, until I went to the airport and nearly made a fool of myself." She followed Carrie into the family room while Ray went upstairs to check on the children. Jillian dropped down on the sectional sofa that graced the back wall.

Carrie frowned as she sat down beside Jillian. "What happened?"

Lowering her voice, she whispered, "I thought I saw Kaitlin."

Carrie was speechless in her shock.

Twisting her hands in her lap, Jillian conceded, "I know it sounds crazy, but just for one instance, I thought for sure she was still alive. If you could've seen this woman . . . I'm sure you would agree."

"I miss her, too. It's been six months since the plane crash and I still miss her. There are still times I reach for the phone to call her . . ." Carrie changed the subject when her husband strolled into the room by asking, "Where are the children?"

"In Bridget's room. Leah's getting her clothes together." Ray studied Jillian's face. "What are you not telling me, Sis? I can tell something happened. It wasn't just seeing John today, so what is it?"

Ray and Kaitlin had been very close, and she didn't want to upset him. "It's nothing. I guess I'm just really tired, that's all."

"You're lying," he accused.

"Ray . . ." Carrie began.

"Jillian, you look pale," Ray asserted. "Now tell me what happened."

She took a deep breath and exhaled. "I thought I saw Kaitlin today in the Houston airport. I know it sounds crazy, but this woman looked so much like her."

They sat silent for a few minutes.

Sighing, Jillian maintained, "I wish I could just let her rest in peace. I know she's gone."

"I think with Matt off somewhere searching for her, we're never going to lay her to rest. Not totally." Ray leaned over and took Jillian's hand. "Sis, we can't do this to ourselves. If Kaitlin were still alive, she'd be right here with us. Besides, the airport is the last place I think we'd find her."

"Everything you're saying makes sense. John practically said the same thing." Rising to her feet, Jillian strolled across the room and stood before the brick fireplace. "Did Leah behave herself?"

Carrie smiled. "She's a sweetheart. Leah practically took care of Bridget all by herself. She's helping Mikey with his bath. They should be down shortly."

"She loves babies."

"Mommy!"

Jillian turned at the sound of her daughter's voice. "Come here, sweetness. I missed you so much." She bent down to hug Leah.

"I missed you, too. Did you bring me anything back from Houston?"

Laughing, Jillian tickled her daughter. "I sure did. I

also have something for my handsome nephew and niece. Where's Mikey?"

"He'll be down in a few minutes. He's in his room getting dressed."

Carrie stood up. "I'd better go up and check on him."

"Here I come, Mom. I'm done." Mikey bounced into the room wearing a basketball-theme shorts set. "Hey, Auntie Jill."

"Hey, yourself," Jillian responded. "Are you going to give me a hug or what?"

Mikey rushed to her, hugging her tight.

Gesturing toward the kitchen, Carrie announced, "I'm going to check on dinner. It should be about ready."

Ray rose to his feet. "I'm going to check on my little girl. She should be waking up right about now. I'll be back in a few minutes."

Leah and Mikey followed Ray upstairs.

Jillian chewed on her bottom lip.

"What's the matter?" Carrie asked.

Sighing heavily, Jillian said, "I just wish Leah's father loved her the way Ray loves his children. She needs him."

"Do you ever hear from him?"

"No, and I really don't expect to. Byron was adamant about not having children. He's never wanted them."

"One would think he would change his mind. Especially once he got to know her. Leah is such a sweetheart."

Squaring her shoulders, Jillian played with the fringe on one of the sofa cushions. "He's not interested. Anyway, I keep telling myself that it's better this way. If Byron doesn't love her, then it's his loss. She's my daughter and I love her enough for the both of us. We don't need Byron."

"It's definitely his loss and I think he's stupid for not wanting to get to know his little girl. But like you said, she's better off without him in her life." Lowering her voice, Carrie added, "However, it still hurts like hell."

Jillian nodded. "That it does." When Carrie stood up, she rose to her feet. "Can I help you with anything in the kitchen?"

"No, just come keep me company. Now tell me how you liked Houston," Carrie said as she headed to the kitchen. "I've never been there, but it's a place I've always wanted to visit."

While they talked, Carrie prepared the children's plates. When she was done, Jillian carried them out to the dining room table. Her mind traveled to John Sanders, and she wondered how he was spending his evening. Briefly she wondered if he was alone.

Two

She loved coming home to Riverside. It had been ten days since her return from Houston. Jillian took the exit that would lead her to her mother's house. If her job hadn't taken her to Beverly Hills, she would never have left the Riverside County area. Jillian didn't relish the idea of commuting on a daily basis.

"Uncle Laine's here," Leah announced, gleefully. "Mommy, did you know he was going to be in town? I wonder if Aunt Thelma's with him."

Jillian parked her black Ford Explorer beside Ray's car. "No, honey, I didn't. I don't think he told anybody he was coming." Secretly, she doubted her sister-in-law was here. Laine and Thelma were already having problems in their short marriage of four months.

"Well, I'm glad he's here. Maybe he brought me a present." Leah rushed out of the car before Jillian could respond. She climbed out and followed.

The newly painted front porch with its railing made a bold statement. Another covered porch ran the length of the rear of the house. A row of Philadelphia Windsor armchairs lent an air of stateliness and formality to the broad front porch. Large Boston ferns flanked the front door.

Jillian stepped into a foyer bordered by the living room and the formal dining room, and proceeded past the open staircase to the family room.

When she entered the living room, she found Laine surrounded by children. As usual, he came without his wife and bearing gifts. Jillian waded through her nieces and nephews to plant a quick kiss on her brother's cheek. "Hello, stranger. I haven't talked to you in weeks."

Grinning boyishly, Laine nodded. "I know. That's one of the reasons I came home. I've been real busy with a case up until now." He gestured to a man standing nearby. "Do you remember my friend, Marc Chandler?"

Jillian glanced up at the handsome man standing beside her brother and nodded. "I sure do. It's good to see you again."

"You, too. It's been a long time." While they made small talk, Jillian heard the sound of another car pulling up.

"Uncle John's here," Mikey called out. All of the children raced outdoors to greet him. Jillian's sisters, Allura and Ivy, ran to a nearby window and peeked out.

"Humph. Here he comes with yet another woman," Allura observed. "Doesn't John date anybody more than once?"

Her attention perked up at the mention of John, but Jillian refused to let it show. Chewing on her bottom lip, she resisted the urge to peek along with the rest of the Ransom women.

Still standing before her, Marc was shaking his head and laughing. "John gets around."

"Yes, he does," Jillian muttered. She excused herself and moved across the room to speak to Ray. "Did you know John was bringing a date?"

Ray looked puzzled. "What's going on between you two?" He studied her face for an answer.

"Nothing." She answered a little too quickly. "Why would you ask a fool thing like that?" Shaking her head, Jillian mumbled, "I don't know about you sometimes." She made haste out of the room, her long denim skirt flaring.

"What was that all about?" Laine questioned.

Ray shook his head in confusion. "I don't have a clue."

Alone in the kitchen, Jillian gathered up all her strength

to keep herself in check. Ever since she'd run into John at the Houston airport, her emotions had been in constant turmoil.

"Why are you hiding out in the kitchen?"

Jillian turned around to face her older sister. "I'm not hiding, Ivy. I came in here to see if I could do anything to help Mama."

Her voice in a conspiratorial whisper, Ivy said, "You should come out and meet John's latest. She's a bankruptcy lawyer."

Jillian scoffed at the idea. "Why do I need to meet her? I'm not in financial trouble." In her opinion, the woman didn't look like John's type at all. She refused to acknowledge the fact that she'd only caught a glimpse of his date.

Observing her with a questioning gaze, Ivy reached for a carrot and stuck it into her mouth.

Jillian looked through the oven window. "I think the bread's almost ready." She stuck her hands in a pair of mitts before opening the oven. She was jealous, and there was no denying it. Picking up a butter knife, she stabbed the freshly baked cornbread.

"What did the bread do to you, dear heart?" Ivy asked.

Before Jillian could respond, John entered the kitchen. He greeted Ivy and moved forward, stopping in front of her.

His dark eyebrows arched mischievously. "I wondered where you were hiding."

Ivy took another carrot. "I'm going to check on the children."

John never took his eyes off her.

Grinning, Ivy left the kitchen.

Nervously, Jillian moistened her dry lips. "Hello, John. How are you?"

"I've been waiting for you to call me."

Her eyes dodged his. "I've been busy. Besides," Jillian gestured toward the family room, "looks like you have, too."

"Who—Karla? She's just a good friend."

Jillian nodded. "I'm sure."

The beginning of a smile tipped the corners of his mouth. "Sounds like you don't believe me."

"It doesn't matter, John. You certainly don't owe me any explanations."

"Jillian, I'm not trying to run some game on you."

She smiled. "That's because you can't. I know you much too well. Now go on and entertain your date." Putting both mitten-clad hands on his shoulders, Jillian pushed him out of the kitchen.

Half an hour later, everyone navigated into the huge dining room for dinner. Two long tables had been set up. The children were seated at a table in the breakfast nook. Jillian's youngest sister and housemate, Elle, decided to sit in there with them.

Much to her dismay, John sat directly facing Jillian. She knew he delighted in making her uncomfortable. She stirred uneasily in her chair and chewed her bottom lip.

"Stop that," he said softly. "You're going to ruin your lips."

She glanced nervously around the table to see if anyone was paying attention to them. They weren't and, for that, Jillian was grateful.

Why am I having such a hard time keeping my emotions under control? she wondered. *I've always managed before.* Jillian glanced over at Karla. The woman really was gorgeous. Perfect hair, perfect body . . . She was absolutely perfect and she made Jillian sick.

Her eyes met John's and held. From the amused glint in his brown eyes, he seemed to know what she'd been thinking. Jillian picked up her fried chicken and took a bite.

Laine nudged her in the arm. "You feeling okay?"

"I'm fine. Why?"

"You seem unusually quiet today."

"I noticed that myself," John commented.

Jillian gave him a narrow glinting glance. "I'm okay. I just haven't had much to say."

She was glad when dinner was over. Jillian rose quickly to assist her mother in clearing the table. Half an hour later, she and Allura had the kitchen clean. They moved to join the others.

Jillian entered the den in time to hear Karla announce she needed to leave.

"I'd better be heading home. Brad's going to meet me there," Karla announced. "It was so nice meeting all of you."

"Brad?" Jillian repeated. "Who's Brad?" she asked John, in a hushed whisper.

"Her fiancé," he whispered back. "I told you she was a good friend of mine. We used to work together. I'm going to drop her off and I'll be back. She just lives in Corona, so it won't take me long." His gaze traveled over her face and searched her eyes. "Will you be around for a while?"

Ignoring the tingling in the pit of her stomach, Jillian answered, "I'll be here."

John turned to leave. "I'll see y'all in a few minutes. I'm going to drive Karla home."

Jillian reluctantly took her gaze off him. When she did, her eyes met Ivy's. "What?"

"I didn't say a thing."

Wanting to escape the amused look she was getting from her sister, Jillian strolled outside. She hoped the brisk weather would help clear her muddled mind. John was getting under her skin. In truth, he'd been there for a long time.

"We can only be friends," she whispered. "Only friends." She pulled her denim jacket together, shutting out the nippy air. Watching Leah run around with her cousins brought on a rush of tears. Her daughter would never know her father. Byron wanted nothing to do with her.

Leaning against the bars of the iron fence surrounding the house, Jillian watched the children playing a game of hide and seek in the back yard. Her mother's house was nestled in the shelter of picturesque mountains and embraced by the endless heavens. It was chilly but her pre-occupation held the cold at bay.

"I think you owe me an apology," a bass voice whispered in her ear.

Jillian knew without turning around that John was standing there. She'd been so engrossed in her thoughts and watching the children play, she hadn't noticed his return. "For what?" She turned around slowly to face him.

"For thinking that I'm such a jerk. You think that after trying to get you to go out with me, I'd bring another woman out here. Karla and I are only friends."

"Okay, I admit I shouldn't have been so judgmental. I'm sorry."

"I forgive you."

Concealing her smile, Jillian returned her gaze to the laughing children. Sighing, she murmured, "They're so carefree. Sometimes I wish I could go back to being that way."

"You can, Jillian. Just relax and let go. Sweetheart, life's too short."

"I know all of that," she replied, a little too quickly.

"Laine's right. You seem different somehow. What's going on?"

"I've been thinking about Leah, and what I'm going to tell her about her father. She's starting to ask about him more."

"Why not tell her the truth?"

Jillian was quiet. She knew John had no idea why she and Byron had divorced. "Maybe. We'll see." Turning to face John, she said, "I'm getting cold. I think I'd better head inside."

Grabbing her hand, he pleaded with her. "Don't run away from me, please. There's something between us, Jillian. You know it and I know it. It's been there for ten years and I'm pretty sure it's not going to go away."

"John . . ."

His fingers stroked her arm sensuously. "Give us a

chance. For the first time, we're both free of any entanglements."

John looked as if he were about to kiss her. Backing away, Jillian chewed nervously on her bottom lip. "It wouldn't work."

"How do you know?"

Ray interrupted them, sparing further conversation. "Oh, there you are," he said to her. "I wondered what was taking you so long. Mama needs your help with something."

Without another word, Jillian rushed off. Another minute, and she wasn't sure what would've happened between John and herself. Her body was aching for his touch.

After seeing to her mother, she felt like she had her emotions under control. Jillian was a little disappointed to find that John had already left without saying good-bye. She decided to leave as well. "It's time Leah and I headed home."

"I'll be leaving within the next half hour, but I need to stop by Nyle's place, so don't wait up for me," Elle announced.

"I'll see you later then. Be careful," Jillian murmured. She bid farewell to her siblings and led Leah to the door.

"Call me before you leave," she demanded of Laine. "We need to talk."

He nodded. "I know, Sis. I'll call you this week. I'm going to be here until next Monday."

Jillian turned to Marc. "Take care of my brother. And talk to him."

"I'm trying." Marc leaned over and planted a kiss on her cheek. "Good seeing you again."

"You, too."

Leah ran ahead of her to the car. After unlocking the door and getting her daughter settled, she heard footsteps. Turning around, she found John standing a few feet away. "I thought you were gone."

"I wouldn't leave without saying good-bye."

"Bye, Uncle John. I love you."

He strolled around the front of the car. Reaching into the passenger window, John tickled Leah. "I love you, too, little miss. Now you be a good girl for your mom, okay?"

"I will."

Jillian climbed into her Explorer. "I'll see you later, John."

A sly grin spread over his face. "Is that a promise?"

Her heart gave a little jump and hung in her throat. Swallowing the lump and shaking her head, Jillian turned on the car. "Good night," she murmured, before driving away.

An hour later, they were home and she'd just gotten Leah settled into bed.

"Mommy, will you read me a story?"

"It's nine-thirty, Leah. No story tonight. You won't want to get up for school in the morning."

Folding her arms across her chest, Leah pouted.

Hiding her smile, Jillian murmured, "Goodnight, baby."

" 'Night, Mommy."

She stood in the portal of the doorway for a moment. Leah's room had been transformed into an airy oasis, with soft lavender paint and a nineteenth century Irish brass and iron bed dressed in periwinkle floral linens by Ralph Lauren. Jillian had spared no expense when decorating this room for her daughter.

When Leah closed her eyes, she turned off the lights and closed the door before heading to her own room. She stifled a yawn as she undressed. Showering quickly, she readied for bed.

Her thoughts of John brought on an unwelcome surge of excitement. Jillian had nothing against men or dating, but she had to be reasonable about this. She counted off the reasons on her fingers: John was a carefree bachelor; they'd been friends for years; he was her brother's best friend; John loved women—all women.

His words, spoken earlier, traveled to her heart. Perhaps he *was* ready to settle down. Maybe he was right. Their attraction had survived ten years. Feeling the heat of desire coursing through her veins, Jillian wondered if perhaps one night in his bed might do the trick. She shook her head in the negative. One night with John would only make matters worse.

John stood in the doorway of the physical therapy room at the Beverly Hills Physical Therapy and Sports Medicine Institute, watching Jillian work with a patient. He recognized the injured NBA player immediately. The man was paying more attention to Jillian than her instructions. John couldn't blame him.

Jillian's flawless ginger complexion reminded him of smooth satin. Her chin-length, medium-brown hair seemed to have a life of its own as it swung back and forth. He especially loved the honey-blond streak that softly framed her face. Many people paid to have streaks like that, but for Jillian, it was natural. She'd had that golden streak of color in her hair from the day she was born. Her well-shaped body offered no proof of her ever having given birth.

Spotting him, she turned her patient over to her assistant. She crossed the room in feminine strides, causing John's heart to pound faster. "What brings you here?"

He rewarded her with a playful pinch on the arm. "Hello to you, too. I came by to see if I could persuade you to have lunch with me."

Running her hands down her jeans, Jillian seemed to be struggling with a response. Finally she said, "I don't think we should, John. It wouldn't be a good idea."

"Why not?"

Folding her arms across her chest, she stood with her back against the wall. "You know why. We should just leave things the way they are."

"So two friends can't have lunch?"

"You want more than that."

"So do you," he threw back. John knew Jillian had every

right to be cautious where he was concerned, and he'd anticipated this reaction. However, he'd never been one to give up. This time he fully intended to make Jillian his.

"I need to get back to work, but thanks for the invite, John."

He grinned devilishly. "Okay for now. I'm not going to give up, you know."

Her lips curved into a smile and Jillian nodded. "Knowing you as well as I do, I wouldn't expect you to."

"Enjoy the rest of your day, and kiss Leah for me." Blowing her a kiss, John walked away. He could feel the heat of her gaze on him. Smiling, he knew that warmth would carry him through the rest of his day.

Ray and John were seated almost immediately after arriving at The Garden Room. Situated in the Westwood Marquis Hotel, the bright room, with its latticework design and green carpet, provided a garden-like setting.

Ray picked up his menu. "John, I need to ask you something. Is there anything going on between you and Jillian?"

"No, but it's not for lack of trying on my part." He downed the last of his beer.

"Jillian is my sister. I don't want to see her hurt." He laid the menu back on the table.

John's dark gaze met Ray's. "I wouldn't do that. I really care about her."

"If you're not ready to settle down, then it's best you leave her alone."

Ignoring Ray's warning tone, John pushed forward. "How would you feel if we started dating?"

Ray's expression was unreadable. "Jillian's a grown woman. She can see whomever she pleases. I just want her to be happy."

"So you won't have a problem with it?"

"Not as long as you treat her the way she deserves. You're my friend, John. My best friend. I know you have had your share of women, but I hope that's all in the past. If not, leave my sister alone."

"So then you won't have a problem with us seeing each other?" John asked again.

"It'll take some getting used to," Ray admitted. "But I know Jillian's had a thing for you for quite some time now."

"I want you to know something. I love your sister. I've been in love with her for a long time."

Ray was clearly surprised by his admission. "Does Jillian know?"

"She won't stop running long enough for me to tell her."

Ray threw back his head, laughing.

"Your sister and I are destined to be together. She's the only woman for me."

"It's not me you have to convince. It's Jillian." Shaking his head, Ray added, "I sure don't envy you."

Without replying, John returned his gaze to his menu, trying to decide between the roasted monkfish or lobster. He was going to need his strength for the chase.

Three

"Do you want me to get the phone, Mommy?" Leah called out.

"I'll get it, sweetheart," Jillian yelled from the kitchen. "It's probably for Elle anyway." She reached for the receiver. "Hello."

"Since you won't call me, I figured I'd just give you a call. I'd like to take you to dinner. It can even be an early dinner."

Jillian felt a warm glow flow through her as soon as she recognized John's voice. "I can't believe you're being so persistent, John. I thought by now you'd have moved on to someone else."

"What is it going to take to convince you that I'm ready to settle down with one woman?"

"I don't really know." She threw the last of the chopped onions into the large pot of simmering spaghetti sauce. "I'm not even sure you could ever convince me of something like that."

"Give me a chance, please. I know you're crazy about me. We need to do something about it."

Stirring the sauce, Jillian burst into a bout of laughter. "You really need to quit. That line is not going to work on me."

"I'm serious," he said, with quiet emphasis. "I thought you knew this but I'll say it anyway. I love you."

"Yeah, right."

"Name it. I'll do anything to prove how serious I am about you."

"Anything?"

"Anything. I mean it. I know you're the woman I want to spend the rest of my life with."

"I bet you say that to all of your wives."

"Ooow, that hurt."

An idea formed in her mind. Grinning from ear to ear, Jillian snapped her fingers. "I just thought of something. I know how you can prove it. Let's just get engaged right this minute. It shouldn't be a problem since we're both so ready to settle down."

John was quiet.

She waved at her sister, who'd just arrived. "Well, I've got to get off the phone. I need to help my daughter with some homework. Think about it and give me a call." Hanging up, Jillian threw back her head laughing. "I won't ever hear from him again."

"What's so funny?" Elle asked, as she laid her backpack down on the sofa in the family room. She entered the kitchen and immediately washed her hands in the sink.

"It's nothing," Jillian murmured, as she drained the water off the cooked pasta. "I think I just came up with a way to get John out of my hair for good."

Elle pulled out a head of lettuce, two cucumbers, and a tomato from the refrigerator. "You'd have to kill him for that."

Laughing, Jillian shook her head. "No, I think I came up with a great idea. I told him we'd have to get engaged."

After taking a quick breath of utter astonishment, Elle asked, "You did what?"

"You heard me right. I told him that we'd have to be engaged." Jillian prepared the garlic bread while Elle made the salad.

Elle's soft brown eyes narrowed. "What are you going to do if John agrees to your demand?"

"It wasn't a demand, and John agreeing to it is the last thing I have to worry about." Jillian opened an oak cabinet and reached in. "Would you call Leah down for dinner please?"

John's mouth was still hanging open when he hung up the phone. Was Jillian serious? He rose to his feet and strode over to the bar to pour himself a brandy. *No, she couldn't be. Not Jillian.*

Mulling over his drink, John couldn't shake the image of being married to a woman like her. She was every man's dream: a wonderful cook, a devoted mother, and fiercely independent. She maintained her own cars and owned an impressive collection of tools that could rival even the most devoted craftsman. Although he had yet to make love to her, John knew that she was a very passionate woman.

The more he thought about Jillian, Leah, and marriage, the more the idea appealed to him. He loved them both and couldn't imagine being without them. John had been there when Jillian gave birth. Leah was as much a part of his life as she was her mother's. Selfishly, he wished that she had been his daughter.

His thoughts jumped to Jillian's ex-husband, Byron. He didn't deserve a daughter like Leah. He'd never liked the way the man treated Jillian during their separation and divorce. He'd never even bothered to show up at the hospital the night Leah was born. John couldn't understand anything being more important than the birth of a child.

Carrying his drink with him, John headed into the kitchen to make dinner. By the time his fish and baked potato were ready, he had given himself enough reasons to walk away.

By the time he'd finished eating, his heart had convinced him to give Jillian what she wanted. Knowing her as well as he did, John knew she hoped he would just run the other way. Smiling to himself, he shook his head. *Running away is the last thing I'm going to do where you and Leah are concerned,* he thought.

* * *

"Hello, Elle." John embraced her when she opened the door. "How are your classes coming along?"

"Great. I graduate next year." She held up a thick textbook as she stepped aside to let him enter. "I'll be so glad when this year ends. I'm tired of studying." Frowning, she stated, "I don't know why Nyle wants to be a doctor. He's going to be in school forever."

He laughed. "I understand. I wasn't sure I was going to make it through law school." Turning around to face her, John asked, "Is your sister here?"

Nodding, Elle gestured upstairs. "She's trying to fix the sink in the bathroom."

"She still fancies herself a plumber?"

"You know it. Miss Fix-it. I'll see if I can pry her from the toolbox." Elle ascended a railed staircase that led to the upper level. "Jillian, there's someone here to see you," Elle announced.

Easing from under the sink, Jillian asked, "Who is it?"

Smiling, Elle responded, "Guess."

"John?"

Elle nodded.

"He's downstairs now? I . . ." She stood up, surprised, more uncertain than ever.

"Why don't you go downstairs and see what he has to say? Maybe he decided to turn you down in person."

"You're probably right."

Pointing to her sister's disheveled appearance, Elle suggested, "You should probably change out of your overalls."

"I don't think so. I don't need to dress up to get dumped." Jillian rushed down the stairs. After greeting John, she asked, "What are you doing here? I thought you'd be the last man I'd ever see again." Noting the heart-rending tenderness of his gaze, she felt a little nervous. Self-consciously, she ran her fingers through her hair.

Slowly, John sank into a nearby chair. "I'm sure you

know me well enough to know that I don't give up that easily."

Arms folded across her chest, Jillian remained standing. "And I hope you understand that I'm not going to change my mind," she said, as firmly as she could manage. "Before I'll go out with you, I have to know this relationship is going somewhere. Getting engaged will be proof."

Jillian made sure she wasn't standing in the path to the front door. She didn't want John knocking her down in his rush to leave. When he made no move to leave, she had no choice but to sit down on the sofa facing him. "Did you hear what I said?"

Leaning forward, John grinned. "I didn't think you would, and that's exactly why I'm here." Reaching inside his jacket, he pulled out a small black velvet box.

When he opened it, Jillian gasped. She wasn't prepared for this. This couldn't be happening. John was supposed to run the other way—not buy her an engagement ring. She moved to sit next to him for a closer look.

"Well, do you like it?"

The heart-shaped diamond glared defiantly at her. Jillian raised her head slowly, meeting his gaze. "It's incredible. John . . ." She paused, searching for the right words. "You shouldn't have—"

"You wouldn't be trying to back out of the terms you originally set, now would you?" His eyes raked her over.

"Well . . . er, no. Not really. It's just that . . ." Jillian frowned. "John, this is insane. I shouldn't have said what I did. I really didn't expect you to run out and buy me a ring. It's—"

"No," John interjected. He took her hand in his. "It makes perfect sense. We've both been through bad marriages, but it hasn't destroyed our belief in love and matrimony. I loved being married. I just want the right wife this time. I know you want the same thing. We both want to share our lives with someone. I care for you a great deal.

I've always cared for you. This ring is a token of just how much I care."

Unnameable sensations ran through her as his fingers caressed her hand. The pit of her began to burn. Jillian snatched her hand away. "This is so crazy!"

"What's crazy about it? Honey, I'm agreeing to your terms. Will you honor your terms and consent to marry me?"

Her head spun. "John . . ."

"I'd hate to have to take you to court."

Jillian stared at him before bursting into laughter. "Fine. I'll go out with you, but we don't have to get engaged."

"Yes, we do. You said you wouldn't change your mind. Well, neither will I. I want to marry you, and I want to be a father to Leah."

His admission nearly took her breath away.

"Will you agree to marry me? We don't have to rush. We'll take our time."

She opened her mouth to speak several times but no words would come. Jillian propelled herself to her feet. Rushing out of the living room, she ran upstairs to her bedroom, nearly knocking Elle down.

"Jillian, what's wrong?" Elle followed her into the master suite.

The rear wall of the room was made of glass and provided a view of the pool, the waterfall, and spa. Jillian stared out, seeing nothing.

"Jillian, are you alright?"

She turned around and walked toward her sister. "Elle, you're not going to believe this, but John asked me to marry him." She wasn't sure she believed it herself. Placing her hands on her face, Jillian massaged her temples. She eased down to sit on the edge of her king-size bed.

"You're kidding."

"He has an engagement ring. From the size of it, I'd say it's about two or three carats."

Elle was shaking her head in disbelief. "It's probably a fake. Remember what Carrie told us about Martin and when they were engaged? John is probably just using it to get you to go out with him."

"You know what, Elle? That's right." Waves of relief swept through her, but she also felt a thread of disappointment. "I wouldn't put it past him to do something like that." Jillian pushed off her bed. The more she thought about it, the more it made sense. "He knew I'd freak out. Well, two can play this game."

"What are you going to do?"

"I'm going to say yes to John." Hugging Elle, she mumbled a quick thank you, before heading back downstairs.

"I thought I was going to have to come upstairs to get you," John said, when she joined him. She sat down next to him.

"I'm sorry I ran off like that. Seeing the ring along with your proposing . . . It took me by surprise. I have to admit that I really wasn't expecting this."

"Do you have an answer for me?"

"I can't believe I'm about to say this, but, yes. Yes, I'll marry you."

John blinked twice and his mouth dropped open. "Did you just say yes?"

She burst into nervous laughter. "This is so crazy."

"You don't know how happy you've made me." Taking her hand, he placed the diamond on her finger.

Biting her bottom lip, Jillian stared down at the ring. It certainly looked real to her. The first thing she would do would be to take the ring to a jeweler and have it appraised. Then she would give John pure hell for trying to run a game on her.

Before she realized what was happening, John's hand held her chin and tilted her face up to his. Leaning forward, he brushed his lips gently against hers.

Jillian gave in to the unleashed desires of his mouth against hers. She kissed him with a hunger that sent flaming sparks through her.

John moved his mouth over hers, devouring her softness. His calm was shattered by the hunger of her response. Jillian wanted him as much as he wanted her, and the thought thrilled him.

His lips seared a path down her neck, exploring her soft velvet skin, and made their way back to her mouth.

She tried to speak, but her words were smothered on his lips. Her mouth parted eagerly beneath the crush of his, accepting the thrust of his tongue.

Like a fever, the wanting escalated between them both. Jillian pulled away reluctantly. "Elle's right upstairs." Her voice was somewhat strained.

John nodded his understanding. "I need to get back to the office myself." Breathing heavily, he rose to his feet. "I'll call you later. Kiss Leah for me."

Nodding, Jillian followed him to the door. There, he kissed her once more before he left. A few minutes later, she had changed clothes and was on her way to see a jeweler.

Jillian entered her bedroom in a daze, followed by a concerned Elle.

"That was quick. What did you find out?"

"It's real. The damn ring is real." Near tears, she dropped down on her bed. "John gave me a real engagement ring."

"I guess that means you're really engaged."

"And it's all your fault, Elle," Jillian snapped. "I never should've listened to you."

"I didn't tell you to go and accept John's proposal," Elle argued. "I only hinted that the ring may not be real. As it turns out, I was wrong."

Jillian looked bewildered. "What am I going to do?"

"Start planning your wedding?" Running, Elle dodged the pillow Jillian sent flying her way.

Jillian massaged her pounding temples. "I think I'll lie down for a while. Maybe sleep will help me think clearly."

"I'll pick up Leah from school," Elle offered. "That's the least I can do for you."

"Thanks," she mumbled, as she closed her eyes.

Jillian woke up an hour later to the sound of her daughter's laughter. She climbed out of bed and headed downstairs.

She found Elle in the kitchen preparing dinner and Leah in the family room playing a game on the computer.

Leah glanced over her shoulder and grinned. "Hi, Mommy."

Leaning over, Jillian planted a quick kiss on her daughter's forehead. "Hey, baby."

"Feeling better?" Elle asked when she joined her in the kitchen.

Jillian threw her hands up in despair. "I don't know how I'm going to get out of this mess. John and I can't be engaged."

Leaning against the formica counter, Elle eyed her sister. "Jillian, get a grip. John obviously loves you. He wants to marry you."

"I just don't know. Sometimes I think he does love me but then again, I'm not so sure."

"How do you feel about John?"

"I'm crazy about him. It's just that he's been married and divorced a couple of times. I know he wasn't at fault, but the fact remains that he's never been with the same woman twice—at least, I've never seen him with anyone more than once. I don't think he can be happy with one woman."

"Maybe they weren't the right ones. Maybe it's you."

Lounging carefully against the door frame where the large breakfast room flowed into the family room, Jillian expressed, "I don't know if I can afford to be so generous, Elle. I have Leah to think about."

"What about Leah? John treats her as if she's his child anyway."

"I know that. It doesn't change the fact that I don't want to bring men in and out of my daughter's life. And then there's the fact that Leah's very close to John. What if things don't work out between us?"

"John will always be there for you and for Leah. Sis, I believe he loves you. Personally, I think you should give the man a chance. He's made it known for a long time how much he cares for you."

Four

I'm getting married. Jillian and I are getting married. The thought played over and over in his mind. John couldn't believe that the woman of his dreams would finally be his. She had actually said yes.

A part of him wanted to do somersaults, his happiness was that great. Ray and Carrie skipped through his mind. They were a close and loving couple. He'd never envied Ray because his friend had gone through hell and back to have Carrie, and he deserved every ounce of happiness she gave him. But every moment he spent with them made him aware of an emptiness he'd never had filled inside him.

Whenever John drove to Riverside for the Ransom gatherings, he experienced the same hollow feeling. It was just a small hole, one he usually could overlook or ignore. It wasn't something he could ease by going from one woman to the next. Only Jillian could ease that lonely ache.

Cup of coffee in hand, John sank into one of the living room chairs and stretched long legs out before him. His mind traveled back to the kiss he'd shared with Jillian. It was like the soldering heat that joined metals. John's lips still burned in the aftermath. Their union would be a passionate one.

Smiling, John reached for the telephone. He wanted to hear her voice again. When Jillian answered, his heartbeat throbbed in his ears.

"It's funny that you called. I was just thinking about you."

John smiled. "You don't know how happy you've made me by saying that."

They sat silent a moment until he spoke up. "Do you have any plans for tomorrow night?"

"No, actually I don't."

"I'd like to take my fiancée to dinner, if you don't mind."

"What time should I be ready?"

"Eight o'clock fine with you?"

"Great. Should I dress any special way? I know your penchant for the dramatic."

He burst into good natured laughter. "Put on your best dress."

"I'm actually looking forward to this."

"I'm glad to hear that. I want to make our date one you will never forget." They talked for a few minutes more before hanging up.

John downed the last of his coffee before reaching for his telephone book. He had to make arrangements for his date with Jillian.

"So you and John are actually going out on a date?" Elle asked Jillian from the doorway of her bedroom.

Stretching out on the bed, Jillian nodded. Propping herself up on pillows, she stated, "We're doing things backward, I guess."

"So when are you two going out?"

"Tomorrow night. Leah's spending the night with Kelsey."

"Hmm. Does that mean I need to stay over at Ray's?"

Jillian gave an exasperated sigh. "No, it does not. John and I may be engaged, but I'm not jumping into bed with him." She didn't confess that she'd been giving the idea some consideration not more than a few minutes before. She'd begun lately to feel the emptiness of her life without a man with whom she could share it. Jillian often sought out solitude, but it was quickly becoming a state of loneliness.

She longed to feel the strong arms of John around her, and the thought of the two of them married excited her. She had always dreamed of marrying John and having more children.

Her hair was a mess! Groaning, Jillian pulled her fingers through the tight curls. It wasn't supposed to be this curly. Dressed only in a robe, she sat down on the plush cushion of her vanity bench and took deep breaths to calm herself.

She was nervous about her date with John. Jillian wanted to look her best, but her hair simply wasn't cooperating. She looked like she was trying to reinvent the afro. Eying a turquoise-colored spray bottle filled with water, she decided to try something she'd seen Elle do. Spraying a light mist, Jillian smiled as the curls began to loosen.

Ten minutes later, with her hair styled to perfection, Jillian rose to her feet. Crossing her bedroom, she slipped her dress off the hanger and stepped into it.

The phone rang. Muttering a string of curses, Jillian answered it.

"Hi, it's Allura. I know Elle is at the library on campus studying. But what are you doing tonight? Trevor and I want to spend some quality time alone and we need a babysitter."

"Then you need to call Carrie or Ivy. I'm going out." Jillian pulled the phone away from her ear when Allura screamed.

"Going out? YOU? With who?"

"Yes, I'm going out, and it's none of your business with whom."

"Well, who's watching Leah?"

"She's spending the night with a friend from school."

"Oh, I see. Girl, it's about time you got your groove back," Allura stated, in bubbly exultation.

"It's not like that. Get your mind out of the gutter, will you? Leah's sleepover has been planned for two weeks."

"Come on, Sis. Who is he? He has to be pretty special if you're going out with him. You haven't dated in years."

"Thanks for reminding me, Allura. Look, call Carrie or Ivy. I'm sure one of them will babysit for you. I'll see you all on Sunday."

"Have fun."

"I will. Thanks." Jillian hung up. The heart-shaped diamond caught the light of her bedside lamp, casting a rainbow of blazing colors onto the wall. Rising to her feet, Jillian whispered to the empty room, "What in the world am I doing?"

The man was an African-American work of art. Jillian's eyes traveled up and down the length of John. When her eyes met his, she gave him a big smile.

He gave her a chaste kiss on her cheek before saying, "You look exquisite, as always."

"Thank you, John."

As they headed out to the car, Jillian noticed he was watching her intently. "What is it?"

"I keep pinching myself. I can hardly believe that we're actually going on a date together."

She tried to suppress her laughter. "I can hardly believe it myself."

"You have a beautiful laugh. I love hearing it."

Jillian's eyebrows rose in amazement, but she said nothing.

After she was seated in the car, John presented her with a beautiful corsage. Reaching up, she guided his face to hers. Jillian kissed him. "I never knew you were such a romantic. Thank you."

"This is your night, sweetheart." John walked around to the driver's side and climbed in.

"Where are we going?"

"It's a surprise."

Jillian knew John was trying to make their first date special, and she was touched beyond words. She had a feeling that this was indeed a night she wouldn't soon forget.

She recognized the restaurant immediately. It was La Maison. When they entered, she glanced around the dining room. "Are we the only ones here?"

"Yes. Tonight I don't want to share you with anyone. Your beauty is for my eyes only."

Jillian's mouth twitched with amusement. "I take it we're cooking our own dinner, then?"

Delight flickered in the eyes that met hers. She loved his gentle camaraderie, his subtle wit. She enjoyed the friendly bantering as much as he did.

John threw back his head and laughed. "Okay, so I'll have to share you with the waiter and the chef." He pulled out a chair for her. After Jillian was seated, he took a seat across from her. Pulling out a thick envelope, he said, "I have something for you."

"What is it?" She opened the envelope and removed a set of papers.

"It's copies of my medical history. I want you to know that everything you may believe about me isn't true." His voice broke with huskiness. "I'm not the player you think I am."

"Really?"

"I know I've dated a lot of women. I've been married twice, but I don't sleep with every woman I meet. And for the most part, I've always practiced safe sex." Pointing to the papers in her hand, he added, "As you can see, I've never had any type of sexually transmitted disease."

"I see." Jillian looked up at him.

"Why are you looking at me like that?" John stared back in waiting silence.

Handing him back the papers, she asked, "Do you really think this was necessary?"

His eyes darkening with emotion, John nodded. "Yes, I do. When you become my wife, I don't want you to have any worries. I have no children and I've never had anything for you to worry about. I don't smoke, and I drink on occasion. I don't eat red meat, and I'm very healthy. I even have a healthy sperm count."

Jillian burst into embarrassed laughter. "I don't know if I needed to know all that."

"Of course you do. I want children and I know you want more."

"I also want the father around to help raise them. Your batting record with marriage is horrid."

"It wouldn't be that way with us." His gaze came to rest on her questioning eyes.

"How can you be so sure?"

"Because I've never loved anybody the way that I have loved you these past ten years. Do you know that one smile from you brightens up my whole day?"

She was a little stunned by his admission. "I don't know what to say. I've never heard you talk this way."

"You've never given me the chance."

"Don't you think we're moving much too quickly, John?"

He shook his head. "No, sweetheart. I don't think we should wait another moment. We've wasted ten years, Jillian."

Jillian groaned as she glanced around her home. Bold columns and large windows added style and elegance to the design of her condo. It was Saturday and her weekly cleaning day.

The doorbell rang.

She opened the door. "Ivy! I didn't know you were coming by today, especially this early." Moving aside to let her sister enter, she asked, "Do you know what time it is?"

"It's eight in the morning. Now that we've gotten that

out of the way, why didn't you tell me that you were going out with John Sanders?"

"How did you find out?" She glared over at Elle, who was standing nearby with the vacuum.

"I didn't say a word."

"Ray figured it out and told Carrie. And she told me and Allura."

Shaking her head, Jillian muttered, "I should have known." She resumed her dusting.

"Why are you being so secretive? You've had the hots for him forever."

Glancing over her shoulder, she snapped, "What?"

"Surely you didn't think nobody knew? Everybody knows, even Mama."

"Great."

"Anyway, that doesn't matter. Now tell me this. Did you and he—"

"Don't even go there, Ivy," Jillian interjected quickly. She was glad she'd taken off the ring earlier. Her sister would have a field day with that little piece of news. She was somehow going to have to break the news to her family, but Jillian had no idea when.

"But you did kiss him, right?"

"If you are going to hang around, you might as well help clean up."

Frowning, Ivy glanced around the room. "What is there to clean? This house is always spotless."

Throwing her a cloth, Jillian said, "You can help me dust. Start over there on the glass sofa table."

"Okay, I'm dusting. Now tell me about your date."

"There's nothing to tell, Ivy. We had a nice dinner. Have you been married so long that you've forgotten what it's like to go out on a dinner date?"

"Well, yeah. It's been a long time."

The three women burst into laughter.

"I guess I'd better have a little talk with my brother-in-law."

"Humph. Somebody needs to give the man a hint." Ivy

moved on to the coffee table situated in the center of the room. "I couldn't have all this glass in my house. You must clean these tables every day."

"No, just every other day."

An hour and a half later, the three women had the house spotless.

"Now that we've cleaned your house, how about we go to mine and you help me clean up. I'll take you two to lunch afterward."

Grinning, Jillian nodded. "As long as we're going to Aunt Kizzie's Back Porch. I'm dying for some beef short ribs and collard greens."

"What about you, Elle?"

Pulling the vacuum, she replied, "Let me put this away and I'm ready. Do you think we should invite Carrie and Allura?"

Jillian picked up her purse and keys. "It's okay with me. Just don't tell them about the cleaning up part. They can just meet us at the Marina. I don't think I want to spend the entire day as a rotating maid."

"So how was your date with John?" Allura asked, as soon as Jillian stepped into her mother's house the next day. Most of her other brothers and sisters were already there.

She glanced over at Elle and rolled her eyes heavenward. "We just got here. Can I please sit down and rest a minute?"

"Why are you stalling?" Allura insisted. "You know we all want to know what happened."

"If you hadn't been too busy to have lunch with us yesterday, maybe you would've heard all the details."

"Don't even try it. Carrie said you wouldn't even talk about your date. What's the big secret?"

"It's no secret. John picked me up. We had dinner. He took me back home. End of story."

Pointing to the ring on her finger, Ivy shook her head.

"Oh, no, you don't, dear heart. There's a lot more to this story. Come on, out with it, Jillian."

She turned around, looking to Elle for help.

Shrugging, Elle suggested, "I think you'd better tell them. They're going to find out anyway."

"Tell us what?" Ray asked.

Playing with the ring on her finger, Jillian prayed for courage. This was not going to be an easy task.

"What is it, dear?" her mother probed. "Is there something we should know?"

Jillian was aware that Elle had eased away to leave her standing alone to face her family. All eyes were on her.

"Jillian?" Ivy prompted. "Don't keep us in suspense."

"It's quite simple really. John and I are engaged."

Five

"YOU'RE WHAT?" they all chorused.

Jillian swallowed hard, lifted her chin, and boldly met each gaze. "You all heard me. It seems that John Sanders and I are engaged."

"Congratulations, I think," Carrie offered. "John is a very nice man."

Giving Jillian a narrow look, Ray rose to his feet. "Where is John? I want to talk to him."

"He just pulled up," Ivy announced. "Boy, I can't believe this."

Handing Bridget over to her sister-in-law, Daisi, Carrie rose quickly to her feet. "Ray, it's not our business, honey." She grabbed him by the arm. "Stay out of it."

"I'm going to have a talk with him. This is my sister. I don't know what John's up to, but I'm going to find out."

Jillian blocked his exit. "Listen to your wife, Ray. This is between John and me. Now I want all of you to listen up, my well-meaning but nosy brothers and sisters. I love you all but this is my life and I will live it as I choose. Understand?" Her tone brooked no argument.

"But—" Ray began.

"But nothing," she cut in promptly. "You wouldn't listen to me when I told you not to marry Lynette. Laine wouldn't listen when I told him not to marry Thelma . . ."

He enfolded her in a gentle embrace. "Sis, we're not

trying to tell you what to do," Ray argued. "We're just concerned for your happiness."

"I know that and I appreciate your concern. However, I will not allow you all to gang up on John. If he hurts me, I'll deal with him personally—I don't need your help."

At that moment John stepped into the house. In his usual charming manner, he greeted everyone. Crossing the room to stand beside Jillian, he asked, "Did Jillian tell you our news?"

"That and more," Elle muttered, before seating herself beside Daisi and Garrick.

Ray held out his hand. "Congratulations, John. Take care of my sister."

"Ray . . ." Jillian's tone held a warning.

Garrick rose to his feet and crossed the room in quick strides. "Welcome to the family, John."

After everyone congratulated them, Jillian took John by the hand and whisked him outside. She wanted to talk to him away from her family.

John turned her to face him. "Why do I get the feeling that I've walked in on something?"

"That's probably because you did."

"I take it they didn't take the news too well."

"I think it's because it happened so fast. They weren't expecting this. I'm sorry I put you in this predicament."

John pulled her into his arms. "I love you, Jillian, and I plan to be the best husband and father I can be. I've wanted you my whole life, it seems."

Wrapping her arms around his neck, Jillian stood on tiptoe to plant a kiss on his lips. "You know something, I believe you. I really do." After giving him another kiss, she said, "I'm so glad you're in my life."

Standing on the porch, Amanda Ransom cleared her throat loudly.

Embarrassed, they pulled away from each other.

"I would like to talk to you two. Could you come inside?"

Jillian and John exchanged nervous glances.

"I guess we should go on and get this over with. Your brothers didn't bother me but your mom . . ." John shook his head. "I don't ever want to tangle with that lady."

Jillian agreed wholeheartedly. She'd take on her siblings any day of the week. Her mother was a different story. "Let's go. We shouldn't keep her waiting," she mumbled under her breath.

They followed Amanda into her downstairs bedroom. She waited until they were all seated before asking, "Are you two really engaged or are you two playing a joke on the others?"

"It's not a joke, Mama. I know this happened quickly, but I want you to know that we're not going to rush into marriage. We're going to take our time."

Amanda relaxed visibly. "I'm so glad to hear that. I know that you two have been fighting your attraction to each other for years, but I think you should spend some time together as a couple. You've already built a foundation based on friendship, but now you've added a new level to your relationship. There's an adjustment period."

"Does that mean we have your blessing?" John wanted to know.

"Yes. John, you may not know this, but Jillian's father and I got married seven days after we met."

His look was one of surprise.

"It was love at first sight for us and it lasted up until his death twelve years ago. However, it was hard, and we separated three times within the first five years. We didn't really know each other. He was set in his ways and I in mine."

John nodded his understanding.

"We became good friends. In fact, he was my best friend. But mostly, we had a wonderful marriage. And that's the way it should be."

"It's what we both want, Mama. We're not taking this lightly."

Amanda looked relieved. "Welcome to the family, John." She gave a tiny laugh. "I don't know why I'm saying that. You've been a member of this family since you were knee high to a duck." She rose up slowly with the aid of her quad cane. "I guess we should go out and join the others." Her voice rose an octave. "I wouldn't be surprised if their ears were glued to the door."

Hearing a scuffling noise outside the room, Jillian, her mother, and John burst into laughter.

"Uncle John, are you busy right now?" Leah asked.

Putting down the empty paper plate he'd been holding, he said, "I always have time for you, Little Miss. What's the matter?"

"Are you really going to marry my mom? I heard Uncle Ray talking to Uncle Garrick."

"Yes, I am. Remember what I told you a few months back?" When she nodded, he continued, "Well, I meant it. I love your mom very much."

Looking down at her hands, she asked, "Do you w-want children?"

"Yes. But you know something else? I really want to be your daddy. I want you to be my daughter."

Leah's eyes were bright. "Really? You want me, too?"

"Of course. You and your mother are a package deal. I don't want one without the other. I love you both. Hey, I was there when you were born, remember? I've even changed your diapers, Little Miss."

"Uncle John . . ." Leah burst into embarrassed giggles.

"I'm going to tell you a little secret. But you can't tell anyone, okay?"

"I won't Uncle John. I promise."

His voice became hoarse with emotion. "In my heart, you've always been my little girl."

Wrapping her arms around his neck, Leah murmured, "I love you, Uncle John."

"I love you, too."

She bent down to retrieve the plate he'd laid on a nearby table. "I'll throw this away for you."

John's eyes followed her until she left the room. Once more he wished she'd been his.

"You're a good man, John," a voice behind him said. Garrick strode around the sofa and took a seat beside him. "It's about time you stopped playing around. I don't know why you and Jillian didn't hook up a long time ago."

John couldn't help but grin. "You know your sister. You can't make her do anything until she's good and ready."

"You're right about that."

Laine soon joined them. "When did all this come about? I didn't even know you and Jillian were dating. I guess I've been out of touch for a while."

"Not really. We weren't dating. In fact, we got engaged before we ever went out."

"Excuse me?" Laine glanced over at Garrick. "Is this for real?"

John broke into laughter. "This is what happened. The official story. When Jillian and I saw each other in Houston—"

"Hold up, John. I want to hear this story myself," Ray announced. "When we talked, all you mentioned was dating. Nothing about marriage ever came up."

Soon the entire Ransom family was gathered around. When Jillian pulled up a chair and sat down, John began his story.

When he was done, everyone sat staring at the couple in amazement. All of a sudden, Laine burst into laughter. The rest of the family immediately joined in.

"Dear heart, I'm impressed," Ivy commented. "Most men would take off and run the other way."

Gazing at Jillian, John nodded. "But you see, that's what your sister planned. It just kind of backfired."

"In a good way though," Jillian admitted.

Daisi spoke up. "I can't say I'm too surprised. Jillian's never been one to put up with much from anybody. She likes to cut away the fat and just get to the meat of the matter."

"You two are off to a rather spirited beginning,"

Amanda stated. "Your marriage should be anything but boring."

Jillian rewarded her mother with a smile of gratitude. It meant a lot to have her mother's blessing. If Amanda Ransom was at ease about her impending marriage, then her siblings would follow her lead.

Six

Standing just outside her door, John kissed her lightly on her forehead. "What are you thinking about, sweetheart? You were so quiet on the way here."

"I've been thinking about Mama and what she said. Are you sure that you're ready to settle down, John? I don't want another divorce."

He wanted to wipe away all of her fears. Following her into the family room, John answered, "Yes, honey. I'm very sure that you're the only woman I want."

"I overheard your conversation with Leah earlier. Thank you for saying what you did. It meant a lot to both of us."

"It's the way I feel. I've loved Leah from the first time I saw her in your arms. Byron doesn't have a clue as to what he's missing. One day he will though, and it's going to be too late."

"Byron's never wanted to be a father," she replied thickly. "He made that clear before we were married."

"The man's a fool." John spit the words out like they were a bad taste in his mouth. "I don't know what happened between you two, but the man shouldn't dismiss his own child."

She felt an instant's squeezing hurt. "He's never tried to have a relationship with her. He just sends money each month." Jillian tried to swallow the lump that lingered in her throat.

"Leah's not hurting for love, sweetheart. She has your

entire family wrapped around her finger and she's even got me. You know, I used to try to imagine what it would be like to hold my own child for the first time." He shook his head in wonder. "It has to be the most incredible feeling in the world."

"It is." She exhaled a long sigh of contentment. "Leah is the one thing I've done extremely well. She's all the good in me."

"You're a magnificent mother, Jillian." He inched closer. "That's why I want you to be my baby's mama."

His hands slipped up her arms, bringing her closer. "Nothing can ever break us up, honey. I want you to know that. You own my heart, Jillian. And although you have yet to admit it, I know I have yours. Heart to heart."

She wound her arms inside his jacket and around his back. "I do care a great deal for you, John. It's just that love is not a word I've ever used lightly. I do have strong feelings for you—"

"You love me," he interrupted. "You love me and you're afraid to say the words. That's okay. When the time is right, girl, you'll be yelling them across the ocean."

"I don't know what I'm going to do with you."

John moved closer. "Why don't you kiss me, for starters?" She kissed his cheek. "How's that, Mr. Sanders?"

"I know you can do better than that with those sexy lips of yours."

Jillian pressed her mouth to his, savoring every moment. For the time being, she was glad she'd decided to ride with John and let Elle drive her car home with Leah.

John showered kisses around her lips and along her jaw. His lips were warm and sweet on hers, setting her body aflame.

Suddenly she was lifted into the cradle of his arms and carried to the sectional sofa, where John placed her down gently. Parting her lips, Jillian raised herself to meet his kiss. She had a burning desire, an aching need for him.

John started to unbutton her shirt, until Jillian stilled his hand.

"What's the matter, sweetheart?"

"Elle and Leah are going to be home pretty soon. I don't think they should find us like this."

Groaning, John raised himself up.

"I'm sorry."

"It's okay, sweetness. I understand completely. Besides, I'll have you for the rest of my life." He strode across the room to stand in front of the fireplace. John pointed to a photograph of a younger Jillian in her military uniform. "I love this picture of you."

"It's okay. I look scared to death."

"I think you look beautiful." John crossed the room, taking his keys out of his pocket. "I'd better head home before I'm not able to leave."

Jillian laughed and followed him to the door. "Call me tomorrow."

Standing in the doorway, John glanced over his shoulder and blew her a kiss. Right before he closed the door, he whispered, *"Ich liebe dich."*

Having spent two years in Germany during her stint with the Marines, Jillian knew he'd just proclaimed his love for her. Wrapping her arms around her waist, she smiled and headed upstairs.

Leah had finally drifted off to sleep, and Elle was in her room studying. Jillian decided to work off her sexual frustration with aerobics. She'd been celibate for the last five years, but tonight she'd wanted to throw it all away by making love to John.

She panted harder, as she pushed herself with the weights. All those years of fantasizing about John and what it would be like . . .

Jillian laid the weights down and picked up a towel. She gave herself a mental shake. She'd done the right thing by waiting, she told herself. She had to be sure of her feelings for him. She always thought with a clearer head after a vigorous workout.

Jillian did one last stretch before calling it quits. John was right. She was in love with him. She had been for years but for so long she'd denied it, even to herself. She was afraid—afraid that John would wake up one day and decide he wasn't ready to settle down.

She forced herself to think positively. If anything, John was a very honest man. He wouldn't tell her something he didn't mean. A warm sensation filled her as she recalled his declaration of love in German. He loved her and he wanted to marry her. He even wanted to have babies. Jillian giggled. She felt like pinching herself. Her dream was coming true.

Turning on the shower, she decided John was right. He was her future. She would never love another man the way she loved him.

"Mr. Sanders, here's the motion for dismissal." The secretary handed John the stack of papers.

He glanced over them, nodding his approval. "Thanks, Becky."

She headed toward the door then stopped and looked over her shoulder. "Oh, Miss Woods is here to see you."

John frowned. "Sara?"

Becky nodded.

"Send her in. And Becky, hold all of my calls please." John stood up and greeted the slender woman as she entered. He and Sara used to work together and for a time they were lovers. When he left to start his own practice, they parted ways.

John hadn't seen her again until three months ago. After a couple of sexual encounters, he decided not to travel down that same road with her, and he ended the relationship once more. His mind wondered at the purpose of her visit. He waited for her to sit down before reclaiming his seat. "Sara, what are you doing here?"

"I needed to see you, John. I came here because I have to tell you something." She took a long breath before continuing. "I really don't know any other way to say this except to come straight out with it. I'm going to have a baby."

He sat straight up in his chair. "What?"

"I'm pregnant. It must have happened our last night together."

John counted back in his mind. "That was two months ago. Besides we used a condom." Twisting his face in a frown, he said, "I thought you were on birth control."

Sara shrugged. "The condom broke, remember? Anyway, I didn't have my diaphragm in that night. But regardless of how it happened—it did."

John rubbed the palm of his hands over his face. "I don't believe this."

"It's true, John. You're going to be a father." Sara stood up. "I did a lot of thinking about this, and I decided it's time I had a child. I'm thirty-five years old. I'm not getting any younger, you know."

Stunned, John mumbled, "I always figured you to be a career woman."

"I am. However, I'm sure I can manage my career and a baby. Women have been doing it for years."

"You've never talked about having a child." He eyed her warily. "In fact you've always said you didn't want any."

"I know. It's the way I felt at the time. I admit the timing's off, but there's nothing we can do about it. We are going to have a child."

John could not believe what he was hearing. This could not be happening to him. He didn't want to believe it. Panic raged inside him. He and Jillian . . .

"You can wipe that panicked look off your face. I'm not looking for marriage, if that's what you're thinking." She sighed heavily.

"But," he prompted.

"Well, you know how stuffy some of the partners can be. You've worked there. This could seriously affect my chances for being a partner—not being married and having a child."

John shook his head. "They can't do that."

"Yes they can, and they will." She sat down in one of the chairs facing him. "We've always made a great team—"

"Sara, I'm seeing someone," he asserted.

"That's nothing new. John, I'm not looking for love. We could be married in name only. After a year, we'll get quietly divorced."

"You don't understand. I'm engaged."

Sara's big eyes grew even bigger. "You're kidding. YOU?" She burst into laughter.

"It's true. I'm getting married, Sara."

"How's she going to feel about your little bundle of joy? Do you think she's still going to be willing to marry you?"

"I don't know," he replied quietly.

"I hate to break it to you like this, but I don't think so. I know I wouldn't."

John had a feeling she was enjoying every minute of this. "You've always been selfish."

"Tsk, tsk. No need to get nasty, John. I didn't plan this, nor did I do this by myself."

"I'll do all I can for the baby, Sara. You don't have to worry about that."

"This baby and I are a package deal. You can't have one without the other. You'd do well to remember that." She rose to her feet. "I've got to go. I'm due back in court shortly." Swinging her purse on her shoulder, Sara strode out, leaving him alone to digest the news.

Becky peeked in. "Are you okay?"

He glanced in her direction. "I'll be fine. Did you need something?"

"No, Miss Woods told me that I should look in on you. Did something happen?"

"Nothing I can't handle," he lied. John was scared. For the first time in his life, he was afraid of losing someone.

He found Jillian with her head stuck beneath the hood of her Explorer. His eyes grew wet as he watched her check the oil. This was not going to be easy, and although he'd prayed fervently, he had a strong feeling that he would lose Jillian over this.

Clearing his throat noisily, John reached for her. "Hello, sweetheart."

She turned around in his arms. "John, what a surprise. I didn't know you were coming over. Look at me, I look a mess." She set a quart of oil on the ground.

"You look beautiful. Come over here. I want to talk to you."

"Sure. I was going to call you later and invite you over for dinner. Now that you're here, I can scratch that off my list." She glanced up. His expression was one of sadness, and it prompted her to ask, "You can stay for dinner, can't you?"

"Jillian, do you think you could take a few minutes to sit down, so we can talk?"

He could read the fear in her eyes.

"What is it, John? You look horrible."

Rubbing his face with the palm of his hands, he uttered, "I don't know how to say this. I can hardly believe it myself."

She reached for his hand and he knew she was searching for a way to comfort him. "Well, what's wrong? Tell me."

He turned to gaze at her. "It seems that I'm about to become a father."

Jillian drew back her hand as if she'd been bitten. "Excuse me? What did you say?"

"I'm going to be a father."

Seven

Jillian was speechless. At the moment, all she could think to do was rise to her feet and head into the security of her house. She walked briskly to a bathroom downstairs and washed her face and hands. When she came out, John was waiting for her in the living room.

"Honey, this doesn't have to change things between us. I'll do right by my child, but I still want us to get married."

She gave a massive sigh and rubbed her palms over her face. Jillian paced back and forth in her living room, her arms flying. "I don't know, John. I really don't know."

"What are you talking about?"

Her expression was one of disappointment but not blame. "I don't think you should be focusing on me. You should try and work things out with your baby's mother." In a defensive gesture, she folded her arms across her chest. "Being pregnant is an emotional time for a woman. She shouldn't have to go through it alone. Lord knows I know how that feels."

"Sara will be fine. That woman's nothing but a barracuda."

"Why do you say that?"

"I wouldn't put it past her to have gotten pregnant deliberately. She's selfish and manipulative. If she wants a baby then she goes for it. The hell with what someone else wants."

Jillian clenched her fists in anger. "You know, that's just

like a man. Why do all men think we women have nothing better to do than to get pregnant on purpose?"

"Why are we fighting?" John stared at her, baffled. "What's really going on with you?"

Her lower lip trembled as she returned his stare. "Do you know why Byron and I got divorced?"

"No, not really."

Restlessly, her hand stroked the back of a club chair. "Because I refused to have an abortion, that's why. Byron didn't want children and before we got married, we agreed not to have any. Well, I was on the pill and, at some point, it stopped working. I became pregnant and Byron accused me of tricking him."

John reached out and caught her hand in his. "I never knew that."

"He divorced me, and he wants nothing to do with Leah. That's why he was never around during my pregnancy and why he never showed up at the hospital."

"What a bastard."

Pushing back a wayward strand of medium-brown hair, Jillian uttered, "It doesn't matter anymore. Right now, the only thing you should worry about is your child and its mother. Leah and I will be fine." She pulled her hand away. Without warning, John's hand closed on her right shoulder.

"I can't stop caring about you like that, Jillian. I love you."

Moving out of his reach, she retorted, "And you're having a child with someone else."

"Don't shut me out, honey. This is a shock for both of us, but we can get past this. I know we can." His eyes pleaded with hers. "Don't let this be the end of us."

Holding back tears, Jillian closed her eyes. Putting her hand to her face, she turned away from John. "I need time to deal with this. Would you mind very much leaving? I can't think with you here. Not right now."

From behind her, she heard John move toward the door. *"Yo te amo,* Jillian."

She nodded but didn't turn around. She heard the door open and close and knew John was gone. Only then did she permit herself to fall apart.

"Jillian must have called you," John stated, when he saw Ray standing at his door. He didn't want company, but he knew sooner or later he would have to deal with his friend. Sighing, he decided it might as well be now. The day surely couldn't get any worse.

"Yes, she did." Ray followed John into the den. "What are you going to do?"

This line of questioning was not at all what he was expecting. Ray seemed strangely sympathetic. "I don't know. I want to do right by my child but I don't want to lose Jillian and Leah." Flinging out his hands in despair, he stated, "I'm in a hell of a fix."

Nodding, Ray agreed. "That you are."

"I love your sister. I can't lose her."

"Have you ever considered that it's just not meant to be?"

John was keenly aware of Ray's scrutiny. "I don't believe that. Look at you and Carrie. I remember when you were ready to give up on her. You two are married and you have two wonderful children."

"I can't argue with you there. I really believe that anything worth having is worth fighting for. That includes my sister."

"I'm not going to give up on Jillian. Although she's never told me, I know she loves me. I see it every time she looks at me."

"So do I. That's why I came by. Jillian is upset right now, but she's fair. Give her some time to absorb the shock, then talk to her. I'm sure she'll feel differently."

"It's all I'm praying for."

"How do you feel about this baby? I know you and Sara have some serious issues to deal with. Hell, I thought you left her alone years ago."

"Libido, man. It was stupid. That's all I can say. But it's not my baby's fault. I'm going to be the best father I can be. I just don't want to lose Jillian over this."

By the time Ray left, John felt better. As long as Jillian loved him, there was still a chance to have a future together.

"I really don't feel like shopping," Jillian complained.

"Dear heart, we've got to get you out of this slump. It's been a week since you've talked to John, but it'll get better." Ivy embraced her. "I promise."

Allura nodded in agreement. "There's a car show a few blocks away from here if you'd rather go there."

"I'm okay. I would rather go home and catch up on my reading or watch TV." Jillian turned to speak to Ivy, but her sister's attention was elsewhere. "What are you looking at?" she questioned.

Ivy was standing with her hand raised to shelter her eyes. "Isn't that John?"

Jillian followed her gaze. It was indeed him coming toward them. As he neared, she resisted the urge to bite her bottom lip.

After greeting them, he asked, "Would you ladies please excuse us?" John placed a restraining hand on her arm. "My fiancée and I need to talk."

"Sure, don't mind us. We'll just be over here, in the bridal department, looking at the bridesmaid dresses."

Jillian glared at her sister. "Ivy . . ." She didn't continue, because she planned to deal with her sister later. For now, she turned her full attention to John. "Well, here I am."

"Sweetheart, I've missed you."

"I've missed you too," she admitted.

"I'd like to do something with you this weekend. I think we need to get away."

Jillian folded her arms across her chest. "And go where?"

"We could drive down to La Jolla," John suggested.

"We'll need separate rooms, of course."

"I'll get a two-bedroom suite." His eyes softened. "I love you, Jillian. That won't ever change."

"That may be true, but Sara's carrying your child. She will always be a part of your life."

His dark eyes never left hers for an instant. "I don't love her."

"It doesn't matter. You love your child. And Sara is going to need your support throughout her pregnancy. She's going to need you, John."

"This weekend, we're going to spend time together and we're not going to talk about Sara or the baby, agreed?"

"John . . ." She was about to add that not talking about Sara or the baby wouldn't make the situation disappear, but his silent plea stopped her.

"Agreed? We need this time for us."

Against her better judgment, Jillian listened to her heart and agreed.

La Jolla, California

The villa John had rented was absolutely stunning and sheltered by a lush palisade thick with palms and other flora. Jillian was in awe.

"We can do whatever you want, honey. There's a guided walking tour of historic buildings and Sunny Jim Cave."

"To be honest with you, all I really want to do right now is just spend the evening here in this gorgeous villa. It would give us a chance to talk about us. We can take the tour tomorrow."

"Are you sure?"

She nodded. Jillian sank down on the sofa and patted the space beside her. "Come sit down."

"I will in a minute, but first I want you to see something." He extended his hand to her. "Come with me."

John led her by the hand to one of the bedrooms. "This is where you're sleeping."

She surveyed the room. In soft pastel colors, an old-world rose checkerboard quilt covered an elegantly carved pine bedframe that had been lightly distressed and painted in a cream color. "It's exquisite," she murmured, almost to herself. Jillian ambled over to an artistic display of flowers that had been placed on a round table. There were eleven red roses and one lavender placed in the center of the arrangement.

"There's a note attached," he pointed out.

Jillian removed the tiny envelope, immediately recognizing John's handwriting. Glancing over her shoulder, she said, "These are from you." Smiling, she read the contents:

You are one of a kind and my love for you is true. I'm offering you true friendship, affection, and devotion.

                                                      John

Jillian's eyes teared up. "I never knew you were so romantic."

He came up behind her, his arms locking around her waist. "I want you to be sure of my feelings for you. It's important that you feel secure in our relationship and in my love. The last thing I want or need is another divorce."

Turning around in his arms, Jillian contended, "You're doing a splendid job of making me feel special."

"That's because you are special." Giving her a pat on her behind, he ordered, "Now go on and get ready. We're going to have an early dinner and then we're coming back here to spend the rest of our evening in each other's arms—"

"Talking," Jillian threw in.

An hour later, she was running her comb through her hair when she heard a light rap on her door. "Come in." She spun, an expectant smile on her face.

"Wow! Girl, your smile lights up the entire room."

Jillian came to John, offering an exuberant hug. "Let's go. I'm starved."

They returned to the villa an hour later, having decided to pass on dessert. While John made a phone call, Jillian stared out of a window, admiring the picture perfect view of the ocean and the beaches of La Jolla. As much as she tried, she couldn't put Sara Woods and her unborn child out of her mind totally. Being with John like this—in such a romantic setting—made it that much more difficult.

As if John sensed what she was thinking, he placed his arms around her and whispered, "It's going to be all right, baby."

Her head nudged against his shoulder and he drew her closer.

I love you, John Sanders. The realization beat strong within her like a drum, but she didn't have the courage to speak the words. Instead she tried to show him by the sweetness of her kiss.

They pulled apart slowly.

"Honey, that was some kiss. You don't know how many times I've dreamed of kissing you like this."

"I think I do." Jillian led him over to the sofa. "Let's talk."

"As long as it has nothing to do with Sara or the baby."

"I just want to talk about us."

Jillian spent the rest of the evening in John's arms. When they felt they could no longer control their passions, Jillian decided to call it a night.

John left her at her bedroom door with one last kiss. Jillian was a bit surprised that he hadn't persisted in staying with her. When she heard the light rap on her door fifteen minutes later, she smiled knowingly. Tying her robe, she called out, "Come in."

John strolled in carrying a tray of hot tea and cookies illuminated by the soft glow of a silver and satin tea light candle. "I thought this might help you sleep."

"Thank you, John."

"I have to warn you that this is no substitute for me,

however. I'll leave my door unlocked just in case you change your mind." He kissed her quickly and left the room.

Smiling, Jillian fingered the delicate string of seed pearls and the petal pink roses that adorned the creamy hand-sewn shade of the tea light.

The next morning they rose early to take the guided walking tour of historic downtown. Mid-afternoon, they decided to have lunch at George's At the Cove on Prospect Street. The town's only triple-decker eatery, John and Jillian dined on the roof terrace, which provided a full view of La Jolla Cove.

After a sumptuous lunch, they strolled hand in hand along La Jolla's answer to Rodeo Drive. They spent the greater of the afternoon perusing the stores along Girard and Prospect, where they selected gifts for the Ransom family and several outfits for Leah.

A sunny day and the Pacific Ocean gleaming nearby was a blissful experience for Jillian. She made a mental note to bring Leah back here very soon. After finishing her second roll of film, she and John headed back to the villa.

Jillian threw down her camera on the sofa. "I really had a good time and I think the pictures will come out perfect."

"I'm glad." Unbuttoning his shirt, John said, "I'm going to take a shower."

"Me, too." Jillian headed to her room. Twenty minutes later, she was dressed and ready for dinner. When she walked into the living room, she found John was still in his bedroom.

"Your cell phone's ringing," Jillian called out, from the living room.

"Can you answer it for me?"

"Sure." She picked it up and said, "Hello."

"Who is this?"

Jillian answered the question with one of her own. She

recognized the voice of the caller as none other than Sara Woods. "Would you like to speak to John Sanders?"

"Yes, I would." She paused. "Is this Jillian?"

Uneasiness overtook her. "Yes, it is." The suite seemed to swell with tension.

"It's been a long time, hasn't it? I think the last time I saw you was at our high school reunion."

"Right."

"Did John tell you about the baby?"

"Yes. Congratulations."

"Well, that's the reason I'm calling. I'm not feeling well, and I need John to come home. I may need to go to the hospital and I don't feel well enough to drive."

She wondered silently what in the world John could do, but she decided to keep her thoughts to herself. If the woman was sick, she should call an ambulance.

John came into the room and she handed the phone to him without comment.

"Sara?" He looked pensively at Jillian. "I wouldn't be there for a couple of hours. Why don't you call one of your friends?"

Her hands on her hips, she could hear Sara screaming into the phone and knew his suggestion had been met with anger.

"I know I'm the father . . ." John massaged his temple with his left hand. "Sara, calm down."

Jillian crept out of the room, unable to bear listening to any more of their conversation. She pulled out her carry-all and started to pack. When John came into the room a few minutes later, her body tensed like a tightrope.

"What are you doing?"

"I'm packing," she lashed out. "Don't you have to go home and babysit Sara?" She could hear the jealousy in her voice and hated herself for it.

John broke into laughter. "I told her I'd see her tomorrow. We're not leaving, sweetheart." His arms slid around her waist.

Ignoring the heat of their closeness, Jillian asked, "Aren't you worried about her?"

"It's just morning sickness. What can I do for her besides hold her head over the toilet?"

"She's probably scared."

"Sara scared? I doubt that." He shrugged in a dismissive manner. "We don't have to shorten our weekend."

"Yes, we do," Jillian decided. If she stayed with John, what happened today was just the beginning of many more incidents. She and Sara didn't like each other, and she knew the tension would not be good for the baby.

"Why, sweetheart?"

Taking him by the hand, Jillian led him over to the bed and sat down beside him. "John, I have to be honest with you and myself. I don't know if I can handle your being there for Sara."

Shaking his head regretfully, he said, "I can't abandon my child. You know that."

"I know, and I wouldn't expect you to, John. I'm just saying it would be very hard for me to handle. Besides, Sara and I aren't exactly friends. I'm not sure I can, so I think it's best that we go our separate ways. Starting now. I think we should go back home."

He rose slowly. "If we love each other, we can get through anything, honey." He walked out of the room, his movements stiff and awkward.

Her heart breaking, Jillian knew once they returned to Los Angeles, John would walk out of her life forever.

Eight

Bridget was finally asleep. Jillian laid her down in her crib. She and Carrie eased out of the bedroom and went downstairs.

"Since you came all the way here, why don't you just stay and have lunch with me?"

"Thanks. I was just going to pick up a burger on the way back to work."

In the kitchen, Jillian prepared a salad while Carrie heated up left-over baked fish from last night's dinner.

"I hate it when Ray has to transport prisoners. I worry until he's back home with me and the children."

"He's going to be fine. I don't think the Lord will take my brother after the way Kaitlin . . ." Her voice faltered. "It just wouldn't be right, and I don't know if any of us could bare it."

Carrie removed the fish from the microwave. "I pray for his safety every day. I don't want to lose him."

Handing her a plate, Carrie asked, "Are you sure you just want to hand John over to this other woman?"

Jillian lifted her gaze and her eyes were large and wet, her tone wavering pitifully. "No, I'm not, but what choice do I really have? He's the father of her child."

"He doesn't love Sara. John loves you. You're the one he wants to marry."

Following Carrie over to the dining table, Jillian acknowledged, "Maybe, but the fact remains that he's going to be a father. I can't handle having him run off to Sara every time she calls. I know it sounds selfish, but I'm being honest about the way I feel. It would bother me." She took a sip of iced tea.

"I know what you mean. The first time I met Lynette, she said that she was carrying Ray's baby. Even though they were divorced, it bothered me. I guess we're both selfish people."

"But it's not just that, Carrie. A child needs two parents. I really believe that."

"Oh, I agree totally. However, a child can have two parents who aren't together."

"I'm not forcing John to marry Sara. I just think he needs to be with her at this time. If something more comes of that, then he was never the man for me."

"Okay, I understand that, but what happens after the child is born? Will you take John back then?"

"I don't know. In truth, I don't think he'll want to come back to me." Jillian played with the base of her glass. "Carrie, you should have seen his face. He wants this baby."

"And you're jealous, aren't you?"

"Yes. I wish . . ."

Giving her a knowing smile, Carrie asked, "You wish you were the one pregnant, don't you?"

Jillian nodded. "Isn't this so crazy? John and I haven't even made love."

"I think it's sweet."

"Carrie, it really bothers me that this other woman is carrying John's baby. It makes me so mad that once again something's come between us. I guess it's just not meant to be."

"It's not over yet."

"Yes, it is. John and I were never meant to be a couple. We're to remain friends. Nothing more."

Carrie rose to her feet and shook her head. "For some reason, I don't believe that." Pointing to Jillian's hand, she added, "I don't think you really believe it's over either. You're still wearing his engagement ring."

"I'm going to give it back to him this evening. I just wasn't quite ready to take it off."

"I understand. Really I do. I just wish you two could work something out. I refuse to believe it's over."

"Neither does my heart," Jillian pronounced, sadly. "Thanks for lunch and for listening. I guess I'd better get back to work."

Jillian headed to the door, where she and Carrie embraced each other. "Kiss the children for me."

"I'll call you later," Carrie promised. "Give it some more thought before you give John the ring back. You two may be able to work things out."

Jillian nodded, but she knew in her heart that she could not remain engaged to John.

John was standing by Jillian's car when she walked out of the rehabilitation center later that evening. Her initial impulse was to run to him and throw herself into his arms. But knowing what she had to do held her back. Instead she asked, "What are you doing here?"

"I'm not going to give up on you, sweetheart. I love you and I know you feel the same way."

Her chin quivered. "I guess it's a good thing you're here. I was planning on coming by your house after work."

"I'm glad to hear that—"

Holding up her hand, Jillian stopped him. "It's not what you're thinking. I need to give something back to you." She slipped the ring off her finger and held it out to John. "This doesn't belong to me anymore."

He was shaking his head and backing away. "No . . ."

"John, please don't make this any h-harder." She kept her tears at bay.

A tense spasm jumped along his lean jaw. "Why do I feel like I have to choose?"

Taking his hand, she said in a hoarse whisper, "You

don't. I would never make you choose between your child and me."

"It really bothers you this much that Sara's having my baby?"

Jillian nodded. "Yes. I think it would bother any woman." In his hand, she placed the ring.

Gazing into her eyes, he whispered, "I wish it were you."

Shrugging, she responded, "But it's not."

"*Je t'aime,* Jillian. Doesn't that matter?"

"That's why this hurts so much." Unable to resist, she kissed him one last time. "Good-bye, John." Climbing into her car, she waved and drove away. Jillian wouldn't let herself take one last peek at the man whose heart she'd just broken. "I love you, too," she whispered, before bursting into tears.

Tossing the ring into his pocket, John walked to his car. His head throbbed with pain as he unlocked his door to get in. It was after he started the car that reality set in. He and Jillian were not getting married. They would never be a family. Leah's face flashed before him and his eyes grew wet with unshed tears.

Instead of going home, John drove to Sara's house. They needed to have a long talk.

She arrived home just as he pulled up. Climbing out of his car, he went to assist her with the groceries. They carried them through the garage and into the kitchen. Sara babbled on and on about how hectic her day had been. She never once asked about his. Not that John had expected her to. She was very self-absorbed, and he was no longer sure what had ever attracted him to her in the first place. When he grew tired of her tirade, he interrupted her. "Sara, I need to talk to you."

"What is it, John? I'm really tired and this damn morning sickness seems to only come at night," she complained. "This is not what I had in mind when I decided to have this baby. So, if what you have to say is going to end up getting me upset, then forget it. I'm not in the mood." Sara navigated to the den and dropped down on a leather sofa.

John took a seat on the matching recliner. "I'm not trying to upset you, but I have to be honest with you. I'm in love with Jillian and that's not going to change. Not ever."

She stared over at him, then coaxed, "I know you want to be a part of the baby's life. But you do understand that this is a package deal, don't you?"

Sara seemed to be waiting—waiting for the right words to come. John could only nod in response. He wasn't sure what she wanted to hear.

"I'm not looking for love, John. And if I were, you'd be the last person I'd have in mind. I handled both of your divorces, remember? And let's not forget how you broke my heart years ago."

John frowned slightly. "I've said how sorry I was over and over. I wasn't looking for anything serious back then. I told you—"

"I'm not holding some type of grudge, John," Sara cut in. "We made a baby together. I can't change that. If you don't want to be a part of this," she pointed in the direction of the door, "then leave."

"Neither one of us wanted this, but we have this situation and we have to make the best of it. That's what I fully intend to do. I want to be a part of my child's life. I'm not the kind of man who'd walk away from his responsibility."

"I know that. You've always been honest with me and I respect you for that. We work extremely well together and we have great sex."

"Why don't we just take it one day at a time and see what happens?"

"As long as you agree to give us one hundred percent. I'll accept nothing less."

John eyed her warily. "You make it sound like a threat, Sara."

"It's not. It's the simple truth. You've been honest with me and I'm going to do the same for you. I want to make partner. I've worked for those male chauvinists for almost fifteen years. I've earned that partnership. Since you left, I've been the only black lawyer there. I've kissed enough white butt and I want my due."

"Whether we're married or not shouldn't affect your getting a partnership."

"John, you haven't been gone long enough to forget the rules. They're stuffy old men who think any woman my age should be married with a couple of children. You know how family oriented they are."

"Sara, I'm not going to marry you. I am going to be a father to my child."

"Never say never, John. You should know that by now."

"I'm not in the mood for your games."

She smiled. "I'm not playing games, John. I'm playing for keeps. Once the shock wears off, you'll come to your senses. I'm sure of it."

Nine

Amanda checked the tall steaming pot of mixed greens. "I wonder what happened to John. He's usually here by now."

Standing beside her, Ray lowered his voice to a whisper. "He's not coming. In light of everything that's happened, he feels it's best he not come out here anymore."

Handing a bowl of freshly shredded cheddar cheese to Jillian, Ivy asked her, "Are you okay?"

"I'm fine. It's going to take some time getting used to not seeing him, but I'll be okay." She took the bowl that Ivy offered and poured the cheese into another bowl, which was filled with macaroni.

"I'm so sorry."

Shrugging, Jillian replied, "It just wasn't meant to be." She cracked an egg and tossed it into the bowl. Pouring in a cup of milk, she worked steadily until the macaroni and cheese casserole was ready for the oven. When she was done, she strolled over to the sink and washed her hands.

Allura pointed to her bare hand. "You gave him the ring back?"

"Yes, it didn't belong to me." Turning to her mother, Jillian asked, "Is there anything else I can do?"

"Everything's under control. Why don't you take a walk? I think the air might do you some good."

She gave a hint of a smile. "You're probably right."

Giving her mother a quick hug, she whispered, "Thanks."

Outside, Jillian walked around the quiet neighborhood where she grew up. After walking a couple of blocks, she turned around and headed home, feeling utterly alone.

When she reached the house, Jillian wasn't ready to go inside, so she sank down in one of the chairs. It was late and the air was cool, but she was numb to both facts. She never thought she'd ever hurt like this again. Byron had done a number on her but she survived. So she knew she would also survive this heartache. Her thoughts jumped to Leah. But would her daughter survive? How was she going to explain this to her?

Sara wanted to visit every single baby store in Los Angeles. John fought to hide his impatience and boredom. He thought it was much too soon to be shopping for baby furniture, but Sara would not listen.

She ran her fingers across the top of the oak crib. "What do you think about this one?"

"It's nice," he mumbled. John missed driving to Riverside and being around the entire Ransom clan. He missed Jillian and Leah most of all.

Sara broke into his thoughts. "John, where are you really?"

"What are you talking about?"

"Forget it," she snapped. "You know you never told me what happened between you and Jillian Ransom. Are you two still getting married?"

"No, we're not."

"Hmm, I guess that means she didn't take it too well. But then, I didn't think she would."

"What does it matter, Sara?"

Shrugging, Sara said, "It doesn't matter at all to me. Not really. I've never liked Jillian."

"Why don't we change the subject?"

"You know, they offered me a partnership. They don't know about the baby though."

"I thought you were going to tell them."

"I'd planned to but when I went in to talk to Steve Weinberg, he stopped me and then offered me partner. This would really work out if I could announce to them that I'm also getting married."

John was silent.

Clutching his arm, she suggested, "You know, we could fly to Vegas and get married tonight. I'd rearrange my schedule so that we could take a couple of days off—"

"Sara, let's get something straight. I don't love you."

"I think love is much too overrated. We make a great team, John."

"We have too many issues to deal with to even consider marriage. There can't be anything so permanent between us."

"You don't think having a child is permanent?" Sara demanded.

"Yes, I do." People were starting to stare, so John lowered his voice. "Don't make a scene, Sara. We can discuss this when we get home."

During the drive back to her house, Sara was sullen. After a couple of failed attempts of trying to draw her into conversation, John gave up. It was better this way. Maybe it would give them both a chance to calm down.

On the way home, Leah asked, "How come we never see Uncle John anymore?"

Awkwardly, Elle cleared her throat.

"He's been busy, sweetie," Jillian sputtered.

"He's never been too busy for us before. Is he mad at us?"

"No, Leah. John's not mad at us. He's just very busy.

There are some things going on in his life right now that he needs to deal with." She stirred uneasily in her seat. Jillian didn't want to lie to her daughter.

"Will he be back?"

"I don't know."

"Are you still marrying Uncle John?"

Jillian swallowed hard before responding, "No, sweetheart. John and I decided not to get married, after all. We think it's for the best."

"But it's not. You can't do this, Mommy. Uncle John said he'd marry you any day of the week. I know he hasn't changed his mind."

"I know you don't understand, but—"

"You two have to get married. *You have to.*"

Jillian heard the panic in her daughters voice and it crushed her.

They rode the rest of the way home in silence. She was grateful that Leah hadn't persisted in talking about marriage and John.

While Elle helped Leah prepare for bed, Jillian worked on her notes and a report she needed for a meeting tomorrow morning.

After giving the papers one final review, she stretched and yawned. Weary, she climbed the stairs. Stopping at Leah's room, she peeked inside.

Jillian brushed away a lone tear as she watched Leah sleep. Feeling a tap on her shoulder, she turned to find Elle standing there. "She's so upset," she whispered.

Nodding, Elle whispered back, "I know, but she'll adapt. Children always do."

She stole another peek at her daughter before closing the door. Jillian prayed Elle was right.

John pulled away from a scantily clad Sara. "I'd better get home. I'll call you in the morning."

"You're leaving? I thought you might want to stay over."

John shook his head. "I'm sorry, Sara."

"What? You're not turned on by me now that I'm carrying your child? You certainly had no problem getting me pregnant."

"Calm down, Sara. It's not what you're thinking."

"Then tell me. Why is it I suddenly repulse you?" Her voice broke miserably.

"I never said that."

"Then what is it?"

"I told you earlier. We have some things we need to work out. I can't stand the way you try to manipulate me." Shaking his head regretfully, he warned, "It's got to stop, Sara."

"I don't try to manipulate you—"

"Yes, you do," John interjected. "Sara, I'm not going to argue with you."

She spoke calmly, with no lighting of her eyes, no smile on her face. "It's not me, at all. It's Jillian. You love her that much?"

"We don't need to talk about Jillian. She's out of my life."

"But she'll always be in your heart, right?"

"Sara . . ."

A look of tired sadness passed over her features. "Am I right? Tell me, John."

"Yes. I never lied about my feelings for her."

"Tell me something. You have this undying love for her and she just blew you off. Doesn't it make you wonder whether or not she feels the same for you?"

"I know she loves me."

"But not as much as you love her," Sara countered.

"Jillian and I are over. She's the kind of woman who won't stand in the way of my being a good father to my child. I don't think there is any need to discuss this further." He walked briskly to the door. "I'll call you to-morrow."

Driving home, John had to wonder whether or not Sara had a point. Perhaps Jillian didn't love him the way he loved her.

Ten

Where was Sara? She never mentioned having to go out of town.

John glanced at the clock. Where had Sara gone? Something about this didn't sound right. Worried, he tried her number again. No answer.

He felt bad over the state he'd left her in last night. John knew he had to find a way to get over Jillian and make some kind of life with Sara. He owed his unborn child that much.

Whenever they connected, he decided he would take her out for a nice dinner. They would go back to his place and decide on the plans for the nursery. He decided it would be best to have a room set up in his home as well for his child.

Throughout the day, John tried to reach Sara but to no avail. As the hour grew later, the more he couldn't shake the sense of foreboding he felt.

Elle peeked into the kitchen. "Jillian! What on earth are you doing?"

Dressed in a pair of faded blue overalls and a white T-shirt, Jillian removed a cabinet door off its hinges, laying it on the counter with the others. "I thought I'd remodel the kitchen, starting with the cabinets. I think I want to try a royal blue and oak theme."

"Oh." Elle glanced around the room. "I think it'll look real nice, Sis."

Jillian handed her sister a sample to look at. "This is the tile that I'm thinking of putting in here."

"You're going to put in the tile? By yourself?"

She gave a choked, desperate laugh. "No. A friend of Ray's is going to do it for me. I'm going to redo the cabinets myself though."

"Why are you doing this? For the last day or so, you've been running yourself ragged."

"I need to keep busy. It takes my mind off . . . things."

"You mean John, don't you?"

Her misery was so acute that it was a physical pain. "I miss him so much, Elle. I feel like I'm not going to make it." A lone tear rolled down her cheek. "With everything Byron put me through—it didn't hurt this much."

"I wish there was something I could do for you . . ."

"I'm just glad you're here with me," Jillian replied, in a low, tormented voice.

"How is Leah?"

"She's not accepting the fact that John and I are over. She won't even discuss it. I've been thinking about taking her to a therapist."

Retrieving an apple from the refrigerator, Elle told her, "Give her some time, Jillian. Who knows, you and John may work this out."

Jillian reached for her screwdriver. "My future with John is over, Elle. It's time we all moved on."

"Sara, I was worried about you. Why didn't you tell me you were going away?" John asked, as soon as she let him in.

Taking her time, Sara walked slowly over to her couch and sat down carefully. "I took a few days off and I decided to go away."

Still standing, John inquired, "But why? Why wouldn't you call me or something?"

"I wasn't ready to talk to you."

For the first time, he noticed that she appeared to be in pain. "What's wrong, Sara? You look pale. Are you feeling okay?"

"I'm a little tired, but I'm feeling much better." Waving her hand in a dismissive gesture, she added, "I've gotten rid of that morning sickness and everything."

Icy fear twisted around John's heart, and he dropped down into a nearby wing chair. "Meaning . . ."

"I had an abortion," Sara stated, without emotion.

He glared at her with burning, reproachful eyes. "What? How could you?"

"It's my body, John." Rancor sharpened her voice. "Besides, you didn't want this baby or me. Did you think I couldn't tell?"

"We should have discussed this." A sudden chill hung on the edge of his words. She took away his child without one word to him. He was angry.

"Why? John, it's simple. I'm letting you off the hook. I'm not exactly ready to change diapers, do midnight feedings, or be a mother—period. You're not ready to be a father—"

"That's where you're wrong." He interrupted her vehemently. "I wanted this baby. I'm not a fool, Sara. You got rid of our child because of that damned partnership. You didn't want me any more than you wanted that baby. It was all a ploy to get the partnership. You thought having a family would better your chances and then when you didn't need us . . ."

"Think what you like. I really don't care."

John rose to his feet. He'd never hated the sight of anyone the way he hated Sara at this moment.

"You're in love with Jillian Ransom. So go to her. She's the woman you really want. Who knows, maybe she'll give you the child you so desperately want." Placing her hand on her flat stomach, Sara said, "Please let yourself out."

His face twisted with rage, and John slammed his fist against a table bearing some of Sara's prized possessions.

Satisfied over the sound of her crying, he left without one backward glance.

Ray called Jillian at work. "Sara had an abortion."

Jillian was shocked. "Oh, no. How is John?"

"He's fine, I think. He called me last night and told me."

She hurt for John. "He wanted the baby."

"I know. He also wanted you. Sis, John needs you right now."

"Did he say that?" Jillian asked.

"No, but I could hear it in his voice."

"Well, I'm on my way home. I'll see if Elle is busy tonight. If she's not, I'll go by his house. If she has plans, then I'll just give him a call."

As soon as Jillian hung up, she raced home. She released a sigh of relief when she glimpsed Elle's car in the driveway.

In the house, she found Elle working on her laptop computer in the family room.

"Elle, do you have any plans tonight?"

"No, I'm staying in. What did you need?"

"I need a really big favor. Could you make sure Leah does her homework and that she makes it to bed on time? I need to see if John's okay."

"Is he sick or something?"

"No. Sara had an abortion."

"Oh, I'm sorry. I know he wanted that baby."

"I need to check on him."

Nodding, Elle agreed. "Leah will be fine. Take as much time as you need."

"Thanks, sweetie. I owe you."

Eleven

John was clearly surprised to see her. "Jillian, what are you doing here?"

Holding up a white plastic bag containing two dinners, she said, "I thought you might need some nourishment and, most of all, a friend."

"Come on in and have a seat. You're looking as beautiful as always."

Jillian took a seat across from him. Laying her purse down beside her, she said, "You don't have to put on a front for me, John. Ray told me what happened."

John's eyes filled with tears. "I wanted that baby."

"I know."

"She did it without talking to me." Anger flashed in his eyes. "I had no say whatever. But what really gets me is that she tried to blame me for it. The truth of the matter is that she thought having a baby and a husband would help her make partner. When she didn't need us . . ." He couldn't continue, he was so angry.

"I'm sorry, John."

He was leaning forward, with his hands on his face. With a groan, he cried out, his shoulders shaking. John buried his face against her breasts, harsh sobs tearing out of his body. Jillian moved to sit beside him. She pulled him into her arms and held him while he grieved for his child. Her own face was wet but Jillian didn't care. All that mattered right now was John.

Later, when he was feeling better, she coaxed him into eating. Having finished her meal, she cleaned the kitchen and readied to leave. "I'll call you tomorrow, John. For now, I want you to take a long, hot shower. Get into bed and try to relax."

He grabbed her, crushing Jillian to his chest. For a moment he didn't say anything; he just held her. When he did speak, it was from the soul. "Please don't leave. I need you."

Jillian didn't respond at first. Her breath gave a tell-tale hitch as she rubbed her face against his shirt. Looking up at him with misty eyes, she whispered, "I'm not going anywhere. Just let me call Elle."

While she made her call, John took his shower. Jillian made a couple more calls before he was done. When he walked into the bedroom, he found her sitting on the edge of the king-size bed. He gave her a silk pajama shirt to sleep in.

John was in bed by the time Jillian came out of the bathroom. Crawling in, she laid next to him. He moved closer to her, his hands moving up and down her back. John stared at her, then reached out to stroke her cheek with his thumb. "Jillian," he said in a soft whisper, before covering her mouth with his own. Kissing her passionately, he murmured, "As much as I want to make love to you right now, I really think we should wait."

"Why?"

"You're mine in my heart, but before I make you mine in body, I want us to be married. Believe me, it's not going to be easy to wait, but I want to do this the right way."

"I understand. Besides you probably need the rest anyway."

For the first time in days, John laughed. *"Mimi nakupenda,"* he murmured softly. "If I have to, I'm going to tell you I love you in a hundred languages and dialects. People probably think I'm crazy. I'm always asking how to say the words 'I love you' in their language."

She sat up. "What language or dialect was that?"

"Swahili."

"I wasn't sure whether or not you were putting a curse on me or something."

Pulling Jillian down, he kissed her deeply. "I don't know if I'll ever be able to tame you, sweetheart. But I'm going to spend the rest of my life trying. This time though, we're not going to rush this relationship. We're going to take our time."

She lay in John's embrace while he slept. Jillian realized that it wasn't the need for physical gratification that rose so insistently within him—it was the need for an intimate union of spirit. She wasn't disappointed in John's desire just to hold her. Sleepily, she sighed contentedly as he sidled closer to her.

"Throw the ball to me, Mommy," Leah yelled. She stood right under the basketball goal.

John was crouching down, trying to guard Jillian. Laughing, she stepped around him and threw the ball to her daughter.

Leah caught it and attempted to throw it up to the basket, but John picked her up and swung her around.

"Cheater," Jillian called out.

"I have two WNBA players out here on the court and it's just me. I need to win any way I can."

Leah tickled him under his chin. Laughing, he put her back on the ground.

Jillian picked up the ball and tossed it into the basket. "We win."

"Oh, no, you don't. We still have two minutes game time." John caught the ball and made his way down the court with two screaming females on his heels.

Later, as they headed to the car, Jillian spied John and Leah in a huddle.

"Hey, what are you two whispering about?"

Leah giggled. "Nothing, Mommy. We're just talking."

"Yeah, right." Jillian didn't believe that for a moment. She had a feeling they were up to something.

* * *

Elle handed Jillian a stack of freshly washed sheets. "You're in love with John. It's as clear as day."

"I haven't told him yet."

"Why not?"

Tucking in the corners, Jillian murmured, "I don't know. I guess the time's not right. When it is, I'll tell him. Besides, he has me whether I tell him or not."

"What are you afraid of?"

Shrugging, Jillian sat down on the edge of the newly made bed. "I don't know. John and I have had this attraction for one another for ten long years. I'm not even sure John feels the same way as he did before. He says he wants to take it slower this time. He didn't even want to make love to me."

"I find that hard to believe."

"He says he wants to wait until we're married. On one hand I appreciate it, but then I start to think that maybe he's bored with me already. Maybe I don't even love him the way I think I do. Maybe it's just lust."

Tossing her a pillow, Elle asked, "Who do you think about before you go to bed?"

"John."

"And who do you think about when you wake up?"

"John."

"Who do you dream about?"

"John. I'm getting your point." Jillian stood up and proceeded to apply the finishing touches to the bed.

"No, you're not. Yes, there is a physical attraction, but I'm sure there's more."

"There is. John is so easy to talk to and he makes me laugh. He's my best friend. I think about my life and it seems so empty without him. When I sent him out of my life and into Sara's, I thought I would die. It was as if a part of me was missing."

"You love him in a big way. That kind of love is not going to go away."

"You're right. My heart is not happy without his. Errgh! I can't believe I'm being so corny."

"I think it's really special. I want a love like that someday."

"You're going to find it and more. Have you met anybody yet?"

"Actually there's this man that I have the biggest crush on. He doesn't know I'm even alive."

"What's his name?"

"Brennen Cunningham."

"Is he that millionaire who's always in the news?"

Elle nodded. "He's a friend of my boss."

"Well, little sister, if you catch that man, all I want you to do is send Leah to college."

"It's a promise."

"I want you to know that I spoke to John, and he's fine with you living with us."

"I've found an apartment and Nyle is thinking about sharing it with me. You don't have to worry about having me underfoot."

"You don't have to do that, Elle." She snapped her fingers. "I don't know why I didn't think of this before. Instead of my putting this place up for sale, why don't you and Nyle just stay here? You two can rent this place from me."

"Actually, this would be perfect. The other place costs about the same as your mortgage and it's a lot smaller. Nyle and I both can have an office . . . this would be perfect."

"Great. Then it's settled. Nyle can even move in here immediately. I know he hates where he's living."

"I'll give him a call right now." Elle stopped mid-stride. "You are going to put the doors back on the cabinets, right?"

"Happy Valentine's Day."

"Same to you, John. I really appreciate you including Leah."

"Why wouldn't I? Even little girls deserve Valentines."

Jillian smiled at her daughter. "I think so, too."

"Balloons. Someone's getting balloons," Leah announced. "I love balloons."

Jillian and John shared a laugh. Stroking her daughter's cheek, she said, "We know."

"Look, Mommy, he's coming this way!"

She glanced over at John. "What have you done?"

He merely shrugged and returned his attention to his plate.

As the waiter neared, Jillian lowered her voice. "Why don't I believe you?"

Jillian couldn't help but smile when the bouquet of heart-shaped balloons were presented to her.

"They're for you, Mommy. Are you surprised?"

"Did you know about this, little lady?"

Leah burst into giggles.

While they waited for the waiter to return with dessert, Jillian smiled as she gazed into John's eyes. "You're something else."

He shrugged. "I just want to make you happy."

Leah downed the last of her lemonade. "This is the best Valentine's Day ever."

Taking Jillian by the hand, John stared into her eyes. "This is the beginning of many more, I hope."

At that moment, the waiter appeared with dessert and two stuffed bears holding red hearts. On the hearts were the words: *Will you marry me?*

Jillian read it again. "John . . . I thought you wanted to wait." Her eyes filled with tears. "I don't believe this."

"I want to know that our relationship is going somewhere." Touching his heart, he said, "I need this. So what is the answer, love of my life? Make all my dreams come true."

"Yes, I'll marry you. I love you."

"He wants to marry me, too," Leah interjected.

Through her tears, Jillian smiled. "Well, what's your answer, sweetheart?"

"Yes. And you know what else? He's not going to be Uncle John anymore. He's going to be my daddy because he wants to adopt me."

Through her tears, Jillian looked to John for confirmation.

"I've already spoken to Byron. He's agreed to terminate his parental rights so that I can adopt Leah. He thinks it's best and so do I. I know I should have discussed this with you, but—"

"I love you, John."

Twelve

Valentine's Day
One year later

"You look beautiful," Amanda murmured.

"I still can't believe I'm getting married." Jillian stared at herself in the full-length mirror. Her ivory satin dress was strapless and dotted with pearls. Stopping just above her knee, it complimented her figure. In the back, a pale peach and nude organza bow with floor-length streamers added a subtle touch of color and gave her the elegant look she wanted.

"They really did a good job decorating. The scenery on Catalina Island is gorgeous."

"John came up with the idea of having the wedding here and renting the Casino Ballroom. He took care of everything."

Amanda nodded. "He's certainly planned an elegant affair. Girl, you've got yourself a good man this time. Hold on to him tight."

"I plan to. He's wonderful with Leah, too."

"I've watched those two together. I think he's always had a soft spot where she's concerned."

"I think so, too." Jillian stood still as her mother placed a double strand of pearls around her neck. On her head, she wore a simple pearl encrusted headband.

Elle, Allura, and Ivy rushed into the room. They were all dressed in peach and each one looked lovely.

"They're almost ready to start," Allura announced. "How about you?"

"I'm ready. What do you all think?" She needed to hear their assurances. Jillian wanted to take John's breath away when he saw her coming down the aisle.

"You look so beautiful," Elle reassured her. "John is going to be so proud."

"I agree," murmured Ivy.

"Sis, you're stunning." Allura reached over to hug her. "I'm so happy for you."

Amanda Ransom reached for the doorknob. "And this is a perfect day for a wedding. God's smiling over you and John. It's a good sign."

Taking Allura by the hand, Jillian asked, "You know what would really make this day perfect?"

"What?" they all chorused.

"If Kaitlin were here bossing everyone around." Her eyes filled with tears. "Remember how she was at Allura's wedding?"

Wiping her own eyes, Amanda said, "Kaitlin's here in spirit, sweetheart. She's here with all of us."

"Come on and let's get you married. I hope Prescott won't be as stiff as he was when he walked me down the aisle."

"Well, at least he didn't faint at your wedding, Allura. I couldn't believe he passed out right before he took his vows."

Carrie met them at the door. She was dressed in the same gown as the rest of the Ransom women. "I was just about to see what was keeping you all. They're ready to start."

"Where's Prescott?" Jillian asked.

"I'm right here, Sis," a voice behind Carrie responded. "Let's do this."

* * *

As they waited to make their grand entrance into the ballroom, Jillian nudged Prescott. "Feeling okay?"

Tugging nervously at his bow tie, he nodded stiffly. "You know I wouldn't have been offended if you'd asked Ray or Garrick to walk you down the aisle."

She laughed. "You should be used to it by now. Besides, you only have one more to walk down the aisle and that's Elle."

Smiling, Elle declared, "Don't worry, Prescott. It's not going to happen for a long time."

Daisi gestured to Elle. It was time for the maid of honor to make her entrance. She was escorted by her twin brother, Nyle.

Mikey, dressed as ring bearer, and Leah as flower girl made their way down the aisle next.

It was time for the bride to make her grandiose arrival.

Holding onto Prescott's arm, Jillian walked gracefully down the narrow white runner that had been littered with peach roses.

Meeting John's eyes, she smiled at him. He looked so handsome in the ivory tux he wore. She could hardly believe that they were about to become man and wife.

Jillian felt movement and glanced down. Mikey was fidgeting with his suit. She couldn't help but smile when John bent down to adjust her nephew's bow tie.

"That's better, Uncle John. It was choking me to death," Mikey exclaimed loudly.

Fighting laughter, they both turned their attention to the pastor. When it was time for them to say their vows, John turned to face her. Taking her bouquet from her, he handed it to Elle.

John took both her hands in his. Looking deeply into her eyes, he spoke. "Jillian, nothing happens without cause. Our union did not come about accidentally but is the foreordained result of God. From the first time we ever met, our hearts spoke to one another. You have become mine forever. I have become yours. Heart to heart, we are partners, lovers, and friends. We are word and meaning, united."

His eyes glittered bright from unshed tears, causing Jillian to reach out and softly stroke his cheek. "John, I give you my heart into your eternal keeping just as you have given yours to me. Together we will share not only the joys but the sorrows as well. Love and compassion are built upon trust, patience, and perseverance. As long as we remember this, our marriage will remain firm and lasting. I promise to be your best friend, your lover, your partner forever."

The pastor spoke up. "Leah Michele Winters, John has something he would like to say to you."

Wiping away her tears, Jillian stepped back so that John could take her daughter by the hand. She glanced over at her siblings and found that they were all crying, too.

"Leah, I want you to know that I love you as my very own daughter." He pulled a tiny wedding ring from his pocket. "With this ring that I place on your finger, I promise that my love for you will never end. Like this ring, our bond can never be broken or dissolved. I promise to be the best father that I can be. I want you to know I will always be there for you, during good times and rough times. With you as my daughter, there can never be any bad times."

Leah raised her hand. "Pastor Stanley, I have a vow."

Jillian and John exchanged puzzled glances. This wasn't part of the ceremony.

Pastor Stanley nodded. "Go ahead, child."

"I promise to be the best daughter that I can be because I have the best mother and father in the whole world. I love you both and I'm glad you two got married. It's what I've always prayed for. I want to thank God for answering my prayers, and I haven't forgotten that I said I'd be a good girl. I'm going to keep my promise."

Leah's vow touched Jillian, and when she glanced over at the man who would soon be her husband, she could tell that it had touched him, too. John's eyes were wet with tears.

A few minutes later, John and Jillian were pronounced husband and wife.

Amidst period antiques and a magnificent view of the Pacific Ocean and San Pedro, John had arranged for them to spend their wedding night in a romantic luxury villa known as the Wrigley Mansion that had been built in 1921 by the chewing gum magnate.

John heard a noise and looked up. The sight of Jillian took his breath away. Wearing nothing but a pair of sexy high heeled slippers, she sauntered toward the bed, saying, "I'm no blushing bride, and you are certainly no inexperienced groom, so I thought I'd forego the virginal peignoir and bare all."

"I love the way you think, Mrs. Sanders." John moved over to make room for her as she climbed into bed.

Stroking his cheek, Jillian stared into his eyes. "We already have one child, but I think we should work on baby number two."

His dark eyes smoldered. "Oh, I love the way you think." Reaching for her, John pulled her closer to him. He kissed her and then again, this time more possessively.

As his head moved to her neck, a shock of sensation rocketed through her and Jillian clutched his head, anchoring him there as John continued to taunt and tantalize her to a near frenzy.

When their sparks of desire ignited into flames of passion, John took possession of her body, setting off an explosion of ecstasy for them both.

Afterward, as they lay together in each other's arms, Jillian softly stroked John's cheek. "What are you thinking about right now?" she asked.

"You were definitely worth the wait. And I'm not just talking about making love. I think if we'd gotten together all those other times, I would have found some way to blow it. It seems like forever, but the timing was perfect.''

"I don't know. I think no matter when we would've gotten together, it would have worked out.''

"What makes you say that, sweetness?''

"Because I would have loved you to perfection or killed you dead.''

Roaring with laughter, John pulled her on top of him. "Baby, I love the way you think.''

Dear Readers:

I hope you have enjoyed Jillian and John's story. You will be meeting more of the Ransom family in books to come. The next story, *Family Ties,* will feature Marc Chandler and McKenzie Ashford. You may recall meeting Marc in this book. After *Family Ties,* the next book will be Laine Ransom and Regis Melbourne's story. Kaitlin and Matt's story will be released in 2001.

As always, I love hearing from you. You can write to me at: PO Box 7415, La Verne, CA 91750-7415 or feel free to e-mail me: *jacquelinthomas@usa.net*

Coming in March from Arabesque Books . . .

__FORBIDDEN HEART by Felicia Mason
   1-58314-050-65 $5.99US/$7.99CAN
When savvy Mallory Heart needs someone to oversee construction of her
first boutique, she turns to Ellis Carson. Although he has little in common
with the college-educated men she's used to and he thinks she's a snob,
soon enough they start concentrating on their shared interest in each other.

__PRECIOUS HEART by Doris Johnson
   1-58314-083-2 $5.99US/$7.99CAN
Burned by love, Diamond Drew is determined never to trust another man
again. But after meeting handsome Dr. Steven Rumford, everything
changes. Since he comes with a disastrous past as well, the couple must
learn to trust each other if they can ever hope to find happiness together.

__A BITTERSWEET LOVE by Janice Sims
   1-58314-084-0 $5.99US/$7.99CAN
When Teddy Riley secures an interview with reclusive author Joachim West,
she never expects that a freak accident will lead to her being mistaken for
his wife . . . or that she might find an irresistible passion that promises
a future filled with a joyful, healing love.

__MASQUERADE by Crystal Wilson-Harris
   1-58314-101-4 $5.99US/$7.99CAN
Offered a chance to housesit in Miami, Madison Greer soon meets Clint
Santiago, the most handsome, mysterious man she's ever encountered.
But Clint is really a federal agent trying to bust a drug dealer and to do
that, he'll have to get close to Madison and risk losing his heart forever . . .

Call toll free **1-888-345-BOOK** to order by phone or use this
coupon to order by mail. *ALL BOOKS AVAILABLE MARCH 1, 2000.*
Name _____
Address _____
City _____ State _____ Zip _____
Please send me the books I have checked above.
I am enclosing $_____
Plus postage and handling* $_____
Sales tax (in NY, TN, and DC) $_____
Total amount enclosed $_____
*Add $2.50 for the first book and $.50 for each additional book.
Send check or money order (no cash or CODs) to: **Arabesque Books,
Dept. C.O., 850 Third Avenue, 16th Floor, New York, NY 10022**
Prices and numbers subject to change without notice.
All orders subject to availability.
Visit out our Web site at **www.arabesquebooks.com**